# INTO the AIR

# Into the Storm Trilogy
# Book Three

Serene Conneeley

Blessed Bee Books

INTO THE AIR: Into the Storm Trilogy Book Three

First edition copyright © Serene Conneeley 2019

Conneeley, Serene
Into the Air by Serene Conneeley
ISBN: 978-0-6484016-1-2

Website: www.SereneConneeley.com
Email: serene@sereneconneeley.com

Published by Blessed Bee Books
PO Box 449, Newtown, NSW 2042
Australia

Cover artwork: *Light and Dark* by Selina Fenech
www.SelinaFenech.com
Illustrations: Daniella Spinetti and Justin Sayers

Doubt whispers to the warrior:
"You are broken, so you are weak."
The warrior roars back:
"I *was* broken and weak,
so now I am stronger than you will ever know."

# Contents

"Out of your vulnerabilities will come your strength."
*Sigmund Freud, Austrian psychoanalyst*

## Chapter 1

# Out of the Fire

The pain was almost more than she could bear. She tried to let go, to dissolve back into the dark, into the nothing. Into that place where there was no thought, no feeling, no... anything.

*No her.*

And yet a tentative thread of starlight was holding her. Trapping her, she knew not where, or how. There was a pulling at the core of her, and a pushing from outside. A force trying to reassemble her. What was it? And *why* was it?

Swimming in a lake of incoherence and confusion, Beth was unable to form words or thoughts, let alone find answers to questions. The world was blurred around the edges, her mind vague and foggy, as though she was trying to peer through a veil of mist. A mist that swirled around her, drawing her down, drawing her under, trying to drown her. Panic clutched at her. She tried to fight it, to form herself back into some semblance of herself. Which was...

*A ghost.*

She was dead, and yet something – the yearning of her family perhaps, or her own guilt – was keeping her here. Which was its own kind of torture. In this strange half-existence, she was able to see just how much her death had devastated her husband, confused her young son, and broken her daughter's heart.

*Her daughter.*

The evening before Beth died, Rhiannon had stolen out into the dark woods to work a healing spell with an older witch. A male witch. Beth had thought her awful premonition had rescued her in time, but she was wrong. So wrong. Last night – or last week? – she'd discovered that the guy had assaulted her sweet, innocent daughter, within the sacred boundary of the circle no less, and Rhiannon had allowed the grief at losing her mother the next day bury her trauma deep within, and beneath. For eighteen months she had repressed the memory, ignored its impact – until she ran into her attacker on the High Street and fell apart.

Beth had borne horrified witness to her daughter's breakdown. Watched as the memories of that night slammed back into her and brought her to her knees. Walked with her as she wandered, blind with tears of pain and anger, down deserted lanes, too scared to go home. Seen her submerged in a flower-strewn bath, wrestling with whether or not to allow herself to drift off into the peace of oblivion the warm water offered.

Beth understood the pain and suffering that made it feel like a good option – she'd felt that despair as the cancer had eaten away at her own body – but she refused to let it happen to her child. Somehow she'd managed to pull her molecules together enough to reach into the water and drag her daughter above the surface, although whether she'd actually achieved some kind of physicality, or just projected her terrified emotions and psychic will to Rhiannon, she had no idea.

The effort had torn Beth apart. She'd exploded into a million tiny pieces and scattered to the four directions. But she was glad to pay the price, to no longer exist, in whatever shaky form she'd been in, in order to help her daughter. She'd thought that was the end.

And yet here she was, a searing heat forcing her mouth open in a silent scream of anguish and agony. Was she in hell? Was she really the awful person she'd always feared herself to be?

The heat intensified, scorching every part of her, then she heard a loud crackling. Her eyes snapped open. She was in the woods, in the hour after the gloaming, and there was a furiously burning fire dancing on a witch's altar. An eerie woman with long black hair, deep ruby lips and a flowing scarlet dress was seated on the forest floor, her piercing eyes looking as though they would incinerate the person sitting across from her.

*Rhiannon.* In the billowing red dress she'd found in her wardrobe right after her bath. Looking terrified. Of the fire, of the woman, of herself.

No time had passed. Beth saw the chamomile flowers still twisted through her daughter's hair from the bath, saw the dampness of her curls, and knew it was the same night.

But what was she doing out here, back in the woods, in the very place she'd been assaulted? Being challenged by... Who was that woman? *What* was she?

A wrenching sob dragged her attention back to Rhiannon, and the pain etched into her face, clawing through her shoulders, ripped at Beth's heart. She couldn't hear what was being said – she still felt as though she was underwater – yet she could see its impact. She tried to move, to float down to her daughter and fold her in her arms, but she was frozen in place.

*Completely helpless.*

Beth wanted to scream at the woman to stop, to leave Rhiannon alone, to realise the damage she was inflicting with whatever she was saying, but she could only hover there, powerless, as she watched her darling daughter collapse in on herself all over again.

*And yet...*

Slowly she became aware that Rhiannon was changing. She was sitting up straighter. Her head was no longer bowed, and whatever she was saying to the mist-wreathed woman crouched across the altar from her, she was speaking with more confidence.

Beth's heart lifted. Expanded. It seemed the strange woman in red was helping her daughter in some way, healing her. Gratitude coursed through her, that she'd been able to witness this before she faded away to nothing. Because, crushed and defeated just an hour ago, Rhiannon's fortitude was beginning to emerge. Beth could sense her spirit blossoming, feel the courage spiralling out from her centre, and she felt great pride as she watched her daughter rise up, transformed, and head determinedly, defiantly, home. She moved to follow her – until the red-clad woman stared up at her, mouth open in an O of surprise. Or was it alarm?

Her dark, glittering eyes pinned Beth where she hovered above the altar, then she felt herself implode, and collapse down in a fiery jumble at the woman's feet.

"Who are you?" she hissed. "*What* are you?"

Beth stared at her in shock. "You can see me?"

A hand shot out and grabbed Beth's arm. "And you can see me. Very few people can."

"My daughter can." A sob escaped Beth, as the helplessness she'd experienced earlier returned. It devastated her that she could no longer help her children. Know them, and be known.

The woman peered more closely at her, just as Beth realised her own ghostly form had become solid. Her arm was being held, and she could feel the sensation, feel the pressure of the woman's grasp – a cruel, tight, grasp – and the warmth of contact.

"You are her mother." It wasn't a question.

Terror pulsed through Beth. Who was this woman, this stranger, who was clearly so close to her daughter? Was she a new priestess from Rose's circle? But why had she never heard of her? And what did she want with Rhiannon?

"I am called Aideen by some," the woman conceded, as though she'd read her mind. "I am... a guide of sorts. You do not need to fear on her behalf."

*Easier said than done.*

"I am more concerned about you Beth."

Shock made her tremble. How on earth did Aideen know her name?

Shrugging a delicate shoulder, the woman leaned in closer. "You are supposed to be dead."

"I *am* dead," Beth insisted angrily, then the fight went out of her, and she sighed. "To be honest, I don't know what I am, or why. I just want to help Rhiannon, and help my husband, but I can't seem to make myself known to them." There was desperation in her voice, and deep pain.

In an instant, the strange woman was by her side, one arm around her, and her touch this time was a sweet comfort in this moment of confusion, her presence a soothing balm.

"Can you help me?" Beth implored her. "Tell me why you can see me. Tell me how I can make my family see me too..."

As quickly as she'd arrived, Aideen was back across the altar, and Beth felt the absence physically as a deep chill, and emotionally as though she'd dropped into a freezing ocean of isolation. She shivered – and then she saw, out of the corner of her eye, a flash of gold. Squeezing her eyes tightly shut, she tried to breathe slowly in, then out. Tried to calm her mind, and steel herself against hallucinations. But when she finally opened her eyes and looked up, Aideen was gazing curiously at the spot where the gold had been, and Beth wondered again if something was following her. Chasing her. Sent to lure her back to the emptiness of real and final death.

"Did you see that?" she demanded.

Aideen gazed at her, perplexed, then shrugged it off. "We must close Rhiannon's sacred circle, and return her ritual objects to her," she said. "Will you help me?"

Although the woman had ignored her similarly worded request, Beth nodded numbly and bent to pick up her daughter's wand. For a moment her eyes rested on the black raven feather on the altar, then she raised her arms to thank and farewell the directions and the deities, confident they had assisted Rhiannon in some way.

A smile softened her face. It had been so long since she'd lifted a wand, or taken part in a magical ritual, and she loved the energy that coiled up from the earth and coursed into and through her, and the light from the moon and the stars that illuminated her and the strange red-clad woman. It was a moment to savour, to treasure, to be able to do this again.

Carefully she stepped out the circle widdershins, her daughter's wand held high, closing the sacred space by absorbing the border of the portal between the worlds into her and returning the clearing in the heart of the woods to its usual vibration.

*The circle is open, but never broken.*

The words she'd said so often in the past had lost none of their power, and she felt such a yearning to weave magic with Rose again, to call the directions with Laura, to invite her daughter to join her within the boundaries of the enchanted realm she'd so often been part of.

Desperate with longing, despite the joy from the touch of magic on her brow, she turned to speak to Aideen again, to demand answers. But there was no one there. And it was as though there never had been. The altar tools had vanished, the heat of the fire had been erased, and not even the lush grass appeared to have been sat upon.

Had she hallucinated everything here tonight? She wouldn't accept that, she couldn't. She had to believe that Rhiannon had been here, and that the red-robed Aideen had been with her, soothing her despair, easing her pain, healing her trauma. The alternative didn't bear thinking about.

Blackness swirled up around Beth, and this time she prayed for oblivion.

## Chapter 2

# The New Normal

### Rhiannon

"Kraw, kraw, kraw."

Rhiannon stumbled through the woods, branches smacking her in the face, and twisting vines and ground creepers tangling around her ankles and threatening to send her crashing to the hard earth. The rich scent of mouldering leaves made her recoil, so when the faintest hint of jasmine wafted past on a thin breeze, she tried desperately to focus on that. Jasmine reminded her of her mother, and made her feel safe – but she wasn't safe now. She was trying to outrun *the thing that happened*, and a world of pain.

"Kraw, kraw, kraw."

The sound was louder now.

Suddenly a huge black raven swooped down in front of her, the rush of air from its beating wings hitting her cheeks, and perched on a low-hanging branch. Imposing, intimidating. Gulping nervously, she forced herself to lift her gaze to his. The bird regarded her with fierce, beady black eyes, head tilted to one side. She trembled, but her nervousness faded when she saw the mischief in his expression, then noticed the small silver key he was clutching in his beak.

Hesitantly she held out her hand, then shut her eyes in panic when she sensed him lean down towards her. But she felt no pain, and he didn't bite her – he simply dropped the key into her palm, winked at her, then flew away. A wave of curiosity swept through her as her hand closed around the cold metal. Whose key was it? What would it unlock? Where did she need to take it? How could she figure it out?

A ripple of despair shuddered through her. She had no clue, and no way to discover one. Why would a bird torment her? Desperately she called out to him, begging him to return, to let her know what she was supposed to do with the key.

"Use your imagination beloved."

She gasped in shock at the strange voice. Was the bird speaking to her, or was it just her feverish imagination? Had one of the mist-wreathed women turned up? Staring around herself in growing horror, she realised she didn't even know where she was. And the huge trees around her were closing in on her. How had she ended up in a part of the woods she'd never seen before? A part of the woods filled with darkness and shadows, and ancient trees that seemed to want to harm her.

Struggling backwards to get away from a brooding old oak that was bending menacingly towards her, she smashed her head against the trunk of the birch behind her, then felt its rough bark through her dress as she slid down to the hard, cold ground. The sharp edges of the key bit into her flesh, and when she looked down, there was a bead of blood on her palm.

"Rhiannon, do not be afraid," the voice crooned. "You will discover how to unlock your pain."

She screamed in frustration – and the sound brought her abruptly back to consciousness, torn from a sleep so deep that surfacing made her groggy and disoriented. Feeling her quilt twisted around her legs, relief pulsed through her, that the horror had all been a dream.

Until she realised her waking life was its own kind of nightmare. Her heart raced as flashes of memory and pain from the past few days hit her, one after the other, a relentless flurry of punches to her gut.

Being devastated and betrayed by the break-up with her first boyfriend.

Enduring the horrifying, recurring dreamscape said boyfriend no longer entered to save her from, which triggered the re-emergence of the trauma she'd long buried for so long.

Coming face-to-face with the guy who'd inflicted that trauma, which ripped her apart all over again.

Tears trickled slowly down her cheeks, and her body trembled. With great effort she brought her breathing under control, then impatiently wiped her eyes.

She sighed. This was her new normal. Aware of what had happened to her, but not wanting to dwell there. Working on some kind of acceptance so she could move forward in order to function, yet recoiling from the reality.

Still shaking, she tried to force the images from her mind. She had to focus on what had come after.

The ghost of her mother, somehow dragging her from the bath she'd considered surrendering to.

A strange ceremony in the woods with the woman in red, who had provided comfort and healing, and reassurance that the assault was not her fault.

That was all fading though, and Rhiannon was terrified that she wouldn't be able to cope with school today. Already the insights she'd gained and the forgiveness she'd worked towards felt dreamy, elusive, a half-forgotten notion she could no longer quite grasp.

It scared her that she was now a completely different person than the one who had headed to Scotland a week ago for a holiday with her father and brother. Before they left, she broke up with her boyfriend. When they returned, she broke down. Falling apart, body and soul, as the long-ago trauma resurfaced. And while her spellcasting and ritual making in the woods last night had been soothing, even therapeutic, she wasn't anywhere near put back together.

She didn't know if she ever would be.

Desperately she longed for a week off, alone at home, while she tried to come to terms with what had happened. She felt too raw to be scrutinised by her classmates, or worried over by her teacher Laura. How could she focus on lessons when her heart and mind were torn apart and her soul was trying so hard to repair itself?

Perhaps most difficult of all, how would she keep her secret from her best friend? Try to appear normal to the girl she worked magic, and shared everything, with? She couldn't tell her what she'd endured eighteen months ago. Carlie's mother had suffered through far worse than Rhiannon had at the hands of a brutal man, and her friend was still working to come to terms with that, and reconcile Violet's mysterious past with her own perception and knowledge of her.

Besides, Rhiannon couldn't stand any more sympathy. After her own mum's death, she had resented the looks of pity cast her way, and the awful, hateful isolation she was consigned to as her friends tiptoed around her, or even worse, ignored her completely, not knowing how to deal with her grief.

*Ugh.*

Remembering how ostracised she'd felt from her childhood best friends Debbie and Sue back then made her feel even worse. How would she cope with seeing Debbie in class today, since it was Debbie's older brother who had... hurt... her? A flare of misplaced fury roared to life and coursed through her veins when she considered her old friend, but she took a deep breath and tried to tamp it down. It wasn't Debbie's fault.

Guilt and fear boiled in her stomach as she came back to the thought that had been torturing her. That it was her own fault, *the thing that happened*. She had been so desperate to do a healing ritual to save her mum's life that she'd ignored her instincts, or drowned them out all together, and entered the woods that full moon night with Evan, shedding her black velvet ritual cloak and standing trembling and naked before him when he insisted they must come together as the god and goddess did in order to fuel the spell.

She'd never been intimate with a guy before, never even had a boyfriend, and the assault on her body and her senses had devastated her. Which had been heightened further when her sick, frail mother had come staggering through the trees in an attempt to save her – then died the next day.

Racked by pain, shock and shame, Rhiannon had buried the trauma and let her grief at losing her mum consume her instead. Which had seemed like a sensible idea. It certainly put everything in perspective. But now the darkness had resurfaced, and she couldn't put it back in its bottle and hide it away again.

At first her anger had kept her warm, and lent her strength. During her ritual she had become the heat of the fire. Had felt herself being forged and strengthened in the flames. But now the fury had burned out, and she didn't know what she was left with.

Pulling on her school uniform, she picked up her hairbrush with a trembling hand. How was she going to do this?

A sparkle out of the corner of her eye dragged her attention to her dressing table, and the gold necklace the woman in the woods had gifted her. Stretching out a shaky hand, she picked it up, placed it around her neck and did up the clasp. The deep ruby red of the crystal gave off an eerie glow, even so far from the fire that had ignited between them during her ritual, and she focused on the deep shadows within the gem's surface as she slowly breathed in its steadying calm and power. The same soothing warmth seeped into her body, and she felt steadier.

Stronger.

During her ritual she had felt powerful, invincible, at one with nature and the earth. At one with her self. Now she just had to hold on to that.

*Maybe she could do this after all.*

Determined, she hurried downstairs and out the door, ready to face her first day back at school as a person transformed...

## Chapter 3

# *One Moment At A Time*

### Rhiannon

**D**ragging her feet up the steps of her school, Rhiannon shook off the sprinkling of spring snow that had gathered on her shoulders, and straightened up. She felt older, and colder in some ways, yet she reminded herself that she was stronger too.

At least, she hoped she was.

Her history teacher Laura waved to her across the corridor, and looked as though she was going to come over and chat. Not yet. Ducking quickly towards her locker, Rhiannon managed to avoid her – and bump right into Debbie.

"Hey Rhi, how are you?" her friend asked.

Forcing a smile, she lifted a hand to her pendant and desperately gripped the stone. "I'm fine."

Her voice sounded high, and shrill, and not in any way believable. *Breathe. Just breathe.* "How are you?"

"I'm great! Evan's down at the moment, home from college, and we're planning a party this weekend. You should come! It's been ages since you've seen him."

Rhiannon clutched at her stomach, the words a physical blow, and staggered backwards, up against her locker. She felt hot then cold. Fire then ice. And there was a buzzing in her head. Was she about to faint in front of everyone?

In the distance she heard the bell ring, and she held tight to the sound, an anchor to get her away from Debbie, away from invitations to party with the guy who... hurt... her.

"Anyway, it's on this Saturday, from three o'clock. Bring Carlie too. See ya!"

People swarmed around her, but Rhiannon felt alone. Adrift. As her knees started to buckle, she had a flash of another moment exactly like this. Eighteen months ago, the morning after *the thing that happened*, her back had slid down her locker as she fell to the floor, Evan's friend's taunting words in her ears. She couldn't do this, not again. She turned to run.

"Rhi, hey, sorry I'm late."

It was Carlie, cheeks flushed, breath coming quickly, arms thrown around her in greeting. "How was Scotland? When is spring actually going to start? And did you finish your homework?"

Her friend's touch warded off the darkness, and her casual chatter brought Rhiannon back to this moment, back to herself. Her panic receded, and not even the thought of how embarrassed she would be to not hand in her homework could drag her back under. Sheepishly she shook her head, and Carlie looked at her with sympathy.

"Don't stress, I'm sure Laura won't mind. Are you feeling okay?" She peered at her more closely. "You look, I don't know, not quite right? Are you sick?"

Grasping at that explanation as they hurried off to class, Rhiannon babbled about food poisoning and feeling washed out, and not getting home from Scotland till late the night before. No one need know they'd come back a couple of days early – just in time for her whole nightmare with Evan to resurface.

Laura bought the food poisoning excuse too, and told her to hand her homework in the next day. Smiling gratefully, Rhiannon took her seat and tried to focus on the lesson. If she just concentrated hard enough, maybe she could survive the day. Then maybe the week. And then the one after that.

*One moment at a time. One day at a time.*

*One problem at a time.*

As the week progressed, Rhiannon began to think that maybe she would survive this. Maybe she could find the strength to move forward, eventually. Her journal became her confidante, the repository of her tears, her fears and her wonderings. Writing about it helped, and reminded her of what she had to do.

First up, she had to forgive herself for burying it for so long. She'd had to pretend away *the thing that happened* so she could function after her mother died. Not that she'd functioned well, not for a long time, but it was self-preservation that had made her repress the assault. She wasn't conscious of it at the time – her brain must have worked of its own accord to enable her to cope. She supposed she should be flattered that her inner self now considered her strong enough to deal with it all.

Next, she had to figure out a way to face people and act *normal*, whatever that was. By Wednesday she was able to chat to Debbie without flinching, although she made an excuse to get out of the party. And by Friday she was feeling hope. Impatience even. She was over it. She wanted to be done with it. Which meant moving on.

Despair glittered in her eyes as she faced Carlie across the cafeteria table. "God, I hate being single. When will I meet someone, someone amazing? The mists women said love was coming for me."

Carlie tried to smother her laugh. "Seriously Rhi? It's only two weeks since you broke up with John. I'm sure you'll survive. I'm sure they would counsel patience if they were with us now."

Nodding grudgingly, Rhiannon sighed, and thought back to her dream of the raven with the key in his beak. Months ago, the woman in blue had told her to look for the raven and she would find her love. But where was she going to find a raven? Were her dreams of the mysterious black birds just another way for her to torture herself? Punish herself?

Before she could figure anything out, Jake rushed over to them with his lunch tray and slid in next to Carlie.

"Do you think we could get away with not working on our assignment this weekend?" he asked hopefully. "It's just that my cousin is coming down from London to stay for a few days, and I haven't seen him for a couple of years. So I'd feel bad ditching him and leaving him all alone with Pop to go off and study."

"Of course, we'll be fine," Carlie said. "And we can catch up Monday after school, yeah? Besides, we've got two more weeks, and we're pretty much done, so no worries."

Rhiannon hid a laugh. Carlie and Jake's Australian lingo always amused her, while also making her feel a little left out. These two had so much in common that she desperately wished her friend would see him in a romantic light. If anyone deserved a happy, loving relationship it was Carlie, not her. She was suddenly glad she hadn't cast that spell on Jake to make him fall for her.

"Is your cousin Australian too?" she asked.

"No, sadly he's English," Jake replied, deadpan, then laughed at her consternation. "Just joking! He was born in London, and has spent most of his life there, although he did live with us for a year in Perth when I was, I don't know, ten maybe, and he was thirteen."

"And is he cute too?" Rhiannon pressed.

Her friends both stared at her, and she blushed. "What? Can't a girl ask these things? People need to know!"

Jake grinned. "I'm sorry, of course you can ask. But I'm not sure – I haven't seen him since he was sixteen, and that was only briefly, when I came to London with my parents for a family reunion. He seemed kinda gangly and goofy, but I probably wasn't the best judge. And he might have grown into himself now. I think he's been apprenticing at a tattoo studio the last couple of years, so for all I know he could be a long-haired biker with a huge beard and full sleeve art by now."

Then his eyes widened. "Actually, would you guys want to have lunch with us tomorrow, or do something together? I'm not sure I'm going to be interesting enough for him, and I'm worried he'll be totally bored being stuck with just me and Pop all weekend."

Rhiannon knew Carlie was about to say no, but something within her was screaming that she had to meet him, even if just to practise talking to a male stranger, and work out how she felt around guys she didn't know. "Yes," she blurted out, before her friend could speak. "And there are loads of things we could do…"

By the time the bell for class rang, they'd decided to meet for lunch, then see what they felt like doing after that. Rhiannon consoled Carlie with a promise that they could leave at any point if they weren't having a good time, but what did they have to lose? It was only an hour of their time, it would help Jake, and she could practise her boy-conversation skills. After her short-lived relationship with John, she needed all the help she could get.

And who knows? Maybe it would be good for her to meet a friendly, non-threatening guy, to be able to relate to him on a normal level, and try to change her not-altogether-surprising view that all men sucked.

## Chapter 4

# The Starless Void

Beth

For hours Beth drifted. Barely aware. Barely conscious. Without direction or focus. Pushed and pulled within the starless void, and lacking the strength or will to see where she was or what was happening around her, or to her. She'd watched her daughter enact a healing ritual in the woods, then seen her rise up at the end, transformed, renewed, ready to be free. Healing would take time, but Rhiannon had begun the journey, so hadn't Beth achieved what she needed to do? Couldn't she float away now, and finally go wherever people went when they died?

Instead of the peace of eternal release though, Beth felt the flapping of black wings, and their rhythm swirled her back into being. Dizziness swamped her. When it finally passed, she opened her eyes, and found herself atop the tor. Its soothing magic was reaching out for her, anchoring her to the sacred ground and holding her safe.

"Kraw, kraw, kraw."

The sound of the raven drew her attention skyward, and the physical disturbance of its flight on the breeze pushed against her as it dove right at her. She flinched, then laughed at how pointless that was. She was a being of air now, rather than of the solidity of earth. Wondering if the bird was real, or phantom too, she peered back at it, just as curious about it as it seemed to be with her.

An image of the raven feather on Rhiannon's altar in the woods flashed into her mind. Was it a memory, or had the black winged creature transferred it to her? Maybe this bird was Rhiannon's spirit guide. Ravens appear to people when transformation and transmutation has kicked in. When they are in need spiritual rebirth.

"Will you help her with that?" she asked the raven, and was shocked when the bird nodded.

And even more shocked when it spoke. "Of course."

Despite feeling ridiculous that she was talking to a bird, her relief was palpable. "Thank you," she said cautiously.

"And your butterflies will help you," the raven cawed, then flew off in a flurry of feathers and distorted air currents.

*Her butterflies.*

Beth had forgotten all about them...

An image of a dawn ritual she'd done with Rose and her circle long ago swirled around her. They'd been up on the tor one new moon morning, not long after she and Mike had wed, at that magical moment between night and day, when the first light of the approaching dawn colours the sky, and the whole world thrums with possibility and promise.

She plunged backwards into the memory...

**B**eth placed another tentative foot before her on the darkened path, her long blue cloak eddying around her ankles, her breath coming out in little puffs of white mist. She shivered in the pre-dawn chill, but pushed onwards. Any second now, the path would open out before her, the air would warm slightly, and the steep climb up the side of the tor would bring a flush to her cheeks and heat to her body.

A smile lit up her face as she caught up with Laura, and they hugged hello before beginning the solemn, silent processional to the summit. The faintest wash of pink and gold in the eastern sky silhouetted the hulking hill, and Beth marvelled again that she had returned to this village. She had been born here, and had grown up here, yet was always so desperate to escape. Now though, without her parents in it, it was her perfect home.

"Good morning girls." Their priestess greeted them at the top, smudged them with burning lavender and sage, and welcomed them into the circle with their fellow witches.

There were thirteen of them this morning, and Beth grinned at the synchronicity. Her magic brought her such joy. It had healed her deepest wounds, provided a steadiness and delight to her daily life, and anchored her with such a strong sense of self, one she'd never imagined she was capable of experiencing.

The last person struggled up the hill, breathing hard, and Rose encircled her in the sweetly scented smoke then ushered her into the circle too. As the women joined hands around the altar, the priestess lifted her moonstone-tipped wand high and stepped out around them, moving deosil, and raised her voice to the heavens.

*By my will a circle formed,*
*Between the worlds where magic's born.*
*Please guard without and hold within,*
*The power and energy raised herein.*
*Hold us safely throughout this rite,*
*As we journey within to our own light.*
*This circle is cast, so mote it be.*

After she returned to her starting point, Rose entered the circle and stood at the central altar, then gazed with love at Beth. It was her turn to speak. Voice shaking only a little, she faced the south and lifted her arms to the sky.

*Element of fire, and of the south, with love, respect and gratitude I invoke you. Please burn away our doubts and fears so we may gaze with courage at our inner selves. Instil in us your seeking spirit, and fill us with passion and fiery purpose. Element of fire, welcome.*

Catching Laura's eye, she smiled as her friend turned to the west and raised her wand, then spoke her own words of invocation. Her voice was soft and watery, which was perfect.

*Element of water, and of the west, with love, respect and gratitude I invoke you. Please bathe us in your purity, wash away those things that no longer serve us, and fill us with your power to flow with what life brings us. Element of water, welcome.*

Next Glenda pivoted to face north. Her words were deep and rich, thrumming with an energy that seemed to rise up from the ground and flow into their circle.

*Element of earth, and of the north, with love, respect and gratitude I invoke you. Please anchor us with your strength and grounding as we go within, help us nurture our own hearts and souls, and teach us how to protect ourselves from doubt and harm. Element of earth, welcome.*

And then it was Miri's turn, and Beth gazed at her with wonder as golden light from the slowly rising sun spilled over and lit up her face, giving her an ethereal glow that only deepened her connection to her element and direction.

*Element of air, and of the east, with love, respect and gratitude I invoke you. Please bathe us in your dawning light, illuminate the paths to our deepest heart, grant us your intuition and clarity, and bring us clear insight on this journey within. Element of air, welcome.*

With great reverence, Rose welcomed the god and the goddess to their circle, then they all sank down onto the grass together, thick cloaks beneath them, and the chill of the morning dew balanced by the warmth of the reborn sun as it finally dragged itself above the horizon. They closed their eyes, and the priestess led them on a meditative journey within to discover their animal spirit guide, the creature who was drawn to them at this time to assist their growth and reflect back their spiritual learning.

Beth had been working magic with Rose for more than two years, so she slipped easily into a trance state, a smile flickering across her face as she found herself in the cool green of an ancient forest. The rich scent of the earth grounded her, while the perfume of the wildflowers made her almost drowsy.

Sunbeams filtered through the branches, dancing gracefully and illuminating the path ahead of her. She took a cautious step forward, not wanting to disturb the woodland or its inhabitants. This was a place of faeries and of the Otherworld, and she wouldn't be surprised if a fae being darted out from the shadows.

But it was a delicate winged creature of another kind that swooped down in front of her, then beckoned her forward. She followed, trusting the beautiful blue butterfly to show her what she needed to know.

After a gentle meander through the trees, the forest opened out into a golden green meadow, with a narrow blue stream bubbling through the centre. It was so welcoming that Beth hurried to the bank, slipped off her shoes and plunged her feet into the icy water. She scooped her fingers through it too, then placed her hands in her lap, palms up.

Perhaps she needed to meditate in order to summon her animal guide. Would it be a meadow-dwelling deer, or perhaps a wolf? Or a water creature – a turtle perhaps, or the salmon of knowledge?

A flash of movement out of the corner of her eye caught her attention. A second butterfly had joined the first, and they dove and dipped around her head, making her laugh, making her crane her neck to follow their soaring flight. Then one alighted on her left palm, and one on her right. She peered down at them, touched by their delicate beauty, by the tickling sensation of their tiny feet on her skin, and by their total lack of fear of her. They seemed to be staring at her, almost laughing at her, until suddenly she realised.

The butterflies were her spirit guides.

"Yes." It was a tinkling sound, as much laughter as speech, but somehow she understood it.

"We are here to awaken you to the beauty and lightness of life. We will remind you of the joy you already have in your heart, that you share with others without even realising. And we will guide you along your path of transformation, helping you heal, and work through issues, on the way."

She tried to remember what she knew about butterflies and their deeper meaning. "I've heard that you symbolise change and metamorphosis. Does that mean I will transform, that I'll burst forth from my cocoon into a magical new life?"

The butterfly on the left looked so saddened by her words that Beth felt tears well in her eyes. But the one on the right uttered the strange high-pitched laugh again. "Sweet Beth, you have already emerged. Look at you! You have been transformed by the love of your husband, by the nurturing of the priestess, and by your own hard work and inner strength. You are a light in the world, a light to others, and we can see the inner beauty that illuminates you."

The other one swallowed its sadness and nodded. "You are a healer and a messenger, and we are here today to remind you that you must still make time to be playful. To laugh and love. That is a vibration the world desperately needs, and it bubbles up within you and spills out with such clarity and joy."

A blush stained Beth's cheeks. She'd spent her whole life being told she wasn't good enough, wasn't smart enough, was just plain not-enough. It was too challenging to her view of herself to accept any of the praise these winged creatures were heaping on her.

"That is why we have come to you. To remind you to listen to your beloved, and to your priestess. They see your true self, and will help you see it too. And they will help you let go of the past that still affects you, even though it is over." The voice was almost stern this time, and she had to stifle a giggle at the thought of a grumpy butterfly.

"But you are correct," said the shyer, gentler butterfly. "You are approaching a time of transition, physically and emotionally, and we want to remind you that you will be supported throughout it. This new chapter will bring you great joy, and you will blossom into an even more complete version of your lovely self."

Puzzled, she tried to figure out what they could mean...

"Kraw, kraw, kraw."

The sound of the raven catapulted Beth back to the present, back to when she was dead, and she realised those long-ago butterflies had been talking about her transition to motherhood. Not long after that ritual she'd discovered she was pregnant with Rhiannon, and she had blossomed and grown, her magic increasing as she felt life swell within her.

The message of those butterflies had brought her comfort over the years. She hoped, if this raven was Rhiannon's guide, it would help her just as much.

Chapter 5

# The Call of the Raven

Rhiannon

Groaning, Rhiannon dragged herself out of bed and pulled on a pair of jeans. Yesterday when Jake had asked her and Carlie to hang out with him and his cousin she'd said yes, even though she knew it was the last thing Carlie wanted to do. But now she couldn't remember why she'd been so eager.

Maybe she just wanted to be reassured that not all guys were like her ex, who'd smirked while he told her witchcraft was, how had he so condescendingly put it? "Superstitious nonsense that ancient peasants believed in because they didn't understand what made the sun rise and the earth turn," and that anyone who was interested in it "was seriously lacking in intelligence".

She could laugh now, but it had really hurt at the time, so the idea of a boyfriend like Jake, who accepted magic and came to rituals with her, was incredibly appealing. Unfortunately she'd realised that Jake was in love with Carlie, so for a moment she'd dared to dream that his older cousin would be even more perfect, even more accepting, even more into magic. She definitely didn't miss John, yet part of her longed for the companionship, the being held, the kissing for hours, of her first relationship. But how could she even think about kissing someone while she dealt with the fallout of her past trauma revisiting her?

Pulling herself together, she headed downstairs for breakfast with her brother and her dad, trying to breathe out her nerves. She'd drive herself crazy with her overthinking. All she had to do was have a quick lunch with Jake and his cousin, then she and Carlie could leave and hang out together for the rest of the day.

*Piece of cake.*

The girls were still working out their excuses when they reluctantly opened the door of the cafe – but the moment Rhiannon laid eyes on Jake's cousin, she was transfixed. Her breath caught, and all thoughts of their prearranged departure plan in case of boredom were instantly forgotten. This guy was everything she'd ever dreamed of, right here in her village, right here in this cafe, and staring right at her.

"This is Tom, although apparently he prefers to be called Raven now," Jake said, as he nervously made the introductions.

Rhiannon gasped. Raven! What had the woman in blue said? *Love is coming for you Rhiannon, but you must recognise it, and grant it entrance to your heart, mind and life... Just look for the raven.* And on her way to the fire ritual in the woods, as she began to come to terms with her past and free herself from its despair, a raven had swooped down and gifted her a feather for her altar. Could this be the guy the mist women had told her was coming for her? The love she deserved?

Shaking her head to shake off the distracting thoughts, she tried to focus back on the guy in front of her – every six-foot-tall, long-dark-hair-and-muscled inch of him.

"Hi Carlie," Tom was saying, as he extended his hand to her. "And you must be Rhiannon." He turned to her, his gaze electric, and a shock zapped through her. "Jake's been filling me in, but he didn't tell me how gorgeous you are."

He stared at her, down deep in her soul, and she froze. Heat shot through her, and panic, and she was terrified she would sound stupid if she opened her mouth. Yet saying nothing would surely be worse.

Nervously she giggled, silently cursed herself for it, then mumbled a shy hello. But when Tom took her hand and held it to his lips, she shrugged off her hesitation, gathered her courage and hugged him. "It's lovely to meet you. Any friend of Jake's is a friend of ours!" she gushed, sliding into his side of the booth so she was close to him.

Carlie and Jake smiled in amusement as they sat down opposite them, and Rhiannon flushed red. Oh god. *Any friend of Jake's is a friend of ours?* What a stupid thing to say.

Before she could make a bigger fool of herself, the waitress came over, and Rhiannon pretended to focus on the menu while trying to compose herself. Alarm bells were ringing, because she had to stop herself from reaching out to touch Tom's face or hold his hand. There was a magnet pulling her towards him. A connection that throbbed through her and made her heart race. It was so much stronger than anything she'd felt for John, and it shocked her, that while the thought of John touching her now made her shudder, she wanted Tom to drag her into a passionate embrace.

What was wrong with her? It was only a week since she'd been shivering with anger and sobbing with pain as her memories of being assaulted resurfaced, yet here she was, wanting to kiss a stranger.

Dimly she heard Jake apologising to his cousin. Apparently last time they'd seen each other, Tom was a big meat eater, hence Jake choosing the cafe best known for its burgers, but since he'd started exploring paganism three years ago, he'd become vegetarian. Rhiannon's ears pricked up. He *was* into magic!

Excited, she turned to face him. "Are you in a coven, or is it less structured for you? Have you been studying? Do you have a particular focus – witch, druid, shaman – or are you more eclectic?" she asked, then paused. "Sorry for the twenty questions, but I'm always excited to meet other magical folk."

He smiled at her, and it was definitely a flirty smile. Rhiannon's cheeks reddened, and she tried not to drown in his mesmeric gaze. Not that that would be a bad way to go. She smiled back, ignoring Carlie's puzzled expression, although she could guess what her friend was thinking. *Magical folk.* Where had that even come from?

"I've been attending public rituals with a group near where I live, and studying with a priest and priestess I met last Mabon. They were initiated into Wicca years ago, but are more broadly pagan now, so I guess I'd just say I'm a witch," Tom replied. "I love the discipline of learning from them though, and I've been doing a lot of self-study too. Why, do you know much about magic?"

Rhiannon's eyes lit up. This was her chance to impress him. "I've been celebrating the wheel of the year and the phases of the moon since I was a kid. Carlie's grandma Rose is a priestess, and one of our teachers at school is part of her circle. So was my mum – it's all quite open here, attending rituals is just part of life."

Okay, yes, she was exaggerating a little. Well, a lot. She hadn't been practising for long at all – in fact she'd turned Rose down when she'd tried to include her. Turned her back on magic. And if Carlie hadn't arrived and begged her to accompany her to her first ritual, she wouldn't have turned back.

She didn't know why she was lying to Tom, but she couldn't stop. And oh god, that was a lie too. She *did* know why she was lying. She wanted to impress him. She wanted to seem worldly and experienced. *She wanted him to like her.*

Carlie had raised her eyebrows at the lie, but hadn't given her away, and she was grateful for that. She'd try to explain it later.

Then a terrible thought shook her. What if Tom liked Carlie, not her? Rowan had chosen her friend. Hell, even Jake had a thing for her. Was it the foreign accent? The air of mystery she carried with her without even realising? Or the sense of tragedy that clung to her, expressed in her big, sad green eyes, which seemed to engender sympathy in everyone?

*Argh!* Now she was hating on her friend for no reason at all – and thereby proving why people *should* choose Carlie over her. Luckily she didn't seem interested in Tom though, in fact she looked a little repelled, so maybe she stood a chance.

Relieved, Rhiannon turned her attention back to Tom, falling more and more under his spell with every moment. He was everything she wanted in a guy – smart and well-read, mature, magical, a little wild and untamed, creative, independent, tattooed. A memory floated back to her, of sitting out the back of Rose's cottage with Carlie not that long ago, rattling off that list.

*Perhaps Tom was the answer to her love spell.*

Forcing herself to concentrate on what he was saying, she stared into his gorgeous eyes, and felt herself falling again. As though reading her mind, Tom caught her gaze and smiled right at her, one corner of his mouth quirked up knowingly. Then he winked. Blushing scarlet, she looked down at her coffee in embarrassment and confusion – was he reading her mind?

"I consider myself a witch too," she blurted out, trying to keep her voice even. "We celebrate the sabbats and the new and full moons with Rose – and Jake and your grandad even came to the last one, at Imbolc. And Carlie and I formed a coven six months ago, and have been studying together and doing our own private rituals ever since."

Jake shot her a look half curious, half hurt that they hadn't asked him to join them, but she couldn't think about that now. Tom was looking at her with new respect, and more interest.

"Perhaps we could work some magic together," he said, eyebrows raised and tone suggestive.

She batted her eyelashes at him. "I'd love to."

For a moment she felt herself float out of her body and look down at herself, wondering why she was pretending to be more mature than she really was. From his sultry voice and intense gaze, she knew he was talking about sex magic, and part of her was mortified, while another part was secretly thrilled. There was challenge in his eyes though. Was he just teasing her? Making fun of how young and inexperienced she was? Desperately she wanted to prove him wrong.

To pretend, even for a little while, that she was grown-up enough, and confident enough, to slip out of her clothes in front of this sexy guy and work a spell like her mum had worked.

A vision hit, of sitting atop the tor with the blue-clad woman while white angel terns wheeled overhead. Rhiannon of the birds, she'd called her. Maybe that was their link. Maybe she and Tom both had spirit animals that were birds. Was that their connection? She certainly *wanted* to have a connection with him.

And she'd been noticing ravens every day for the past week. Was this a sign they should get to know each other better? She hoped so.

When the waitress brought their burgers, Rhiannon noticed Carlie staring at her. Did her friend think less of her that she was flirting with a stranger so soon after her break-up? But there was something so compelling about Tom. She was so drawn to him, and his witchyness was a big part of it.

Suddenly all the things Carlie had told her about Rowan started to make sense. The incredible instant attraction. The weak at the knees sensation. The heart connection. The falling so hard and fast that she couldn't catch her breath. This was so much more intense than what she'd felt with John, so much more real.

Sitting here with Tom made her feel hot and cold all at once. All grown up, yet woefully young. Shaken to her core, yet calmer and more centred than she'd ever been. And when he stared at her the way he was doing now, she felt naked, like her soul was being laid bare, and he could see to the very essence of her. Her strengths and weaknesses. Her frailties. Her mistakes. Her pettiness. Her cruelty to Carlie over Rowan.

As she thought her friend's name, Tom turned to look at her across the table. "So Carlie, how do you see yourself?" he demanded.

"I suppose I'm a witch," she stammered. "But I don't take the goddess as literally as Rhiannon and my grandmother do, so I'm not sure I can actually claim that word for myself..."

She trailed off, looking uncomfortable. Looking like she wanted to run. For some reason Tom was making Carlie uneasy, and Rhiannon was scared her friend would flee at any moment.

"Her boyfriend was a druidic shaman, or a shamanic druid, and they worked a lot of magic together," she said quickly, trying to drag Tom's attention away from her friend, while also letting him know they dated witches. She desperately wanted to impress him.

But she soon wished she hadn't opened her mouth. Tom was staring at Carlie, then at Jake. "Where is he today?" he asked, suspicion seeping from his voice, and Rhiannon groaned. The judgement in his tone was palpable, as though he thought Carlie was two-timing with Jake and was beneath contempt.

Carlie looked as though she'd been punched in the stomach, and Rhiannon felt awful that she'd brought it up. She tried to think of something to say, a way to distract Tom, but before she could, Jake put a comforting hand on Carlie's arm and faced his cousin.

"He died," he said simply, coldly, and with no room for further questions. There was a note of warning in his eyes as he glared at his cousin. Yep, Jake was head over heels for her friend.

"Rhiannon."

Her head snapped around to Tom. He hadn't said her name out loud, yet she'd felt it, burning her up inside. He'd called to her, and was drawing her to him without a word. Without even looking at her. She marvelled at his power, at his confidence, at his strength. Felt him absorbing something from her. Was he feeding on her growing feelings? Was he encouraging them?

Her tummy tightened, and she felt the most incredible attraction to the guy sitting next to her. He was talking to Jake and Carlie, yet he was in her head, asking her what she wanted from life, from him. Asking her if she was ready to leap into the fire. She felt breathless. Oblivious to the conversation happening around her. Consumed with this shadow world communication between her and Tom.

Closing her eyes, she shut out everyone and everything else, and allowed her mental barriers to fall. And she saw Tom, in her mind's eye, standing before her, in a long cloak tipped with raven feathers. His eyes smouldered, and his lips quirked up. An invitation. A challenge. When he held out his hand, she raised her own to meet his, almost against her will. If she had any will left. The strongest sense of yearning enfolded her, and she wanted to throw herself at his feet, or pull him into her arms, she wasn't sure which.

As he moved towards her, his cloak shifted, revealing his bare chest. When he took another step, his naked thigh slipped through. She shivered, terrified yet excited. The moment their eyes locked, she transformed into flame. Burned into smouldering embers. Crumbled to ashes, incinerated in his arms. Yet not a single thing could stop her wanting it to happen.

She had to say something, had to break this mind connection somehow.

"How do you feel about working skyclad?" she blurted out, then groaned as all eyes turned to her. Such a great way to shift the focus from the sexual charge between them – talk about working magic with no clothes on.

But Tom was delighted by the diversion, gazing at her with another flirty smile. "It's my favourite way to work." He grinned. "And you?"

Blushing again, she tried to channel some confidence, to seem unperturbed by the conversation. "Well, it's been really cold of late, so I've favoured practicality. And of course it depends on who you're working magic with."

"Of course," Tom said, and this time his charged gaze melted her insides. He leaned in close, voice dropping to a whisper. "I wouldn't want just anyone to have the privilege of seeing you naked."

Rhiannon gasped, and he grinned, but then he leaned back and dialled down the intensity, and for a while the four of them chatted about less contentious things. She allowed her mind to wander again as she imagined Tom standing atop the tor with her, hand in hand, chalice held high, cloaks slipping free from their...

"Rhiannon?"

It was Carlie, asking her something, and she sounded worried. She looked up at her friend, but wasn't able to avoid glancing at Tom. He smirked at her, but she saw something else in his eyes. There was danger there, but also... *Surprise?* Had he seen something in her she wasn't even aware of?

She focused on Carlie, then jumped as Tom's hand ran along her thigh. Despite the denim between his hand and her skin, it felt like her flesh had been branded. Like her soul was on fire. She concentrated her attention on Carlie and Jake, but all she wanted to do was throw herself into Tom's arms and let him burn her up.

She'd wanted to dance in the fire, and now it seemed she had met her match. Met the flame that would transform her – or totally consume her. She wasn't sure which. She wasn't sure she cared either. When he removed his hand to pick up his coffee, she almost cried out, almost snatched it back. She wanted to feel his hands on her, all over her. She wanted him to touch her, body, mind and spirit.

God, what was wrong with her? She started to shake, terrified of what she was feeling. Horrified by the need in her. Scared of what she would do for this guy she'd just met. Who wasn't even looking at her, yet was burned into her soul. Seared into her flesh. She wanted to give herself to him, lose herself in him, and that frightened her more than anything.

When the waitress came over to announce they were closing to prep for dinner, Rhiannon panicked. She couldn't leave now. Couldn't leave Tom, and whatever this... thing... between them was. Swallowing down her nerves, she turned to him.

"There's a cafe down the road that has the best chai in town – we should all go there," she said. And was secretly relieved when Carlie made her excuses, as she'd known she would, and Jake insisted on walking her home. He was so sweetly predictable. Rhiannon's heart started beating faster, relief and fear combining into a heady mix.

"It was lovely to meet you Tom," Carlie said, holding out her hand. Always the polite one.

He smiled at her. "It was wonderful to meet you too, and I'm so sorry about –"

She shook her head, cutting him off. "It's fine, you didn't know," she replied stiffly, then hugged Rhiannon.

Relieved that Tom had made amends with Carlie, and excited that they'd be alone together now, Rhiannon said goodbye to her friends then gazed at Tom. Who looked just as delighted as she was to be left on their own. Relief coursed through her, that he hadn't wanted to go home with his cousin.

"I've got a key to get back in, so don't worry if I'm late home," he said to Jake with a wink.

A shiver swept over Rhiannon. Of excitement, or fear? For a moment she hesitated. But she was supposed to be the new Rhiannon, right? Taking a stand. Reclaiming her power, her strength and her magic. Confident enough to speak to anyone, be alone with anyone. Filled with the courage of fire, and brave enough to trust herself, and risk her heart.

She took a deep breath. "Let's go."

Chapter 6

A Rising Fire

Rhiannon

*U*ntethered. *Unbound. Free.*

Carlie and Jake walked off up the street, and Rhiannon suddenly feared she would float away, off into the air.

As though sensing her conflict, Tom took her hand. They stood on the pavement, facing each other. "Are you sure you don't need to leave too?" he asked, staring into her eyes as he gave her an excuse to back out. Taking a deep breath, she nodded. He smirked again, and part of her wanted to slap him, wanted to tell him she wouldn't just do whatever he wanted. And yet, she would.

*Mixed up. Confused. Intoxicated.*

She knew she wasn't thinking clearly, yet she wanted to never think straight again. She was ready to fall. Was this the way to get over her resurfaced trauma? Fill herself with the love of a good man, to blot out the bad?

*And, um, love? What was she thinking?*

His voice broke the spell. "So, you mentioned amazing chai?"

"Yes. This way." She was relieved to have a task, to have to move, and she quickly took Tom down the road to Kylie's Cafe, where they settled together at a small table and ordered tea. But now they were alone, Rhiannon suddenly had no idea what to say. Fear clutched at her heart. *What was she doing here with a guy she didn't know?*

While she busied herself with the teapot and tried to will her cheeks to stop blushing, Tom picked up the conversational slack. Gratefully she listened as he chatted about his and Jake's grandfather, what it was like staying with his cousin in Australia one long-ago summer, the music he liked and the book he was currently reading. An hour later, when their next pots of chai arrived, he shared about losing his grandmother eighteen months earlier.

Moved by his genuine sorrow, Rhiannon hesitantly confessed that her mother had died around the same time. Tom's hand reached for hers, and the empathy in his eyes, in his voice, was genuine – yet his touch sent her heart rate spiking, and she had trouble concentrating on his words, too focused on his lips, and their physical connection.

Reading her mind again, he broke their contact, picking up his mug and taking a sip. "Tell me about the land here," he said, sensing she needed to ground. Relieved, she told him about the energy of the tor, and the power of the mists, and he looked spellbound when she described the Otherworldly woman she'd met on the summit, who had helped soothe her pain in the first awful weeks of her grief.

"Will you take me there?"

She nodded, excited that he didn't want the afternoon to end either, and stood up cautiously, careful not to knock anything over. She was so nervous around him. Taking her hand again – which sent a rush of goosebumps up her arm – Tom let her lead him back up the High Street, and she thought her heart would burst with joy.

When they got to the meadow at the bottom of the tor, Rhiannon indicated the path to the top, but he shook his head, and gently pulled her off to the side. Puzzled, but willing to go wherever he wanted, she followed him around the lower slope of the hill.

Apple blossoms scented the air, and she stared around herself with new eyes. She was embarrassed that she'd never come this way. Usually she took the front path up, and at her coven dedication with Carlie she'd made the climb from the back of the tor, up the steep side, which was stunning and dramatic. But this way was so sweetly magical. There was a gentle energy rising from the earth, and a sense of enchantment in the air.

When they reached a small gate, Tom stopped abruptly, and she almost ran into him. Quickly he slid through, then closed it behind him and held up his hand. "It's a kissing gate, and you have to pay me with a kiss in order to pass."

Her breath caught as she stared at him. He wanted her to kiss him? Her face flushed with excitement, and shyness. What if she was a bad kisser? Or she slipped and fell on her face as she reached for him? Even worse, what if he was joking, and he laughed when she attempted to lock lips with him?

"No need to look so serious Miss Rhiannon," he teased, then leaned forward and kissed her on the cheek, before ushering her through the gate and continuing onward through the trees.

In a daze, she raised a hand to her cheek, then grinned. Surely he must like her a little, if he'd kissed her! Her head spun with possibility and hope, the pale light surrounding them became brighter and more radiant, and a deep hum from the earth vibrated up through her body. Of course it could just be the unfolding of spring within the ground beneath her feet, but she *felt* her blood thrumming in her veins, felt alive in a way she hadn't before, and she knew in her heart it was because of Tom.

Tom who had paused at another gate, and this time kissed her lightly on the lips before allowing her through. Before she could float away, made weightless with her joy, he took her hand again, and they meandered through a lush, magical woodland on the lower slopes. There was a chill in the air within this grove, a touch of magic that saturated her skin and seeped into her body, and her mind. Being with Tom was enchanting, like a faery tale.

And then, after one more kissing gate, they wove their way upward, following an almost invisible pathway to the summit. It folded back on itself at times, then hit the steep side, where they had to stop holding hands and cling to the grassy earth, before it evened out and spiralled around, like a labyrinth or a maze.

Dizziness overwhelmed Rhiannon, and dimly she remembered Rose mentioning a labyrinth on the tor. How strange that she'd forgotten it. Or not seen it, since the pathway, though faint, could certainly be discerned if you looked. Did something Otherworldly hide it from eyes not ready to see it? From minds not aware of its purpose? Was it an initiatory path, and if so, was she equipped to handle it? And was Tom going to initiate her into something?

A blush enveloped her whole body as she imagined what that might be, and she got even hotter when he turned to her and winked. Oh god, who was this guy? How deeply magical was he? What powers did he have? *What powers was he going to use on her?*

Eventually her heartbeat settled back into its normal rhythm, the slope levelled out, and they reached the top of the tor. The view always took her breath away, and this afternoon was no exception. Her whole body was buzzing, and she could feel so much raw energy coursing into her from the earth. Or was it coming from Tom? He was so powerful, she knew that already. So knowledgeable. So magical.

Sensing movement overhead, she gazed up at the brilliant blue sky. Ravens were wheeling above them, and a flash of her time with the angel terns played out in her mind, so it looked as though the white birds were dancing through the sky with the black ones. It was a beautiful image, and she prayed it meant she and Tom would be dancing together at some point, echoing the graceful movements of these winged creatures.

Suddenly she felt a hand on her shoulder, and he spun her around, into his arms, and dipped her in a strange slow rhythm. Dizziness shot through her again, along with a moment of panic. Could he hear her thoughts? Then she grinned. Did it matter? She felt so warm, so safe, so loved.

Shaking her head, she tried to dislodge that thought. Who was she kidding, thinking Tom could ever love her? He was amazing. Smart. Artistic. Inspiring. Magical.

Sensing her distress, he gently untangled her from his arms and sat down on the grass, pulling her down with him, then letting go of her hand.

"It's so beautiful up here isn't it," he commented, looking off over the green fields and gentle hills. Rhiannon breathed a sigh of relief, grateful that he was backing off and giving her some breathing space. Even though she felt bereft now that he was no longer touching her.

"It is." She forced herself to focus on him and this moment, rather than the loss of his touch. To be here now.

"You must have had some amazing experiences." He gazed at her expectantly, so she nervously told him about her coven dedication with Carlie, when they'd each encountered a woman of the mists atop the tor, who'd gifted them their first ritual tools.

"That's incredible, that they came to both of you," Tom said, and he looked at her in a new light, like she wasn't some silly schoolgirl, too young and naive for his notice. Warmth spread through her, just as the sky started to turn all pink and gold as the sun began to set. It was so breathtakingly beautiful, more beautiful than it had ever seemed before, and she wondered if it was because she was seeing everything with new eyes because she was with Tom. Or was it part of her own magic, her own knowledge? Something that taking the labyrinth path up the sacred tor had unlocked within her?

Before she could ask, Tom leaned over and kissed her. Properly kissed her. Not just the feather-light peck from the kissing gates, although it was gentle too. At first. And then he deepened the kiss, and she felt her mouth opening to him even as her heart did. Felt a stirring of desire in the pit of her stomach. She was floating, yet was more grounded than she'd ever been. He pulled her to him, until she was sitting in his lap, legs wrapped around him and body pressed close. His arms encircled her, one hand tangled in her hair, and she moaned softly, her body on fire where they touched.

Faintly she was conscious of the sunset colours, of the sky aflame, but she was disappearing into him, melting against him, until all her awareness was concentrated in the touch of his fingers on her skin, his lips on her throat, his chest pressed against hers. She had no idea how much time passed – it could have been a single moment, or eternity. The world around them turned dark, but they kept kissing, and she felt as though they were the only two people on earth.

His kisses became more insistent, and she felt her own fire rise to meet his. She wanted to burn up in his arms, wanted to smoulder to ashes with him. His hand was pushing her t-shirt up, and a trail of fire played across her naked stomach where his fingers swept across it.

Her breathing became ragged, and there were tears in her eyes, but they were tears of want and wonder, not fear.

Just as she thought her heart would melt within her, thought about ripping his shirt off so she could feel his bare flesh on hers, he gently pulled back. His breathing was as uneven as hers, his lips swollen from their kisses, and there was lust in his desire-darkened eyes.

"You're beautiful Rhiannon," he whispered, voice hoarse.

She blushed as she tried to get her breathing under control, but the star-speckled night had fallen, so he couldn't see the colour of her cheeks. Drunk with emotion, she leaned forward and kissed him, just for a moment, then swayed back. "You are too."

He grinned at her. "I'm sorry I've kept you out so late. Will you be in any trouble?"

She shook her head, then looked at her watch and gasped. Where had the day gone? They'd met at the cafe with Carlie and Jake nine hours ago, although it felt like a lifetime now. How long had they lingered over chai? How many hours had it taken them to make their way through the labyrinth? How long had they been kissing?

"I like kissing you," he said softly, then helped her to her feet and drew her into his arms. She could hear his heartbeat as she leaned her cheek against his chest, and it made her smile. Then she remembered how late it was, and groaned. Her dad would assume she was with Carlie, but she should get home before he checked.

Regret knifed through her, and she silently swore – and Tom nodded as though she'd spoken it out loud. Had she? No, it was just that he was inside her head. And her heart, and her physical self too. Just the thought of his lips on hers was making her whole body tingle. She couldn't bear to be torn away from him.

"Could I walk you home?" he asked her, and she smiled with joy.

Looking out at the lights of the town twinkling below them, she felt like she was floating again. Or had been in another dimension. Peering ahead, she saw the light change and the atmosphere ripple before them, as though the mists that had closed so gently around them were releasing them back to the real world.

The boring world. The world without Tom in it. Reluctantly she headed for the path back down, determined not to break down until she was alone in her room.

Outside her front door he kissed her goodnight – kissed her goodbye – and a wrench of disappointment jolted through her. But Tom drew back and smiled at her, and she drowned all over again in his piercing gaze. "It's not goodbye Miss Rhiannon. I've loved being with you today, and I'm grateful that you showed me the magical places of your town."

Laughter bubbled up and out of her. "I think you showed me more than I showed you," she said softly, then blushed. "I mean, showed me the sacred places and pathways of this town."

"They reveal themselves to those who are worthy," he insisted, then leaned down and kissed her again. "More importantly, can I see you tomorrow?"

Gasping in surprise and delight, she nodded eagerly.

"Same cafe?"

She nodded again.

They made plans, then Tom finally tore himself away. After watching him disappear into the darkness, Rhiannon drifted dreamily inside. Her dad called out to her, saying he'd saved her some dinner, but she shouted back that she'd eaten at Carlie's, surprised at the ease with which the lie fell from her tongue, and hurried upstairs to her room. Flopping down onto the bed, she stared at the pale green stars on the ceiling and smiled as she replayed every second with Tom, from the moment he'd taken her hand in his and kissed it when they'd been introduced at the first cafe, to sharing their hopes, dreams and grief over chai, then their magical hours on the tor.

*Had* they fallen through the mists into a different realm, an Otherworld? A place where time moved differently, and hours of kissing passed in a heartbeat? Finally though she gave up on trying to find an explanation, to rationalise the magical, and focused on the sensation of his lips on hers.

She couldn't wait to see him again.

Tomorrow was way too far away.

Chapter 7

### Beth

Her head was still filled with the sound of beating raven wings when Beth found herself back in Rhiannon's room. And noticed, for the first time, the artwork on her wall. She swooped closer to investigate. It was a spirit guide piece, no doubt with a reading to match, clearly created for her daughter. She wondered when she'd had it done, and who had painted it for her.

It was beautiful.

In the middle was a vision of Rhiannon, all long golden hair, piercing blue eyes and floaty white dress, but her form was merged with that of a white swan, and you couldn't tell where the girl ended and the regal snow-coloured bird began. A white feathered cloak was slung over her shoulder, and there was a blurring around the edges of both human and creature, which evoked such a strong feeling of magic that Beth could feel it emanating outward even to where she hovered.

And in a corner of the artwork was a small white horse, with a trail of golden stars making a glittering bridge from the centre of its brow to the centre of Rhiannon's forehead, connecting the two on an etheric level. Dappled sunlight added to the mystical impact. The white horse was one of the goddess Rhiannon's companions, a symbol of love, grace and dignity, of perfect trust, and of enduring through hardship. Anxiously she hoped that it had been able to lend her daughter that strength, those qualities, when she was healing from her grief at losing her mother, and now as she worked through the resurfacing of her other trauma.

Beth was stunned by all the connections in the painting to the Celtic deity she'd named her daughter for. Rhiannon of the birds, guardian of white horses, was the goddess of love, transformation, wisdom and inspiration. She was connected with the cycles of the moon and the stars, and with healing and forgiveness, inspiring people to discover their own ways to survive trauma, work through their hurt and find joy again. She was about movement and change, and remaining steadfast and comforting in times of crisis and loss.

That was why Beth had started working with this goddess when she first joined Rose's enchanted circle. With her help, she'd been able to let go of the pain and damage of her childhood, so when she and Mike had a daughter, she didn't even have to wonder what to name her. They'd both been so proud as they watched their Rhiannon grow up, embodying so many of the qualities of this maiden goddess.

Floating over to the painting, she peered more closely at the swan, where it melded and became one with Rhiannon. She didn't know where the raven she kept hearing fit in, but she was relieved that the swan was with her daughter as a guide. It would help her work through and let go of pain, focus on hope, and find balance. She was only seventeen, and had already been through so much. Beth prayed her animal guardians would lend her strength as well as encouraging her to move forward and celebrate all the good in her life – her friendship with Carlie, her magic with Rose, and her loving family with her dad and her brother Brodie.

The painting touched Beth deeply, and she smiled as she reached out a ghostly hand to trace the pattern of the swan. There was another reason she loved these graceful creatures.

The train was speeding towards London, and Beth laughed with delight. "When will you tell me what we're doing? Or where we're staying? Or anything at all about the next four days?"

Her voice was playful. She *was* incredibly curious, but she also loved the romance of this wild and spontaneous adventure, and didn't mind that it was a mystery.

Mike smiled at her. "Patience sweet Beth. Everything will be revealed soon enough."

Tucking one of her long blonde curls behind her ear, he leaned across and kissed her, then pulled out a thermos from his bag and poured her a cup of hot, milky coffee, just the way she liked it. *Ah, she could get used to this.*

For six wonderful months she and Mike had been dating, and she loved him even more now than when they'd met again eighteen months ago. She'd fallen for him right away, but for a year she'd silently pined over him, until he finally realised he had feelings for her too. The wait had been for the best though. Mike had been devastated when his childhood sweetheart, Rose's daughter Violet, had disappeared without a trace, and although it had been difficult for Beth to hide her love and just be his friend, she was glad she hadn't seduced him into what could have been just a rebound fling. Now, for the most part, she was confident that he genuinely cared for her. She still had the odd moment of insecurity, but that was her own issue, and no reflection on him or how he treated her.

Since he'd confessed his feelings for her, they'd had lots of romantic nights out, and even more cosy nights in. They'd been to music festivals, done rituals together, and written long letters to each other every day when he had to travel to Edinburgh for work. But this was the first time they'd gone away together.

A grin lit up her face as she recalled the morning's events. At 9am there had been a knock on the door of the apartment she shared with Laura. A delivery guy was standing in the hallway, arms filled with a huge bouquet of pink roses. He thrust the flowers, and a card, into her hands, then left.

Laura had sighed dramatically when Beth wandered back to the kitchen, but she was happy for her friend, despite her own lack of success on the dating front. As she lifted their only vase down from the top of the cabinet, Beth had read the card, and gasped.

"What does it say?" Laura asked impatiently.

*Dearest Beth,*
*I know you have a long weekend off from college, so I took the*
*liberty of arranging three nights in London for us.*
*I'll pick you up at 11am today, if that's okay.*
*Lots of love, Mike xx*

Her friend squealed with excitement. "Quick, you have to get ready, he'll be here in two hours. What will you wear? What will you take? Ooh, what do you think you'll be doing?"

Beth's mind whirled. What *would* she take? What would she need? And two hours? Should she be annoyed at the lack of notice?

"Oh Beth, that's the most romantic thing ever," Laura gushed. "You're going to have the best time. I'd be jealous if I didn't know you two are absolutely made for each other."

Hugging her friend, Beth dragged her into her room to help her pack, then jumped in the shower. When Mike knocked on the door at eleven, she was sitting calmly at the kitchen bench drinking coffee and reading a book, although her mind was racing with all the possibilities. She hoped she'd packed the right things.

When they pulled into Paddington Station she was none the wiser, but she followed eagerly as they jumped on the Tube towards Kensington and Westminster. Memories of her year at college in London flooded back, and she was overwhelmed by how much her life had changed since then. She was happy, for a start. And she was in love – and loved – by this gorgeous man.

A thrill raced through her when they got off at St James's Park Station. Surely they couldn't be staying in this beautiful, glamorous area, so close to the Palace and Parliament, as well as the parks where she used to sit and watch the swans? Yet it seemed they were. Mike took her hand as they emerged from the station, and she tried desperately to control her excitement, because surely they weren't staying at...

But they were. As he guided her up the long tree-lined courtyard to St Ermin's Hotel, she gasped. She'd walked past this place often when she'd lived in the city, in awe of its history and old-world glamour, but she'd never gone inside.

She turned to Mike, her eyes alight with joy. "How did you know?"

"That you'd always wanted to stay here?" he asked.

Beth nodded.

"I remember you mentioned it once, when you were talking about the bees."

"But that was a year ago! Before we were even dating."

Mike shrugged. "I always listen to what you say."

So touched by his words that she felt she might burst, she followed him into the opulent, light-flooded lobby, and gazed around in wonder. White marble columns, velvet-upholstered chairs, huge pots of flowers, and a grand staircase spiralling up to the next floor. There was an elegance to it, a charming touch of European style, but Beth was most impressed that her boyfriend had remembered her desire to see it from a single long-ago conversation, when they were still just friends.

Their room was beautiful too, and she threw her arms around him as soon as they were inside. "It's gorgeous Mike, thank you so much. This is the best surprise ever."

He smiled, his eyes crinkling at the corners in that way she loved. "This isn't the whole surprise."

He would say no more on the topic though. He just set her bag in the corner, then opened the closet door, revealing a flash of white. "I'm just popping out to a little bakery around the corner, which makes the best cupcakes in the world, so we can have one with our coffee and chill out for a while. We'll have to leave by 6:30 tonight though, if that's all right with you?" When she nodded, he paused, and his cheeks flushed red. "And I hope it's okay, but Rose helped me choose a dress for you, if you'd like to wear it."

And he quickly left the room.

Beth's head spun. Where were they going? Rushing over to the closet, she peered inside, then pulled out the dress hanging within. It was stunning. So much better than anything she'd brought with her, but still very much her, with swirling layers of different fabrics that managed to look a little witchy, despite being white.

Hurrying into the bathroom, she stepped into the shower, grateful for the luscious gardenia-scented gels and lotions laid out for her. When she emerged half an hour later, the new dress swirling around her ankles as she walked, her long curls still damp, Mike handed her a cup of coffee and a cupcake, and she sank into the comfy chair with a groan of delight.

Mike grinned. "You look like a fallen angel. In a good way!"

Biting into the cupcake, Beth laughed, spraying a few crumbs. "Thanks, I think. But seriously, thank you for the dress, it's gorgeous. And thank you for the coffee and cake. Now, are you going to tell me where we're going tonight?"

Shaking his head, he lifted his own coffee to his lips, and asked her about her time living in London. Beth was surprised by how quickly the time flew, and how comfortable she felt with him.

As the sun lowered and lights began to turn on across the city, they tore their eyes away from the window and headed out into the magic of the night. They wandered through the glittering streets hand in hand, then down a narrow laneway that emerged at St James's Park. They followed its perimeter, laughing in delight as a squirrel paused right next to them. She gazed around, wide-eyed, loving the energy that pulsated from cafes and spilled out of taxis as people tumbled out onto the pavement.

As they passed the lions of Trafalgar Square and wandered alongside the National Gallery, Beth tried to figure out where they were going. Before she could ask again, Mike paused to buy a rose from a street vendor, wove it into her hair, then leaned down to kiss her. "Ready for dinner?"

Nodding enthusiastically, she surrendered to the not knowing, and they had a beautiful meal in a cosy, romantic restaurant. She was so grateful to be there, in that moment, with the man she loved, drinking red wine and eating exquisite food. But when the waiter asked them if they wanted coffee and dessert, Mike said there was no time, and they were off again. As they continued their walk through the glittering city, Beth hardly dared hope, but when they came to a stop outside the glamorous old Royal Opera House, she sighed with pleasure.

"Really?" she whispered hopefully, eyes twinkling with excitement.

Mike smiled as he nodded. "Swan Lake. You said you'd always wanted to go."

Hugging him fiercely, she repeated her thanks, then spun around on the pavement, feeling the layers of white lace and chiffon swirl around her like feathers. "It's all so perfect."

"Like you," Mike said. "Ready?" He took her arm, and they hurried inside, caught up in the crush of people heading for their seats.

A uniformed usher led them to the front row, and Beth grinned again. "You've been planning this for ages, haven't you?"

"A little while," he admittedly bashfully. "I just wanted to make the perfect night for you. It's our six-month anniversary after all."

Beth kissed him, more passionately than she usually would in public, then drew back as the lights went down. As soon as the curtain rose, she was focused entirely on the stage, spellbound by the story, and the dancers, and the enchantment they wove with physical expression rather than words. Sitting in the grand old building, the whispers of generations of performers around her, she felt transported. And so grateful for the wonderful man at her side.

The next morning they woke late and ordered room service, relaxing in bed until Mike suggested they head out to explore. Hand in hand they entered the cool green of St James's Park, grinning at the squirrels scampering across the meadow, and the sleepy owls nodding on a low branch. They headed for Duck Island Cottage, admiring the flowers, and the lake filled with a variety of birds of various colours. But it was the swans that drew Beth, and she hurried down the bank until she was close to them.

"Did you know the Queen owns all the swans in England?" she asked Mike.

He smiled at her, the smile that lit her up from within, to know that this man could love her. "I find it more interesting that swans fall in love for life, and that they stay together forever," he replied, leaning down to kiss her.

The sunshine, the scent of the freshly mown grass and the sound of bird calls surrounded

Beth as she surrendered to the kiss. She'd never been happier than she was in this moment.

For three hours they wandered, through Green Park and Hyde Park, and into the Italian Gardens with its carved historic pools, fountains and sculptures. It amazed Beth that there was this huge oasis of nature in the middle of the city, with occasional glimpses of buildings in the distance. She always saw new things, in new ways, when she was with Mike, and she loved that about him.

Just as Beth was starting to get hungry, Mike suggested they head back. When they reached the hotel he led her up to the third floor terrace, and out to the kitchen garden that overlooked the London skyline and the parks they'd just wandered through. Noticing Beth's enthusiasm, the guy working there took her over to where the beehives and the "bee and bee" hotels were set up – home to more than three hundred thousand bees. She gazed in wonder at the busy community, and lapped up every word she was told about honey production, green gardening and sustainability.

When she'd absorbed all she could, Mike took her back down to the Tea Lounge, at the top of the grand staircase, where they were seated at a small table in a cosy corner and served an exquisite high tea. Honey sponge cake in the shape of bee hives, layered chocolate pudding in tiny flower pots, green chocolate apples filled with cinnamon-apple mousse, mango jelly and jasmine panna cotta, delicate sandwiches and savoury treats, and warm scones with lashings of jam and cream.

The waiter filled their water glasses then poured two glasses of sparkling wine, and Mike lifted his in a toast.

"To us, darling Beth."

As they clinked glasses, she hoped he knew just how happy he made her. "This is all so beautiful. I'm just... I'm blown away. Everything is so thoughtful."

He shrugged, like this amazing weekend was no big deal. Like all he did for her was no big deal. "I love you."

"I love you more."

Laughter shook Mike's shoulders as he shook his head. "You couldn't," he insisted.

A waiter glided to the table to refill their glasses, and they grinned at each other, relieved that their "who loves who more" argument had been interrupted.

Mike took Beth's hand. "I got you a little something..."

"Mike! You've already done so much, got me so much..."

"It's just little."

Taking a small purple-wrapped package from his pocket, he handed it to her with a shy grin. "I hope it's not overly mushy..."

Beth tore the paper off, too impatient to open it politely, then stood up and leaned over to kiss him. It was a delicate gold chain, with a golden crescent moon dangling from it, and a full moon nestled within that. Etched into its surface were the words *Love you to the moon and back*.

"Celebrating the phases of the moon with you up on the tor, and at Rose's circles, they're some of the happiest moments of my life," he said, voice quavering with emotion. "You've brought so much magic to my life Beth."

"No," she whispered. "You've brought it to mine. You introduced me to the priestess circle. *You* brought the magic to me."

Suddenly it was really important to her that he know this, that she could impress upon him just how grateful she was to him for the incredible way he treated her, for the kindness he offered, for the power of his love to transform her life and her view of herself. She knew from bitter experience that not all men were like that.

Before she could speak, he'd moved around to her side to do up the clasp of the necklace, then returned to his seat.

Gently her finger traced the shape of the crescent moon. "It's beautiful Mike, thank you so much. *You're* beautiful."

He blushed, but was saved from replying when the waiter returned with an antique silver coffee pot and a jug of cream.

After he left, Beth reached into her bag. "I got you something too, although it's only small," she said, wishing desperately she had something more elaborate for him, more personal. More reflective of the depth of her feelings for him.

But when he opened the package, his appreciation was genuine. "How did you even find this?" he asked, thumbing through the first edition of his favourite book that she'd finally managed to track down. "Thank you so much Beth, it's gorgeous. This means so much to me, really. I love it."

"I'm glad."

He raised his glass to her, took a sip, then placed it on the table. "I'm not sure I should tell you this Beth, it sounds so soppy..."

Smiling encouragingly, she motioned for him to speak.

"You are just the sweetest person I know. That anyone could know," he said.

A flush of embarrassment stained Beth's cheeks. "No, that's you," she protested.

But Mike was insistent. "You do so much for people, without being asked, and expect nothing in return. You help Rose more than you'll ever realise – she thinks of you as a daughter, and she wouldn't do that with just anyone. You have a goodness that radiates from you, and lifts everyone around you, and a light that shines from within. You're so supportive, and encouraging – I know you will be the best teacher anyone could hope for. And I see you when you don't know anyone's watching, when your face lights up with joy at the smallest thing. You make everything around you more magical. And you see everyone, and offer kindness when others ignore a situation, or don't even see it to begin with..."

Beth shook her head, more vehement this time. "No Mike. If I'm like that, it's because you have brought it out in me. I was bitter and resentful before I met you, so if I'm any of those things now, it's only through your eyes, your gaze. Through your love. You have made me that way, *if* it's even true. Please don't sell yourself short. You are everything to me, and through your love I have been transformed."

Now, as she floated, disembodied, around her daughter's bedroom, Beth laughed. Their most common argument had always been over who was lovelier, kinder, sweeter, more devoted. Who loved who more. She'd never managed to convince Mike that it was he who was more deserving of love, but she still believed it with all her heart...

Chapter 8

# The Wild Heart

### Rhiannon

A bird's wing beating against her window jolted Rhiannon awake, and she sat bolt upright. She'd been dreaming of ravens again, which made her instantly think of Tom. Was he real? Had yesterday actually happened?

Hugging her knees to her chest, she went over every moment of the day in detail, from their shy first meeting to sitting next to him throughout lunch talking about magic – and working skyclad. She blushed. Had she really asked him about doing rituals naked? Carlie must have been horrified. And what about Jake? She cringed. Was he annoyed that she was flirting with his cousin? Had kept him out all day and into the night? She hoped it wouldn't affect their friendship.

Stifling a giggle, she thought of their time at the next cafe, drinking chai alone together, before Tom had taken her hand and led her up the winding labyrinth path to the summit of the tor, stopping at each of the gates to press his lips to her cheek, then to her lips.

Lifting her fingers to her mouth, she sank back onto her bed, marvelling at how tender his kisses had been. And how passionate they'd become when they were sitting atop the sacred hill, watching the light change as birds wheeled overhead and night slowly fell.

Up there she'd felt alive in a way she never had before, like absolutely everything has changed – yet it was only her that had.

It was the best and most magical day of her life, and she was about to do it all over again.

Which terrified her. What if he'd changed his mind? What if he didn't even show up? What if he thought she was a silly little schoolgirl? Anguish swamped her, but she pushed it aside to focus on a more immediate concern. What should she wear today?

Throwing several outfits in her bag, she raced over to Carlie's, knocked, and stood on her front step, bouncing up and down with excitement. When the door opened she threw her arms around her friend, almost sending them both sprawling onto the hallway floor.

"Oh, sorry! I've just got so much to tell you!" she cried, cheeks flushed with happiness and anticipation as she followed Carlie through to the kitchen.

Rose was there, looking amused and cheered by Rhiannon's high spirits. "Would you like a cup of tea?"

"I'd love one, thank you," she grinned. "Oh, isn't it a gorgeous day! I feel so alive!"

There was a twinkle in the priestess's eye. "The joy of youth," she said, and there was the faintest note of regret in her voice. "And love, if I had to guess."

Rhiannon glared accusingly at her friend.

"I didn't say anything, I swear. I don't *know* anything," Carlie protested. "But you do look all excited and filled with the thrill of new love."

Crinkling her nose in embarrassment, Rhiannon grinned. "I'm meeting Tom at ten o'clock for a chai, and hopefully lunch after that, and I wondered if you wanted to come with us? Jake will be there, so you won't feel left out if we, you know..." She gazed at her friend hopefully. She knew it was the last thing she wanted to do, but she was too scared to go on her own. "Please?" she pressed.

Carlie shook her head, mumbling that she had to help Rose in the shop that day, but her grandmother refused to let her use that excuse. "It's okay Sweetheart, Laurel's coming in today, so we'll be fine. You go and hang out with your friends."

"Awesome!" Rhiannon shrieked, trying to ignore the disappointment on Carlie's face. "Can you help me work out what to wear? I brought a few options over." She grinned again, holding up her huge, bulging bag.

Following her reluctant friend upstairs, she vowed to tone down her enthusiasm – but once she'd flopped down on Carlie's bed with a melodramatic sigh, she couldn't help herself.

"He's so wonderful," Rhiannon gushed. "And isn't he gorgeous? Just take-your-breath-away stunning. I totally know what you mean now, about the difference between Rowan and John. John was just a friend, almost a brother, compared to how I feel about Tom. He's just so amazing. My tummy feels all fluttery when I think about him, and when he stares into my eyes, oh my god! It's so intense."

She knew she was raving, and that Carlie didn't want to hear about it, but she kept going anyway.

"So, you really hit it off, huh?" her friend offered sarcastically when Rhiannon finally paused for breath.

It was all the encouragement she needed. "I know, wasn't it amazing! From the second he took my hand when Jake introduced us, I could feel it, this incredible energy between us, like fire. Like our Imbolc fire ritual. Maybe Aideen sent him to me," she squealed.

That thought filled Rhiannon with joy. And she remembered that before she'd encountered the mysterious red-robed woman in her healing ritual in the woods, she'd met her during her Imbolc coven night with Carlie. Aideen had given her a gift, something to illuminate her own light when she was drowning in darkness, and Rhiannon had implored her for the passionate, all-consuming love that burns you like a fire. Tom was certainly that.

"It was like we were connected, heart to heart. And just everything about him is perfect. He's magical, he's smart, he's independent, he loves music, he plays guitar, he has tattoos, he's wild – everything on my list! He's just so cool." She sighed, drifting off again as she recalled the feel of Tom's hand on her arm, on her shoulder, in her hair. And it made sense, that he would be the answer to her love spell, even if he had taken his sweet time to find her.

"Oh god, sorry, where was I?" she finally said, when she realised Carlie was staring at her in alarm. How long had she been fantasising this time?

"Whenever he brushed against me I got all shivery inside, and we kissed for ages up there, and oh my god, it was so intense. Like I could have just melted into him, dissolved into him, merged into one being with him. Is that what it was like with Rowan?" she asked.

Carlie stiffened, and Rhiannon felt awful as she remembered the lectures she'd given her friend, the warnings that her boyfriend only wanted one thing from her, and that she'd better not have sex with him, because once she did he'd dump her for someone else.

She moved closer and took her hand. "I'm so sorry Carlie." Her voice was heartfelt, and full of regret. "I realise I sound like the worst kind of hypocrite, and that I was out of line with you and Rowan, in so many ways. I just had no idea it could feel like this. And I'm aware that I just met Tom, and I hardly know him – and again, I can only apologise for not understanding that it could be so instant and so total, because already I feel the most amazing connection to him. It's like, this could be real love, you know what I mean?"

Trying not to see the hurt in Carlie's eyes, Rhiannon continued. "I remember you trying to explain all this to me when you were with Rowan, but I couldn't even comprehend it. So I'm really grateful to you for sharing your letters with me, and making me realise that being with John was nice, but not enough to bring me to life like this does. Because otherwise I would have been with John yesterday, and I never would have met Tom. And the weird thing is, even if I never see him again after this weekend, I'll feel blessed to have known him, to know this feeling, to know that this depth and passion is possible."

But as they left the house, she wondered if that was true. Would she really be fine if he'd just been leading her on, and had no intention of ever seeing her again? As they approached the cafe, she started shaking with fear and nerves. What if he thought she was a silly schoolgirl, and laughed at her hanging off his every word?

As usual, Carlie picked up on her feelings, and only sounded a little exasperated with her. "Rhi, he was very clearly into you, even just at lunch, with us, let alone what happened in the six hours after. So you don't have to worry, I promise."

"I know, I just… how could he like me?" she whispered, suddenly distraught.

"How can you even ask that?" her friend demanded. "You're amazing! And gorgeous! And a wonderful friend! And apparently an awesome kisser," she joked, and Rhiannon managed a smile.

"Now come on, let's go see the boys," Carlie insisted, pulling open the door of the cafe and pushing her friend inside.

Rhiannon felt her eyes drawn directly to Tom, as if by magic, or by his will, and she stared at him, terrified, excited and nervous all at once. Had she just imagined all that had passed between them up on the tor? But the expression on his face steadied her, and she bounded over to squeeze in with him on the narrow two-seater couch.

He leaned in towards her and they kissed, eliciting rolled eyes from Carlie and Jake, but she was oblivious as she fell over the precipice into a vortex of passion and want. She felt like she was floating outside of her body, tethered to the earth, and to this moment, by the heat of his lips alone.

When the waiter came to take their orders, they reluctantly broke apart, although Tom kept his arm slung around her shoulder as he spoke. "I was talking to Jake about the spring equinox, and we thought it would be awesome if you both came up to London to join us for our Ostara ritual. The Body Mind Spirit Festival is on during the day, then we'll be having a small gathering in the park that night."

Rhiannon's face was transformed with joy, and she turned to Carlie, eyes sparkling with hope. "Can we? Will you come with me? We can stay with my cousin again, like we did last time. Oh, please say yes!" she begged.

Dread flitted across her friend's face, but she nodded reluctantly, and for a while the four of them chatted about the equinox and what would be involved in the ritual, which kept them all involved in the conversation.

After lunch and a few rounds of coffee, Tom announced that he had to head back to London for a late shift at the tattoo studio that night.

"Walk me out?" he asked Rhiannon, who leapt to her feet and followed him. They stood at his motorbike, talking for a moment, then he pulled her into his arms and placed his lips on hers.

"I wish I didn't have to leave," he whispered between kisses.

"Me too." She sighed, wondering if she would ever see him again.

She felt the same sensation of falling as she had yesterday, felt herself responding to him in a way she'd never even imagined before, a sense of wildness and strength consuming her as his lips greedily possessed hers. She felt herself opening up to him – physically, where his mouth was hot on hers, and emotionally too.

A small part of her was whispering caution, whispering fears that he must have a girlfriend in London, that he was just playing with her, that she wasn't good enough. But the desire thrumming through her veins drowned it out, screaming louder with delight and the first faint stirrings of love.

When Tom shifted away from her, she felt bereft, as though she'd never be whole again, and she smiled unsteadily as her body trembled. As if sensing her lack of stability, he held her close again, and their kisses deepened, their passion igniting, Tom holding her ever tighter against the length of his body. Just as she wanted to abandon all self-control, she suddenly remembered where she was. Standing on the High Street, in full view of anyone who was walking past – her dad included – kissing a guy most would consider a total stranger, and getting raunchier by the minute.

She pulled away, and swore under her breath. Tom peered at her, curious, then understanding dawned. "Wanna come for a ride?" he asked, a glint of mischief in his eyes.

She peeked into the cafe, where Carlie and Jake were staring at her in shock. Before she could second-guess herself, she squashed the helmet Tom was offering onto her head, threw a leg over the back of the bike and wrapped her arms around his waist.

They roared off down the road. The wind rushed against her face and her hair streamed out behind her, and exhilaration made her laugh and grip Tom's strong frame even tighter. She'd never been on a motorbike – it was one of the very few rules her dad insisted on – but she liked it. As the motorbike slid around a corner, she clutched him even closer, loving the feel of his strong chest. A thrill of excitement and rebellion raced through her, and she laughed again. Tom was the answer to her spell. *Magical. Smart. Independent. Creative. Mature. Tattooed. Slightly wild. Witch.*

He was perfect, and most importantly, he seemed to really like her. She wasn't going to get ahead of herself, but if nothing else, he was breathing life back into her shattered heart, and letting her know for the first time that pure, wild love was possible. She hadn't felt like this with John, that was for sure.

Just as she was getting used to the bike, Tom pulled over and cruised to a stop. He jumped off and turned around, taking off her helmet and resettling so they were sitting face to face, his arms wrapped around her, a cheeky glint in his eyes.

"Sorry, I just couldn't say goodbye to you there, in front of everyone else. I wanted you to myself a bit longer."

She'd never heard anything so sweet.

"And believe me, I do want you Rhiannon."

A shiver raced up her spine, part fear, part anticipation, part desire, but when his lips came down on hers and he crushed her body to his, she stopped thinking and revelled in the steady burn of the fire between them.

The naked desire coursing through her shocked Rhiannon, and she moaned and inched even closer to him. Then her eyes snapped open. She was in way over her head. She had so little experience with guys, except for... *the thing that happened...* and a few afternoons of kissing John. And Tom, well, he was no shy, nervous schoolboy.

As panic threatened to overwhelm her, Tom released her, and tenderly pushed a lock of her hair, wild from the wind and their crazy ride, behind her ear. "I really like you Rhiannon," he said, voice gentle. "And I'd love to see you again, if you want to." He sounded suddenly, adorably, unsure of himself, which endeared him to her even more.

"I'd love to see you again too," she said quickly, before she lost her nerve.

He beamed at her. "What if I come down for the new moon on Friday? Would... is it Rose, the priestess? Is she running a ritual for it? Would she mind if I came too?" He paused, and looked uncharacteristically nervous. "Would *you* mind?"

"I'd love that," she whispered. Relief washed over her. He really did want to see her again. Enough to drive back down from London to do it. Her heart was so full she thought it might explode.

"I wish I didn't have to leave now, but I promise I'll be back. And if you can come up for Ostara, that would be amazing."

She nodded as he stared down at her, his kiss-bruised lips all she could focus on. He touched his lips to hers one more time, then grudgingly turned around and drove back to the cafe. Rhiannon reluctantly slid off the bike to stand with shaky legs on the pavement. Oblivious to the world around them, they clung to each other again, then sadly said goodbye, and Tom drove away.

Rhiannon stared longingly after him until he was out of sight, then floated back into the cafe and flopped down on the couch with her two friends, hair windswept and cheeks flushed, and a wide, joyous smile lighting up her face.

"Oh Jake, your cousin is so lovely, thank you so much for introducing me to him. And Carlie, my god, now I get it!" she said, sighing dramatically.

"Get what?" Jake asked. Carlie looked uncomfortable, and tried to send her friend "shut up" vibes, but Rhiannon was oblivious.

"Well, what she and Rowan had together was amazing – it was totally real, true love, the whole let's-get-married-right-now-and-be-together-forever trip. He just adored her, and was cutting back on his work so that he could spend more time with her. And he put up with me being a total bitch to him because he loved her so much, and she loved him just as desperately," she raved.

"It was the most beautiful romance ever, cut tragically short. I didn't understand at the time though, I guess because I'd never felt anything like that. I was dating John, and he was nice, but there was no passion, not like they had. But now I get it!" she said again, drifting off with a dreamy smile on her face.

Jake was suddenly quiet, his posture rigid and cold. Rhiannon was blissfully unaware of the effect of her words though, and ploughed on. "Oh, how will I survive the days until I see him?" she moaned. "I can't wait to be with him again. You'll both come to London with me for the equinox won't you? Dad will let me go if he knows I'm going with you Carlie. God, how will I get through the next week?" she wailed.

"I thought the spring equinox wasn't for another three weeks," Jake said stiffly.

"That's right, but Tom is coming down next weekend so we can do our own ceremony on the tor, and go to Rose's new moon ritual at the healing centre together as well. You and your grandad should come too, they're really lovely evenings," she enthused.

"We probably will," Jake replied, his aloofness cooling. "Pop said he really wanted to go to that one, and he'll be happy to see Tom again – not that he ended up seeing him much this weekend," he said, then laughed as Rhiannon blushed.

"Just joking," he grinned, good humour restored.

Chapter 9

# Black As Night

Rhiannon

"**D**arling!"

Rhiannon jolted in her seat, and gazed up at her dad in confusion.

He laughed. "Where on earth were you just then? You've looked like you're a million miles away since you sat down to eat."

"Yeah Rhi-Rhi," her brother grumbled. "You didn't hear a word I said about my adventure with Ben, did you?"

Her cheeks flamed, and she smiled apologetically. "I'm so sorry, I've been obsessing over an assignment. But I'm here now."

Alarmed at how easily the lie had slipped out, she made an effort to push her Tom obsessing to the back of her mind and focus on her family. It was hard though, and she was relieved when she could finally head upstairs on the pretext of finishing her homework. Which she really did have to do, but first she allowed herself a little time to daydream about Tom.

Feeling inspired, she dug around in a drawer and found a sketch pad and some pencils, and settled down on her bed. It wasn't Tom's face that emerged on the paper though, but a series of sketches of birds. A swan took shape first, its neck long and elegant, its feathers more detailed than she'd thought she was capable of. She looked up at the painting Rowan had done for her, of her and her white swan spirit guide merging, and the white horse in the corner. But the swan she was drawing got darker and darker, until it became black. She'd never seen a black swan before. Weren't they Australian?

Turning the page, she tried to evoke the white angel terns she'd seen up on the tor, but soon they too morphed, and she was sketching black ravens. She was surprised by how real they seemed, and she shivered as the largest one seemed to stare at her, deep into the depths of her soul, challenging her beliefs and her doubts, and her very self.

Standing up and moving to the nearest shelf, she pulled down one of her mum's books on spirituality, and thumbed through it until she found a chapter on animal meanings.

*A black swan symbolises the Mysteries and the unknown. Something coming into your life that is forbidden, yet tempting...*

Putting down her pencil, she laughed. That summed up Tom, and her feelings for him, perfectly. She wasn't sure how her dad would react to him being a few years older than her, and she really wasn't looking forward to having *those* chats with him again. It had been awkward enough discussing John as a boyfriend, and he was every father's dream date compared to long-haired, motorbike-riding, tattooed artist Tom.

*Black swans represent the mysteries that are within you, that you've avoided examining, and the intuition you may have ignored, all of which are waiting to be revealed and set free...*

She gazed up at her wall, where her white swan spirit guide drawing was framed, and pondered whether seeing a black swan in relation to Tom meant they were two halves of one whole – or if it was a warning to her that he was darker than would be good for her. Yet swans were healing, no matter their colour, and signified intuition and knowledge, which was always a good thing, right? And ravens? She flicked through the pages.

*Ravens are the guardians of sacred mysteries and secret wisdom, and represent intuition as well as spiritual rebirth, change and transformation.*

Mysteries again. She grinned. Perhaps Tom would inspire her own rebirth as she released the pain of her remembered trauma, and moved forward with her wonderful, magical, love-filled life. She couldn't believe how differently she felt about *the thing that happened* now. As though just meeting Tom had given her hope, and strength. It had certainly reassured her that there were men who were kind and considerate, who wouldn't take advantage of her.

School on Monday was unbearable, creeping by minute by ever-long minute. All Rhiannon could think about was Tom, but she managed to make it through the day. And her art teacher was so impressed when she caught sight of her bird sketches, as Rhiannon flicked past them to find her assignment piece, that she asked her to enter them in the art prize. Maybe daydreaming about Tom hadn't been a total waste of time after all.

Tuesday wasn't much easier, and she knew she was boring Carlie senseless with her unceasing chatter and speculation about Tom during lunch, but her friend was putting up with her, with just the occasional eye roll. She vowed to be more subtle at their coven meeting that night. She would force herself to talk about something, anything, other than the object of her affection.

"Jake really likes you," Rhiannon blurted out as she settled herself on a green cushion on Carlie's bedroom floor after dinner. Her friend looked up from the herbs she was sorting, panic on her face, before she quickly masked it and shook her head.

"Yes he does, I can see it in the way he looks at you," she insisted. "Plus Tom told me. And I hate to admit this, but I was really jealous when I realised this a few weeks ago, because it seemed like all the cool guys wanted you."

"Oh Rhi, that's not true –"

"It's okay," she interrupted. "I'm glad now that he didn't like me, because Tom is even *more* amazing – gorgeous pagan tattoos, a motorbike, a career, an artist, a witch! He's even better than I could have dreamed up with a love spell. And I know he's three years older than me, so I'm not sure when to break it to Dad, but I really appreciate you having my back on this, especially after what I did to you."

"About that..." her friend said, and Rhiannon stared at her in horror, worried she wasn't going to keep her secret after all.

"Of course I will Rhi, don't be silly. No, it's just, well, I think maybe I was a little unfair to you with the whole Rowan thing."

Confusion washed over Rhiannon. "What do you mean? I was the one who was out of line."

Her friend took a deep breath. "I was angry that you kept pointing out the age difference, and trying to convince me that he only wanted me for sex, and would cheat on me and all that," Carlie said.

Rhiannon grimaced. "I know, and you had every right to be angry. I'm really sorry about that."

"No, *I'm* sorry," Carlie continued. "I know now that you were just worried about me, and looking out for me, in your own unique way. I realised when you rode off on Tom's bike with him the other day – suddenly I was asking Jake all the same questions you challenged me with. 'Is he just playing her?' 'Is the making-magic-together, sky-clad-ritual promise a line he uses on lots of women?' 'Is he taking advantage of her innocence?'" she admitted reluctantly.

"All of which Jake rejected by the way – he told me that Tom is totally smitten with you. And I was only asking because I care about you and I was worried for you, but it made me realise that when you were asking me those questions, which made me so angry, it was coming from a place of love too."

Rhiannon smiled. "Well, thank you for caring about me – and for finding out the answers to those questions from Jake, because I've got to be honest, I've been wondering about them too. That's why I can't wait to see Tom again, to work out whether our feelings are real, or if I've just imagined it all."

"Oh Rhi, you didn't imagine it. Jake said Tom never gets up early, especially on a Sunday, yet he got up early just for you, and was so eager to see you that he beat us to the cafe. And he raved about you non-stop on Saturday night, after he finally got home to spend a few moments with his grandfather."

Rhiannon's face lit up, and she hugged Carlie tight. "Thank you for telling me that, it's such a relief. I wouldn't have blamed you if you'd wanted to smother me with a pillow rather than listen to one more thing about Tom, and I will try to talk about other things too, I promise!"

For a while they did. Carlie pulled out her mortar and pestle, and Rhiannon lifted the drawer of herb-filled glass jars down onto the floor next to them. "We need a spring-time new moon blend for Friday night's ritual, so I was thinking a little sandalwood as a base, because of its ability to bring peace and assist with wishes, and because it's not too heavy, yet it helps purify and protect, and set sacred space," she said. "And can we put a little orris root in?"

Carlie gazed at her, eyebrows raised.

Giggling nervously, Rhiannon rushed to explain. "It's a lunar herb, right? And it's great for divination and dreamwork, plus it smells beautiful, like violets, and I know they're your favourite flower."

"And?"

"And yes, it's often added to love spells," she conceded bashfully.

Her friend laughed as she started to grind the sandalwood resin. "Of course you can add it. It *is* one of my favourites, and it will fit well for this ritual. I just liked seeing you squirm a little."

"Hey!"

"Sorry," Carlie said, although there was still laughter in her voice. "What else?"

Rhiannon moved her hands over the glass jars, tuning in to the vibrational essence of each herb. "Some lavender and verbena, and a touch of lemon peel too. And is there anything you'd like to add?" she asked, taking off the lids and adding a scoop of each to their blending bowl.

Carlie's voice was so quiet that Rhiannon had to lean forward to hear it. "I'm going to do some healing with Laura as part of the ritual, if I find the courage, so could we pop in a bit of rosemary and lemon balm for bravery?"

Reaching for those two jars, Rhiannon unscrewed the lids and poured a little of each herb into the bowl, whispering a prayer to the goddess as she mixed everything together with her fingers to add her intent, then handed it to Carlie to do the same. It smelled beautiful, and would be a heady mix of love and healing from the two of them, to accompany the energy of new beginnings of the new moon.

Rhiannon felt so proud, and honoured, that Rose was letting them create the incense for the upcoming ritual. She and Carlie had been baking for them for a while, for the traditional cakes and ale portion of the ceremony, but this task was far more witchy, and she was eager to impress their priestess with her knowledge and wisdom.

A pang of regret sliced through her, that she never got to do this with her mum, but having Carlie and Rose to work magic with was the next best thing.

After writing all the herbs they'd used and their various properties in each of their Book Of Shadows, they searched for a new moon cookie recipe to bake on Thursday night, then headed downstairs to make a fresh pot of tea and chat with Rose.

After half an hour of magical small talk, Rhiannon kicked Carlie under the table.

Her friend gulped, and her voice shook a little. "Um, Gran, we were wondering, would you mind if we got the train up to the city for the Body Mind Spirit festival on the 22nd? We'd stay the night with Rhi's cousin again, and be back in plenty of time for our Ostara ritual with you the next day."

Rhiannon waited with bated breath for the answer, fingers crossed at her side for luck. She couldn't miss this amazing opportunity to spend time with Tom, maybe even see where he lived. But Rose was staring hard at her granddaughter, a strange look on her face. For a moment Rhiannon was worried that it was suspicion, as though trying to gauge what Carlie was trying to get over her.

Then she realised it was concern. Of course. Her friend had met Rowan there six months ago, and Rose was worried that going back there would be too painful for her, so soon after his death. Regret stabbed into her again, and she berated herself for not considering that before pressing Carlie to go with her. Although, if she was brutally honest, she *had* thought about it for a second, when Tom had first mentioned it. But her desperation to see him far outweighed anything else.

Did Rose know this? Would she say no in order to help Carlie – and punish her selfish friend?

But after a brief glance at Rhiannon, which had her squirming under the priestess's hawk-like gaze, Rose gave her permission, and the two girls sighed, one in relief, the other quite possibly in dread.

Deciding she should head home before anyone changed their mind, Rhiannon hugged them both goodbye and quickly fled.

When she jolted awake on Thursday morning, Rhiannon was a nervous wreck. Awful visions of the assault had tormented her all night, interspersed with a raven swooping at her at breakneck speed to attack her, and she felt wrung out and blurry around the edges. Her eyes were gritty and red, and she felt inexplicably angry, not to mention upset, exhausted and scared. Tomorrow night she would see Tom, and while she'd been panicking all week that he wouldn't turn up, and that even if he did, he couldn't possibly like her, now she was more worried that she wasn't ready to face him. That *she* didn't want *him* to come.

He was amazing, and worldly, and that's what worried her. He'd flirted with her shamelessly, and she'd flirted right back, but she was terrified of it going any further than their admittedly wonderful kissing, and worried she wouldn't have the strength to stop herself. Wouldn't want to stop herself. And that could only end in disaster.

All day at school she tried to force the nightmare images from her mind, but they taunted her, flashing vividly to life every time she thought of Tom.

When Carlie leaned over to touch her arm in class, Rhiannon jumped, her heart racing in panic, but she was grateful to have been brought back from the darkness of her swirling imaginings.

"Are you okay?" her friend asked.

Trying to focus on the present, Rhiannon nodded.

"Dark moon getting to you? Don't worry, as soon as we start baking the new moon cookies tonight, the energy will lift."

Of course. It was the dark moon today. No wonder she was feeling so grim. But she could use that.

When she got home from school, relieved that her dad was at work and Brodie was with his friend Ben, she pulled her mum's huge Book of Shadows down and started flicking through the pages. The dark moon was the ideal time in the lunar phase to do a ritual to banish her fears and release her anger and hurt, and let go of the emotional residue of the trauma she could still feel within her body.

Soon she found the perfect one, so she quickly ground up the incense she would need, found a blue candle, pulled out her own Book of Shadows to record everything in, and grabbed a notepad and pen.

She ran a hot bath, sprinkling in some chamomile flowers and lavender oil with a scoop of salts, then relaxed into it, letting the perfumed steam clear her mind, and feeling the ritual head space slowly descend. After a long soak she emerged from the warm water, dried herself and pulled a soft, pale blue dress over her head. Then with great reverence she set up her altar and performed the ritual.

By the time she finished, she felt stronger, more powerful, and more able to cope. The doubts that had been plaguing her had dissolved, she felt calmer and more at peace with the assault, and when she thought of Tom, she felt warm and safe, and couldn't wait to see him.

Inspired now, and eager to start planning her new moon wishes, she headed over to Carlie and Rose's to bake the biscuits for the following night's ritual, feeling so much lighter than she had all day.

## Chapter 10

### Beth

The sharp citrusy scent of lemon and the floral sweetness of lavender drew Beth back together, into some semblance of her former self, and she spent long moments drifting, eyes closed, as she inhaled the soothing aromas.

Lemons brought back memories of warm summer nights in a tiny cottage in the south of France with Mike. Dancing naked on the tor under the full moon with him, clad only in the uplifting perfume of citrus oil. Weaving purification rituals and love spells with Laura and Rose. Long, much-loved hours in her garden. Picking the heavy fruit to bake tarts and make hot drinks for her family when they were sick.

Lavender encircled her with visions of picnics in springtime fields with her beloved. Her hands in the warm earth while bees buzzed around her with their messages of celebration and community. Late summer evenings drying the herbs she'd grown. Crisp autumn nights grinding them for protection charms, sleep spells and dream pillows.

And the two scents combined? That heady blend transported her across the sea to an ancient forest, where she walked along sun-dappled paths, and talked long and hard with a kind-hearted witch who'd taken her in and given her the first clues to her true self.

Smiling with the light of the magic wrapping around her, Beth opened her eyes – and was shocked to find herself in the kitchen of

Rose's cottage, not across the seas in the French kitchen where she had baked syrupy lemon and lavender cake with Celia, and gazed into the swirling patterns made by tea leaves.

It had felt so real.

Curious, she peered down at Rose and Carlie from her perch in the beams of the ceiling. The priestess had just walked in, her arms filled with flowers and plant cuttings. "Sorry I'm late Sweetheart," she said to her granddaughter, and Beth wondered if it was guilt she detected in her tone.

"Where were you?" Carlie asked, voice sharper than she'd probably intended. "I was getting worried."

"I'm so sorry, I was just over at Richard's, and didn't realise how late it had become. He needed some help to plant out his herb garden, so I offered him a hand, and then he asked my advice about a recipe his wife used to make, and I showed him how to get it right, then we had a cup of tea, and all of a sudden it was dark. I'm sorry you were worried though."

Carlie smiled. "That's okay, it sounds like he really needed you today. And Jake will be glad he had a friend over to talk to."

Understanding dawned, and Beth grinned. Richard was Jake's grandfather, and Rose was just being as kind and neighbourly as ever.

"Well, it wasn't all one sided," Rose admitted. "His garden is really amazing, and he gave me some great cuttings so I can grow them too, as well as these gorgeous lilies." Gently placing the flowers on the bench, the priestess reached for a vase, turning her face away from her granddaughter. Beth giggled. Rose's cheeks were definitely pinker than usual. Was there something going on?

Suspicion darkened Carlie's gaze as she stared at her grandma. "Are you blushing?"

Rose laughed, a high-pitched, not-quite-natural laugh. "No Sweetheart, why would I be blushing?" she replied, although she ducked her head behind the flowers she was carefully arranging. "Now, I'll just go and get washed up..." And she fled.

Beth raised her eyebrows, mirroring Carlie's expression, and wondered if it was possible that Rose had found someone to care for, someone who would care for her. When she'd returned to Summer Hill after her year in France, Beth had become close to Violet, and had loved spending time at her cosy, homely cottage with her and her parents Rose and Louis. They were the sort of parents she'd always longed for – kind, accepting, encouraging, supportive. They'd welcomed her into their family without question, gaining Beth's undying gratitude.

But four months later Violet had disappeared, and a month after that, her dad had downed a handful of sedatives with a bottle of whisky, and driven off the bridge. In four short weeks Rose lost her only child then became a widow, and she had remained alone for the twenty years Beth had known her.

The priestess had nurtured Beth like a daughter, had been more grandmother to Rhiannon and Brodie than their blood relative ever was, yet she'd never welcomed anyone into her life romantically. Now that struck Beth as strange. How could the kindest, wisest, most loving woman she'd ever known be incapable of finding love? It didn't make sense.

She watched Carlie, and it seemed she was thinking the same thing, because there was a mischievous twinkle in her eye as she finished making dinner. Was there a way Beth could help Carlie help Rose with this?

Swooping down closer, she tried to talk to Carlie, but whatever magic had made her appear to her in that cafe a month ago was no longer with her, and she slumped against the kitchen bench, feeling helpless all over again.

When Rose returned and they sat down to eat, Beth's mouth watered at the sight of the rich chickpea vegie curry Carlie had made, and she was distraught at yet another reminder of what she'd lost. Simple pleasures – eating, gardening, holding hands, hugging. She knew this half existence was better than nothing, but it could be so frustrating!

For a while she forced herself to focus, to push her essence out towards Rose, in the hope that the priestess would recognise her, *see* her, but she had no luck with her either. When she started to feel like a spy for eavesdropping on their conversation, she floated off down the hallway to Rose's altar room. She was still hopeful that she'd find a way to communicate with the priestess and get a message to Rhiannon. And being in this room was so soothing. She wafted around, peering at books, then pushed her nose through the glass into the many jars of herbs. With each new scent she was transported to a different ritual, a different sabbat, a different time. Jasmine for love. Rosemary for remembrance. Sandalwood for protection. Sage for purification. Lemon peel for love and new beginnings. Lavender for relaxation and release.

A knock on the front door brought Beth abruptly back to the present. Curiously she peered out into the hallway as Carlie opened the door, and her heart swelled. Rhiannon was standing there, eyes glittering with excitement, pale blue dress swirling out around her, and a cloud of frankincense and cinnamon and a wisp of magic enveloping her. She was beautiful, with a sparkle of confidence and joy Beth hadn't noticed before.

Her heart warmed. Had Rhiannon already done a ritual tonight, before coming to Rose's? She looked different, like she'd flung off the cloak of pain and anger she'd wrapped so tightly around herself. Intrigued, Beth reached out her arms to hold her daughter, but they swept right through her, leaving Beth more dejected than ever.

With a sigh, she trailed the two girls out to the kitchen. Rose was putting the kettle on, and greeted Rhiannon warmly, embracing her before she pulled another cup from the pantry. Although it pained her that Rose could connect with her daughter physically and she couldn't, gratitude swamped Beth again — not just that she'd had the wonderful priestess in her own life, but that Rhiannon had her too. The mother to the motherless ones. Robbed of her own child, but adopted parent to many others.

"Ready to help us bake all the new moon cookies for tomorrow night, sweet girl?" Rose asked.

Rhiannon nodded happily. She looked so at home in the golden warmth of this kitchen, kneeling down to pat the little black kitten under the table, then grabbing the milk from the fridge while Carlie poured the tea. She clearly spent a lot of time here, and it soothed some of Beth's disquiet, to know that her daughter was accepted as a part of this cosy family, and loved and treasured. It couldn't make up for losing her mum, but it was something.

Hovering in the corner of the room, Beth watched the three witches as they grated the rind of the lemons and squeezed the juice from them, measured out the flour and sugar, creamed the butter and stirred the dough, then shaped the biscuits into crescent moons and popped them in the oven.

Then they started on the delicate lavender shortbreads, using fresh flowers from the garden. Beth's mouth watered again as she remembered making them with Rose not long before she died. Between the two of them they'd eaten so many while they drank several cups of tea that they'd had to whip up an extra batch to ensure there were enough for the ritual.

A laugh rippled through her, before her attention was drawn back to the conversation. "And what will you be wishing for this new moon?" Rose asked Rhiannon.

"Well, um..." Rhiannon paused, and looked too scared to speak. Carlie smiled encouragingly at her friend, and Beth leaned in closer. What on earth was her daughter too scared to tell Rose?

Anxiously she watched as Rhiannon took a deep breath, psyching herself up. "Um, well, I'm hoping that Tom will make it down in time to join us for the ritual, if that's okay with you?" she finally said, gazing at the priestess with wide, fearful eyes.

Beth gasped. Who was Tom? And how did Rose know about him, yet she didn't? Jealousy stabbed at her, but she tried to push it aside. She had to focus, had to learn all she could. Was this guy the reason Rhiannon was looking suddenly happier, and less traumatised? Was he the key to her healing – or would he hurt her even worse? Fear throbbed through her, but surely if the priestess knew about him, he must be okay?

"Of course sweet girl," Rose replied, eyes twinkling. "So, it sounds as though things are going well with this young man?"

Rhiannon blushed. "Um, I hope so," she said shyly. "But I won't know until I see him tomorrow night. That's why I haven't told Dad about him yet – I wanted to wait until I knew a

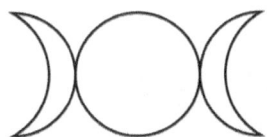

bit more before I mentioned it. Because who knows, Tom may just not turn up, or he might see me and change his mind, or... I don't know." She sighed, and Beth's heart broke for her daughter's doubt and insecurity. *This* was why she'd reformed here at Rose's tonight, rather than at home, so she could listen to Rhiannon talking about this new guy she was too scared to mention to her father.

"I'm just not confident enough that anything will come of it right now. Part of me thinks that last weekend was just a wonderful dream, and he doesn't really exist. So if it's not putting you in too awkward a position, could you not mention this to Dad just yet?" Rhiannon begged. "I promise I'll tell him soon, if there's anything to tell. And if there isn't, he will have been saved the trouble of needing to react."

Rose smiled at the nervous young woman in front of her. "Yes, I can keep your secret for a few days sweet girl, until you've decided whether or not it's worth sharing. But please don't leave it too long until you tell Mike."

Rhiannon nodded, her relief palpable.

"And I think you'll be surprised," Rose added. "Your dad knows that you're growing up, and that there will be boys. All he wants from you is honesty, and for you to deserve the trust you already have. This goes for you too Carlie. We would rather know that you're dating someone, and have the chance to meet them so we know that you're safe."

The priestess's voice was heavy with regret, and Beth's heart ached for her. If only Violet had been able to share her secret boyfriend with her mother, how different all their lives might have been. Rose would still have her husband and her daughter... And Mike would have married Violet. A shudder rocked Beth. What would have happened to her then? Would she have returned to Paris, and her job as a nanny? Or would she have remained in the village, friend to both of them, yet secretly pining after her beloved?

For a while she drifted, feeling far removed from the actions of the three below her as they put more biscuits in the oven and drank more tea. She tortured herself with the idea of other lives, other possibilities. Would she have still practised magic, in this parallel world? Would she have made another family, with someone else? Would she have somehow ended up in Australia in Violet's place? It horrified her, that her entire life could have been so changed if a single moment in time had played out differently. If she'd warned her friend about the shaman, would Violet have never left the village? Never left Mike?

Distraught, Beth felt herself coming undone, her molecules beginning to shatter, and scatter. The lure of the darkness, of the starless void, tugged at the edges of her consciousness. But just before she dissolved, Rhiannon scraped back her chair and stood, bringing Beth back to the present, to the real world, the physical world. The world that made her ache with pain at its loss. Depressed, she followed her daughter out to the front door, where she stood with Carlie in the beautiful dark, stress causing her voice to shake.

"Oh god, I'm so nervous about tomorrow night," Rhiannon confided. "What if Tom has forgotten, or he met someone more interesting than me this week, or he realises that I'm just a boring schoolgirl, and decides to avoid Summer Hill altogether – that would upset Jake and his grandfather no end."

Carlie took her friend's hands and stared into her eyes. Her voice was firm. "Rhi, come on. You know how much he likes you – hell, Jake and I know how much he likes you, going off your very public displays of affection last weekend," she said, unable to hide a giggle. "Now go home, get a good night's sleep, and you'll be hanging out with him in no time."

Beth wished she could hug Carlie, could tell her how much she appreciated her being in her daughter's life, and the amazing support she offered her. And she wished she could thank Violet for raising such a wonderful girl. When she'd first become aware that she was dead, Beth had searched for Violet in the darkness of the void – she'd searched for anyone she knew – and had also tried hard to communicate with the living. But so far she'd only been able to converse with Carlie that night in the cafe, and with the strange red-robed woman in the woods one other time. She'd encountered no other person, living or dead, and been seen by no one either.

But she could worry about that later. For now, she was with her daughter, and she was determined to make the most of every moment. Floating along beside her as Rhiannon walked home, Beth moved through the cool dark with her, wishing she could stroke her hair or hold her hand, but content at last just to watch her, and be near her. And hope and pray that this mystery guy was good enough for her.

Chapter 11

# In An Unguarded Moment

Rhiannon

Heart racing, Rhiannon rushed up the stairs to her room. Excitement warred with the terror that was threatening to make her pass out. Tonight she would see Tom again, and discover whether he liked her as much as she liked him.

Or liked her at all.

If he turned up.

*Argh!*

Throwing her school bag on the floor, she quickly weighed up having a shower or a bath. A "good" witch would submerge herself in a relaxing, emotionally cleansing pre-ritual bath, but she didn't have the patience. She'd only lie there fretting. And she still hadn't worked out what to wear.

*Shower it was.*

A few minutes later, wrapped in a fluffy towel, she peered into her wardrobe. She wanted to look pretty, and glamorous, and grown up, but she also needed to feel comfortable, or she'd end up with one more thing to stress about. Thankfully this afternoon – when she'd been obsessing again – Carlie had reminded her that when she met Tom she was wearing jeans and a t-shirt. There had been no make-up or glamour. If he liked her, he must actually like *her*.

Not that that was helping her butterflies right now.

Reaching in, she pulled out a long, forest green velvet dress. It was an old favourite, perfectly coloured for spring and the new moon, and warm enough for the top of the tor. Most importantly, she was fine with sitting on the grass in it, yet it was dressy enough for a ritual. Relieved, she slipped it over her head, threaded ribbons in various shades of green through her hair, slicked some cherry gloss across her lips and headed downstairs.

Brodie was just home from soccer practice, so while he sat at the table asking her homework questions when he got stuck, she made nachos and salad and prayed her dad would be back soon. She was meeting Tom at Jake's place, so they could go to the healing centre together, and she didn't want to be late.

"You look really pretty Rhi-Rhi," her brother said when she took him a glass of milk. "Are you going to a ritual with Carlie tonight?"

She smiled and ruffled his hair. "Thanks buddy. And yes I am, with Carlie and Jake, and Rose of course."

He gazed up at her with wide blue eyes. "It's because you're happy I think."

"What is?" she asked, surprised.

"That you look so pretty. Your eyes are sparkling and stuff."

Leaning down, she hugged him. "Thank you Brodie. That's just what I needed to hear."

The front door banged shut as she popped the nachos in the oven, and she sighed with relief that her dad was home. She would make it to Jake's in time. Which made her heart race with nerves and anticipation. Would Tom have even driven all the way down here? And would he still like her after a week apart, or would his face fall with disappointment when he saw her?

Her father's voice broke into her thoughts. "Hi darling. You look lovely."

"Thanks Dad. Dinner's nearly ready, and Brodie's finished his homework. I shouldn't be too late home, unless Rose wants me to help pack up." Again the lie slipped out so easily, and Rhiannon shuddered. She hated keeping things from him, but there was no point telling yet. Twenty minutes from now she might be in floods of tears, her heart broken, and she didn't want to have to explain that.

Her father frowned. "You're not eating with us? I thought the ritual didn't start until eight."

*Damn.* Rhiannon thought fast. "I told Carlie I'd help her set up. She's really nervous about a healing ritual she's doing tonight."

"Okay darling." Mike kissed her on the forehead then turned back to Brodie, and she picked up her bag and fled. Her little white lies were harmless enough, weren't they? Part of her wished her mother was alive so they could talk – about boys, and magic – yet for the first time she wondered if doing rituals with her mum would make her more self-conscious. Less herself. Would she have been too scared to invite Tom tonight if her mum was in the circle?

More urgently, was she too scared *now*? Could she do a public ritual in front of him – let alone a private one? And would he expect more from her up on the tor than she could give? Her mind veered from yes to no, fight to flight, until she was at Jake's house, knocking on the door then standing anxiously as she waited. Was it too late to turn around and run?

As she vacillated between staying or going, the door opened and Jake stood there, a welcoming grin on his face.

"Hey Rhiannon, come in. Tom's just showing Pop some of his books on magic. Do you want a tour of the place? You've never been here before, have you?"

Heat rose in her cheeks, and she suddenly felt bad for using Jake to get close to Tom. "Um, sure, I guess."

He laughed. "Don't worry, I know you're here to see Tom, and in a minute you'll be sitting in the lounge room with him drinking coffee while Pop and I finish icing the cake he baked for the ritual."

"Thanks," she muttered, feeling increasingly uncomfortable and out of her depth.

Jake took pity on her, and as he showed her through the living area and out to the kitchen, he leaned in close. "Don't stress. Tom's really looking forward to seeing you. You're all he's talked about since he arrived this afternoon, so there's no need to worry."

Impulsively she hugged her school friend, grateful for the confidence boost as she prepared to see the object of her affection after a week apart.

The scent of baking reached her first, then as Jake walked into the kitchen, Tom charged out, caught her in his arms and spun her around. When he released her, he ducked his head. Almost shy.

"It's so good to see you. I was worried you wouldn't come, or that you'd see me and want to flee," he muttered, then led her back through to the lounge room.

Swallowing her laugh, she smiled up at him, relieved that he was just as vulnerable as her. "I was thinking the same thing," she reluctantly admitted.

When Jake came in with two mugs of coffee, she sprang away from Tom, and Jake rolled his eyes. "Seriously? I've seen you both kissing on the High Street. You don't have to leap apart on my account." Laughing, he headed back to the kitchen, and the murmur of voices drifted out as he and his grandfather chatted.

"Sofa?" Tom asked.

Nodding, Rhiannon sank down onto the cushions gratefully, not sure how much longer her legs would hold her up. Unfortunately they ended up at opposite ends though, and the distance between them seemed huge. They stared at each other in silence, the awkwardness growing, and Rhiannon tried desperately to think of something witty to say. As time stretched out, she figured she'd settle for *anything* to say.

"So, how was your week?" she finally blurted out.

Just as Tom spoke. "Did you make it through the dark moon energies okay?"

They both laughed, and Tom moved closer to her. "My week was good. All the tattoos I had to do were pagan, which is always a delight, I got some time to paint, and I did a wonderful dark moon ritual last night with my coven."

Rhiannon smiled. "I had a great coven meeting too – Carlie and I created the incense for tonight's ritual, and last night we made the new moon biscuits with her grandma. Oh! And Carlie asked her if we could go to London for Ostara, and Rose said yes."

When she realised they were talking normally, her body relaxed. And as soon as that happened, her mind relaxed too, and conversation flowed. They talked about art, and herbalism, and the design course Tom was doing at college. Before they knew it an hour had passed, and Jake and Richard had appeared to tell them it was time to leave.

A soothing, citrusy scent swirled around them. "That's not a lemon and lavender cake is it?" Rhiannon asked sharply.

Richard's eyes widened in panic. "It is. Tom suggested it would be appropriate for tonight's ritual. Is that wrong?"

"No, not at all, it's perfect. It's just... my mother used to make that for the new moon, so it brings back a lot of memories. Good ones though!"

Glancing at Tom, she wondered if this was a sign. Had her mum somehow put the idea in his head, to reveal to Rhiannon that she was still with her, still around her, and that she approved of her choice of...

*Was it too early to say boyfriend?*

A hush descended on them as they climbed the stairs at the healing centre and gazed in at the candlelit ritual room. "It's beautiful," Tom whispered, and Rhiannon sighed with relief. She'd worried that he would think their magical workings unsophisticated compared to his big city coven, but as she watched Rose standing at the central altar, wrapped in the strength and authority of the goddess, she wasn't sure what she'd been so nervous about. The priestess exuded power and Otherworldliness, and Rhiannon sensed Tom's own power reaching out towards her. Abruptly Rose looked up and right at them, and she and Tom exchanged a glance that quivered with electricity. Rhiannon shivered. What would Rose think of the guy she was holding hands with? And would she keep her secret?

Her attention slammed back to the present when she heard Carlie welcoming Tom and Jake and their grandfather, then give each of them a green pen, a few small white cards and a beeswax candle. A huge grin lit up her face as she leaned in to whisper to Rhiannon. "You look so happy. I hope that means all is well?"

Trying to suppress a giggle, she nodded, then watched anxiously as Rose came over to shake Tom's hand and hug Richard and Jake. Catching the speculative glance Carlie and Jake shared as her grandma embraced his grandpa, Rhiannon gazed at them curiously. Was something going on between Rose and Richard?

Before she could ask Carlie, the priestess turned back to the rest of the room and instructed everyone to make themselves comfortable on one of the jade green cushions that had been arranged in a large circle around the altar. Then she moved back to the middle as everyone linked hands.

"Welcome. Tonight you are creating the sacred circle yourselves, with your own bodies, and have imbued it with just as much magic and protection as I ever could," she announced. "It's wonderful to see a few new faces. Thank you for bringing your energy and intent to our gathering." She smiled at Tom, then her eyes lingered on Richard for a long moment.

Rhiannon was ecstatic. Perhaps she was getting ahead of herself, but it would be wonderful if Rose had finally found love. For as long as she could remember, the priestess had been like a grandmother to her and Brodie, had cared for everyone in the village, yet she'd always been alone. For the first time, Rhiannon wondered if she'd been lonely, especially before Carlie arrived to live with her. Rose deserved love more than anyone.

As the ritual was outlined, Rhiannon felt Tom's eyes on her. "Where did you go?" he murmured.

*Oops! Time to be present.*

"I'm here," she mouthed, tightening her grip on his hand then turning her attention back to Rose. A delicious shiver snaked up her spine. She'd been yearning to do a ritual with someone she... cared about... and finally she was.

*Oh goddess, please let Tom like her as much as she liked him!*

Grinning, she kept holding his hand, even as others in the circle let go, and watched as four of Rose's coven sisters stood up to call the directions and invoke the elements.

A hush fell over the room, and people gazed at the women in wonder. It fascinated Rhiannon to watch her teacher Laura clad in the air of a priestess, to see the light shining from her eyes, and the self-assurance and strength spilling out of her. Tom squeezed Rhiannon's hand, and her heart swelled with pride at just how magical this circle was. She didn't have to feel like a fraud next to him, like a kid playing dress-up and inventing a more enchanted reality than was true. This was her life, and she was overcome with gratitude for it.

When Rose raised her arms skyward to invoke the deities, Tom gasped, and Rhiannon sensed his awe as they watched her transform into their high priestess, her own self melding with something more, something other. Her voice deepened, and throbbed with power. Tom's reaction gave Rhiannon a secret rush of satisfaction, and a confidence she gathered to herself, determined to remember it when they stood on the tor together later that night. She was terrified of coming across as a silly schoolgirl, or magically naive, so she clutched tight to the knowledge Rose had instilled in her, and the enchantment that swirled around her and within her now.

As the priestess's words died away, a sense of great reverence wove its way through the space. Rose's voice gentled, and she led them through a new moon meditation, guiding them to focus on their intent for the coming month, and what they would need to do to dream their goal into being and manifest it into the world.

Closing her eyes, Rhiannon let go of her worries and allowed herself to simply feel.

"Whatever your heart yearns for, we will sow the seeds tonight, fuelled by our combined energy and powered by this beautiful moon phase," the priestess concluded, then lapsed into quiet herself. As the silence swelled around her, Rhiannon picked up the green pen and started writing.

*Sweet moon goddess, thank you for the blessings you have showered on me, and for crossing my path with Tom's.*
*Tonight I pray we will sow the seeds of a relationship that will grow strong and true over the coming month, with mutual*

*respect, and a mutual love of magic that makes my heart sing. Thank you for the lessons I learned with John, and the inspiration to move forward with love and hope. Blessed be.*

When she finished, she stood up and slowly approached the altar, then held her slip of paper in the cauldron fire until it caught alight. Reverently she watched her intention carried up and out into the universe with the smoke.

As she turned to go back to her place in the circle, a gold-clad figure rose out of the flames and locked eyes with her. Time stood still around her as the woman lifted a delicate hand to her own chest, then extended it to Rhiannon. Her whole body tingled, the sensation rippling outward from where the mist-wreathed woman's palm lay over her heart.

"Trust," she whispered, her mouth curving up in a gentle smile. Then her face started to blur, and for a moment it was Beth standing in her place. Beth with her hand on her daughter's heart.

Desperately Rhiannon reached out to her mum, but as the flames rose higher, a blast of heat forced her backwards. She blinked a few times, trying to focus, trying to see the woman again, see her mother again, but the cauldron just smouldered now, with not a lick of fire, and certainly no gold-robed woman within its depths.

*Was she going mad, to have imagined a woman with her mother's face reaching out to her from the flames? Infusing hope in her barren heart?*

Suddenly she became conscious of Carlie across the altar, feeding her new moon wishes into the cauldron. Her friend looked up and grinned at her, then glanced at Tom, and Rhiannon spun around in panic. For a moment she'd felt outside of time, and had forgotten Tom was with her. Had forgotten herself, in the desperate longing to see her mother. Embarrassed, she hurried back to him, but he was still writing on his paper, his long dark hair hiding most of his face, but his intensity clear in the set of his shoulders.

As though he could feel her gaze on him, he looked up, and his smile made her melt. She was desperately curious about what he'd written. Was he asking the goddess about her too, or were his wishes unrelated to love? Was there something more important that he longed for?

Sighing, she returned to her cushion, and tried to push her doubts and fears from her mind. Tonight was focused on intent, and she didn't want to confuse the universe about what she wanted and instead manifest all her anxieties into reality.

She was soothed by the healing energy Carlie and Laura sent around the circle – and by Tom's steadying presence beside her. Somehow he managed to stay totally present within the ritual, while also reassuring her that he wanted to be here with her. He was a rare gift, and she really hoped she wouldn't stuff things up too quickly.

*No, she hoped she wouldn't stuff things up at all.*

By the time Rose closed the circle, Rhiannon's head was spinning and she was worried she might float away. Tom pulled her to her feet and kissed her cheek, then laughed.

"You really need some grounding, don't you?" he asked, leading her over to the table set up with tea, juice and treats. He offered her a new moon biscuit, and she ate it hungrily. By the third one she was far more grounded, back in her body and ready to face people.

Hands full of lavender shortbreads, they headed over to where Carlie and Richard were deep in conversation. "These are the yummiest ones we've ever made," Rhiannon said, and Richard laughed as he agreed, not seeming to mind the interruption.

Tom planted a kiss on Rhiannon's forehead, then became serious. "It was lovely to do a ritual with you Pop," he said, leaning in to embrace his grandfather. "I'm looking forward to doing more of them together, and spending more time with you."

At that moment Jake walked over to join them, a slice of cake in hand, and rolled his eyes at his cousin. "And I suppose that would have nothing to do with wanting to spend time with Rhiannon?" he said, but his tone was friendly.

Rhiannon beamed at the implication.

"Hey, there's nothing wrong with having two reasons to get out of the city, now is there?" Tom retorted. "Or three I suppose, if I was to count hanging out with you, Cuz," he teased.

Rhiannon laughed along with them, but her tummy tingled with nerves. Soon she would be alone with Tom, properly alone, and although she desperately wanted it, she was scared too. She admired him so much – his confidence with magic, his ease at slipping into her world and, as Rose joined them, his self-assurance as he spoke to a high priestess he'd only just met. She would be a blushing, stammering wreck if she met his.

*Oh no! She was going to meet his priestess soon.*

Just as her anxiety threatened to spiral out of control, Rose turned to her, eyes twinkling. "Trust, sweet girl," she murmured, too low for anyone else to hear. "Now, isn't it time you two left?"

An image of the gold-clad woman swirled around Rhiannon, making her dizzy, but she pushed it away and took a deep breath. Nodding to Rose, she turned to Tom, who was gazing at her with such intensity it made her shiver.

He slipped his hand into hers, and she grabbed it and held on tight.

Chapter 12

# Under A New Moon

### Rhiannon

It was cold out on the street, and the sky was inky black, yet now that Tom was holding her hand, Rhiannon wasn't scared. She felt warm, and safe. It was strange, how comfortable she felt with him, especially in the dark. It was only a few weeks since the trauma of her night in the woods had slammed back into her and broken her apart. She didn't understand how she'd been able to bury the memory and its impact for eighteen months, but after being forced to face it, to dance in the fire and burn the pain away, she was starting to feel a little more at peace with it. And was relieved that kissing Tom last weekend hadn't freaked her out or triggered her further.

Wrapped up in her thoughts, she stumbled and almost fell, but Tom caught her, and used it as an excuse to let his hands linger on her waist.

"You okay?" he asked, his sexy voice sending a thrill through her.

She laughed. "Yeah, I'm fine, just a little clumsy. Guess I should have brought a torch."

Tom's arms tightened around her, making her grateful for the lack of a light to show the way. "I'm not afraid of the dark. Are you?"

"Not when I'm with you," she said softly. "Although perhaps I shouldn't admit that."

She felt his lips on her forehead, and a flash of heat pulsed through her when he pushed a stray curl behind her ear.

"I'm the same," he whispered, his breath warm on her cheek. "So I reckon that together we can climb this hill, right?"

"Right." She hoped she sounded more confident than she felt.

Tom laughed softly. "You might have to take the lead though – you know the way far better than I do."

She gulped nervously, inhaled a deep, calming breath, then stepped out of the circle of his arms. "Okay, let's go."

Sternly she reminded herself that she could do this. She and Carlie had climbed the tor in the dark before, although they'd had candles. Shutting off her logical brain, she peered into the darkness. Perhaps a fae creature would light their way.

The sky overhead was black and moonless – the tiny gold crescent wouldn't rise until morning – and as they passed the final street light, Rhiannon tried not to focus on the inky shadows closing in around them. Winter had loosened its hold a month ago, at Imbolc, yet a chill lingered. Doubt filled her mind. Was it stupid to be climbing the hill in the dark, in the cold? *With a stranger?*

"Wow, the darkness is intense. Can I hold your hand?" Tom's voice was loud in the silence, and a shiver ran up Rhiannon's spine. Not of fear though. It was anticipation, and joy, and it pushed away the last wisps of trepidation.

Smiling in the starless dark, she extended her hand to him, and felt a shock of heat, and desire, when his fingers interlaced with hers.

"That's better. I don't want to fall off the pathway and disappear into the land of the fae or anything."

Rhiannon giggled at the image of Tom being dragged off into the woods by magical creatures, then quickly sobered. This was the tor,  and it had long been considered a portal to another dimension, another world. And she'd seen women emerging from the mists here herself. It wasn't out of the realm of possibility that some Otherworldly being would want Tom for themself. She had to keep her wits about her.

Ears straining, she thought she heard a laugh from higher up the slope, but maybe it was just the wind. Cautiously she put one foot in front of the other, and stepped out of the trees and onto the path upward.

"What was your new moon wish?" Tom's voice pierced her concentration, and she felt herself blush at the question. Thank god it *was* so dark.

"I can't tell you that!" Rhiannon tried to sound firm, and in control, but her voice came out as a squeak, and she knew if he pressed she would spill her guts and admit how much she wanted him to like her. *To want to be with her.*

"Do you do lunar rituals with your coven?" she asked quickly.

"Nice dodge." Tom laughed. "We do, although when I told Jasmine I wouldn't be able to get to this one, she was relieved, because she couldn't either, and now she doesn't need to feel guilty."

"Jasmine?"

"She's our priestess, and a wonderful woman and friend. I was glad tonight's ritual with Rose wasn't too different to one of hers – I was scared I'd make a fool of myself in front of her, and you."

Rhiannon giggled in disbelief. "How on earth do you think you could have made a fool of yourself? You're so experienced, so worldly, so magical…"

"So are you Miss Rhi, but you don't acknowledge it…"

Smiling at the endearment, she basked in the compliment, then focused again on feeling her way up the path. When they finally reached the summit, an icy wind sliced through her. Dropping his hand, she pulled her coat more tightly around herself and tried to stop her teeth from chattering. Then she felt Tom's arms wrap around her, and she leaned gratefully into his body, the cold as well as her mind soothed by his proximity.

"Are you okay?" Tom asked.

Twisting out of his grasp, she nodded, then realised he couldn't see her. "Yes, of course. I've just never been up here without a full moon to light the way, but I love it. There's something so liberating about the darkness. Too dark even for shadows."

Tipping her head back, she gazed up at the sky, at the tiny pinpoints of light that sparkled across the black expanse, yet shed no illumination on them. They were so far away. For a crazy moment she pictured her mother sailing through the velvety heavens, trapped forever in a void, on the altar of a dark star. Pain pierced her heart. She felt completely alone and bereft. A tendril of panic shot through her body, then started to wind its way around her, freezing her where she stood, constricting her throat, stealing her voice, and binding her in a prison she couldn't escape.

Then suddenly Tom's hand was on her arm, connecting them physically again, and she was released from the whirl of despair.

"It is strange, this darkness," he murmured. "So isolating. I'm here with you now though. You're not alone or bereft."

Even as she panicked that he'd read her mind, relief swamped her. It wasn't just that he was here with her now, holding her close in the late-night cold. His presence was also soothing an ache she'd long felt but never articulated, a pain she hadn't known she felt.

Slowly they sank to the ground, his hand still on her arm, and settled on the grass, sheltered from the wind in one direction at least by the crumbling stone tower atop the hill. Once her breathing returned to normal, Tom released his hold on her and opened the bag slung over his shoulder.

"I hope this is all right," he said, voice gentle as he took out some ritual tools. "I can still feel the circle of protection from our ritual, and the presence of the elements that were invoked, but I thought we might need a little light up here, and a little something to focus on."

Rhiannon watched, impressed, as he lit a white candle in a glass holder, then set out four objects around it – a black feather in the east for air, an athame in the south for fire, a dish he filled with water in the west, and a piece of rose quartz in the north for earth.

*And for love, she hoped…*

While the candle flame danced between them, he leaned across his makeshift altar and took her hand. "I'm happy to share my new moon wish with you," he offered, and his voice vibrated through her body, warming her heart. "As the dark moon fades and the new moon prepares to rise, I'm planting the seeds of spending the coming month getting to know you."

Rhiannon beamed, overjoyed that his wish had been about their relationship too.

Then he turned serious. "And I want to apologise for coming on so strong last weekend. I shouldn't have presumed that was okay."

"It was though," she whispered. *And there she went with the embarrassing admissions again.*

He smiled. "Still, I didn't ask, and I should have."

Just as she was about to say it would be perfectly fine to come on strong right now, up on the sacred tor, on the velvety grass, in the beautiful dark, Tom spoke again. "I want to prove to you that I'm genuine, and sincere. I want to take things slow. There's all the time in the world for us. So I thought a new moon exercise would be better than a second new moon ritual."

"Um, okay…"

"So Miss Rhi," he began, voice rich and powerful, the way Rose's went when she took on the mantle of the priestess. "At this liminal moment, in the darkness of this moonless night, when we're hidden by the void, tell me something about yourself. Something hidden. Something true."

Rhiannon froze. She'd worried – a little – that she'd be trying to fend off sexual advances up here, alone in the dark, yet he wanted her to reveal herself, not her body. Which was so much more terrifying. So much more intimate. And yet, if she could bring herself to do it, would it be so much more liberating too?

Reaching out across their altar, Tom stroked her cheek. "Don't be afraid. You don't have to tell me anything you don't want to, don't have to reveal any piece of yourself that you're not ready to share. I can go first."

Shadows played across his face as the candle flame flickered, and for a moment Rhiannon was overwhelmed with the desire to tear off his clothes and feel the heat between them as their bodies connected. But he was offering more than that. He was offering truth, and acceptance, and vulnerability. All the things that had been missing from her relationship with John. He was challenging her to be as honest as she'd claimed she wanted, and he was prepared to cut open his chest and offer his heart before she did. Slowly she smiled, and nodded.

He smiled in return. "Let's start with something easy. I love tattooing people, especially when they want pagan or spiritual symbols, because then it becomes a really deep and powerful ritual. But in my secret heart I want to be an artist. I want to paint. And I do, when I have time, that's my labour of love. Most people say it's impractical and self-indulgent, that I'm wasting my time because I'll never make money doing it. And don't worry, I'm not trying to convince you to date a starving artist who lives in a tiny, draughty garret – I love my day job too. But when I dream, it's of canvases I want to paint, not designs I want to tattoo. And it's when I paint that I feel the most free. The most me."

An image flitted through Rhiannon's mind, of Tom in an airy, light-filled loft, curtains fluttering in the breeze, a huge canvas on an easel, and him with a paintbrush in hand, surrounded by jars of brushes and tubes of paint. She longed to insert herself into the scene, reclining on a couch perhaps, draped in a floaty, translucent dress, his eyes taking in every inch of her as he transformed her into art.

"I'd love to see your paintings some time," she said shyly. "And I must admit – or reveal – that I'm jealous you have something you love so much. To have such passion for something, to really know what you want to do, that's such a gift."

"There's nothing you love doing?"

She shrugged. "I guess after Mum died, everything seemed a little pointless. Or superficial. And I had so much more to do, making meals, cleaning up, looking after my little brother, trying to help him and Dad cope, when I was barely coping myself." Her throat tightened, and tears started to well. Huh. She hadn't realised she still felt so emotional about that. So resentful.

"I'm so sorry Rhiannon. That you lost her, and that her loss has impacted you so much."

Shaking her head, she tried to make sense of the emotions surging through her, and the impact his sympathy was having on her. All her defenses were lowering, and there was a tidal wave rising within her, ready to pour out of her and drown them both. "No, it's fine," she muttered, embarrassed. "I shouldn't exaggerate. I'm sorry, it's not so bad now. It wasn't bad then. Forget I said that."

He reached over again and took her hand. "Never apologise for your feelings Rhiannon. They're part of you. You can't control them, and nor should you. You have to allow them, and acknowledge them, and let yourself *feel* them."

Shock surged over her in a flood, knocking her sideways. She'd tried so hard to hide her feelings, to deny them even to herself, mortified by the anger inside her. Surely she couldn't just give that up. Couldn't reveal the ugliness of her emotions. "But I can't feel resentful about everything I had to do after Mum died – there was no one else to do it. People were right to say I was selfish to complain."

"Oh babe," Tom said, and the compassion in his voice made Rhiannon tear up again. "No one has the right to tell you how you should feel in any situation. Whatever you're feeling – anger, resentment, grief, fear – it's all valid, all real, all perfectly understandable. No one else can decide what you should or shouldn't feel, whether you get to be hurt or offended, or diminish your genuine reaction to anything."

"But I *was* selfish…"

"Did you not do all those things though? Cook and clean, and care for your family?"

"Well, yes, eventually, but I did resent it."

"But you did it. You can control how you act in a situation – and you acted by doing what you felt you had to do – but that first, pure response? That resentment? You can't control how you *react*, how you *feel*, and no one has any right to tell you that you're not entitled to your feelings, or that your response is wrong. How dare anyone tell you what and how to feel? Those emotions are real, and true, and instinctive. They're part of you. Promise me you won't ever let anyone tell you how to feel, or diminish your honest reaction to something."

Shivering at the vehemence of his tone, Rhiannon slowly nodded. "I promise."

A dark shape swooped down at them, so close they felt the ripple of the air it disturbed in its flight. Tom grinned at her, just before the candle was extinguished by the creature's beating wings. "Bats show themselves to those who have wonderful powers of perception."

"Not that it actually showed itself to us," Rhiannon said, giggling. "Not technically."

Tom laughed. "That's true, it's too dark for us to see him, but I can sense him, can't you?"

She nodded. "I can. And I've always loved bats. They're so sweet and mysterious, and surely not as dark as people think."

"Yes! They're not dark, they just help us when we need to summon the courage to *face* the dark. But we've already faced that tonight, so maybe this one was just a sign that it's time for me to take you home."

Disappointment rose in Rhiannon, and she tried to quash it – until she remembered that she was allowed to feel whatever emotion came over her. She was *supposed* to feel it. So, she would acknowledge that she was disappointed the night was over. She just wouldn't allow it to make her sullen and uncommunicative. And she should be brave and ask for what she wanted.

"I guess I should get back, just in case Dad waited up. But, um, will I be able to see you tomorrow?" she whispered.

Leaning over and drawing her into his arms, Tom kissed her forehead, then lifted her chin so she was gazing into his eyes. The darkness was still intense, but she could just make them out. Glittering like stars. Like a promise.

"I hope so," he said, voice husky. "I told work I wouldn't be back until late Sunday, so you have some entertaining to do."

She grinned. "I can handle that."

## Chapter 13

# The Enchanted Forest

### Beth

When she heard the key turn in the front door, Beth leaped out of her husband's bed and rushed down the stairs. Glancing at the hall clock, she saw that Rhiannon had been up on the tor for several hours, and she waited anxiously for her to come inside.

Time moved strangely to a ghost. It felt like only a single moment had passed since she'd been lying in bed with Mike, dreaming with him, yet it was also an eternity. It was worth the wait though, to see her daughter's sparkling eyes and exquisite happiness. Beth followed her upstairs, laughing that they were both floating tonight.

Earlier, she'd had a wonderful time at Rose's new moon ritual, hovering around Laura as she and the other women welcomed the elements, soaring above the altar while the priestess invoked the deities, and watching in astonishment as Rhiannon sat in the circle holding hands with a tall, dark and gorgeous young man, her face beaming with joy. It soothed Beth's fears when Tom spoke with Rose afterwards, hugged his grandfather, and was so sweet to Rhiannon.

Although she'd wanted to follow them as they weaved their way up the tor through the late-night darkness, she headed home instead, determined to trust her daughter and not act like an over-protective mother. Rhiannon was seventeen, and deserved privacy. Beth just hoped her gut hadn't failed her, and Tom was a decent guy.

And it had been wonderful to spend time with her husband, as he put Brodie to bed, cleaned the kitchen, then curled up in their bed with a book. It was some comfort that Mike wasn't quite as distraught as he'd been four months ago, when she'd first become... whatever she was now. This strange phantom, blessed with the ability to spend time with her family, yet cursed to not have them know she was there. Desperately she hoped that her presence was helping them on some level.

She still had no idea how long she had left. It would be wonderful if she could stay here forever, in this half life that was frustrating, yet so much better than the alternative. But she knew she could be snatched away at any moment, dissolved back into the void permanently, and she didn't take this second chance for granted.

It was her dearest wish that she could help her family move forward without her, so she was relieved that their pain had lessened a little since Samhain. Most of all she wanted to see her beloved find someone to share his life with, and she knew he'd need help with that, since he was too loyal to even think to look. If she could assist him with that, and know that Brodie was okay and Rhiannon was healing, she would have no regrets when she disappeared.

What she'd seen of her daughter at the ritual tonight had been encouraging – she'd glowed with happiness, smiled readily at everyone there, and lit up from within whenever Tom looked at her. Most importantly, he seemed to cherish Rhiannon, the way Mike had always cherished her.

Flitting back along the hallway to her husband's room, Beth curled up around him and prepared to drift off, back to the void. But Mike was restless, and finally he threw back the covers and headed down to the kitchen. She followed close on his heels, desperate to take his hand, or stroke his forehead, to forge any connection that might soothe him, but disappointingly unable to. Defeated, she watched him heat some milk, then sat opposite him at the table while he slowly drank it, his eyes staring out into the darkness, sadness etched in every line of his face.

Shimmering across the space between them, she wrapped her arms around his body, and wanted to cry in frustration when she fell right through him. Determined, she tried again, gathering her essence together to imprint herself on his heart. And slowly she felt herself sinking into him, becoming part of him.

"Beth," he whispered, voice broken. She gasped. Could he feel her? She reached out again, trying to connect with his mind, with his heart. He inhaled a ragged breath, and for a moment she dared to hope – until he sighed deeply, expelling every molecule of her back out into the room. While she tried to pull herself back together, Mike stood up, squared his shoulders, and forced a rueful smile. Returning upstairs with him, Beth was relieved to see his mood had shifted, even a little, and convinced that he had sensed her on some level.

As they entered the bedroom, the clothes she'd been wearing at the ritual changed. Before, she'd been wrapped in a long green robe, her golden curls tumbling loose down her back, with flowers woven through them. Now her hair was in a sleek ponytail and she was clad in a striking red dress that swung out around her as she moved, the skirt full and cinched at the waist. It had been one of her favourites. She often wore it at Yule, because of its festive vibe, but as she raised a hand to her throat and felt the beautiful, delicate ruby pendant, she knew the occasion she'd travelled back to.

It was Brodie's first birthday, and Beth had spent days cooking and shopping for gifts, knowing it was for her own benefit, since Brodie was too young to sense the importance of the day, but pleased regardless. Twelve-year-old Rhiannon had helped her bake the cake – although she used the term *help* loosely – and was just as excited as she was, running around setting the table, putting out placemats and cutlery, and organising games. The perfect little host.

"Thank you so much for all your help today darling," she said, heart bursting with love and gratitude.

"You're welcome Mummy," Rhiannon said, long blonde hair in pigtails with bright red ribbons to match Beth's dress. "I just want it to be special for Brodie."

"He might be a bit too young to remember it all."

"I know silly, but there will be photos, and there will be guests too, who will notice what it looks like. And Rose is coming isn't she?"

Beth nodded, grateful as always for the woman who had stepped in to be a grandmother to her two kids. Her own mother had sent a card with a hundred pounds on the birth of each child, then broken contact again. Beth had seriously considered not telling her parents about Brodie's birth, but Mike had convinced her to try. Her sweet husband, always knowing the best thing to do. Understanding that she would have been racked with guilt if she hadn't made an effort, torturing herself with what-ifs and might-have-beens. At least once she'd sent the letter she could try to forget about them, try to let go of her expectations and focus on all the love she *did* have in her life.

For a moment she thought of Celia, her friend from the enchanted forest of Broceliande in Brittany, who she'd stayed with during her French adventure in the year before she returned to Summer Hill. She wondered what the kindly wise woman was doing now, whether she was still in her little stone cottage on the edge of the woods, communing with faeries and the spirits of Viviane and Morgaine.

A knock on the door interrupted her musings, and she wiped her hands on a tea towel and handed the plate of cupcakes to Rhiannon, then went to open it.

"Parcel delivery for you."

Signing for it, she stared at the unfamiliar handwriting, then noticed the French stamps. Turning it over, she saw an address in Brittany. Filled with anticipation, she slipped her finger under the seal and pulled it open. Inside was a white card and a red-wrapped gift with her name on the tag.

"Who is it Mummy?" Rhiannon called from the kitchen.

"Just the postman honey."

Tearing open the parcel, she smiled as she saw the beautiful faery artwork on the cover of a huge Book of Shadows. A woodland sprite with long red hair and a golden gown to match her wings was kneeling at a wooden door in an ancient oak tree, standing guard over the book that was bulging with spells, rituals, recipes, drawings and pressed flowers.

Turning to the first page, she found a handwritten message from Celia.

*Dearest Beth,*

*I sincerely hope you are well and happy, and enjoying your love-filled life.*

*I am so glad you found the perfect man to give your heart to, and create your family with. Our friend Viviane let me know when you met, and when you had Rhiannon. And now, as I fade from this world, she has told me of your son, and I am so delighted for you.*

*Please know I have thought of you often over the years, and still treasure the time we spent together. And so I want you to have my book of "recipes", and hope they will bring you peace and healing when it is needed.*

*All my love,*

❀ *Celia*

When Rhiannon came to see what was keeping her, there were tears in Beth's eyes.

"Mummy, Mummy, what's wrong? Why are you sad?"

Sinking to the floor, she drew her daughter into her arms. "I love you so much darling, you know that don't you?"

"Of course silly. I love you too."

"I will always love you."

Rhiannon drew back, panic in her eyes. "Why did you say that?"

"Sorry darling, it's just a letter from an old friend, who is very sick. It's brought back memories, that's all. I miss her."

Brodie's cry interrupted them, and Rhiannon raced up the stairs to get him up from his nap and ready for the party.

Smiling after her, Beth got to her feet and gazed out the open door at the bright sunshiny sky. A faery-shaped cloud blew across the sun, and she laughed. "Thank you Celia," she whispered. "May you rest in peace, wherever you end up."

Perhaps Viviane, the Otherworldly being Beth had met deep within the enchanted woods, would have a place at her side for the sweet kitchen witch who'd tended the plants there, honoured its fae folk, and healed so wisely with its herbs. Was there a way Celia could become part of the forest and the land and the elements when she died? A way for her magic and her kindness and her spiritual support to somehow remain in the world?

Behind her, Rhiannon was carefully descending the stairs with her baby brother in her arms. Beth turned to walk inside, to embrace her family, but stopped when she heard footsteps on the path. Rose was approaching, and Beth's heart lifted – until she noticed the basket that looked alarming like Celia's, and inhaled the warm scent of baking that wafted from it. She paled, the parallels and the emotion almost too much for her. The priestess rushed forward and drew her into her arms, and as Beth felt the safety and security of her comforting hug, she broke down.

"Dear one, it's okay. Those we love are never really gone."

Shocked, she stared at the priestess, at the all-knowing gaze and the deep love in her eyes. Rose smiled, and looked up at the fae-shaped cloud. "A magical one's passing?"

Tears trembled on Beth's lashes, and she nodded sadly. Dimly she felt her daughter's hand on her back, and heard the snuffling and cooing of her baby boy as he fought off the drowsiness of slumber. Taking him in her arms, she bent down and scooped Rhiannon to her, holding her family tight.

"Hello sweet girl," Rose said to Rhiannon.

The little girl's face lit up. "Hi Nanna Rose!" she replied, then tugged on her skirt. "Will you help me finish the birthday cake?"

"Of course."

Beth cradled Brodie to her, smiling down into his sweet blue eyes, and felt such appreciation for her time in the forest. It had, in a roundabout way, brought her back here. When she'd left home after school she was convinced she had to live far away for her own sanity, but it was not her surroundings that had to change, it was herself. And that had begun in Broceliande Forest, with a kitchen witch called Celia who baked lemon and lavender cakes and saw people's futures in their tea leaves.

When she headed through the dining room, Beth gasped. Rose had lifted the covering from her basket, and the sweet aroma of lavender and the crisp fragrance of lemon assailed her senses. The cake she placed on the table was beautiful, delicately risen, with lemon syrup poured over the top, and lavender and lemon blossoms wreathed around the base.

"How could you know?"

The priestess grinned. "Magic, my dear girl. Now, I have a gift for the birthday boy, and one for you Rhiannon." While Beth took a silver-wrapped parcel over to the sideboard and added it to the pile of gifts she'd bought for her son, Rose stooped down to Rhiannon's level and handed her a small velvet pouch.

She looked up at her with huge blue eyes. "But Nanna Rose, it's not my birthday."

"I know sweet girl, but I just want you to know how much I adore you, and how precious you are to all of us. You should be celebrated every day, just like your brother, and your mum and dad."

Beth stared hard at her young daughter. Was she jealous of all the attention Brodie was getting today? Now she remembered the litany of warnings from the women at her mothers' group, of older children acting out when their once-sole claim on the household was diluted. She gazed down at her daughter anxiously.

"Thank you so much, that's very kind of you," Rhiannon said politely to Rose. "But I don't mind Brodie getting presents, because I know I'll get some on my birthday." She flashed a cheeky smile. "But I can't wait to see what it is."

Pride suffused Beth, and she watched curiously as Rhiannon opened the bag, and pulled out an antique silver charm bracelet.

"Oh, I love it! Thank you," she said, hugging Rose, then holding out her arm so she could do up the clasp for her. "It's so pretty. Look Mummy! There's a faery and an oak leaf, and a little purple crystal, and a sun and a crescent moon, and a swan too."

"It's lovely darling," Beth replied, then her eyes shifted to the priestess. They were all items she associated with Broceliande, but how could Rose have known that she'd be thinking about that now? That she would receive a spell book straight from the forest on this day of all days?

The priestess winked at her, then turned to face the doorway, seconds before Mike walked in.

"Rose, hello," he said, coming in and embracing her. Then he lifted Rhiannon up and spun her around, eliciting a wave of giggles, before kissing Beth and tenderly stroking his son's cheek. "How's it all going?" he asked. "It looks amazing, very festive, and I made it just in time – they'll be arriving any minute, won't they?"

Glancing at the clock, Beth nodded, but she didn't feel as anxious as she'd expected as she passed Brodie to her husband and headed to the kitchen to finish plating up the last of the party food. Mike followed her in, Brodie in one arm, and a small red box in the other.

"For you my darling. You have made me the happiest man alive. I know you bought heaps of gifts for Brodie, but you're the one who deserves to be showered in presents today."

She ducked her head, all of a sudden shy, but Mike lifted her chin and leaned in and kissed her on the lips. "I adore you Beth Stark, and I am grateful every day that you allowed me to be your husband, and the father of your children."

*Goddess, this day was determined to make her cry.*

Swallowing down her tears, she opened the box, and gasped. It was a rose-gold charm bracelet, almost the twin to Rhiannon's, with an oak leaf and a faery, a rose quartz crystal, a sun, a moon and a star. "And that white bird is for Rhiannon, since she was named for Rhiannon of the birds," Mike explained. "And the four-leaf clover is for Brodie, because this family we've created is my life, and I feel so blessed to have you all."

Beth couldn't stop the tears this time, but she started laughing when Brodie stuck his pudgy little fist up and tried to grab at the four-leaf clover charm.

"And this," Mike added, pulling another box from his pocket and opening it for her. "This is for you."

Inside lay a beautiful heart-shaped ruby pendant on a delicate rose-gold chain, and she stared at it in wonder. "It's beautiful."

"Not as beautiful as you, beloved. Here, let me help you put it on."

Raising a hand to the pendant at her throat, she marvelled at the warmth emanating from it. She felt so lucky to have her family, her friends, this home and this *life* that she'd never imagined could be hers. And the magic. She smiled at Rose as she poked her head in to let them know the first guests had arrived. Taking Mike's hand, Beth headed out to welcome them, and spent the day surrounded by those she loved. And as she ate a slice of lemon and lavender cake, she raised a glass of champagne in honour of Celia.

When Beth fell into bed with Mike that night, she thanked the goddess for the life she had created, and the amazing people who had helped her on her way. She even spared a thought for Andrew, the boyfriend she'd met while she was living in Paris, after her time in Brittany. He'd treated her terribly – and later dated her friend Violet with devastating consequences – yet she couldn't regret being with him, because in its own way it had set her on the path that had led her to here. And there was nowhere on earth she'd rather be.

A tear welled in Beth's eye as she remembered, and she watched in surprise as it fell through her and onto the blanket. In his sleep, Mike turned towards her, as though he'd heard the tear drop, and reached out a hand towards her.

"Those we love are never really gone," he murmured, echoing the priestess's words. Shocked, Beth felt herself break apart into a million tiny pieces and disperse back into the star-strewn universe.

## Chapter 14

# The Silver Wheel

### Rhiannon

Rhiannon's eyes snapped open long before her alarm went off the next morning, and she grinned as she replayed every moment of the previous night. Doing a ritual with Tom at her side had been amazing, even more than she'd expected. She'd always wished John would come with her, but in the face of his indifference had reluctantly decided it didn't matter. Now she knew it did. To be able to share such a beautiful, magical experience with someone she cared about was indescribable.

It reminded her that her parents' relationship had begun when her dad invited her mum to one of Rose's rituals. Although Beth had ended up being the more active of the two magically, sharing such a deep love for nature, and the power of the moon and the turning of the seasons, really deepened their connection.

Being up on the tor with Tom after the new moon ceremony, alone together in the beautiful dark, had been even more special, and made her fall for him even harder. Because it turned out that he actually cared about her, and wanted to know her, and know about her life and her feelings.

When they first met they'd flirted and joked about sex magic, so that ever since, Rhiannon had vacillated between worrying that he'd expect her to go through with it, and hoping that he would. Yet he was interested in intimacy of a different kind. The talking kind. The revealing your self, not your body, kind. Which blew her mind.

*Could he be more perfect?*

His farewell at her front door had been passionate, but then he'd reminded her that they had all the time in the world, and she had floated upstairs, dazed from his kisses, and relieved that he was happy to take things slow.

But now she was drowning in impatience. How could she wait until midday to see him? It was sweet that he'd promised to spend the morning with his grandfather, but she longed to feel his arms around her again, and listen to his stories, and watch his eyes light up when he talked about his passions.

*Only four more hours…*

Punching her pillow with frustration, Rhiannon dragged herself out of bed and headed downstairs for breakfast.

"Hey Dad, hey Brodie," she said, stifling a yawn as she spooned cereal into her bowl then poured a large mug of coffee.

"Hi darling. How was last night?" her father asked. "I didn't hear you come in."

She smiled, remembering the feel of Tom's hand in hers as they'd sat in the ritual circle – and then as they'd climbed the tor. "It was wonderful. I never get sick of watching Rose do her thing. And there was so much beautiful, loving energy. Plus the cookies we made were a big hit."

"Did you save any for me?" Brodie asked.

"I'm sorry buddy, they were all eaten. But I can make you some today if you'd like?" she offered guiltily.

Their dad grinned. "That would be great. I have to go in to work, so would you mind hanging out with Brodie this morning, and dropping him off at school at half past eleven? He's got rehearsals for the play."

Rhiannon cursed under her breath.

Her panic must have shown, because her father quickly reassured her. "Ben and his mum will be there – she volunteered to direct it, crazy, brave woman – so Brodie will go back to their place afterwards, and I'll pick him up on my way home this afternoon. Is that okay?"

"Yes, of course," she said, relief coursing through her. "It's just that I promised I'd meet Carlie later to do some homework and hang out. I'll probably stay there for dinner too."

Swallowing the last of his coffee then grabbing his briefcase, Mike stood up, ruffled Brodie's hair, and kissed Rhiannon's cheek. "I'm so proud of you honey. You're doing so well at school, and still doing so much for us, but keeping up with your friendships and your magic too, which is really important. I don't want you to sacrifice all your time for me and Brodie."

"Thanks Dad," she muttered. Ugh, she felt terrible, for lying to her dad, and for using her friend as an excuse. Especially given how impatient she'd been when Carlie had asked her to be an alibi so she could see Rowan once. Why was it all so complicated?

"Rhi-Rhi, will you come to watch me in the play when it starts? And Carlie too? I'm playing Peter Pan, so I'm really nervous today because I have to practise my flying!"

Her brother's words jolted her back to the present, and she shook off her anxiety and spent the next few hours giving him her undivided attention. They baked cookies, read *Peter Pan* together, then she dropped him off at school and headed off to meet Tom.

Her heart rate sped up as she turned into Jake's street, and butterflies swooped around in her belly. She remembered how vulnerable she'd felt up on the tor, when she'd revealed her secret thoughts, and stopped abruptly. Did she really want someone to know her inner self, her true self? Would Tom even like her when he got to know her? And what if he ever found out about *the thing that happened*? Wouldn't it be safer to go over to Carlie's and hang out with her, and forget about this guy who was going to challenge everything she'd ever believed about life, and love, and her very self?

Before she could decide, Tom came out onto the street and hurried towards her. Scooping her into his arms, he held her close and kissed her gently, and suddenly walking away from him seemed like the stupidest idea she'd ever had.

"Hey babe. Has this been the slowest morning ever? I swear I checked three times to see if the clock had stopped."

Rhiannon grinned. "So slow!"

His smile made her melt. "Is there anything in particular you'd like to do today?"

Hmm, she probably should have given that some thought. She shrugged helplessly, feeling like an idiot. "I'm easy, I'm just happy to be with you to be honest." She blushed. "I mean, there are loads of things we could do, but do you have something in mind?"

"Well, I did have an idea... Do you mind if we drive?" he asked, motioning to his motorbike.

"Um, sure." She tried not to sound nervous. Her dad would kill her if he knew, but she'd survived the terrifying but exhilarating ride last weekend, so she figured it would be fine. *What he didn't know wouldn't hurt him, right?*

"We don't have to..."

"No, it's fine. Let's go." There was a mischievous glint in her eye, and Tom stared at her for a moment, assessing, then shrugged and handed her a helmet. This time he'd brought a spare.

The ride was just as thrilling as last time. Rhiannon clung tightly to Tom at first, then slowly relaxed as they headed out of town, enjoying the feel of the wind in her hair, and her body so close to his.

"Where are we going?" she called out, but her voice was snatched away and drowned out, so she closed her eyes and gave herself over to the sensation, determined to enjoy the mystery.

About ten miles out of town Tom turned off onto a side road, then onto a dirt track. A large wooden sign announced The Silver Wheel, and she gazed around, wide-eyed and puzzled, as they got off the bike in a small, green-shadowed courtyard.

"What is this place?" she asked. "And how come you know about it, when I've lived here all my life and never even heard of it?"

A woman her dad's age came out to greet them before he could reply. "Welcome, I'm Deidre. How can I help you today? Were you wanting to check out the studio, the gardens or the exhibition?"

Tom thrust out his hand to shake hers. "Hi Deidre, we spoke on the phone. I'm Tom, and this is Rhiannon. You mentioned that we could book some time in the studio."

"Oh yes, come right this way. We have a class at four o'clock, which you're welcome to join, but it's all yours until then. I'll show you around, and set you up."

Still perplexed, Rhiannon followed them into a large, light-filled room. There were twelve small wooden benches, each with a pottery wheel on top, alongside a jar holding strange objects.

Handing them both aprons, Deidre told them to take their pick of work benches. "There's clay over here, more tools, and jars for water and sponges are over there. You said you're experienced, so you know how to use everything?"

Tom grinned. "We'll be fine, thanks so much."

"Have fun. And I'll just be through that door, setting up the exhibition, so shout if you need anything."

Rhiannon's head was spinning. They were doing pottery? Or making pottery? What was the correct terminology? And Tom was so familiar with it that he was going to teach her? She hoped so anyway. She couldn't remember the last time she'd handled clay.

Once they were alone together, Tom turned to her and smiled. "Is this okay?"

She nodded, still a little unsure, but happy to give anything a go if it meant spending time with him. She just hoped she wouldn't make a complete fool of herself.

"Have you ever made pottery?"

"Not since primary school," she admitted sheepishly. "And that was just with our hands, no wheel or other tools involved. What made you think of this?"

Eyes twinkling, he tied on his apron. "Last night you mentioned that you haven't had time to do anything crafty, anything artistic, in ages, so I thought this might be fun. Painting can be daunting if you're put on the spot, but working with clay is really satisfying, regardless of whether you consider yourself an artist or not, and whether you like the end product or not."

Rhiannon gulped. Okay, she could do this. Without getting competitive, or being embarrassed that whatever Tom made would be so much better than hers. "Let's do this."

He took her hand. "Hey, this is just for fun, okay? No competition, no stress."

Laughing that he had read her mind again, she nodded and put her apron on too, then sat down at one of the work stations. Tom got her a hunk of clay and filled a jar with water, then pulled up a stool opposite and started to explain what to do.

Self-conscious and unsure of herself, at first Rhiannon regretted not choosing something more normal, and controllable, for them to do. As the clay slipped around the wheel, and at one point almost flew right off, she blushed and swore. It was harder than it looked.

"Let me help," Tom said, and moved his stool so he could perch right behind her. Gently he leaned against her, his arms loosely around her, squeezing her elbows in closer to her body, and his breath soft and warm on her ear.

"Slow the wheel a little, and try to relax your arms," he murmured. He placed his hands over hers and guided them up and down the clay, and Rhiannon watched in astonishment as a shape started to form beneath her palms. She wasn't sure how long she could hold it steady though, because the feel of Tom's body behind her was driving her to distraction. Slowly she leaned back into him, loving the sensation of his arms around her, his heart beating in time with hers. Which was increasing in pace as she melted into him.

"Now add a tiny trickle of –"

"Oops!" A giggle escaped Rhiannon's lips as her vase-like creation collapsed in on itself and bits of wet clay flew from the wheel. "I'm so sorry."

She twisted around to face him, and found his eyes sparkling with laughter. Tentatively he reached out his hand and pulled a piece of clay from her hair, wiped a smudge from her cheek, and tucked a stray blonde curl away from her eyes. Then he leaned down and kissed her, and she felt the room tilt and start to spin.

Clashing sensations warred within her – comfort and challenge, fire and ice – pulling her away from all that anchored her to her perceptions of herself. Stripping her bare. She knew she should be terrified, but she wasn't. She felt safe. She felt wild.

She felt revealed, yet understood.

Soon she was sitting on his lap, held close in his arms, her legs wrapped around him, and the world sliding away as she lost herself in his kisses, in this heat that was burning them up, breaking them down and melding them back together. Stronger. Better.

She never wanted the moment to end.

Suddenly there was a sound in the doorway, and Rhiannon jerked backwards, almost tipping them both over. Tom grinned as he steadied her, placed her back on her stool, then stood up. Deirdre hovered in the doorway for a moment, then brought two mugs over.

"Sorry to interrupt, I just thought you might like a coffee," she said, thrusting the cups at Tom then quickly exiting.

Rhiannon's cheeks blushed fiery red, but Tom just laughed as he handed her a drink then took a swig of his. The coffee calmed her, until she saw the clock and realised how long they'd been kissing, and the sorry state of her dried out lump of clay, and was embarrassed all over again.

"So, shall we have another go at that vase?" he asked, with an adorable smirk.

"I guess we should. If the clay isn't too ruined."

All serious now, Tom sorted out the clay and returned it to its spot in the centre of the wheel. While he was still just as attentive, his arms guiding hers as before, they managed to control themselves, and ended up getting a half decent vase finished just in time to clean up before the students arrived.

"Did you want to stay and do the class?" Tom asked.

Rhiannon shook her head. "I'm not sure I'd find any other teacher quite as effective," she said, before blushing again as she recalled his lips on hers.

"I should hope not." He winked at her. "I'm getting a bit hungry anyway, so would you like to grab some food? Or do you need to get back home?"

"It's okay, I told Dad I'd probably have dinner at Carlie's," she replied, then cringed. She hated lying, but there was no point telling her father about Tom if there was nothing to tell, and she still wasn't entirely sure of their relationship, if that's what it even was. The signs were looking hopeful though.

Tom didn't say anything as they made their way out into the late afternoon light, and Rhiannon's initial sliver of awkwardness grew with every step. Had she said something wrong? Done something foolish? As she climbed onto the back of his bike, she prayed he hadn't decided she was just a stupid kid after all. But when they hit the highway he turned left instead of right, and she was relieved they weren't going home yet. She wondered where they were going, but he wouldn't hear her ask over the wind and the roar of the engine, so she closed her eyes, leaned against him and tried to relax. She would discover where they were going when they got there.

A short time later, Tom pulled over outside a rustic little cafe on the outskirts of Smithfield, and she followed him inside. "I figured we should eat a few towns over, in case anyone sees us and tells your dad," he said, and Rhiannon shrank in on herself, totally mortified.

"I'm sorry, I didn't mean anything by it," she murmured. "And it's not that I don't want people to know about you or anything, I just figured I'd wait until... well, to be honest, I wasn't even sure you'd actually come down last night, so there was no point telling Dad about you if that was the case."

"Hey, it's totally fine," Tom said, smiling at her and taking her hand. "I've met your best friend, and you took me to a public ritual, so I know I'm not your dirty little secret."

She blushed scarlet, and he laughed. "I'm just joking babe."

A waiter brought menus over, and Rhiannon was relieved that they could focus on something else for a moment.

"Will your grandfather mind that you're out with me all day?" she asked tentatively. "Or Jake?"

"Nah, they're fine with it. I'm glad I spent the morning with them, but I wouldn't have come down if it wasn't to see you, so Pop is just thrilled I'm back so soon after last weekend."

"Oh."

His forehead wrinkled as he frowned. "I came down to see *you* Miss Rhi, if that's what you're wondering, and I'm hoping I can spend time with you tomorrow too. Were you still doubting me, even after last night on the tor, and today's passionate pottery class?"

She squirmed in her seat. "A little. I guess it's just hard for me to believe that you could like me," she admitted.

Tom looked stricken. "Why on earth not?"

"Because you're amazing! You have a career, and a life. You're an artist, and are studying something you're passionate about. You've travelled, and done incredible things, and you make magic. I'm just – "

"Stop it babe, please. That's crazy," he said, scooting around to her side of the booth and hugging her tight. "You've done all of that too. You *do* all of that. It's early days, and who knows, you might decide you don't like me before I go home tomorrow. But I really like you Rhiannon, I like hanging out with you, and you have absolutely no reason to doubt my sincerity. At the very least, I know how important you and Carlie are to Jake, so I would never hurt you and make things awkward for him. But that's *not* why I'm here."

Their coffees arrived then, and he moved back to his side of the table, but he reached over and took her hand. "Is that all it is? That's why you don't want to tell your father about me?"

She sighed. How honest did she want to be? "It's just, I was sort of seeing someone before, and Dad finally met him – then we broke up right after that. So I guess I just want to be sure there's something to actually tell him when I do..." Was that enough? She didn't want to admit how recently that break-up had been. Then she groaned. For a moment she'd forgotten that Jake knew all about her dating history, and exactly when, and why, she'd ended things with John.

Tom shrugged. "I don't expect you to have never dated anyone. I imagine guys would be fighting to ask you out..."

Emphatically she shook her head. John had been her first and only boyfriend, although admittedly that was more to do with the timing of her mum's illness and death than her being so unlikeable that no one would ask her out, or so uninterested in dating that she had refused all offers.

"Well, it's their loss, *if* that's true," he continued. "And I've had girlfriends before, but I'm not dating anyone else at the moment, in case you were speculating."

Rhiannon blushed, embarrassed to have to concede that she had been worrying about that, but grateful that he'd brought it up.

"And you?"

She stared at him, puzzled. "Me?"

"You're not dating anyone else?"

"No, of course not!" she replied, horrified at the very idea. "I couldn't kiss you like I just did if I was seeing someone else."

A smile lit up Tom's face. "I'm glad. And I look forward to more of that kissing."

They kissed some more that night. After lingering over coffee and dessert for as long as they could, they'd reluctantly headed home. Tom stopped down the street from Rhiannon's place, and they leaned against a tree and kissed for what felt like hours, before she finally dragged herself out of his arms and into her house. Fortunately her dad was already in bed, so she tiptoed up the stairs to her room and curled up on her window seat, knees clutched to her chest and eyes staring out into the darkness.

Desperately she wished her mum was still alive, so she could tell her all about Tom, and how sweet and considerate he was. To have picked an out-of-town cafe so she wouldn't be stressed about being seen was so thoughtful. And then there were his kisses...

The next morning she had to look after Brodie for a while, but she managed to escape in time to meet Tom and Jake for lunch. Then, just like the week before, they rode off on his motorbike so they could say their passionate farewells alone together.

Chapter 15

# Lose Yourself To Find Yourself

### Rhiannon

It hurt Rhiannon physically to be apart from Tom during the next week. The longing was a dull ache in her body, and she knew her constant pining made her not much fun to be around. Tom had wanted to come down and meet her after school one day, but she'd had to regretfully decline, since she had a major joint history assignment due on the Friday, and had to spend every afternoon with her classmate partner so they could get it written.

Thankfully Tom drove to Summer Hill early on Saturday morning, so they could steal some time together. Her dad and Brodie were out, so Tom spent the whole day at her place, snuggled up watching a movie, curled up on the couch reading, drinking ridiculous amounts of coffee, and talking non-stop.

Unfortunately he had to leave that night for work though, and the next week was just as hectic for Rhiannon because she had to study for a major test. Not that she managed to commit much of the information to memory, since all she could think about was Tom. The only consolation was that he seemed just as sad as she was to be kept apart – and that her trip to London to see him was approaching, albeit painfully slowly.

But finally, after feeling the time would never pass, the spring equinox rolled around, and Rhiannon was on the earliest train to the city with Carlie and Jake. She knew she was expecting a lot of Carlie to return to the place she'd met the boyfriend she'd loved and so tragically lost, just so Rhiannon could fall deeper for a guy who must remind her of Rowan in so many ways. But Rhiannon had asked her anyway, the flicker of guilt drowned out by the excitement that she'd be seeing Tom soon.

*And doing a group ritual with his coven.*

She wondered what it would be like. Did the witches Tom shared sacred space with work together like Rose's circle, or were they more serious? And would she make a fool of herself? Rose's rituals were open to anyone who wanted to attend, no experience necessary, so they were a magical overview of each seasonal celebration rather than a deeper, darker journey into the shadowy depths of each sabbat. And the group's lunar rites were about healing and wishes and wellbeing, rather than seeking the dark and hidden parts of each person's truth. She wondered if Tom's coven would be more like hers and Carlie's – challenging and personal and serious and complex, and far too intimidating and revealing for a stranger.

"Do you think I'll embarrass myself tonight?" she asked her friends nervously.

Carlie stared at her, perplexed. "What do you mean?"

"Well, I've only done public rituals with Rose, and hers are so welcoming and inclusive. I'm sure Tom and his group are way more advanced than I am magically. What if I do something wrong?"

Her friend smiled. "Rhi, it's not a competition, or a test. And Tom said it's a public sabbat, so there will probably be others who haven't worked magic with their group before either. Besides, it's just about honouring the cycles of nature and the seasons, of bringing ourselves into alignment with the earth, and you're great at that. It will be like Jake's first ritual with Gran, surely?"

That made Rhiannon feel a little better. She turned to Jake. "Were you terrified? Was it awful or scary or hard? Did you feel stupid or out of place or out of your depth?" She felt panic rising as she spoke, heard her voice getting fainter, her breath coming faster.

"I was a bit nervous," Jake admitted, which didn't help her anxiety levels. "But I was more excited than anything else. And as soon as

Pop and I got there, we felt totally at ease. I don't know if it was a spell Rose was weaving, or just how welcoming she is anyway, but the moment we entered the room we were transported to a magical dimension almost, a place of enchantment where we felt we belonged. There was no judgement, no feelings of insecurity, no fears we didn't know enough, and believe me, Pop and I knew nothing. You will be absolutely fine tonight – you could probably take part in running the ritual, you know so much about it and have so much experience. Besides, Tom wouldn't care if you singlehandedly ruined the entire night. He just wants to spend time with you."

Pleasure settled over Rhiannon, and she grinned and forced herself to relax. Despite the occasional shiver of fear, she couldn't wait to see Tom performing the ritual. He was magical every second of the day, whether he was sitting with her reading a book, watching TV or staring up at the moon. To see him dressed in his ceremonial clothes, invoking the god and calling the directions, would be amazing. And nerves aside, she *was* looking forward to meeting the other members of his coven and working with a new priestess.

But best of all, they'd get to hang out together all day at the festival. She was so glad Jake had come with them, so he could keep Carlie company while she lost herself in Tom.

At last the train pulled into London, and they made their way to the festival. As they stood at the entrance, Rhiannon hovered near Carlie, trying to envelop her in peaceful thoughts. She knew her friend was dreading the memories of Rowan that were so strong here, as well as the bright flashing lights and the crush of people swarming through the huge hall. It could be overwhelming at the best of times.

"You okay?" Rhiannon asked softly, putting an arm around Carlie's shoulder as they walked in. "Thank you so much for coming with me. I know this isn't easy for you, and I really appreciate it."

"I'm okay," Carlie replied, although she sounded as though she was trying to reassure herself as much as her friend.

It was all for nothing though, because as soon as Rhiannon saw Tom, she let out a shriek of excitement and rushed towards him.

She'd missed him terribly, and desperately wanted to kiss him. He was just as eager. He caught her up and whirled her around, and when his lips found hers, her head spun from the lights, the noise surrounding them, and the heady aroma of incense and essential oils, not to mention the feel of his body against hers, and what being so close to him did to her. Whenever he held her, she wanted to surrender to the passion that burned between them.

His kiss deepened as that thought crossed her mind, and a thrill shot through her, that he always knew what she was thinking – and that he so clearly wanted her just as desperately as she wanted him.

"I've missed you so much," he growled against her throat between kisses, and desire ignited within her.

"I've missed you too," she finally gasped, pulling back slightly so she could look into his eyes. She had to get a grip. "But you should probably say hi to Jake, right? And I should see if Carlie's coping. I'm sure they're horrified by our display."

"It turns me on, just how much you *don't* want us to have to do those things." Tom grinned, then kissed her again, a kiss so filled with passion and longing that she trembled with need.

"But you're right," he conceded, with a dramatic sigh. "This will definitely be continued though."

"Promise?"

"Absolutely."

Reluctantly they disentangled themselves and walked back to the entrance, but their friends had given up on them and were heading into the next aisle, Jake guiding Carlie through the crowd, a gentle hand on her elbow. A wave of guilt swept over Rhiannon, and she wondered if she should go after them.

"She's okay with Jake," Tom murmured. "And we'll catch up with them soon, but there are a few things I want to show you, and a talk I think you'll love."

Conscience soothed, Rhiannon took Tom's hand when he offered it, and they wandered down the first aisle, catching up on their past week in between looking at the products on display. It was a huge hall, with so many different stands to pore over, and she loved listening to Tom describe all the healing methods being demonstrated, as well as peeking at the gorgeous crystal jewellery that sparkled in every row, and all the books, candles and ritual tools on offer.

Time quickly slipped away, and soon they were racing upstairs to listen to a talk about magical names by someone in Tom's coven. Afterwards they collapsed into chairs at a table in the cafe area, and Rhiannon realised how hungry she was after their early start.

"What did you think of the seminar?" Tom asked, after they'd ordered sandwiches, coffee and cake.

"It was fascinating. And it reminded me that Jake mentioned once that you sometimes use the name Raven. Is that your magical name, for coven work?" Rhiannon asked curiously. "I never thought to use another name, and as far as I know, nor did Mum, or Rose."

"You don't need a magical name because you already have one," Tom said, grinning. "What could be more sacred than being named for a goddess?"

She shrugged. "I guess so. I didn't even know about that until last year though, when we had to do a history project on a deity, and our teacher said it would be easy for me and Carlie."

"Wow, that was for a school assignment? How awesome!"

Rhiannon nodded. "Laura is a member of Rose's circle, which helps. I think you met her at the new moon ritual."

"Maybe. There were so many people there though, and I was only interested in you."

Rhiannon glowed at the compliment.

"And of course Carlie was named for the goddess Kali. Did she know before then?"

She shook her head. "No, she had no idea. Her mum Violet grew up in Summer Hill, and went to rituals and practised magic, as you would as Rose's daughter. But after she fled to Australia, she must have given it all up, because when she and her husband died, not only did Carlie have no idea she had a grandmother, she had no clue about magic. Her mum had completely cut herself off from it, so it was a real shock for Carlie when she arrived in a country she'd never visited, to live with a grandmother she'd never met – who had no idea of her existence either – and discovered that said grandma was a witch and a priestess."

Tom was staring at her in disbelief. "Why would someone give up their magic? And how could Carlie have no idea about any of it?"

"It's a long story, and Carlie and Rose are still trying to figure out the details, but I can tell you what I know." While they ate, Rhiannon explained some of Rose's history. Her daughter's disappearance, her husband's subsequent breakdown and suicide, her own devastation – then, twenty years later, her confusion and joy when a sullen, heartbroken Carlie turned up on her doorstep.

"Wow, that makes my life seem so much less traumatic than I'd convinced myself it was," Tom said.

Rhiannon raised her coffee to her lips. "Yeah, and you can imagine how self-indulgent I felt about spending three months being a selfish brat after my mum died, when Carlie was dealing with losing *both* of her parents as well as her home, her friends and her school, and being sent across the world to live with a stranger. She was so much more pleasant than I was. Not to mention that she was under the mistaken impression that it was her fault her mum and dad were dead. It wasn't of course – a drunk driver went through a red light and smashed into their car – but Carlie carried that for a while too."

Tom stared at her, gaze sharp. "Why do you feel responsible?"

A blush stained Rhiannon's cheeks. "Not for that," she whispered. "But I do feel somewhat culpable for her boyfriend's death." She hadn't told Tom about the circumstances of Rowan's accident, or the part she'd played in it. She was too scared of what he'd think of her.

Taking a deep breath, she hesitantly revealed what had happened on solstice eve, and why. Then, dread snaking up her spine, she waited for him to berate her, or get up and leave, but he surprised her by leaning forward and kissing her.

"Miss Rhi, do you honestly believe that Carlie would still be your friend – and that she would have come today, given how painful it is for her to be here – if she believed that?"

Shock made Rhiannon's blood run cold. What did he know about Carlie and Rowan?

Tom smiled, sympathy in his eyes. "When I asked Jake why Carlie seemed reluctant to come, he told me she met her boyfriend here, at the last festival, and a little bit about his tragic death. Which made me even more horrified at how I treated her the day we met."

"You didn't know," Rhiannon said quickly.

He nodded. "Yes, that's true, but I still feel bad about it, even though *it wasn't my fault*. And it's the same for you. Carlie doesn't hold you responsible, so nor should you."

No wonder she was falling so hard for this guy. He made her feel so much better about herself, about everything. Reluctantly she nodded. "Okay."

"Good enough, for now." He grinned. "I know you're feeling a little guilty though, so shall we go and find Jake and Carlie, and spend some time with them? I'd much rather be alone with you, don't get me wrong, but I guess we should pretend we want to see them too," he teased.

They both laughed, the serious, pained atmosphere dissolving in their growing intimacy, and set off to find their friends. It took a while, but they finally tracked them down at a stand of handmade honey-infused lotions and witchy products called Blessed Bee. Jake was buying a basket full of things, and Carlie was blushing at something the woman behind the counter was saying. Puzzled, Rhiannon swooped in and grabbed her friend, calling out to Jake that they needed to show her something.

When they returned to the stand, Carlie was holding a bag and Rhiannon was holding Tom's hand. And when Tom and the woman talking to Jake saw each other, they both started laughing.

"These are the friends you're bringing to the ritual tonight?" she asked him, eyes alight with amusement.

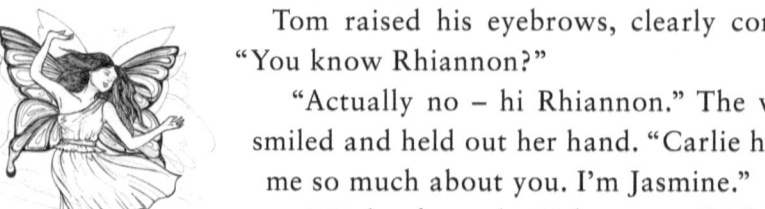

Tom raised his eyebrows, clearly confused. "You know Rhiannon?"

"Actually no – hi Rhiannon." The woman smiled and held out her hand. "Carlie has told me so much about you. I'm Jasmine."

"Right, from the Yule retreat," Rhiannon said, marvelling at the coincidence. "Carlie's mum's friend."

Jasmine turned to Tom. "I knew Carlie's mum many years ago, when she lived in London, and I spent some time with Carlie at the last winter solstice. And I've just been getting to know Jake."

"Small world," Tom said, grinning. "Jake is my cousin from Australia. And that's how I met Rhiannon and Carlie, they're all school friends."

"So you'll be at the ritual tonight too?" Carlie asked Jasmine.

Tom tried to smother a laugh. "Jasmine is our high priestess, like your grandmother."

"Oh! Is it okay if we all come?" she asked shyly. "We don't want to intrude if it's a closed sabbat."

"Of course you're welcome, the more the merrier!" Jasmine smiled. "I was planning to ask if you and your friends could come anyway, but I guess I don't need to now."

A few customers approached, and Jasmine turned her attention to them. Tom dragged Jake off to show him something, leaving the girls to catch up. Rhiannon was bubbling over with joy about her boyfriend and all they'd seen and done in the past few hours.

"He's so beautiful Carlie, isn't he!" she exclaimed. "I'm trying not to rave about him endlessly, because I know you're not quite as excited about him as I am, but I can't even think about anything else. How could you hide how you felt about Rowan the way you did? I want to shout from the rooftops that I love Tom."

Her friend tried to keep her tone light. "Well, I wasn't ready to share it with Gran, and my best friend wasn't his biggest fan, so I kept it inside."

Waves of guilt washed over Rhiannon again. "I'm really sorry," she said, but Carlie shook her head.

"I know you're sorry, and I appreciate that, but it's in the past now, and there's no point dwelling on it. Besides, I remember a wise person once told me to stop saying sorry all the time. And the woman I met in the cafe recently reminded me of that too, and of you. Anyway, I honestly don't feel any bitterness now, so let's put it behind us as we vowed to do at our Imbolc ritual."

Nodding gratefully, Rhiannon hugged her friend, then led her over to a stand of jewellery. "Aren't these gorgeous," she said, pointing at the colourful crystals set in intricate silverwork. "Which one's your favourite?"

Carlie pointed to a large round moonstone with a silver crescent moon on either side of it, representing the triple goddess and the lunar phases. "It's just like Rowan's tattoo, and the crystal is so beautiful – it feels really strong yet also gentle, if that makes sense."

Rhiannon called the stallholder over, pointed at the necklace and pulled out some money.

"What are you doing?" Carlie asked, sounding panicked.

"I'm buying you a present – an Ostara gift of love and new beginnings. And no, you don't have any say in it," Rhiannon insisted, as her friend tried to protest. "You honour the giver by receiving it graciously. Now put it on and show me, because it's so totally you."

Thanking her profusely, Carlie placed the necklace around her neck and lifted up her long dark hair so Rhiannon could do up the clasp. The pendant rested against her heart, and she smiled.

"Are you okay?" Rhiannon asked, suddenly all too aware that today was a painful anniversary for Carlie. The spring equinox was three months to the day since Rowan had died at Yule, and six months to the day since they'd met at the autumn equinox. It pained her that she'd been so oblivious.

But Carlie straightened her shoulders, took a deep breath and smiled at her. "You know, I think I will be okay."

They were engulfed in a wave of energy when Tom rushed over and scooped Rhiannon up to kiss her. "Jake's just grabbing us all coffee, but I missed you too much gorgeous girl," he said, and Rhiannon's heart lifted. As he set her back down, he noticed Carlie's necklace. "I did a tattoo like that a while ago, with the yin and yang symbol within the orb of the full moon, and crescent moons either side. It was really beautiful."

Carlie gasped. "That's the tattoo I want to get. Would you be able to do it for me?" she asked, voice shaky but determined.

 "Sure. We can do it now if you want to, I live close by. I was going to suggest that we go out for dinner before the ritual, but we can hang out at my place and order pizza while I tattoo you."

Joy lit up Carlie's face. "That would be amazing, thank you!"

He laughed. "The pleasure's all mine. I love tattooing people, especially when it means something to them. The tattoo I told you about was for a druid guy, what was his name? Hawthorn? Willow? No, different tree. I think it was Rowan," he finally said.

Rhiannon stared at Carlie. "No way!"

"Even more perfect. Maybe destiny and fate do exist," Carlie said, then trailed off with a sigh.

Rhiannon winced. Yeah, if that sentiment was really true, Rowan wouldn't be dead.

Tom broke into her thoughts. "Is that cool babe? Going back to my place instead of going out?"

Shrugging, Rhiannon forced a smile. Of course she'd rather have a romantic dinner with Tom, even if it was a double date with Carlie and Jake, but she knew this tattoo was important to her friend, and she felt she owed it to her, after she'd endured this long day for her.

When Jake returned with their coffees, they spoke to Jasmine a little longer then headed off. Tom's flat wasn't far, and they were soon climbing the stairs and walking through his door. Rhiannon grinned. She couldn't wait to see what his place looked like, and what it would reveal of him.

## Chapter 16

# A Piece of My Heart

### Beth

A crackling vortex of sound, light and heat swirled around all the fragments of Beth, whirling her back into one piece. Blindly she reached out, trying to feel something, trying to feel herself. The energy was unfamiliar, was too bright, too loud. Tentatively she opened one eye, then snapped it shut again. What on earth was she doing at a spiritual festival in London, so far from her home and her family? How could she even be here?

Reluctantly she forced her eyelids apart and peered around her. Hundreds of stands offering crystals, witchy clothes, spiritual books, herbs, food, faery statues, healing sessions, psychic readings, religious instruction and more stretched out beneath her, pulling her in all directions, tumbling her through the air. Her long floaty mint green dress cascaded around her, and gave her some comfort as she remembered long-ago rituals she'd performed in it. Green indicated that it was Ostara, the festival of springtime and renewal. Which meant it was almost twenty long weeks since she'd first floated into awareness, at the festival of Samhain.

Back then she'd assumed that she'd returned for a reason, some purpose she had to fulfil before she could rest, or ascend, or whatever it was that happened after death. But almost five months later she was still no closer to understanding why she'd been given this second chance, and her head spun as she tried to figure out what had brought her here today.

Closing her eyes again, she tried to centre herself, to ground herself as much as a... *ghost?* ... could. And finally she felt a tugging at her core, and allowed herself to be pulled downward into the crowd near the entrance to the massive hall. Where Rhiannon stood, her arm around Carlie's shoulder, her voice soothing as she asked if she was okay. Her friend looked rattled, not just by the noise and intensity, but by a memory. Beth had seen that haunted look, that naked pain, before, in her daughter's eyes when she'd run into the guy who assaulted her. Her heart ached for Carlie, who had lost so much, but she was so glad the two girls had healed their friendship. They needed each other.

Then, in a split second, Rhiannon's whole demeanour changed. She shrieked in excitement, let go of Carlie, and ran down the aisle without a backward glance. Beth followed, swooping around the people standing in her way, and watched Tom swing Rhiannon into his arms and kiss her passionately. Perhaps a little too passionately for a mother to watch, but her daughter had no idea she was here.

Until now Beth had never worried about whether her phantom presence was too invasive. She'd been careful not to read her daughter's diary while she was writing in it, and had decided not to follow her up the tor with Tom, or pry into her private moments. Yet she was reminded sharply that Rhiannon was growing up. Was no longer the innocent sixteen-year-old she'd been before her mum died. The yearning hole in Beth's chest widened, and started to throb. Why did it hurt so much to see her family?

Turning back to Carlie, she watched her blush at Tom and Rhiannon's passionate reunion. Then the guy with her said something softly, and steered her into the next aisle. Had Rhiannon only invited Jake to keep Carlie occupied while she ditched them both for Tom? She prayed her daughter was still making time for her friends, and not giving up everything for a guy.

It had alarmed her at first, how quickly Rhiannon had fallen for Tom, so soon after breaking up with John, and she'd questioned his motives too, her nerves on edge as he'd flirted with her at the ritual.

The last thing Rhiannon needed was another older guy to take advantage of her during a magical rite.

Yet Tom seemed genuine, and, ardent greeting aside, he was simply holding Rhiannon's hand now as they wandered through the stalls. Chatting to her, and really listening when she spoke. Beth hung back, giving them space, not wanting to snoop, just reading their body language and being impressed with the way Tom sheltered Rhiannon with his own body as people bumped into them and pushed past without apology.

As the happy couple stopped at the performance stage to watch some Tibetan musicians, the noise increased, making Beth's head fuzzy and her vision blurry. She shimmered down one of the aisles to get away from it, and found herself alongside the psychic reading room. Peering in, she saw masses of small tables, each with two chairs, and a vast range of different diviners, from those using tarot or oracle cards to others using a crystal ball, psychometry, complex numerology charts, runes, wax melting or mediumship. She lingered there, fascinated, watching the faces of the readers as well as the people sitting opposite them, who were all searching for answers to their problems or clues to their futures.

Suddenly a shiver ran through her, and she felt someone's eyes on her. A purple-haired psychic near the back of the room was staring right at her. Nervously Beth held her gaze, until the woman smiled, beckoned her over, then turned back to her client. Beth hovered near the entrance, trying to process the fact that someone had noticed her. Carlie had interacted with her once, then been oblivious ever since, and the priestess in the red dress had spoken to her in the woods, but that was it. No one else had seen her.

She floated over to the psychic, who was holding the hand of the girl sitting across from her. "It will definitely be okay. This has just been a test for the two of you, but your hard work has seen you both pass with flying colours, and it is only going to make your partnership stronger. Just remember not to give that other person any of your power or attention, because they only want to cause trouble."

The girl beamed. "Thank you so much. I can't tell you how relieved I am to hear that. I was so tempted to have it out with him, but now I realise that would have made the whole thing so much worse. And I can't believe how accurate you were regarding the situation with my mum. I'm so so grateful!"

A small bell chimed, and the girl stood up and hugged the psychic, then made her way out. The purple-haired reader turned to Beth with a smile. "Would you like to join me on my tea break?"

Nodding over her confusion, she glided at the woman's side as they made their way to an exhibitor lounge at the back of the hall.

"I'm Bev," she said, as she popped a mint teabag into a keep cup and filled it with boiling water. "Sorry I can't offer you one."

Jokes. Beth giggled. "I like the smell, and sometimes that's enough." Sadness engulfed her, but as the woman guided her to a seat, she knew she had to focus, and stay in this moment.

"You look sad. Is there anything I can help you with?" Bev asked. Then her eyes widened in panic. "Um, you do realise – "

Beth almost choked on her laughter. "That I'm dead? Yeah, I figured it out at Samhain. I'd already been dead for thirteen months by then, although I have no idea where I was all that time, or why I came back." A memory came to her, of Carlie walking up the front path of her house with Rose, and wondering even then if it was the stranger girl who'd somehow brought her back.

The psychic took a sip of her tea, and the mint-scented steam soothed Beth. She stilled in her chair. She had to concentrate. She wasn't sure how long she could hold herself together.

"You're the strongest spirit I've encountered in a long time," Bev said gently. "There must be an intense bond holding you here, especially if you'd been at peace for more than a year."

Taken aback, Beth tried to get her head around that. Had she been at peace during the time she couldn't remember? And would she go back to it soon? "My daughter," she said, voice roughened with pain. "I didn't realise how traumatised she was, although she's getting a little stronger now. And my husband. I'm worried that he's so loyal to me that he'll remain alone for the rest of his life, and never open his heart again. But why would that have brought me back after so long?"

"You just had a thought of a stranger."

Beth gasped. This psychic was good.

"I see something related to her. Did you know her mother?"

"Yes," she whispered.

Bev took a sip of her tea and smiled. "You need some closure surrounding the mother. And you will get it. This stranger girl, is that what you call her? She'll set your mind at ease."

This idea didn't totally shock Beth. She'd felt a connection with Carlie since Samhain, was able to sense her emotions, and had already received some solace from her, that night in the cafe.

"And you don't have to worry about your daughter," the psychic continued. "She has been through a difficult period – your death devastated her, but there was something else too..."

Nodding quickly in affirmation, Beth prayed that her new friend wouldn't pry into the details, and sighed in relief when she just smiled at her and moved on.

"She's much stronger than you give her credit for," Bev said softly. "And for the most part, that's due to you and the way you raised her. I also sense a strong energy around her, a really close friend who is guiding her, in magic and in her career choices."

"Carlie. The stranger girl."

"Ah, that explains the link to her. And there's also... a wise woman. Not a spirit guide though, she's still living. She's a huge influence on your daughter, in a good way."

Beth smiled. "Yes, that's Rose. She's been like a grandmother to Rhiannon since she was born, and now she's her priestess, initiating her into magic and guiding her spiritually." Goddess, it still hurt so much, cut so deeply, that she hadn't been the one to bring her daughter into the magic circle and initiate her. But if it couldn't be her, Rose was a wonderful substitute.

"Your magical influence on her was greater than you think," the psychic said. "And she has your Book of Shadows, and uses it often, so you are still with her, guiding her and teaching her. And she does sense your presence surrounding her. Not in a tangible way that she can consciously grasp, but you are definitely comforting her by being around her. Soothing her heart. Healing her pain."

"Thank you, that means so much to me." Beth's throat tightened with emotion, and relief flooded her.

A green-robed man came in and greeted the psychic, then smiled at Beth as he headed to the coffee machine. Another person could see her! Was she getting stronger?

Bev reached out a hand and touched her arm, and she felt the warmth of it, running through her limbs and opening her heart with joy, or some approximation of it at least.

"Some of us are able to see you, yes, although I'm helping to hold you here. But you don't have much time left with me Beth, I can sense you starting to fade. The most important thing you need to know is that this guy with your daughter is genuine. He really cares about her, and he won't hurt her."

Beth felt the sensation of tears, and a lifting of the weight she'd been staggering under. This was huge, and it broke her heart that she couldn't repay this wonderful woman. Somehow she had to impress upon her just how precious this knowledge was to her.

When her voice came out, it was husky with need. "I don't know how to tell you just how much this means to me Bev, you taking the time to communicate with me when I can't pay you in any way."

The psychic laughed, but not unkindly. "None of us do this for the money, don't worry. But I'm honoured that you came to me Beth, and happy that I was able to provide some solace for you. You're not stuck here forever, I promise. You will complete all the things you need to do, and you will find peace. I'm seeing a woman in a gold dress who will be very important to you. She will help you when the time comes."

A flash of gold in the woods. A presence near the churchyard. Had that been a person? Before she could ask, a tugging began at her very core, and Beth felt herself start to waver. There was so much more she wanted to say to this lovely, humble psychic, so much more she wanted to know. "You're a credit to your profession Bev," she called out, but already she was being pulled apart, losing her grip on the physical aspects of herself, and ricocheting back into the vastness of the universe.

Too late she realised that she hadn't asked about Mike. And that the woman had known her name without her telling it. "Thank you Bev," she screamed into the void, hoping the sweet, purple-haired psychic would somehow feel her gratitude.

For a while she floated, only half aware of herself, and too tired and foggy to solidify back into form. She was still so overwhelmed by the sights and sounds, the colour and energy and hustle of the event, and drained by the focus required to communicate with Bev. Then she felt Rhiannon calling to her – not a specific plea, because unfortunately she didn't know her mother was with her, but a flash of yearning that pulled Beth to her. Forcing the molecules of her self back together, she shimmered into being above her daughter, still clad in the flowing green gown she'd been wearing earlier.

Rhiannon was with Carlie at a jewellery stand, buying her a gorgeous necklace and reiterating her apology, which her friend accepted graciously, then said there was no need to dwell on it. Beth sighed with relief. It had devastated her when her daughter had hurt Carlie, and she was proud of them both for how well they'd got through it, talking, sharing, being honest even when it was painful, and both willing to work to fix it, then put it behind them without holding a grudge. They were far more mature than she'd been at that age. A shudder ran through her as she recalled the mess she'd made of things with Violet, and the chain of events her cowardice had set in motion. Desperately she clutched Bev's words to her heart, praying she'd find some closure around her old friend.

Focusing back on the girls, she soaked up every word Rhiannon said, every gesture she made. And when Tom returned, she watched him hungrily, storing it all away, and glad she could stop worrying about his motives and just be in the moment with her daughter.

When Carlie and Tom started discussing a lunar tattoo, Beth tuned out, swooping down to hover right next to Rhiannon, and reaching out her arms to embrace her. For one exquisite moment she thought her daughter could feel her, but then Jake returned with coffees and they all headed outside.

Scared that she would lose her connection with them, Beth hurried after them as they travelled to Tom's place. Taking the train as a ghost was terrifying, but she managed to keep up with them. And while Rhiannon explored Tom's bachelor flat, running her fingers over the spines of his incredible book collection, marvelling at his beautiful witchy altar, smiling at the planter boxes of lush herbs growing on the windowsill, and soaking up the beautiful artwork on his walls, Beth sensed her wonder. She was so grateful that she had this chance to examine his apartment too, and look at his art, and gain some insight into her daughter's boyfriend. Surely that was allowed?

When Tom led Carlie to the small sunroom and got his tattooing equipment out, Beth was torn. Of course she wanted to stay with Rhiannon, but in the end her curiosity won out, and she followed Tom. Would he show another face to the girl he wasn't trying so hard to impress?

At first Carlie seemed nervous, and not even sure that she really wanted a tattoo, then slowly she relaxed, as surprised as Beth by Tom's gentle manner as he wielded the tattoo gun. Carlie closed her eyes and seemed to drift off, until the buzzing of the machine abruptly stopped, and her eyes snapped open.

Tom smiled at her. "You looked like you were a million miles away, in a happy place. That's how I feel when I'm getting inked too," he said quietly.

Shyly Carlie nodded, then glanced down at her wrist.

"I've finished the outline," Tom said. "So if there's anything else you'd like to incorporate, now is the time to tell me."

Curiously she looked up at him. "How did you know?"

Smiling broadly, he tapped his chest, over his heart. "I could see it in your face, and you went into the same kind of trance state that I do while I work, so I could feel some of it."

Carlie gasped and her cheeks flamed red, but Tom shook his head. "Don't be alarmed, please, I don't eavesdrop, and I didn't get any of the specifics. But my tattooing is part of my spirituality, it's the way I express my witchyness, so I seem to be able to tune in when people are getting one as a way to express their inner heart."

While he told Carlie what he'd sensed, and she confirmed he was correct, Beth stared at him in wonder. He was so much more than she had expected. She really had underestimated him.

"I misjudged you," Carlie whispered, uncannily echoing Beth's thought. "I'm sorry."

Tom laughed. "Nah, you were spot on the day I first met you both," he said, and Carlie grinned at his honesty. "I was feeling all superior, and a bit resentful that I had to hang out with my young cousin and his young friends. So I was being silly, trying to impress Rhiannon as a game, just to amuse myself and fill in time – until I realised how much I actually liked her. And how grown up Jake had become. Don't tell them that though, please," he implored her.

Carlie smiled. "Cross my heart."

"Thank you." He paused to switch ink colours. "I misjudged you too, and I'm sorry for that," he continued.

"Well, we're even then. I was suspicious of your motives with Rhiannon, and I apologise for that."

He put the tattoo gun down and took her hand, gazing into her eyes. "No, you were right, and I can't tell you how grateful I am that Rhiannon has such a protective and caring friend. That first day, I had no intention of ever seeing her again. But then after we said goodbye that night she was all I could think about, and by the next morning I knew that I liked her far more than I'd imagined. So from that moment on my intentions have been honourable, I promise."

Carlie smiled. "I can see that now. And thank you for being honest with me."

"She values your friendship more than anything Carlie, and I will always respect that," Tom said.

If Beth had been able to, she would have swooned. What a wonderful thing to express, setting Carlie's mind at ease about his intentions, and also reassuring her that he valued her as Rhiannon's friend. If only she had been so eloquent, so together, so not-insecure, when she was their age, life might have been a lot smoother.

The door bell jolted Beth back to the present.

"That will be the pizza," Tom said. "Perfect timing, since we're all done here."

While Tom put cream on Carlie's tattoo, and she tried to pay him for the work he'd done, the smell of pizza enticed Beth out to the lounge room. Rhiannon and Jake were sitting on the sofa, chatting as they flicked through Tom's magical books. Jake was clearly new to paganism, and his joy at being included was palpable, which made Beth proud that she'd brought her daughter up with such a sacred relationship with nature and the natural world. And even though she hadn't been the one to initiate her into the ritual circle, she had instilled a richness and sense of enchantment in Rhiannon that so many others had no idea about. Sweet echoes of what Bev had told her earlier.

While the four friends sat on the floor eating pizza out of boxes, laughing and joking together, Beth hovered above them, and was reassured again about Tom. He was so respectful of Rhiannon and Carlie, and genuinely interested in what they had to say, and was also the perfect gentleman.

After they ate the last slice, Carlie headed into the bathroom to change into her ritual dress, Jake started cleaning up, and Tom led Rhiannon into his bedroom.

"There's no time for that guys," Jake called out. He was joking, but Beth froze in panic.

*Please no, not after she'd finally decided she could trust Tom.*

But before her fear could spin out of control, Carlie returned to the lounge room, and Rhiannon burst out of Tom's room, her long dress rustling around her ankles, face transformed by joy and excitement, and a huge rose quartz crystal heart surrounded by an explosion of multi-coloured stones nestled around her neck.

"Look Carlie, isn't it beautiful!" she cried, showing off the elaborate necklace. "Tom gave it to me, an Ostara gift."

Beth sighed with relief. This was not the kind of gift you gave to a girl you didn't care about – the rose quartz heart represented love and compassion, and the other crystals all had special significance too. It was not a cheap gift, or a small token of affection. It was a symbol that showed Rhiannon that she was important to him – and let the whole world know too, her ghostly mother included.

"It's gorgeous," Carlie agreed, and seemed genuinely happy for her friend, despite her own broken heart.

When Tom emerged a few minutes later he had an emerald green velvet cloak on over his clothes, an intricate silver headpiece woven through his long dark hair, and a bag containing his ritual tools slung over his shoulder.

"You look so magical," Rhiannon gushed. "I'm so excited that we can share this ritual."

"It's a shame it's not Beltane," Tom replied with a wink.

Rhiannon grinned back. "Don't worry, it's not far off."

Carlie and Jake both rolled their eyes, and Beth felt another pang of fear, but Tom just took his girlfriend's hand and ushered them all out of the apartment, and Beth forced herself to relax. It was a sign that he saw a future in their relationship, that he was planning ahead and committing to time with her weeks from now. She would focus on that.

Swooping along at their side, Beth revelled in the moonlight that painted the city streets in shadowy gold, and smiled when they got to the nearby park. She'd wandered through here when she lived in London during her university days. Not for a ritual though, as she'd been unaware of magic back then, but to see a band play.

As she gazed at the small gathering of people – just as many men as women, she was pleased to note, all dressed in their pagan finery – she felt a pang of envy. She missed all of this so much. Missed the camaraderie and the support, the weaving of magic, the connection with the earth and the divine, and the love these people shared through the bonds of friendship, of family, of enchantment.

With a great effort she shook off her jealousy, and watched happily as Rhiannon kissed Tom then returned to her friends, her face aflame with happiness, while Tom joined Jasmine and a few other witches from his coven for the final preparations.

"Thank you so much for coming with me, both of you," Rhiannon 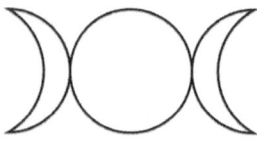 said to Carlie and Jake, her eyes shining with excitement. "It's going to be such an enchanted night, and I'm so glad that the three of us are sharing it with each other."

Beth's heart soared, and relief enveloped her. Her daughter was going to be okay. She had beautiful friends, a wonderful mentor in Rose, and a boyfriend who was kind, respectful and filled with magic. Just like her beloved husband Mike. Now that Rhiannon was okay, she could focus on finding a way to help him.

Soon Jasmine called for everyone's attention, and they all formed a large circle around the central altar. Tom called in the element of earth then welcomed the god to Jasmine's goddess, and while he didn't skip a beat or miss a single word of the invocations, he and Rhiannon couldn't keep their eyes off each other, both totally focused on the other to the exclusion of all else, and both glowing from within as they responded to one another. Beth could see golden threads connecting them, and a bridge of sparkling light flowing between them, from one heart to the other.

This time when she felt the tugging at her core as her form threatened to dissolve back into the night, into the void, she didn't fight to remain. Her mind was at ease over her daughter, one piece of unfinished business drawing to a close.

Letting go of all thought, Beth melted silently away.

## Chapter 17

# Under the Moonlight

Rhiannon

Rebirth and renewal.

Those are the themes of the spring equinox, and as Tom called one of the quarters and welcomed the god, and Jasmine invoked the goddess, this deeper meaning washed over Rhiannon in waves. Tonight marked a new beginning for her. Out of the pain of her mother's death, and the trauma of the unleashing of old memories, she was getting stronger, rising up from the ashes of what she'd burned away. Renewed. Reborn.

The words of the ritual wrapped around her, soaking into her bones, and the beauty and potentiality of the magic she held so dear soothed her heart and healed her soul. Carlie had said she often felt naive and in over her head during ceremonies, having had no idea until she arrived in England about the enchantment of ritual, the impact of invocation, and the connection with nature and the earth that sprang from it. And although Rhiannon had grown up with it, she'd always secretly felt the same. But this ritual, led by a stranger, was a symbol of her new strength, of her growing independence, and of her own power expanding and intensifying.

Happiness surged through her. She'd been worried about crashing someone else's sacred rite and revealing her ignorance – especially in front of Tom, who she was even more awestruck by as he held the energies of the group – but it was not so different from one of Rose's sabbats. The wording was a little altered, slightly more traditional, but she wasn't as out of her depth as she'd feared. So finally Rhiannon relaxed and let Jasmine's voice, and the magic of the night, fill her. Healing, revealing, inspiring.

She gasped when the full moon started to rise, all golden and shrouded in mist. It peeked through the trees edging the park, its light tumbling down over the group. Tom stood silhouetted against it, strong and powerful, yet with a gentle energy that dissolved her residual fear. A tremor shuddered through her, and she exhaled sharply. She hadn't been aware that she still felt the last vestiges of dread, but this was the perfect time to acknowledge then release it.

"When the moon is at its peak, so my heart's desire seek..." As she mouthed the words, Rhiannon remembered the first time she and Carlie had said them together, and was grateful for the friendship they shared. And still shared, despite her almost destroying it.

What did she seek now? Closing her eyes, she swayed slightly but stood her ground. She sensed someone approaching, saw golden sparkles exploding against her lids, and opened her eyes cautiously. A woman clad in gold and wreathed in mist shimmered before her.

"Beloved, you have no need to fear."

Rhiannon gaped at her. Was this the woman from the new moon ritual? Quickly she stole a look around the circle, but no one else had noticed the stranger in their midst. In fact no one seemed to be moving at all. She gazed at the vision before her. "Are you real?"

"What is real?" the figure asked, although her lips didn't move. Then she seemed to take pity on her. "I am sorry Rhiannon, I do not mean to tease. I want only to ease your mind, and ease your worries."

"Why can no one else see you? Or can they?"

The woman sighed. "Is that really what you want to know?"

Reluctantly Rhiannon shook her head.

"Time has slowed for a moment," the gold-clad figure conceded. "So I may reassure you of your own strength, and your ability to choose well and wisely. You worry that past events were your fault,

a consequence of your poor decisions, and that you somehow deserved the bad things that happened. But that is not true. Listen to Thomas, if not to me. Sometimes bad things happen to good people, for no reason at all. And all we can do is learn from them, release them, then move on."

The woman's eyes were hypnotising, and Rhiannon felt herself falling into them. Her words were soothing, absolving her of responsibility, making her feel better, alleviating a guilt she thought she'd already let go of.

"It is an ongoing process, this forgiving of yourself and others. Forgiving yourself for Carlie, for Rowan, for Evan, for John. For your mother."

Anger flickered in Rhiannon's chest, and she stared at the woman in horror. That couldn't be true. She didn't really believe that.

*Did she?*

Reaching out a hand, the woman tenderly touched her cheek. "None of them were your fault beloved. But you feel that they were, each one, on some level."

Rhiannon's throat constricted, and tears welled in her eyes. How could she believe they were all her fault? Did she think that? And more importantly, if she did, how could she *stop* feeling that?

"Breathe, Rhiannon." It was a whisper, a request, a command. She closed her eyes and inhaled deeply, and felt the woman's hand over her heart, and a blast of soft, gentle, healing energy pouring into her, soothing her spirit, and her soul. "You must forgive yourself for supposedly making the wrong choices, or trusting the wrong people. It is all a learning. Step into the light and let it go."

Rhiannon's eyes snapped open. Golden moonlight streamed down from the dark sky and embraced her, engulfed her, enfolded her. It illuminated Tom, where he stood with his arms to the heavens, as well as the woman in gold.

"You can trust him Rhiannon. He will not hurt you. And you will learn much from each other. Yes, him from you as well," she said sternly. "Know that. Know that you are enough, just the way you are." And she faded away, until there was only a faint glimmer in front of Rhiannon's face, a last golden sparkle like fireflies. Sound rushed back in and surrounded her, and movement returned. Tom brought down his arms, and smiled at her. Jasmine lifted a bowl of smouldering herbs, and the ritual continued.

Blinking rapidly, Rhiannon tried to focus, to reorient herself into this moment, in this city park under the golden moon, then she let go of thought and allowed herself to be swept away in the enchantment.

Much later, after the moon had carved an arc across the dark sky, the god and goddess had been farewelled and the elements released, and the circle had been closed, everyone wandered to a nearby cafe, their jewel-hued clothes swirling around them, laughter weaving like golden thread amongst them. A room upstairs was reserved for them, for the social cakes and ale part of the ritual, but Tom took Rhiannon's hand and led her to a dimly lit table in the corner, where they huddled together, oblivious to everyone else.

Anxious that he had duties to attend to, and people he should be talking to, Rhiannon tried to protest, but he told her Jasmine understood, and silenced her worries with his lips. They kissed for what felt like forever, his lips driving her to distraction, at first soft and gentle, then more demanding, more passion-fuelled, more intense. One hand settled on her hip, feather light, while the other was around her waist, crushing her body to his.

Rhiannon felt dizzy with desire. She couldn't kiss him hard enough, deep enough, long enough. As his hand crept upward, leaving tingling fire in its wake, she pressed her body to his, so desperate to be closer to him, to be absorbed by him. She felt their minds melding, their astral bodies merging, and she wanted to surrender to him totally.

Until he pulled back abruptly. "You're beautiful," he whispered, then turned away from her.

The abandonment felt like a slap, like a cloud had covered the sun, and Rhiannon shivered with hurt – until she noticed a waiter standing above them, holding a tray with a pot of tea, cups and saucers, and a plate of scones and other pastries.

"Thank you," Tom said, voice hoarse.

For a while they poured tea and split scones, and joked about whether the jam or the cream should go on first. Then guilt slammed into Rhiannon, and she glanced quickly around the room, looking for her friends. But Jake was having an animated discussion with Jasmine, and clearly enjoying himself, and Carlie was sitting close to the priestess's girlfriend Samantha, wide-eyed and rapt about whatever she was telling her.

"When did you first learn about magic?" Tom broke into Rhiannon's thoughts.

Her conscience about the wellbeing of her friends soothed, she turned back to Tom. "I think I always knew about it. Mum muttered spells as she baked, and sewed me little dresses to match her sabbat ones. And she taught me all about the phases of the moon and the cycles of the seasons before I started kindergarten."

Smiling, she allowed herself to feel the memories, focusing on the moments she'd had, not the ones she'd lost. "Rose, our priestess, used to babysit me, from when I was really young, and I remember being out in her garden with her, talking to the faeries, doing little flower rituals, putting out offerings to the creatures that might eat the plants, to implore them to leave them be."

There was a shard of envy in Tom's voice. "Wow, you're so lucky."

"When did you learn about magic?" Rhiannon asked, suddenly curious about this bewitchingly beguiling witch who knew so much.

Tom shrugged. "About three years ago I guess."

Rhiannon gasped.

"My dad left when I was five, and Mum had to work three jobs to keep a roof over our heads, so there wasn't much room for magic in our lives. Don't get me wrong, I'm glad Dad disappeared, because he's a nasty piece of work, but it was pretty tough without him. I was looked after by the crabby woman across the hall, who dropped me in front of the telly so she could gossip with her neighbours, and totally neglected me. Five years later Mum met Greg, who's a great guy, but I didn't take well to having a stepfather, and it only got worse when they had three daughters. I'd been ignored all my life, but suddenly Mum was the perfect parent, spending all her time with the girls, pushing me away in case I hurt them…"

"I'm so sorry," Rhiannon said, reaching out and taking his hand.

He shrugged. "It is what it is. I was constantly accused of disrupting the harmony at home, so I acted out at school, skipped classes, got drunk with the other three losers in my year. To be honest, if I hadn't literally bumped into Jasmine that day in the park, I would quite possibly be in jail right now."

He looked up at her, and there was sadness in his eyes. "Does that make you want to keep far away from me?"

"Of course not," she cried. "My god, I'm so sorry I was rubbing it in your face about how great my childhood was."

Tom's eyes filled with tenderness. "Don't ever apologise for the precious moments Rhiannon. And you should share them. Everyone has enough sadness in their life, it's nice to hear the opposite. Besides, I still have my mum, and I'm grateful for that. We get on much better now, and I adore my sisters. It was just a difficult few years while I grew into the brother role."

"Do you see them much?"

"Less recently."

Rhiannon stared at him, horrified. "Because of me?"

"No, not at all." Tom laughed. "I see them a bit, but they're busy with school and activities and kid things, and between work and study, I don't have much time for them either. But I still babysit occasionally, or take them out for the day so Mum and Greg can have some time to themselves. Three boundlessly curious girls under ten can be exhausting."

Suddenly Rhiannon didn't feel quite so bad about having to look after her little brother. And her dad had been really good about letting her go away for this weekend, even though it meant he would have to do much more. As she spread jam and cream on a scone and poured another cup of tea, she glanced over at her friends, gratified that they both still looked happy. Carlie caught her eye and grinned, and she heard Jake laugh at something Jasmine had said.

"So how did you meet Jasmine?" she asked Tom. "I'm still getting over the fact that she knows Carlie – and her mum before her. What are the odds?"

Leaning over, Tom kissed her, feather light. "It really still surprises you, after knowing about magic for so long?"

Shrugging, she lifted her cup and took a sip of tea. "I know it shouldn't, but what are the chances that Carlie would sneak off to go to one retreat weekend with Rowan – and start talking to the woman who helped her mum so much twenty years ago?"

"Well, she and her mum apparently looked really alike, right, so that probably sparked the conversation."

"I know, but that she's also your high priestess, that's what really blows my mind."

Tom laughed. "You're right. As often as such serendipitous moments occur, I still find them fascinating, and wonderful. I'm so grateful for them. And so grateful to Jake for inviting you to lunch that day. I might never have met you otherwise, because I wouldn't be visiting Pop so regularly, if at all, without the incentive of seeing you."

"Really?"

Nodding, then cringing at his admission, he reluctantly continued his tale. "It was ages since I'd seen Pop, and Jake had been in England for two months before I finally decided I should fulfil my family obligations. Who knows when I would have next visited Summer Hill, if not for you."

"I'm so glad Jake invited me too." Rhiannon shivered. He almost hadn't. Jake was too embarrassed to ask them at first, and when he finally did, Carlie was about to say no, before Rhiannon quickly blurted out a yes. "I guess it was meant to be."

Tom kissed her again. "Indeed. And it was like that with Jasmine too – well, not the dating part, but meeting her. I was wandering through the park near my house, waiting to meet up with a friend and sneak into the pub. I'd already had a few beers at home, so I was feeling fearless. Anyway, I wasn't paying much attention, until I heard a woman shouting angrily, then suddenly this guy was pelting straight at me, a bag in his arms, and she was trying to catch up with him. So I tackled him – then prayed it actually was her bag, and I hadn't just dragged an innocent guy running for the train to the ground. We grappled a little, and I managed to wrestle the bag from his hands, but then he punched me in the head so hard I blacked out."

Absently rubbing his temple, he gazed off into the distance, then seemed to remember where he was. "When I came to, I was on the ground, my head in this woman's lap, and I realised the horribly loud groaning I could hear was coming from me."

When he saw Rhiannon's face, he laughed. "Don't worry, there was no real damage done – the black eye faded after a few days, and the nose eventually healed. But I'd made a friend for life, because Jasmine was on her way to set up for her Beltane ritual, and the bag had all of her precious magical tools in it, plus the gift she'd bought Samantha for their ten-year anniversary. And somehow she persuaded me to go to the ritual with her."

"Wow, how beautiful for Beltane to be your first magical ceremony," Rhiannon said. "Black eye or not."

"Very true." Tom grinned. "The next day I thought I'd dreamed it all, the result of a concussion or something. Surely nothing so magical could have taken place in the park a block from where I lived. A gathering of people in long velvet cloaks and silver jewellery adorned with crystals, with flowers in their hair and burning lavender wafting through the air. And surely I couldn't feel that connected and at one with the world and with myself, just by standing in a circle with a bunch of strangers. Couldn't be charged up with energy simply by holding hands and having sage smoke breathed over me, and jasmine oil dabbed on my forehead."

When he paused for breath, the sense of wonder was still on his face, and Rhiannon totally understood what he was expressing, and how much it would have meant to someone who'd felt so isolated and alone. It reminded her of Carlie's first ritual. Her friend had lost so much, then suddenly realised she'd also gained something far beyond her comprehension.

"I probably would have relegated it to the back of my mind as soon as my bruises faded – perhaps imagined I'd got in a fight at the pub – but the next day there was a knock on my door, and it was Jasmine and Samantha, with a pot of soup, a bunch of flowers, and a book about paganism." He smiled as he glanced over at them.

"Apparently I was a bit wobbly after the ritual, so they'd brought me home, hence them knowing where I lived. And I think they took one look at me, and my gloomy apartment, and decided they would have to take me under their wing. I haven't been to a pub since, but I've studied witchcraft, spirituality and the esoteric every day."

His eyes sparkled with excitement and purpose, and Rhiannon was glad he'd found something so powerful and life-affirming when he needed it most. "What does your mum think about your path?"

Tom shrugged. "She doesn't know much about it to be honest. I moved out of home at sixteen, into a crappy share house with a bunch of people. I worked on a building site to pay the rent, lived on instant noodles, drank cheap wine in the park with my flatmates. But Jasmine and Samantha had more faith in me than I ever had, and saw something in me no one else could. They recognised my passion for art before I did, and really drew it out of me. They pushed me to apply to art school, and got me working on murals for their coven, then they introduced me to a friend of theirs who owns a tattoo studio, where I'm apprenticing while I study."

Rhiannon's gaze fluttered down to the beautifully intricate black raven tattoo on his wrist, but before she could ask about it, Carlie and Jake were standing above them, telling them it was time to go. Rhiannon was shocked that so many hours had passed so quickly, and devastated that she had to say goodbye to Tom. When would she get to see him again? As they headed downstairs and out to the deserted street, she tried to swallow down her sadness.

But Tom had no intention of letting her go just yet. He hailed a cab and bundled them all in, Jake in the front, Carlie behind him, and his arms around Rhiannon while they clung to each other in the back seat. "Now where were we?" he asked, a glint of mischief in his eyes, and captured her lips with his again.

When they got to her cousin's place, Carlie jumped out, but Rhiannon couldn't bring herself to follow.

"I don't want to say goodbye," she whispered, her heart already aching with the loss.

"Me either," Tom replied, voice just as cracked with longing. "Can I take you out for breakfast tomorrow, before you go home?"

Rhiannon nodded happily, then groaned, crestfallen. "We have to be at the station at midday."

"That's okay, I can pick you up just before six, so we see the sun rise. Or is that too early?"

She grinned. "No, that's perfect. I can sleep on the train home."

Catching a glimpse of Carlie through the window, shivering and yawning while she waited ever-patiently for her friend, Rhiannon quickly said goodbye to Jake, kissed Tom one last time, then clambered out, eyes shining, and full of apologies for keeping her friend standing around in the cold.

Carlie shrugged, and together they crept into the dark apartment and tiptoed down the hall to the spare room and into bed. Rhiannon desperately wanted to tell her friend all about Tom. About this burning fire within her. This igniting of her senses and her awareness. It wasn't just her body he set aflame either, it was her mind too. Everything seemed more interesting, more colourful.

It was all the cliches. She'd never seen such beautiful sunsets, never loved music more, never felt more alive, but it was so much more as well. She enjoyed *everything* more. Playing with her brother, cooking dinner, making magic with Carlie. Spending time with Tom brought her alive in every sense. The highs were higher, and the lows – well, she hadn't had one yet, unless you counted just how hard it was to wait patiently until she could see him again.

But Carlie had fallen asleep, so Rhiannon closed her eyes and went over the perfect day herself. The joy of being at the festival with him. The ever-deepening conversations and sharing of their lives and truths. The intrigue of wandering through his apartment looking at the things he found precious. The incredible beauty of the ritual he led, and the magic of the night.

The morning couldn't come soon enough.

Chapter 18

Rhiannon

Beep. Beep. Beep.

In the darkness, Rhiannon floated slowly to consciousness, head foggy and whole self disoriented as she tried to identify the sound. Her hand thrust outward, her instinct to shut the alarm off and pull the blankets back over her head. But then she remembered. Tom was picking her up soon.

Touching a finger to her lips in wonder, she focused on his kisses from the night before. Excitement and anticipation unleashed a flurry of butterflies in her stomach, and she quickly crept out of bed and pulled on her clothes. Carlie mumbled something, so she half-heartedly invited her along, but was relieved when her friend muttered no, then rolled over and drifted back to sleep.

On tiptoes, Rhiannon snuck down the hall and out into the chilly pre-dawn air, and peered into the swirling gloom. Tom was already waiting for her, lounging in the doorway of the bookstore across the road, with a bunch of pink daisies in his hand. She wondered how he'd gotten them at this hour.

Without looking, she flew across the road and into his arms, and it felt so right, exactly where she knew she should be. When a car drove past and someone whistled at them, Tom broke away and gazed down at her, laughter sparkling in his eyes. "Breakfast?" he asked, and she nodded, although she would have been happy to stand in that doorway wrapped in his arms until she had to leave for home.

Jumping on the back of his motorbike and throwing her arms around his waist, Rhiannon clung to him and closed her eyes, completely content. When she heard him say something, she opened her eyes and tried to listen, but his words were snatched away on the wind. She stared around them in wonder though. She'd never seen the streets of London in this liminal time between night and day, and there was a magic to it that she loved. Or maybe it was just her close proximity to Tom that made the whole world seem enchanted.

Soon he indicated and pulled over next to a stone wall. Helping Rhiannon off the bike, he extended his hand to her. "Come, my sweet, I have somewhere I think you'll love."

Walking to the corner, he looked around furtively, then slid a key into a side door and quickly pushed it open. "My lady," he said, ushering her into a beautiful, almost eerie garden, then quickly closing the door behind them. Cobblestone paths led off in four directions, and the dim illumination from a distant street light created mysterious shadows and pools of darkness that spun away from them in delicate whirls. Then as they stepped onto the middle path, past fragrant night-blooming flowers, the first pale glow of the dawn emerged, and the sky slowly began to lighten.

Hand in hand they walked to a grotto at the centre of the garden. A fountain burbled softly, colourful blossoms waved in the gentle breeze, and the sharp scent of herbs wafted around Rhiannon, adding to the faerytale charm. For a moment her heart squeezed with pain, as she thought about how much her mum would have loved it here, but then Tom pulled her into his arms and she forgot all other thoughts, all other people, all other reality.

Gently they collapsed onto the soft grass, the faraway roar of the traffic sounding like waves breaking on the shore, lulling them into a sense of being out of time, out of place. Wrapped in their own little world, wrapped in each other's arms, lips joined and hearts entwined.

She could have stayed there forever, but the piercing caw of a raven overhead broke into their peace, and Tom pulled away from her, smiling wryly as he gazed up at the bird.

"Sorry Miss Rhi, I promised you breakfast, and here I am trying to devour you," he said, although he didn't sound especially sorry.

"Did you hear me protesting?" Rhiannon asked Tom, leaning in to kiss him again.

He kissed her back, then drew away. "Patience babe," he whispered, and the raw need and desire in his voice sent shivers of pleasure up her spine. "There's nothing I want more, believe me, but my raven friend is reminding me to take it slowly. I promised you that."

Abruptly he turned away, and for a moment she was scared that she'd done something wrong, but he was just opening the bag he'd dropped when they sat down.

"I know it's not exactly breakfasty, but it's a special occasion." He grinned, handing her a thermos of coffee then presenting her with a box of cupcakes, all iced with patterns of hearts and flowers.

"I have no complaints about cupcakes for breakfast," she said with a giggle. "Especially since you brought coffee!" Screwing the lid off, she poured two cups, handed one to Tom, then took a long sip. Sighing with contentment, she selected a cupcake and took a bite. "This is perfect."

Tom grinned. "I'm glad you like it. It means so much to me that you could come to London and spend time with me, and see where I live, and who I work magic with."

"Me too," she whispered, overcome with emotion. She still found it hard to believe that this adorable guy could love spending time with her, but all indications seemed to point to it being true.

Leaning into him, Rhiannon kissed him, then laughed as they fell back onto the grass. They lay there for countless precious moments, holding each other close. As their embrace became more passionate, Tom rolled her over so he was lying on top of her, and gazed down into her eyes.

Time stopped, and a cascade of need and desire raced through her. She stretched her arms up around his neck, then laughed. He had cake crumbs and pink icing in his hair. When he leaned down and licked some from her cheek, she realised she must too. *Oops!* She'd forgotten the cupcake in her hand when they fell.

"It looks adorable on you, but I guess we should eat these before we make a bigger mess," Tom suggested, and she nodded reluctantly. But getting all the cake off each other was a fun way to pass the time, and they spoke all the while, about magic and ritual and future plans, and wanting to do good in the world.

Rhiannon was shocked by how different Tom was from her first impression of him. He was still all the things she'd told Carlie she wanted in a boyfriend – magical, smart and independent; creative, mature, and tattooed; slightly wild, and a witch. But he was far more than that too, so much deeper, more thoughtful and more spiritual than she'd imagined.

And the fact that he liked her, *really liked* her, made her so happy.

"What are you thinking?" he asked, and she blushed.

Her gaze flicked down to his wrist, and the tattoo of a raven. "You were going to tell me about the raven last night, and what it means to you. Jake said you did that tattoo yourself?"

He nodded.

"It must have been tricky, especially there. And didn't it hurt?"

Tom shrugged. "It was... not easy. But pain's relative. And I got into such a meditative state while I was doing it, it was like a ritual. I set up all the equipment and smudged it with sage, then cast circle and called in the elements, and the Morrigan, because the raven is one of her creatures. So it was an inner spirit journey, a rite of passage, and it represents so much to me."

Rhiannon felt a pang of longing. If only she could go that intensely into a magical process, have the courage to let go of her rational mind and delve so deeply within. She'd gone part of the way a few times, yet something always stopped her letting go completely. Fear? Embarrassment? Lack of trust?

"Hey, are you okay? What are you afraid of?"

She stared up at Tom, alarmed by his perceptiveness. But she wasn't ready to delve into her dark heart, not with him, not right now. "Why the raven?" she asked instead.

At her words, a large black raven swooped down at them, and Rhiannon ducked her head as the distinctive kraw-kraw cry broke the silence. She remembered the raven feather she'd been gifted that night in the woods, on her way to meet the woman in red, recalled the cryptic message of the woman in blue, to look for the raven. As the huge bird stared at her with beady, curious, intelligent eyes, the atmosphere changed, and a strange haze enveloped them both. The whole world shimmered and started to bleed around the edges. Panicked, she looked over at Tom for reassurance, but black feathers were blurring around the edge of his face, along his hairline, as though he was transforming into a bird.

"Don't leave me," she whispered, although her voice sounded so far away.

Tom smiled and reached out a hand to her, and she took it, clutching it like a life raft. Comfort and contentment flowed into her, and a knowingness that she was enough for him, for the world, just as she was. There was no need to wish anything else into existence, no need to develop new parts of herself. She was already whole. Curiously she peered at him. She had no idea how he was sending her these messages, sharing this wisdom with her, or whether it was even him.

When the raven cawed again, she spun back around to face it. The bird's strange glittering eyes pierced her soul.

*Then she fell into them.*

Staring around wildly, she realised she was in a different part of the garden, or a different land altogether. Hazel trees grew up around her, and she was standing on a path of tumbled black obsidian, which crunched under her feet as she took a nervous step forward. The sky above her was night-dark, which made no sense, but Tom was just ahead, and beckoning her towards him. Grabbing his hand again, she implored him to tell her what was happening, but though his lips opened, no sound came out. Dizziness consumed her once more.

A warm, soothing breeze swept over them, and she relaxed into it, just as Tom pulled her forward, along the blackened path. Hesitantly she followed, and laughed in amazement as the raven flew down and alighted on his shoulder, its feathers ruffled but demeanour calm as it continued to stare at her, fierce and unblinking.

Soon they reached the banks of a fast-flowing inky black river, and Tom sank to the ground and sat on the soft grass, pulling her down to join him. The bird stayed on his shoulder, head to one side, as though it could understand every word Tom said.

*Maybe it could.*

"A week before I met Jasmine, I noticed a raven swooping around the park. Everyone else was afraid of it, and tried to beat it away, but I liked it. Its ferocity and directness, its persistence. It entered my dreams every night, whispering of transformation if I would just face my shadow side, embrace my own darkness, and let all of it melt away in the light. A year later, during my initiation ritual, I journeyed deep into the earth with a raven companion, who took me through the underworld, and through the death of a part of myself I was not proud of, the one that had resorted to violence and anger, who used alcohol to drown the pain, and who lived without hope. And ever since, it has remained with me, my spirit guide, my ally for embarking on the mysteries, and the one that helped me find my own voice and develop the confidence to raise it."

Tentatively Rhiannon reached out her hand to the black bird perched on Tom's shoulder and stroked its glossy head, amazed that it was letting her do it.

"Ravens appear to you when spiritual rebirth and transformation are about to unfold," Tom told her softly.

Wrapped in each other's arms, they gazed out over the water, until a white swan appeared on the rippling surface, startling them both. "I've never seen a swan here," Tom said in amazement.

Rhiannon smiled. "That's for me. My animal guide is a white swan. It came to me during a spirit journey at the last festival. It was really profound – I felt myself rise up out of my body, out of the hall, and fly off to this incredible place where this huge white bird was swimming, waiting for me. I ended up on its back, soaring over the city with it, cuddling into the softness of its feathers and the strength of its neck, then listening to it speak to me."

"How beautiful. What did it tell you?"

"It said it was with me as a reminder to balance my family commitments and school work with friendship and play, and find a way to recover and re-energise so I didn't lose myself, because for a while I was taking on too much at home, trying to fill Mum's shoes and support Dad and look after Brodie. That was after the first three months though, when I ignored them both and did nothing to help."

She blushed, feeling the usual shame that accompanied her memories of the time right after her mother's death, before she got over herself and started to pull her weight. Before Carlie turned up with her even deeper grief.

"We all grieve differently, and come to terms with things in our own way," Tom said, drawing her into the safety and security of his arms. "You can't judge yourself for that."

"I know. And that spirit journey was a really important part of me getting back to normal. The message was that the swan would be with me whenever I needed strength, and would remind me of my purpose when I felt lost. And it has. Whenever I look at the artwork, which is a depiction of me as a woman half-swan, I feel all the beauty, balance, commitment, dignity and grace it represents, and am empowered to find the balance between work and play in my life. To let go of a little more pain, and focus on hope. The swan also urged me to be fearless, and defend what is right. I'm not sure I do that at the moment, but I hope to. I want to be a grief counsellor so I can help people going through loss, and defend them from the lack of self-worth and purpose that can result."

"You'll be amazing."

A flush of pride coloured her cheeks. "A white horse came to me too, and spoke to me of perfect trust, and reminded me that I am safe, and worthy of love." Her voice trembled, and her eyes welled.

Tom reached out his hand and gently wiped a tear from her cheek. "You *are* worthy of love."

His tender words made her cry, huge wrenching sobs that racked her body. Sadness washed over her, an endless wave of despair, and she couldn't gulp in enough air to breathe.

"What's wrong babe?" he whispered.

"I don't know," she managed to choke out. "I just… oh god, I have no idea. I'm so sorry." Shame heated her body, and she shrank in on herself. She closed her eyes and tried to recall the feeling she'd had that day. When the horse told her she was worthy of love, the words had lodged within her heart. Happiness had washed over her, and she'd felt her body dissolve, transforming into golden sparkles, so she and the horse's essence could dance together in the sunshine, their souls merging, and her consciousness lifting with the sheer joy and sense of freedom. The whole world had slowed as she swooped around the meadow, free of her body, of physical pain, even of grief.

Breathing in that energy now, she felt the golden sparkles wrap around her like a comforting blanket. When she opened her eyes, she was smiling.

"You look radiant," Tom said, awe in his voice. "You are so beautiful Rhiannon, inside and out. And I know this sounds weird, but I can see the outline of the white swan with you, on your left side, merging with you, with your aura."

As he spoke, the white swan on the dark river glided over to them, and Rhiannon extended her hand to stroke its velvety head. "I saw that with you and the raven," she replied, filled with wonder.

"Really?" Tom asked, just as enraptured about the raven as she was about the swan. "They are amazing creatures. The one in the park still follows me every day, and has introduced me to its babies each year. And I still journey with it in my meditations. It's been an invaluable guide in my magical studies, and helped me bring the shadow parts of myself into the light, so I could face my fears, and transform my life and my work. They're shapeshifters and communicators, and messengers too, which I hope I'm able to be when needed."

Rhiannon smiled. "You absolutely are. And you're helping Jake so much – he said you invited him to join your coven, for the teaching side and your study circle, even if he can't make it to all the rituals."

"I think you and Carlie had already sold him on magic, and he's eager to learn more. And to get closer to Carlie," Tom said tentatively. "Do you think he stands a chance with her?"

A rumble of thunder cracked overhead, and they both jumped.

Tom laughed. "Ominous."

"Very. I hope that's not a sign, because I think they'd be wonderful together. They're both so kind and gentle, yet strong, with massive hearts. And I know Carlie cares about him deeply – but she's very careful around him, because she would be devastated if she hurt him. And I think she's worried that she's too damaged to be any good for anyone," Rhiannon finished sadly.

A frown crinkled Tom's brow as he shook his head. "I don't think anyone is ever so damaged that they can't be loved, or be worthy of love, nor so broken that they will be forever incapable of loving someone else. How long has it been since Rowan died?"

Wincing, Rhiannon looked out over the still-dark water. "Three months exactly. He died at the winter solstice. So I feel a bit guilty that I dragged her to London with me, back to the place where she met him. I just wanted to see you so badly." Her voice dropped. "Does that make me a terrible person?"

"Oh babe, of course not," he reassured her, holding her close and kissing her gently on the forehead. His touch soothed her – until the raven that had been shadowing them jumped up into her lap and fixed her with its beady gaze.

"Um, what's it doing?" she asked, alarmed by just how ferocious its beak looked up close.

"Looks like he has a message for you."

*Great. That was just what she needed. Messages from the darkest of birds.*

Tom's lips twitched as he tried to hide a smile, and Rhiannon groaned. There was a downside to having a boyfriend who was a witch and an intuitive.

"There's nothing to be afraid of," he said. "Raven simply asks you what you're afraid of. What's hiding in your shadows? What is holding you back? It can lead you to the realm of the unconscious and walk with you through it, holding you safe as you delve into it, and bring it to the light to burn it away."

"That sounds amazing," Rhiannon said tentatively. But she wasn't ready for that, and she certainly didn't want to be doing it with Tom. She couldn't let him see her shadows, or her shame. She had to change the subject.

"A raven gifted me one of its feathers on my way to a ritual recently, so I used it to represent air," she blurted out. "And I was told by a woman of the mists to look for the raven, but that was about finding love – she said the raven was a sign that it was near, that it was possible."

*Oh god.*

She gasped as her face flamed. *Did she really just say that out loud? To the guy she was falling in love with?*

Her accidental method worked though. Tom backed off from her shadow side and leaned in to kiss her again. "And do you think I'm the one the raven refers to?"

She giggled, and squirmed, mortified by the question, and he took pity on her. "I love spending time with you Rhiannon," he admitted. And then they had no more need for words, as their lips met, their arms went around each other, and the whole world fell away.

The loud cawing of a raven overhead jolted them back to the present, back to daylight, back to the just-opening park, and the increasing rush of traffic zooming around the tree-lined border.

"I guess I should get you back," Tom said, voice thick with regret.

Rhiannon sighed, just as reluctant for this time together, this time-out of-time, to end. She felt steeped in magic, transported from the harsh reality of the bustling city, and a million miles from her two friends. But unfortunately Tom was right. Carlie and Jake would be waiting anxiously for her to return, so they could catch the train back to Summer Hill.

Sadly they packed up, and Rhiannon climbed on the back of Tom's bike again, thrilled that she could drape her body around his and clutch him tight, for these last precious moments together, for now.

Chapter 19

# The Way Forward

### Beth

Sunlight pierced the darkness and warmed her face, and Beth felt the molecules that framed her existence drawing back together, almost against her will. Drawing her back to awareness.

She wanted to resist. Her day at the spiritual festival, buffeted by noise and light and countless people having emotional crises, had left her mentally drained, and sluggish. Yet she didn't know how long she had left before she dissolved back into the darkness of the void forever. So, her urgency returned, she focused on the air she was drifting within.

Eyes still closed, she inhaled deeply, trying to centre herself, then reached out with her senses. The sharp scent of crushed herbs and the chill of morning dew on her bare feet shocked her, and her eyes snapped open. Gazing down curiously, she frowned, perplexed, at her outfit. A fifties-style thrift store dress and black tights. University days. London. Her well-worn but comfy black boots must be nearby.

Looking up, she smiled in recognition. She was in the Chelsea Physic Garden, planted by apothecaries in the 1600s, and still a haven of nature and tranquillity today. For Beth, moving to the teeming chaos of the capital from her countryside village had been a huge change, and while she loved the energy of the city as much as she loved being away from her parents, this peaceful retreat tucked away beside the Thames became a much-needed sanctuary for her.

Before university started, she worked all summer in a nearby cafe, and this beautiful garden was her escape from the madding crowd. When classes began, she still visited whenever she could, recharging and de-stressing before catching the bus back to her cramped share house in London's very outer suburbs. How funny that even then, long before she recognised her witchy heart, she was connecting with nature. Feeling her energy replenished and her centre restored as she breathed in the sweet aroma of lush herbs and pretty flowers, and stared at the calming water of the ponds.

Right now it was dawn, that liminal moment perched between night and day, balanced between dark and light, and filled with potential and promise. The most healing, most magical, time of all. The world was only just beginning to stir, so you could imagine yourself alone, unseen. So many mornings she'd risen before her housemates and gone walking, pounding the shadowy streets, devouring every sight of a flower bursting through the pavement, every lone plant in a concrete block, every small bird squawking or cheeky squirrel hiding.

Some days she was still up from the night before – either from clubbing until the wee hours, or pulling an all-nighter to cram for a test or finish an assignment. Other times she set her alarm earlier than necessary and forced herself out of bed in the dark, lured by the thought of coffee and the beauty of the world waking.

Yet strangely, only once had she been in this garden as night gave way to day. One pre-dawn morning, after they'd had dinner with friends then danced for hours to a rock band in a sweaty dive bar, her artist boyfriend had brought her here to watch the first rays of the sun illuminate the budding flowers. She was pretty sure he'd picked the lock, but she hadn't cared – she'd been on a high from the music and the dancing, and one too many vodkas, and was swept away by the romance of it all.

The moment they entered, they were in another world. The noise and heavy vibration of the city receded, and it was just the two of them, shoes kicked off, dancing along the grassy paths, bare feet connecting to the rhythm of the earth. He'd drawn her down to the ground amongst the poisonous plants, the cold chill of the dew soaking through her clothes, until they dispensed with those, and it soaked through her skin, through her bones, through her heart. Their passion was darkly intense, yet she'd felt so at peace, so at one with the wildness of nature and her self. Perhaps her witchyness was innate. Had already been within her, long before Celia and Rose began to draw it out. She just hadn't known what to call it.

Not long after that night, her boyfriend was offered an artist residency in Portugal, and flitted out of her life. They exchanged postcards and letters for a while, and she visited him in Sagres one weekend, but then he fell for a surf-loving pastry chef and decided to stay on the sunny Iberian Peninsula.

Beth smiled. She hadn't thought of him in years, but she was grateful for their time together. He'd helped her break through the shackles her parents had bound her in, and removed at least one of the chains weighing her down. Wherever he was now, she hoped he was happy.

*But that was so long ago. Why was she here now?*

Laughter sailed over to her from the herb garden, so she floated her way there, to the section where teapots overflowed with mint and basil, cups and saucers were filled with chamomile and lemon balm, and the neat garden beds were already buzzing with bees. Drops of morning dew caught on cobwebs sparkled like jewels, and the crisp, chilly air was soothing, and cleansing.

It was the perfect witches garden, so she shouldn't be surprised that Rhiannon and Tom were there, sitting on the grass together, drinking coffee, eating cupcakes and talking deep and wide – so much more lucid than her drunken adventure all those years ago.

The contrast struck her sharply. All this time she'd been worrying about her daughter, and questioning Tom's motives, yet they were so much sweeter and more innocent than she had been. Creeping closer, she listened as Tom confided in Rhiannon about his struggles, then told her about his connection with his spirit animal guide, how it had helped him, and what they'd explored together. And she watched as her daughter opened up in return, sharing some of her experiences and insecurities.

Beth's heart swelled when Tom tenderly stroked Rhiannon's cheek, and she loved that he hung on her every word, giving her space to share and grow. They made such an adorable couple. And the look on Tom's face as he regarded her daughter reminded Beth so much of the way Mike had always gazed at her, eyes full of love and laughter, and the understanding and acceptance that had underpinned their relationship.

Satisfied that her daughter was happy, and beginning to move forward from her pain, Beth knew it was time to focus on her husband. Feeling a pull in her centre, she closed her eyes and surrendered to the air. And for hours she drifted, floating with her memories, with her regrets, with her hopes.

When she finally pulled herself together again and opened her eyes, she was standing in the woods looking out over a lake. It was Ullswater in Cumbria, where she and Mike had honeymooned.

"**C**ome on darling, I can't wait to show you where we're staying." Smiling at her husband – *they were husband and wife!* – Beth grabbed her bag from the back seat and stared up at the small stone cottage with the peaked roof. A flash of sunlight on water to the side of the building caught her eye. Dropping everything, she ran towards it.

"Oh my goddess! It's *right* on the lake," she squealed. A wooden pier stretched out into the rippling, sun-dazzled surface, and she hurried along it and out to the end, so she could look back at their home for the next ten days. It was breathtaking. Totally isolated, framed by trees, and with a balcony that jutted out over the water.

Mike grinned as he caught up with her, and pulled her into his arms. "You like?"

"It's beautiful!"

"It's an old converted boathouse, so the pier is ours too. There are some kayaks under the house if we want to go out on the lake, and there's no one close by to disturb us, so it's just us. Alone together at last sweet wifey."

"Sweet hubby." Beth's eyes shone. "Oh, I can't believe we're married. And that we're here, on our honeymoon. It's all been such a whirlwind." Leaning into him, she soaked up the tranquillity of the lake and the woodland. "Thank you for this place. I can't tell you how excited I am that it's just the two of us, alone together at last. I know everyone means well, but it felt like the last week, even the wedding, was for everyone else, not us. Does that sound awfully ungrateful?"

"Not at all my love. I've been desperate to get you alone too. Shall we go inside and explore?"

Together they climbed the stairs and entered the apartment through the open-plan kitchen and living area, then pushed through the French doors into the bedroom. They gasped in delight. It was small, with a cosy bed strewn with rose petals and an elegant bathtub under a window, but it opened out on to the balcony, which had a small table and chairs and the most stunning views across the lake.

"I love it," Beth said, sighing in pleasure. "It's perfect!"

"Like you my love," Mike replied, then they sank down onto the bed to test it out.

The next morning Beth woke early, pulled on the toasty warm bathrobe and tiptoed through to the kitchen. Quickly she brewed a pot of coffee, then crept outside with her mug. In the magical hour before dawn she wandered along their pier and sat with her feet in the cold but invigorating lake, soaking up the power of nature and the magic of the earth and of water.

Heart full, she watched the sun slowly sail above the horizon and turn the world a hundred shades of pink-gold-purple, carving a trail of liquid fire onto the dark surface. She marvelled as eagles, kestrels and falcons swooped down over the lake, talons making ripples on the still water, and at the two white swans who glided past her, perfectly in sync with each other.

As she gulped down the last of her coffee and turned to go, she glimpsed two otters splashing in the shallows, which reminded her of how they slept, holding hands so they wouldn't drift away from each other in the night. She giggled. That's how she felt with her beloved, safe and secure, so grateful they had found each other, and never wanting to let him go.

For most of their honeymoon, they stayed holed up inside, moving from kitchen to bedroom to balcony and back again, eating their meals at the little table overlooking the lake, or cuddled up on the couch in front of the fire, soaking up the incredible quiet and bliss of this precious time together.

At night they left the balcony doors open so the moonlight could stream in and turn their naked bodies silver, covering them in a cloak of moonbeams. A few times they got up at midnight and tiptoed out onto the balcony to stare up at the stars, their wash of light and colour glittering like magic painted across the heavens. Occasionally they dragged themselves outside to walk along the shore, delighted to see red squirrels and deer in the woodland surrounding them, and enchanted by the beauty of the golden light on the water on the night of the full moon.

On their last day, Beth rose before dawn, kissed her sleeping husband, and slipped outside. Something drew her away from the lake this time, and she wandered along a narrow uphill path through the trees, breathing in the crisp, clean air, enchanted by the gentle hint of lavender in the sky and the faint beams of light as the sun prepared to rise. She was sad they were leaving today to go back to the real world, and also nervous.

Could she be a good wife? Would Mike be disappointed with her? Was she going to be enough for him? And would she enjoy married life, when the example she'd grown up with was poisoned with cruelty, hatred and wilful ignorance?

Suddenly a red deer materialised out of the tendrils of mist and walked towards her. Beth froze. It was such a majestic creature, and she felt honoured to be in its presence, to be allowed to get this close. A symbol of the horned god, deer represents spiritual authority and regeneration, combining soft, gentle qualities with strength and determination. She wondered what this one's message for her was.

Then the deer shimmered in her vision, and in its place stood a woman with long red hair, and antlers, and a cloak that seemed to have been woven from the leaves and twigs of the woodland they stood within. Her skin was pale, and she glowed, as though she was absorbing all the early morning dawn light and shining it out to Beth to illuminate her way forward.

Was she dreaming, or could this be Elen of the Ways, the Green Lady so closely linked to the land on which she was walking?

The woman nodded in acknowledgement. "Greetings beloved. You are correct. Some people call me Elen, and others know me as the Lady of the Wildwood, protector of the ancient pathways of nature and our selves."

With great reverence, Beth bowed her head, and tried to calm her racing heart. Just a few weeks ago Rose had invoked this goddess during a ritual, and their magical circle had done a guided meditation with her, tracing the path they'd walked as they moved from girl to woman, and on their own witchy journey, and how both had impacted on their personality, experience and happiness in the present moment.

"You are doubting yourself not for your past journeys and past disappointments, but for the new path you are embarking on, no?" The woman's voice was deep, and powerful, evoking images of dark forests and darker times.

Beth frowned. How could this... *goddess?* ... know the dark thoughts she nursed, the fears she still wallowed in?

"You are everything Mike has ever wanted, and you know that." Elen's words were a rebuke, and a warning. "He tells you often, because he knows how insecure you are about love."

Red blazed in Beth's cheeks, and she wanted the forest floor to open up and swallow her whole. The woman took pity on her, and her face softened as she reached out a hand to touch Beth's shoulder. Calm flowed into her, and comfort, and she finally nodded in acknowledgement. If anyone could convince her that she was enough, it was her wonderful, kind new husband.

"That is not the fear at the root of your search though." Elen's voice was less gentle this time, more demanding, and she looked stern and forbidding. "This is not the obstacle on your pathway. Be honest with yourself, if no one else."

A tear welled in Beth's eye, and spilled over onto her cheek. Elen was right. Her biggest fear had nothing to do with Mike. She knew he loved her as fiercely as she loved him, and that they were good for each other. The slow start to their relationship and his endless patience with her had set her mind at ease on that score.

But her biggest fear? She wasn't sure she could speak it. Wasn't sure she could even admit it to herself.

Elen extended her hand and placed it on Beth's heart, and the warmth of courage coursed through her. "Say it Beth, so you can release it. Say what it is that has you frozen in fear and dreading the return home to your wonderful new life."

Clenching her fists and swallowing a huge gulp of air as she tried to summon the nerve, she thought of her parents, and how bitterly unhappy they were, with themselves, with each other, with their daughters. Anger and regret had poisoned their marriage and turned it toxic from the beginning, and her mother's venomous hatred had spilled out of her and scorched everyone in her life. She couldn't let that happen to her.

Finally she managed to speak, although her voice shook. "Will I be able to keep my own self now that I'm a wife? Or will I follow the only patterns I know, and sabotage my chance of happiness, and sacrifice my own needs, so that regret consumes and destroys me?"

Scared, she looked up at Elen, and was amazed by the love and light she exuded, and the confidence burning in her eyes.

"Of course you will keep your self, beloved. You are not your parents, and you will not model the patterns of your childhood. I will be with you whenever you need me. I will guide you down the ancient pathways of your spiritual practice, and help you reveal the Mysteries of the deep, wild woods within you."

An air of freedom, playfulness and fierce, wild energy swirled around Beth, and she saw sunshine piercing the darkness she'd always walked in. She felt so much lighter already. "How do I do that though? How can I connect with you when I need to?" she implored.

"It is already within you Beth. You simply need to trust yourself."

For a moment the shimmering figure looked sad. Disappointed in her ignorance. But she patiently continued her instructions.

"Walk the ley lines, the etheric pathways that throb and pulse through the land where you live, in sunshine and storms. And surrender yourself to the dream pathways in the shadows of night. You will find answers there, and strength. Work with deer too. They move through life and obstacles with grace, and shine the light, just as I do, so that others may find their way home. And you will do this too Beth. You will shine the light for those who are lost, and guide those in need of assistance."

Laughter erupted from Beth. "That's crazy. I can't do that!"

A frown marred Elen's brow for a moment, like threatening black clouds covering the sun, and Beth gulped with nerves. Then the being before her made her expression blank, and her voice gentle.

"Dear Beth, you have no idea of the promise and potential within you. Of the power you will develop, and one day use to help others." Elen took a deep breath, mastering her emotions, hiding her impatience, then smiled. "But you are still young. Wisdom will come, and experience will open you up and help you to see your own radiance. You will one day shine like gold, beloved."

Beth stared at her, flabbergasted by her pronouncements, wanting to deny and contradict, to refute that she could ever be as wonderful as Elen claimed. But she held her tongue. Perhaps this was something she could aspire to.

A flash of triumph crossed Elen's face, as though she had read Beth's mind. "Yes dear one. Deer one." She beamed at her. "Now, this creature will guide you home, because surely you know that Mike is your home Beth, as you are his." And she melted back into the shadows of the forest, until the red deer was standing in her place, gazing at her with deep, unfathomable eyes.

"Thank you," Beth whispered, and allowed the regal creature to lead her back to the boathouse, to her new husband, and to her supposedly golden future.

Chapter 20

# Truly Madly Deeply

Rhiannon

"Um, Dad, is it okay if Jake and Mr Mattherson come over for dinner tonight?"

"Hmm?"

Mike was distracted, searching through a teetering pile of folders from work while trying to eat a piece of cold toast, and barely aware she was there, let alone what she'd asked. Which was how Rhiannon wanted it.

"Dinner, tonight? You don't have to do a thing, I've already shopped, and made a start on the cooking, and Brodie is staying at Ben's, so there's no drama there."

Confusion flitted across her father's face, and he lowered the papers he was holding and gazed at her.

"Jake and Richard? I don't understand. And tonight?"

Guilt thickened Rhiannon's voice. "Well, um, you said at the ritual that we should all catch up, and, um, you know..."

Checking his watch, Mike sighed, drained his coffee cup, then scooped up all the files and shrugged. "Okay, yes, sure. I have to run though. And I have a late meeting, so I won't be home until seven."

Rhiannon grinned. "That's perfect, you'll be just in time. Thanks Dad!" She kissed him on the cheek, grabbed her toast and ran upstairs to her room before he could ask any more questions, anxiety speeding her escape. When the front door banged shut, she breathed a sigh of relief and opened her wardrobe. Now for the most important task. What would she wear tonight?

She'd seen Tom three times in the two weeks since their London adventure, and had fallen even harder for him each time. Twice he'd come down on Tuesdays, since it was his night off, and she'd skipped her coven meeting with Carlie to be with him. She did feel slightly bad about that, but her friend had insisted she didn't mind.

And now it was the next step. Introducing her boyfriend to her dad. She'd promised Rose she would inform her father as soon as there was something to tell, and after spending most of last weekend lost in Tom's arms, with Carlie as a reluctant alibi, there was definitely something to tell.

She was totally, truly, madly, deeply in love.

When she got home from school that afternoon, Rhiannon almost wept with gratitude. Her dad must have come back in his lunch break, because he'd left a note saying he'd try to be home by half past six, and there was a bottle of expensive wine on the dining table they only ever used on special occasions. Pain stabbed her heart as she recalled the last time they'd sat there, for the Samhain dinner with Rose five months ago, in honour of her mum.

Forcing the sad memories from her mind, Rhiannon hurried into the kitchen and lit the oven. Grabbing the vegetables she'd chopped the night before, she drizzled them in olive oil and popped them inside, then added the extra pie she'd prepared the previous weekend and frozen in readiness to the lower shelf. Quickly she made a salad and a herb dressing, set the table with her mum's favourite tablecloth and their brightest plates, picked some flowers from the garden, then ran upstairs to get ready.

Butterflies swooped around her stomach as she showered. What if the dinner tasted awful? What if she embarrassed herself in front of her boyfriend? What if her dad was angry at her for *having* a boyfriend? What if he didn't like Tom? What if *Tom* didn't like her dad – or her?

Her thoughts spiralled and panic started to overwhelm her, until a knock on the bathroom door brought her abruptly back to the present. Oh god! If her dad was home, she only had half an hour until her guests arrived. Shutting off the water, she dried off quickly, pulled her dress over her head and hurried back to her room, deftly missing her dad as he went to shower.

Entreating herself to get a grip, she brushed her hair, slicked some plum-coloured gloss over her lips, then dabbed a few drops of her Confidence essential oil blend on her wrists and behind her ears. She could do this. Jake was a good friend, and she could always ask him about his home in Australia if conversation lulled. His grandfather was lovely too, and had chatted to her dad for a while at a previous ritual. And she knew Tom liked her.

*He had to, or he wouldn't bother driving down from London so often to see her, right?*

Nervously she hurried downstairs, suddenly wishing she'd invited Carlie. Would her friend be mad at her for organising this without her? Feel left out? She and Jake were close. Why hadn't she told Carlie about the dinner, and asked her to come? Initially she'd just thought of it as a family thing, Tom and his cousin and grandfather. And she knew it was tough for her friend to see her and Tom together, since he reminded them both of Rowan. But had she been more concerned that it would be awkward for herself with Carlie there?

When her dad walked into the kitchen, Rhiannon jumped, almost dropping the carafe of sparkling apple juice she was holding. "Dad, hi! Thanks for this," she muttered.

He shrugged, still looking confused. "I never mind you having people over darling, I just don't understand why this was so last minute. Why you wouldn't tell me sooner. And I saw the table, you've set it for five. Is Carlie coming too? I miss seeing her."

"No, she couldn't come," Rhiannon said, almost choking on the lie. "It's actually Jake's cousin –"

At the knock on the front door, she froze. *Why* had she thought it was a good idea to introduce Tom to her dad? What had possessed her? Oh, that's right. Rose was only prepared to keep her secret from Mike for so long. The priestess had agreed to let her wait and see whether their relationship was worth revealing, but that had been a few weeks ago.

Her dad was staring at her. "Are you going to get that, or should I?"

"I will," she squeaked, and hurried down the hallway. When she reached the door she took a deep breath, and forced herself to relax.

*She could do this.*

"Hi Jake, hi Mr Mattherson," she said, ushering them inside. "And hello you," she whispered, as Tom put an arm around her and leaned in for a quick, barely-there kiss, then presented her with a bunch of purple roses.

Heart racing, she took his hand and led him through to the kitchen. Her dad was greeting Jake and his granddad as she drew Tom forward.

"Dad, this is Tom, Jake's cousin. Tom, this is my father."

Her dad said hello and offered Tom his hand, his manner friendly but his gaze piercing. Rhiannon tried to fight the blush rising in her cheeks, to control her nerves, but there was no need to worry. Tom stepped around her and clasped her father's hand.

"Mr Stark, it's a pleasure to meet you. Pop said you really made him feel welcome at Rose's ritual."

"Not as welcome as Rose has made him." Mike grinned, and winked at Richard. "But I haven't seen you there before," he added, voice challenging. He softened when he spotted the roses, and Tom handed him a bottle of wine.

"Dad, why don't you open that for you and Mr Mattherson, and we can all go in and sit down." Rhiannon placed the flowers in the sink then steered everyone into the dining room.

"Wow, it's beautiful," Jake said, gazing around the softly lit dining room. "You've gone to so much effort."

"It's the candles, they make everything look magical," Rhiannon offered quickly, embarrassed. Was she trying too hard? "Now, take a seat everyone, and help yourself to the appetisers."

A wave of guilt engulfed her. She'd never invited Jake to her place before, never hung out with him alone, and she was suddenly uncomfortably aware of how much she was using him tonight. Vowing to make it up to him, she seated Tom and his grandad on one side of the table, with her and Jake on the other, leaving her father at the head. No need to make it too obvious that she and Tom were together, until she'd been able to explain herself properly.

Her dad came in with the wine and three glasses. "Wine for you Tom?" he asked, and Rhiannon looked up in alarm. Was this a test?

"Thank you, but no, I'm driving." Tom smiled and picked up the glass of juice. "Thank you so much for having me tonight."

Mike returned the smile. "I must admit that I was surprised we were having guests tonight, but Rhiannon does most of the cooking, so it's always her call."

Mortified, Rhiannon almost choked on her drink. "Dad!"

"I'm sorry, I didn't mean anything by that, it's just... well, this is the first dinner party we've had since... since we lost Beth."

"I'm so sorry for your loss, Mr Stark," Tom said.

After a brief nod of acknowledgement, Mike changed the subject. "It's wonderful to be among friends, and I'm glad we're finally sharing that meal we mentioned Richard." Then he turned to Tom, before his scrutiny shifted back to his daughter. "So, how do you two know each other?"

Tom smiled at Rhiannon across the table, and a little of his calm flowed into her as he opened his mouth to speak. "We met through Jake. He's in the same classes as Rhiannon and Carlie, and the girls were kind enough to take him under their wing when he got here from Australia just before Christmas. Which was quite a culture shock for him, as you can imagine, trading Perth's sunny beaches and all his friends for snow and strangers."

Mike's gaze moved to Jake, who smiled in agreement. "Rhiannon was the first person to talk to me actually, the first to welcome me, and I'm so grateful for that."

Mouthing a thank you to her friend, Rhiannon offered the plate of spinach triangles, cheese, dips and crackers around the table. Then she steeled herself for the big reveal. She supposed now was as good a time as any to come clean with her dad.

"Jake invited me and Carlie for lunch with him and Tom a few weeks ago, because he was worried he wouldn't be interesting enough on his own."

"Hey!" Jake interjected, although eventually he grinned sheepishly and nodded. "That's true actually. I hadn't seen him for a few years, and I was scared he'd find me boring."

Tom gasped. "Seriously Cuz?"

"Sorry."

"When was that?" Mike asked, and Rhiannon gulped.

"After we got back from Scotland," she admitted. "We all ended up talking for hours, because Tom goes to rituals in London, and –"

"You're from London Tom?"

*Oops.*

Tom nodded. "I'm going to art college there, but I spend a lot of time here with Pop, and of course now Jake is staying for a while, I love seeing him too." Jake and Richard almost choked on their drinks at this exaggeration, but Mike didn't notice, because he was staring so intently at his daughter.

"And you all hung out together in London at the festival?"

Rhiannon swallowed nervously. "Yes, Tom is part of Carlie's friend Jasmine's ritual group, but Carlie and I stayed at Mona's, like I told you." She knew she was babbling, but she couldn't stop. "It was just..."

Her dad reached over and took her hand. "Darling, relax. I'm not accusing you of anything."

Forcing a smile, she took a deep breath, then a big gulp of juice. "Oh, I should check the dinner, back in a second," she said, pushing her chair back and practically running out to the kitchen.

Footsteps behind her made Rhiannon spin around, and she was relieved that it was Jake hovering in the doorway, not her father.

"Can I help?" he asked.

She nodded, grateful again for his calm presence.

"You okay?"

Handing him the salad bowl, she mumbled an affirmative while grabbing a vase for the roses. Then she picked up a tea towel, wrenched open the oven door and pulled out the baked vegies. Relieved they were so well cooked, she followed Jake out to the table, then returned for the pie. It was perfectly golden brown, and she whispered a prayer of thanks as she carried it out.

But she almost dropped it when she heard her dad's next question. "So Tom, what do you do? You mentioned that you're a student?"

"That's right Mr Stark."

"You can call me Mike."

Tom flashed him a smile of gratitude, and Rhiannon felt awful. What was she putting her boyfriend through? Would this night be the last straw for him?

"I'm at art school, but I'm also getting on-the-job training at a tattoo studio."

He paused, tentative, but Mike motioned for him to go on.

"And I paint. I've had a few art exhibitions in small galleries – my most recent one was based on goddesses of the British Isles.

Mike looked wistful. "Beth would have so loved to see that." He took Rhiannon's hand. "And I'm sure you and Carlie would too. Is it still on Tom?"

He shook his head. "It closed last month."

"Maybe Rose could exhibit the paintings at the healing centre, up in the ritual room?" Mike suggested, while Rhiannon almost choked on a piece of pumpkin. "Or is that space too small?"

"It would be perfect actually." Tom grinned. "There's one huge painting, which takes up a whole wall, but the rest would fit across the other two. The most popular series was of ten tiny goddesses, postcard size. I couldn't paint them fast enough to keep up with demand. And I loved the contrast. It was such a challenge doing the largest one, in terms of space and scope – having to fill every inch of canvas, and needing a ladder for some parts – although I absolutely love it. But the small ones had their own difficulties, especially trying to fit the level of detail necessary into a confined area."

"Who's the big one of?" Jake asked.

Tom smiled and looked across the table at his girlfriend. "It's the goddess Rhiannon, with her white horse, merging with her white swan companion. I painted it six months ago, during Mabon, long before I met this goddess."

Rhiannon gasped, thinking of the painting Rowan had done of her last Mabon. What were the odds of him and Tom both painting a half-swan maiden Rhiannon on the very same day?

What did Tom's painting look like? She hadn't seen it at his apartment – not that she was going to confess she'd been there in front of her dad. For a moment she heard Rowan's voice, telling her how strong and brave she'd been, and that her guides wanted her to let her pain and grief transform her and push her forward, and open up to a whole new level of understanding and compassion. Surprised, she realised she had. She'd become strong enough to be with Tom. She wished there was a way to let Rowan know how much she appreciated his wise counsel.

Then she realised everyone was staring at her. "Sorry, I was just thinking of my spirit guide drawing from the Mabon festival, when Rowan drew me as half swan, with a white horse companion."

"Carlie's Rowan?" Tom asked, shocked. "That's who did your spirit guide drawing?"

Rhiannon nodded.

"The guy whose tattoo I did?"

She nodded again, and smiled as he tried to get his head around the synchronicity.

Mike focused back on Tom. "You knew Carlie's boyfriend? You tattooed him?"

"Yes. And even weirder, it sounds like I painted his painting of Rhiannon. The same day. His sounds just like mine. I know there's magic in the world, but this..." he trailed off.

It was Richard who broke the silence. "That's amazing. What a small world. I must admit, I never believed in any of that, um, spiritual stuff. I would have assumed you were stretching the truth to make it *seem* cosmic," he admitted. "Marcy believed in fate and destiny, but I could never bring myself to accept it. But watching Rose facilitate her rituals, feeling the energy and, well, the *magic*, in the room, I can no longer deny that there's *something* to all of this."

He took a sip of wine, then gazed fondly at his grandson. "I would love to see your paintings one day Tom. I still have a few that your mum sent us when you were in primary school. Marcy always kept them on the fridge."

Rhiannon giggled when Tom's cheeks turned pink at that revelation. "I'd love to see those!"

But Mike had fixated on something else Richard had mentioned. "I'm so sorry you lost your wife too," he murmured.

"And you dear Mike." Richard smiled sadly, and the two men stared at each other, a sense of kinship between them.

"Rose is a remarkable woman, isn't she," Mike said. "Her rituals are so healing, so inclusive. I'm so grateful to her. She's been an important part of our lives for, well, forever really, since I was twelve. But after we lost Beth, she was even more amazing. So strong and caring. And such practical help."

Richard nodded, and Rhiannon wondered if he'd just blushed. Did he have a soft spot for the priestess?

"When did you meet your wife?" she asked, curiosity burning away her reticence. "I thought Marcy was more... religious?"

Richard's eyes twinkled. "Marcy was a churchgoer, yes, but she was open to everything. She and her sister used to visit Summer Hill when they were young, and had been to a few of the full moon circles the priestesses here ran. I didn't find out until afterwards that her sister had asked Rose for a herbal remedy to lessen Marcy's pain in her final weeks, and Rose had popped around to sit with her, and offer healing. Religious or not, no one in this village has ever had a problem with Rose. I don't think there'd be a single person who hasn't been helped or healed by her in some way."

"Amen to that," Mike said.

"But I didn't meet her until she invited me and Jake to her Imbolc ceremony a couple of months back," Richard continued. "I only went for Jake's sake, to be honest – I knew he was trying to get me out more, make me socialise a bit..."

"I'm sorry Pop, I didn't mean to push you."

Richard smiled at his grandson. "I'm glad you did. You were right, I'd cut myself off from everyone. I count my lucky stars you wanted to come and stay with me while your parents are away."

"How long have you lived here?" Mike asked.

"I grew up in Perth, but like so many Australians of my generation, we headed off to London after school to make our mark on the world. I met Marcy not long off the plane, and we fell in love immediately." His eyes had a faraway look as he remembered the early days of their courtship.

"We got married in London and lived and worked there for years, although we honeymooned in Summer Hill because Marcy had always loved it here. Then a decade ago we moved to Perth to be close to our son, Jake's dad, and look after Jake when his parents had to travel for work."

Sensing Jake's frown, Rhiannon wondered for the first time how he really felt about his parents jetting off around the world, and abandoning him to his grandparents. It was for a good cause, as they worked for an aid organisation in Africa and were doing important work, and she knew how much Jake loved Richard. But still, being left by your parents would be tough for a kid. She wondered if she could ask him about it.

Then she turned her attention back to Richard, impressed by the romance of his love story. "When Marcy got sick five years ago, we moved back to England so she could be close to her sister and our other kids and grandkids. We have a daughter in London, Tom's mum, who lives with his three younger sisters, as well as a son in Wales, and Summer Hill is halfway between them. We bought a little cottage at the bottom of the tor, and when Marcy died eighteen months ago, I couldn't bear to leave. It probably sounds weird, but it feels like her spirit is still here."

Mike's eyes glittered with tears. "That doesn't sound weird at all. I sense Beth so vividly here, almost as though she's become part of the sacred landscape, embodied in the green fields and the slopes of the tor. I walk there a lot, to try to connect with her..."

A lump formed in Rhiannon's throat at the pain in her father's voice. It was clear that he still missed his wife as deeply and desperately as when he'd first lost her, yet they never talked about it, tiptoeing around each other when it came to emotions. Was there someone he could talk to about his grief? And should she suggest that he see a counsellor? She was so fortunate that she had Carlie and Rose, and now Tom, who understood her pain and grief, and offered her so much comfort and love.

When Richard lifted his wine glass, his hand was shaking. "Finally, I totally understand that emotional connection to the land. And Marcy's ashes are scattered on the tor and in our garden, so she's physically here too. So with Jake's folks in Africa, and Jake here with me, well, there's nothing for me in Australia any more."

"I'm sorry I asked," Rhiannon murmured, but both men said "Don't be" at the same time.

"It helps to be able to talk about them, to know they're remembered by other people as well," her dad said. "It's been eighteen months since Beth died too, and I still miss her every day. The intensity has changed a little – I'm not totally paralysed any more – but I don't think it will ever go away, and I don't want it to."

Richard smiled sadly. "Marcy made me promise I would let love in after she was gone, but I can't see that happening," he replied, although his cheeks reddened again, and Rhiannon recalled her dad's wink earlier that evening, and made a mental note to ask Carlie and Jake if anything was going on between their grandparents.

Mike stood up. "We probably need to lighten the mood a little," he offered. "How about dessert?"

Silently Rhiannon swore. "I'm so sorry, I didn't have a chance to make anything..."

Her dad grinned, and looked proud. "That's why I grabbed something on my way home. Mud cake and ice-cream anyone?"

Later, after Mike went to bed and Jake walked his grandfather home, Tom stayed to help Rhiannon with the dishes.

"Thank you for tonight," she said shyly. "I'm sorry you got the third degree though. I hope you didn't hate every minute of it."

Taking her in his arms, he kissed her lightly and smiled. "I'm glad your dad gave me the third degree. I like to think it's kept other hopeful suitors away. And I loved it, getting to know you in new ways, and Pop and Jake too. It's been so wonderful for both of them to be in Summer Hill, and you're a big part of that."

"Well, it's Carlie who's helped Jake the most," she admitted.

Tom shook his head. "No, he might *like* Carlie the most, but he said it was you who first welcomed him, and made him feel like he belonged. You and Rose."

She was touched by the compliment, but sadness soon overwhelmed her. It hurt physically that she wasn't going to see Tom for two weeks. Before she met him, she'd really been looking forward to going to France for the school holidays, but now she just wanted to stay at home, or go to London. Be anywhere she could see him.

"Hey, why so glum?" Tom asked, taking her hand and swinging her around the kitchen.

"I'll just miss you while I'm away," she said softly.

"Me too." His hand on hers comforted her, and she reminded herself to not ruin this moment with her fears about being apart. She could stew over that once Tom had left.

His eyes were full of tenderness as he pulled her into his arms then leaned down and kissed her. They stayed there, locked together, until they were both dizzy with passion, then she reluctantly tore herself from his embrace and headed back to the sink, plunging her hands into the soapy water.

"What time do you have to go back tomorrow?" she asked, voice soft and unsteady.

Picking up a tea towel and starting to dry the plates, Tom sighed. "I'll need to be on the road by midday to make it to work on time. And I know you have to pack and everything, but could we have breakfast together?"

Relief tingled through Rhiannon, and she leaned into him when he stood behind her and wrapped his arms around her waist.

"Of course we can. How early do you want to meet up?"

Chapter 21

# The Untrimmable Light

## Rhiannon

Shivering as she made her way to the base of the tor in the early morning dark, Rhiannon laughed at how happy she was to get up at stupid o'clock when it meant seeing Tom. Her little brother would have been shocked if he was home, because Saturdays she usually slept in for as long as humanly possible. Well, Saturdays without Tom to get up for.

Her heart leaped when he detached himself from the shadows of the trees and walked towards her. She melted into him, the warmth and comfort of his arms warding off the chill of the morning and the sadness of the impending two weeks without him.

He took off his woollen beanie and placed it on her head, and she smiled at his thoughtfulness. "Ready?" he asked, taking her hand, and she nodded, setting off with him along the tree-lined path, then out into the meadow of the lower slopes.

The slightest glow of lavender gold was apparent in the east as they started to climb, and she marvelled again at just how beautiful early mornings were.

"Not as beautiful as you," Tom said quietly.

"You're more beautiful," she whispered, then cringed and ducked her head, shy again. Why did she always feel so off-centre when she was with him?

And yet, breathing in the colours as they climbed higher and the sky slowly lightened then turned a fiery pink, she felt grounded. Protected. He spun her off her orbit, yet returned her to her self.

At the summit they sank down onto the damp grass, Tom sheltering her from the cold breeze behind them. Grateful, she leaned back against him, luxuriating in his warmth.

"It's not fair, I don't want to go away," she muttered. "The time is going to drag. And what if you forget me while I'm gone?"

Tom laughed. "Like that would happen. But I know what you mean. And it's even more frustrating that I'll be in France for the weekend, but still no closer. Are you sure you couldn't persuade your dad to swing by Paris for a day or two?"

Sadly she shook her head. It was too cruel that they would be in the same country at the same time, yet unable to see each other. Especially since Tom would be in the City of Love, no doubt surrounded by gorgeous, elegant women, while she was traipsing through the countryside with her little brother, trying to keep him entertained and cursing every minute of it.

"Do you think he at least liked me?" Tom asked.

Rhiannon was caught off guard by the anxiety in his voice. "Who?" she asked.

"Your dad."

"Of course he did!"

"But you don't know yet, right? You haven't seen him since last night. Maybe the tattooing thing put him off, or the motorbike, or me being older, or from London…"

She twisted around and stared at him, shocked that he could be so unsure of himself. Was everyone insecure in their own way? Tom always seemed so confident and self-assured, especially compared to her and her constant doubts, but maybe he had deeply buried, well-hidden insecurities too.

"I'm sure he loved you. And it was great to see how well he and your grandad get on. Even if he did have reservations about you – which he doesn't! – knowing Richard would reassure him."

Panic crossed Tom's face, and Rhiannon kicked herself for the last comment. "I promise he loved you. All he wants is for me to be happy, Rose reminded me of that, and you make me happy." She reached up and kissed him, trying to erase the tension emanating from each sharp angle of his body.

"Really?"

Frowning, she tried not to roll her eyes. "How could you doubt that? I've never been happier, I promise. Ask Carlie. Hell, ask Jake. They both know. And I wouldn't have introduced you to Dad if I wasn't sure, if I thought there was no future for us."

Now it was her turn to stress. "Um, if that's not too forward of me to admit?"

But Tom's face had lit up at her words, joy chasing the worry away, just as the sun spilled over the horizon and they were both illuminated by its sparkling golden rays.

The warmth steadied them both, and they talked of other things for a while, solstice rituals and solar spells, and summer nights on previous holidays, then Tom shared his favourite poem with her, one about the ocean's shine, the incredible beauty of the world, and the untrimmable light.

"That's beautiful," she whispered.

Tom grinned. "Like you."

They both laughed, and happiness wrapped around Rhiannon as she basked in the early morning sunshine, and the safety and comfort of her boyfriend's arms.

Then Tom spoke, and her whole world tore apart.

"I have a confession to make."

A chill crept up Rhiannon's spine, and she twisted out of his arms. Adrenaline shot through her body, and her heart clenched, then shattered into a million tiny pieces. Mind racing, she stared at him in horror. Oh god, he'd cheated on her. And now he wanted to break up with her. But they'd been getting on so well, hadn't they? What had she done wrong? How had such a perfect moment burned to ash in the blink of an eye?

Tom reached out for her, hands up in surrender, and she realised she must have swayed a little in her panic. Wouldn't that be great, fainting in the arms of the guy who was dumping her.

"Hey, it's nothing bad," Tom said, leaning over to kiss her.

Eyes wide, she sat facing him on the cold grass, every nerve on high alert. What was "nothing bad", if it came after "I have a confession to make"?

Taking a deep breath, Rhiannon tried to calm her thundering heart and make her voice even. "That's really not a good way to start a conversation." Her attempt at a smile failed miserably.

"I'm sorry." Tom pouted, trying to pull her back into his arms.

"Just tell me already," she snapped. She wasn't sure how much longer she could keep this scream in her throat from bursting forth.

"Before I met you, I'd been hurt a few times, by women playing at being magical, playing at being witches. I would share my magical self, bare my heart, then they would make fun of my beliefs, or expose secrets I'd revealed to them. One assumed I'd be into kinky sex because I was pagan, and tried to get me involved in a threesome with her and the boyfriend she'd never mentioned. Another wanted me to cast spells on people for her, and got angry when I explained about rituals and ethics and the three-fold law. Another accused me of something I didn't – and would never – do, and it was only because her previous partner came forward and revealed that she'd tried it with him too that I managed to escape her."

Absently he ran a hand through his hair, gazing off into the dawn sky as if searching for answers.

"I'm very sorry that you've been through that, but I hope you know I would never do any of that to you," Rhiannon said coldly, offended that he assumed she would.

"Of course I don't think that of you, now. Doing rituals and weaving magic with you and Rose, it's obvious that you're genuine, and that you see it as a path of study and learning, not a shortcut to money or revenge or power. But I was cautious at first, and I wanted you to know why."

Tentatively he leaned in and took her hand. "Outside of my coven friends, you're the first genuine person I've met. And Carlie too, although I was rude and presumptuous when I met her."

He cringed, and Rhiannon's heart softened towards him. "She's fine about that, she said she understood, and she doesn't hold it against you."

Tom managed a wan smile. "Yeah, we talked about that a bit when I was doing her tattoo. We'd both misjudged each other when we first met."

A flash of jealousy jolted through Rhiannon, and she pulled her hand back. "Wait, you've spoken to Carlie about this?" She wasn't sure which of them she felt the most betrayed by. Her boyfriend, for telling her friend things he hadn't told her, or her best friend, for having these suspicions and not telling her, and even worse, talking about it with her boyfriend and *still* not telling her.

"Babe, please don't be mad at Carlie for this. I swore her to secrecy to avoid my embarrassment. I was just grateful that she cared so much about you, and was willing to confront me about her worries – especially since I was tattooing her at the time. She really loves you, and cares about you deeply."

His words didn't placate her. "What did she misjudge you on? She never said anything to me."

Watching as he distractedly played with the pentacle around his neck, Rhiannon grew more worried, more suspicious. Was there more to all this, and he was just leading her into it gently? What wasn't he telling her?

"She said she was suspicious of my motives with you," he began, and Rhiannon felt like she'd been punched in the guts. Carlie had never mentioned that. What was she suspicious of? She stared at Tom with wide eyes, panic making her breath come fast and shallow.

"But then she apologised, because it soon became clear to her how much I care about you," Tom added quickly, and Rhiannon felt some of the tension drain out of her. "She was right to doubt me that first day, but only then, so I was glad I could explain myself and set her mind at ease."

"Okay, well, I'm glad we cleared that up," Rhiannon said.

Then she froze. "Wait, what motives was she talking about?"

Tom sighed, and looked like he really wished he hadn't brought any of this up.

"Hey, you're the one who promised to be honest," Rhiannon said sourly, the sliver of doubt widening into a gaping hole in the pit of her stomach.

"You're right. But just hear me out, okay?"

Rhiannon frowned.

"Don't react to the first sentence."

Gritting her teeth, she nodded.

"That first time, when I told Pop I'd come down and see him for the weekend, I was just doing it out of obligation, because I hadn't seen him for ages. And Mum had been nagging me to spend time with Jake, since he was apparently lonely here – although you and Carlie have been wonderful friends to him."

"He's a wonderful friend to us," Rhiannon said, voice icy. "Keep going."

"I was a bit resentful that I had to hang out with my young cousin all weekend – I hadn't seen Jake since he was thirteen, so I was wondering what on earth we'd have to talk about. And I wasn't impressed when he said he also wanted me to hang out with his young school friends."

Rhiannon shrugged. "Okay, that's not so bad," she conceded. He hadn't met her yet, so she couldn't hold that against him.

"Um, well, it's just that at first – only at first! – I could tell you liked me, so I tried to impress you as a game, to amuse myself and fill in time. I didn't realise right away how grown up Jake had become, or how much I actually liked you. While we had lunch, when we went off to drink chai together, and even while we were climbing the tor that first night, I had no intention of ever seeing you again. I was just having fun, entertaining myself with a pretty girl, and avoiding hanging out with Pop."

Pain gouged Rhiannon, and she gasped, more deeply hurt than she liked to admit by his admission. But when he looked up at her with sad eyes, part of her wanted to reach out and comfort him – although another part itched to rage and scream and vent all her fury at him. She didn't know how to react. Should she stand up and storm off down the hill, and never speak to him again? Or would that just prove to him that his first assumption, that she was young and immature, was correct?

As though anticipating that she might run, Tom took both her hands in his and stared longingly into her eyes, imploring her to listen, and understand.

"I promise you, that was just my first reaction. By the time we said goodbye that night, you were all I could think about, and by the next morning I knew that I liked you far more than I'd imagined. So from that moment on my intentions have been honourable, I swear. When we met up the next day, then left Jake and Carlie on the bike so we could be alone together, that was what I wanted. And when we kissed, it was absolutely heartfelt. What we felt was real – it *is* real. I wasn't acting that I liked you, I absolutely did, and do. Believe me babe, if I wasn't so into you, I wouldn't be spending all my time driving down here to see you."

He looked so sad, his eyes swimming with tears, and Rhiannon wanted to comfort him, to say it was okay. But was it? He had no reason to lie, and no reason to be playing her now. And he could have chosen to never tell her any of this. He was just being honest, which she'd claimed she wanted. And he was right about the travelling. It was a huge commitment, and a huge effort, to drive down from London as often as he did, on the pretext of seeing his grandfather, but really being with her.

And had she known what she felt about him that first day? Wasn't she just using him as a guinea pig to test whether she could talk to a guy other than John? Feel wanted by another guy? That first day she'd only liked him because he was gorgeous and older and a witch, it hadn't really been about him personally, so her motives hadn't been a hundred per cent pure either. Swallowing down a chuckle, she remembered how surprised she'd been later, when she realised how lovely and kind he was.

"Okay," she said finally. "I can deal with that."

Relief made his eyes sparkle, and he beamed at her. "I really care about you Rhiannon, and I guess that I'm risking opening up to you about all of this because I want no secrets. I want to share all of myself with you – my doubts, my insecurities, my flaws and faults."

"You don't have any faults."

He kissed her cheek, then shook his head. "You are very sweet, but no, we all have things we regret, situations we wish had worked out differently, misunderstandings we contributed to, moments we wish we could erase, hurts that have shaped us, character flaws we're working on. And that's a good thing. I want to learn and grow with you, and become a better person. And I want to know all about you, and what makes you the wonderful person you are."

*Oh no.*

Tom drew her into his arms, and she stiffened in panic. Did this mean she had to tell him about what had happened to her before they met? Reveal *her* secret, and the ways she was coming to realise that she was still affected by it?

*There was no way she could do that.*

Trying to relax and lose herself in the sensation of Tom's hands in her hair, and his warm breath on her face as he leaned down to kiss her, she was finally reassured. Nobody knew her secret, not even Carlie, so there was no way he could find out.

Approaching voices drew them back to the real world, and when a few people with their dogs crested the summit, they both stood up at the same time, in unspoken agreement, and started to head back down the hill.

"Do you want to come to my place for breakfast?" Rhiannon offered shyly.

Tom grinned. "I thought you'd never ask."

When she opened the front door and ushered Tom inside, Brodie rushed down the hallway. "Rhi-Rhi! You're back! I just got home too, but Dad's in the shower, and I was hoping you would make me pancakes." He screeched to a halt in front of her, and looked up at Tom quizzically.

"Hello," he said. "I'm Brodie. Will you have pancakes with me?"

Tom squatted down so he was eye to eye with him, and Rhiannon's heart melted at his consideration.

"Hi Brodie, I'm Tom. And I'd love to have pancakes with you, if that's what's on the breakfast menu."

They both gazed up at Rhiannon, and their same hopeful faces made her laugh.

"Sure, pancakes it is." She led them out to the kitchen, and the two boys climbed up on the stools and chatted while Rhiannon pulled eggs and milk out of the fridge then went rummaging through the pantry for flour, cinnamon and maple syrup. She smiled as Brodie told Tom about their upcoming holiday, and how wonderful it would be to have time with his dad and his sister, walking in the footsteps of their mother.

"I don't remember Mumma too well," he confessed sadly. "But Dad said this trip might bring some things back to me, because she loved France so much, and I went there with her when I was little."

Rhiannon's heart lurched. How uncharitable of her to be wishing away her family trip so she could be back with Tom. "We'll remember them together, okay buddy?" she said.

Brodie smiled up at her and nodded, then turned back to Tom. "Rhi-Rhi has been helping me. We started making a book together ages ago, after that night of the pumpkins and ghost plates, and we write something about Mum in it every day."

Tom raised an eyebrow at Rhiannon in question, and she grinned. "We decided to do it last Samhain, after we'd laid out place settings – ghost plates – for Mum, and for Carlie's parents too. It's a book of memories, of the little, seemingly insignificant, things. The first one we recorded was how much she loved jasmine."

"Yes! That's what she always smelled of," Brodie explained. "When she tucked me in at night, I could smell the pretty flowers. That's why I like spring, when the jasmine blossoms."

Walking into the kitchen, Mike caught his son's words, and a cloud of sadness obscured his expression for a moment, before he visibly pulled himself together.

"Hi Tom, it's lovely to see you again." Mike shook his hand, then put the coffee machine on and kissed Rhiannon on the cheek as she flipped a pancake. "Hi darling," he said. "And hello Brodie. How was your night at Ben's?"

As her brother described the games they'd played and the television show they'd watched, Rhiannon poured juice for everyone and got out the plates and cutlery, vowing to make the most of her time away, and help her brother remember their mother.

Once she had a towering stack of pancakes ready, they all pulled up chairs at the kitchen table, and she smiled at how well Tom fitted in, engaging Brodie and her dad in conversation, making them laugh, and sharing stories of his visit to Paris the year before, which filled Rhiannon with a longing to see it with him.

"Paris really is a beautiful city," Mike said wistfully. "Beth lived there before she returned to Summer Hill, and loved it so much. We went there together years ago, and stayed in a sweet little top floor apartment that looked out over the gables to the Seine. We drank endless cups of coffee and ate chocolate croissants for breakfast every day."

He paused, his eyes getting that far away look that always filled Rhiannon with dread. "And that's where I proposed, standing out on a tiny balcony under the stars, Beth gazing out at the lights of the city, and me with eyes only for her."

"How magical," Tom said softly.

Mike blinked, forcing his attention back to them, and his lips curved uncharacteristically upwards. This time his reminiscences about his wife had given him joy, rather than pulling him under and drowning him in sorrow as they had for so long. Rhiannon desperately hoped this was a breakthrough, and he was getting stronger.

"Are we going to Paris?" Brodie's small voice broke the spell they'd all fallen under. "We could see Tom over there!"

Heart skipping a beat, Rhiannon waited with bated breath for her dad's reply, gaze fixed on Tom, whose eyes were also flickering with hope. When her father shook his head, she almost cried.

"Sorry buddy, not this time. It's all beaches and standing stones and enchanted forests for us, but we can put Paris on the wish-list for our next holiday, if that's where you want to go."

"Ooh, beaches! I'll have to pack my bucket and spade," Brodie replied, the lure of the capital already fading from his mind. "Will you help me pack when I get back from football Rhi-Rhi?"

Heart heavy, she nodded to her brother, and took a huge swig of coffee to mask her disappointment. Tom smiled sadly.

Oblivious to their turmoil, Mike swallowed down his coffee, ate the last of his pancake, and took his plate over to the sink. "Okay buddy, I'd better get you down to the oval, so do you want to go up and get changed?"

Brodie shovelled the rest of his breakfast into his mouth, ran upstairs to grab his sports gear, then was gone in a whirl of activity and frenetic energy.

"He's such a great kid," Tom said when they were finally alone. "And he adores you."

Scooping the last pancake onto his plate, Rhiannon tried to smile. "Yeah, I felt quite mean when he was getting so excited about our holiday, and I'd been wishing it away, or praying we could go to Paris so I could see you."

"I wish that too, more than anything," Tom said, taking her hand and bringing it to his lips.

Leaning over, she kissed him, pouring all of her yearning into it, and leaving them both breathless. Pulling away before she got to the point where she wouldn't be able to stop, Rhiannon sighed. "You'll be working the whole time though, so I'd hardly see you anyway, right?" Not that it helped, either way.

"Yeah, I did this event last year, and we barely got a minute to ourselves, let alone time to sightsee. Marie thinks we'll be out at clubs all night, but she's in for a rude shock."

Rhiannon stared at him, eyes wide with horror, stomach tight with dread. "Marie? Who's Marie?"

"Our manager. I told you we both had to go. We'll be there as a team, representing the studio."

"You never mentioned your manager was a woman."

Tom shrugged. "Sorry, I thought I had. Does it matter?"

"Well, it's a bit different knowing you're travelling to the most romantic city in the world with a woman. Sharing a room with a woman?" Breath held, she waited for him to reply, terrified of the answer, head swirling with dark new insecurities.

"Possibly. Last year Brian and I were in a room together – twin share, so there's nothing to worry about." He stared at her, a frown crinkling his forehead.

"Why are you worried? I have no interest in her, I'm with you. And not that it matters, but she has a boyfriend, so she has no interest in me either. But even if she did, it wouldn't make any difference to me."

He sounded flustered, although Rhiannon had to concede that it could just be her strange obsession, and the remnants of their conversation up on the hill, making her think that. Why *did* she care? She trusted him, didn't she?

"Babe, this is crazy. Where's this coming from?"

Fear shot through her, and she stood up, grabbing her cup and heading to the bench. "More coffee?"

She needed to think, to move, to figure out what she *was* worried about. As she waited for the kettle to boil, she stared out the window, trying to focus on the sweetness of the jasmine climbing over the wooden frame, and the calming energy of the tor in the distance.

She jumped when Tom touched her shoulder and spun her around. Tenderly he reached out a hand, cupping her cheek, then stroking her face. So gentle, so sweet. "Hey, you know how much I care about you. Tell me what's wrong, please. I don't understand why you're so upset."

Nor did she, she just knew that she *was* upset. Her whole body was pulsing with anxiety and worry. Which was crazy, he was right about that. Why was she all of a sudden doubting his feelings for her? Just a few short hours ago they'd been up on the tor together, wrapped in each other's arms as they watched the sun rise, navigating an awkward conversation that had ultimately left her feeling even closer to him. And she knew deep in her bones how much he cared about her.

So why hadn't he mentioned that his boss was a woman?

Footsteps coming down the hall weakened Rhiannon's knees with relief, which shocked her. But this was all too much, too intense, on the eve of going away, and she was secretly grateful for the interruption. She couldn't handle the doubt and fear that was swirling around her. Choking her. Making her body tremble.

"Hey darling, hi Tom," her dad said, sauntering back into the kitchen and grinning at them both. "How will you both cope with being apart for two weeks?"

His amusement went down a notch when he stared at the long list on the fridge. "I can't believe we're leaving so soon. Rhi, would you mind throwing Brodie's washing on, and helping him pack when he gets home?"

"Sure." She sighed, but forced a smile when her dad gave her a questioning glance.

"I guess that's my cue to leave," Tom said, and she heard the sadness and regret in his voice. He kissed her lightly, then reluctantly stepped away. "Have a wonderful time in France, and I'll see in two weeks, right?"

Rhiannon nodded, then watched helplessly as he disappeared down the hall and out the door. Her heart raced, the blood thrumming loudly in her ears, and she felt hollowed out. Empty and bereft. Part of her wanted to run after Tom and throw herself into his arms, apologise for her pettiness, and promise him – promise herself – that she was mature enough, and secure enough, to not fall apart because her boyfriend happened to work with a woman. But she stayed where she was, frozen in misery and fear.

"Are you okay darling?"

Turning to face her dad, she gulped down the tears thickening in her throat, and nodded. "Yeah, it's just been a big week at school, and I still have to get organised. What time did you say we're leaving tomorrow?"

Her dad grimaced. "The ferry leaves at half past eight, so we'll need to be in the car and on our way by half past five. Sorry darling, I know it's really early, but you can snooze on the drive down, or on the ferry across. And we have two weeks of relaxation ahead of us."

Forcing another smile, and as much enthusiasm as she could muster, Rhiannon hurried upstairs to throw some clothes in a bag – but ended up throwing herself across her bed instead. Frustration pressed down on her, thick and heavy with regret. She'd handled that so badly, and now she had to wait two weeks before she'd see Tom again, and be able to apologise, and make amends.

For a long time she lay curled up on her bed with the curtains drawn, going over every angry and suspicion-filled word she'd thrown at him, every unfounded, stupid doubt she'd obsessed over, and trying to remind herself of all the beautiful things Tom had said, the wonderful things he'd done for her, the incredible sensation of his lips on hers, and how cherished he always made her feel.

Would he forgive her for her immature outburst, or had she totally blown it? Would he come down to see her when she got back, or had she pushed him away, made him realise she was more trouble than she was worth? Younger and more insecure than he could be bothered with?

She was just about to scream with panic and dread when Brodie knocked on her door, back from football and ready to pack for their adventure. Relieved for the break from her pity party, Rhiannon dragged herself up and followed him to his room, nodding and muttering "uh-huh" and "of course" whenever he paused in his excited holiday ramblings. Once he was sorted, she did a few loads of washing and cleaned the bathroom, then tried to get some of her holiday homework done, knowing she wouldn't spend a single second on it while she was away.

After a hasty dinner – takeout, so they didn't have to worry about cleaning up or washing dishes – Rhiannon headed back up to her room and finally put some clothes in a bag. Then, feeling sad and dissatisfied, she collapsed into bed, grateful that she was so exhausted she fell immediately to sleep.

## Chapter 22

### An Ocean of Stars

#### Beth

𝕯arkness surrounded Beth as she shimmered back into awareness, but it wasn't the black of the void she was becoming used to. Out of the corner of her eye she saw a dim glow, so she floated her way towards it. And found herself in Rhiannon's room, swirling around the small desk lamp that was the only source of illumination in the pre-dawn dark. Her daughter was sitting glumly on her bed, disappointment and regret rolling off her in waves, and Beth spun in confusion. The last time she'd seen her she'd been so happy. Desperately in love with Tom, and with life.

A sharp knock made Rhiannon curse, and hastily stand up.

"You all packed darling?" Mike asked as he opened her door, his own small suitcase behind him. "Brittany awaits!"

Emotion slammed into Beth at his words, sadness and pain warring with joy, and her molecules shuddered and threatened to tear her apart. Her family was going to Brittany, *her* Brittany. Would she be able to accompany them?

Rhiannon pasted a bright smile on her face as she gazed at her father, and somehow her voice came out devoid of the misery she'd been drowning in just moments before. "Yes, I'm good, and I helped Brodie yesterday, so he's ready too. I'll be down in five minutes, yeah?"

Mike nodded, and Beth watched helplessly as her husband's eyes filled with tears. "I'm sure there will be tough moments, but there will be so many memories too, all good ones, so I hope you'll enjoy our time away."

"I'm sure we all will," Rhiannon replied, then turned away sadly. Mike went down the hall to help Brodie with his bag, and Beth peered at her daughter, watching as she picked up a photo of Tom and traced the outline of his face with a finger. Ah, so she would miss her boyfriend. She couldn't blame her. It was hard being apart, especially when the relationship was so new and full of wonder.

Then her heart clenched. *Especially when you could never return.*

Her agony at being separated from her husband stabbed at her, a jagged shard, but she tried to breathe through the pain. Until a new fear paralysed her. Could she travel across the ocean? So far she'd managed to fight her way to awareness as far away as Smithfield and London with Rhiannon, but that was the furthest from her home, and her grave, that she'd been. What were her limits? Would she be able to journey down to the coastal harbour with them, just to be stuck on the shore as their ferry departed?

Panic threatened to swamp her, to rip her apart and strew her across the dark sky, but she focused all her energy on Rhiannon and managed to stay in one piece. Something was really upsetting her, and it looked like it was more than just the two weeks away from her boyfriend. Had something else happened?

Floating over to her daughter's side, she reached out a ghostly hand to her, desperately trying to draw her foggy thoughts and her wispy self together.

The last thing she remembered was Rhiannon inviting Tom for dinner so he could meet Mike. The way she'd sprung it on her dad without warning had amused Beth. That was the first he knew of a new boyfriend, and he'd been terrified, although he hid it well. Beth understood. Tom was a few years older than their daughter, with long hair, tattoos and a motorbike, and Rhiannon hadn't given her dad any hints to prepare – she'd implied that it was just Jake and his grandfather coming for dinner. Which had softened the shock a little, and affirmed that Tom came from a loving family at least.

In the end it hadn't mattered though, because Tom revealed himself to be a fine young man, eloquent and self-assured, and charming too. Beth had loved watching him answer all Mike's questions. He was so polite, yet he hadn't shied away from admitting the truth of who he was. How she wished she was still alive so she could talk to him, and do rituals with him, and watch him display just how much he cared about Rhiannon.

His bravery and confidence, combined with humility, was a beautiful combination, and Rhiannon introducing him to her dad reminded Beth of when she'd finally worked up the courage to let Rose know she was in love with Mike.

They'd been dating for six months before Beth walked into a ritual hand in hand with Mike. She was so scared of upsetting Rose, who had long assumed Mike would be her son-in-law, but the priestess came straight over to them and asked Mike to grab some cushions from the store room, then embraced Beth, kissed her on the cheek and smiled, her eyes twinkling.

"It's about time you let go of the burden you've been carrying sweetheart, and stopped hiding your relationship."

Startled, Beth drew back. "You knew?"

Rose grinned, mischief in her expression. "Of course. I saw the moment Mike fell in love with you. And he did, believe me. You have no need to doubt his feelings. Most importantly, please know that you are worthy of this love."

"But... How? When?" Beth's mind whirled, guilt making her whole body burn as she tried to work out what, when and how the priestess had known.

"Seven moons ago. When I had Laura stay back and help me on her own after that ritual."

Beth gasped, shocked that Rose had been aware of Mike's feelings even before he'd confessed them to her. The older woman smiled, her hand on Beth's arm anchoring her in the room as panic threatened to spin her away.

"I want to thank you for helping heal his heart."

Beth paled. "But Violet –" she whispered, then broke off, unable to form thoughts let alone utter words.

Sorrow flickered across Rose's face, but she swallowed it down, and only kindness and compassion remained. "Darling girl, Violet chose to leave us. And while I'll never understand why, I hope that wherever she is now, she's happy. And I hope that for everyone she left behind too. You and Mike both deserve so much joy, and I can think of no better person to hold his heart. If not Violet, then I am so very glad it is you."

A single tear glimmered on Rose's lashes, harsh and cold like a diamond, then spilled over and traced its way down her cheek. Beth felt the edges of the other woman's pain jut into her own skin. Sharp. Deep. Agonising. Then almost immediately the priestess's expression returned to its usual calm, as though the shadow had never been revealed.

Guilt washed over Beth again, and for a moment she feared she would drown in it, forced under by the weight of Rose's secret distress. But Mike returned at the perfect time, took her arm and drew her away and into the circle, ready to begin the ritual.

Afterwards they'd walked home together, and Beth felt a new peace. She hadn't realised how desperate she'd been for Rose's approval, how scared she'd been of her potential anger. Tipping her head back, she stared up at the tranquil sea of stars arching above them.

"It's a beautiful sky," Mike said softly.

Smiling, she turned to him and saw the starlight reflected in his eyes, pools of silver and black deeper than the ocean. She wanted to dive into them and stay there, caught in this perfect moment of love and acceptance.

When he bent down and kissed her, she happily felt herself drawn under, losing herself in their love and passion.

Rhiannon picked up her bag, jolting Beth back to the present, and she wondered again what was making her daughter so sad. Hopefully the holiday would cheer her up. France had woven a spell around her own heart twenty years ago, and she was sure it could do the same for her daughter.

After her first year of university in London, Beth had set off for the summer break with her friend Priya and some of the guys who had crammed into their sprawling, falling-down London share house. They wanted to celebrate their exam results, practise their French, and see a little of the world.

One of the guys knew of a farm offering summer work, so they stayed there for a few weeks, picking fruit by day, watching their skin tan in the warmth of the sun, and sitting around a campfire each night drinking wine and imagining all the futures they wanted to dream into being.

All her life, Beth had felt lost. Her teenage years were consumed by the driving need to escape her family, and her family's expectations, in order to find herself. But at university she'd flourished, surrounded by fellow seekers, fellow searchers. New friends who accepted her as she was, and liked her for her self. France was another awakening. She met more new people, and felt herself shedding a skin that had restricted and repressed her all her life.

While Priya spent her holiday reading text books for the coming school year, Beth went on adventures with others from the farm. She watched French movies at a tiny cinema, and did a French cooking class in a cute little cafe. She got a lift to the beach one weekend and spent the whole time between sand and sea, soaking up the salt and the sunshine, laughing in delight as the waves broke over her head and she swam in the ocean believed to hold a lost civilisation beneath its surface. She danced in a green field under the full moon, and hiked out to a nearby waterfall rich in legend, where she was the only one with the courage to dive into the icy waters said to be home to an impish water sprite. She soaked up every new experience like a desert sponge, and loved the sense of freedom and daring that cloaked her.

As summer softened towards autumn, her housemates returned to London, but Beth put her studies on hold and stayed, joining new friends to hitchhike around the countryside. Priya tried to convince her to return, to not delay her education, but Beth was too enchanted to listen. She was falling into the patterns and rhythms of nature, feeling a new energy and a new sense of identity as she became the free spirit she'd always yearned to be. No longer tied down by expectations or deadlines, schedules or responsibilities.

She loved that some days she had no idea where they'd sleep that night. Adored the out-of-the-way campsites and occasional youth hostels they stumbled upon. And she was deeply inspired by the late-night gatherings, heart aflame as she argued history, politics and philosophy under the stars, and began to define the things she believed and those she could discard. Most of all she loved being challenged by people who'd grown up in other countries, in other family situations, with religious and spiritual beliefs so different to the ones she was trying to unshackle herself from. Slowly she began to understand the things that mattered to her, and what would give meaning to her life.

When she'd set out on her French adventure with Priya, she'd had no concept of spirituality other than the cruel brand of religion her mother pedalled. Yet as she walked the land and lived by the cycles of sun rise and moon set, a new awareness dawned within her, and in the mist- and myth-drenched forests of Brittany she felt real magic for the first time.

Wandering along twisting woodland paths, she was filled with a new confidence and belief in herself. Breathing in the scent of decay and rebirth, and gazing on tiny scampering creatures and vividly-hued flowers, the numinous swirled around her. Passing under ancient trees, she was filled with a presence that was somehow Other, and a rush of energy that came from the earth itself, which flooded her body with power and peace, and a strange sense of knowing. A new connection with the divine, and with her self.

Would her daughter feel it too?

Chapter 23

A Storm of Tears

Rhiannon

Jolting awake from a nightmare, Rhiannon opened her eyes wide, disoriented to find herself in pitch darkness. The wisps of her dreamscape clung to her like hungry ghosts, vague but unsettling. Yet when she finally managed to force them away, a new horror threatened to consume her whole. She and Tom had unfortunately had their first fight yesterday – if you could call her immature tantrum that – and she had no idea whether they were still together, or when she would see him again. If she ever did.

A storm of tears brewed within her, of rage and frustration, and self-loathing. It was her fault. She'd ruined everything. Tom had been perfectly reasonable, and she was a jealous fool, driving him away and destroying their beautiful relationship.

When her dad knocked on her door, she wanted to scream. She settled for throwing a pillow across the room, which did make her feel slightly better. Then she groaned. She didn't want to go away for two weeks when she desperately needed to see Tom and sort things out.

*Life was so unfair.*

"You all packed darling?" her father asked as he opened the door. "Brittany awaits!"

Rhiannon forced a smile, and told him she was. "I'll be down in five minutes, yeah?"

Throwing on the jeans from her floor, she pulled a long-sleeved top over her head, then slumped back onto her bed. She was so torn, her insides at war. She knew how much Brodie was looking forward to their trip, and she wanted to be a good sister and be enthusiastic for him. But this was the worst time to not be able to see Tom. What if he couldn't be bothered with her now, after yesterday's outburst? What if he forgot her, or met someone more exciting, someone who lived closer to him? What if she'd pushed him into Marie's arms despite him never considering it before? Yet she couldn't refuse to go to France. If only there holiday was at *any* other time.

Sighing, she picked up the photo of Tom from her bedside table, and traced the angles of his face. Tried to convince herself she was being irrational now, that of course he would forgive her foolishness, and not hold it against her. That he would be waiting for her when she returned, eager to see her. But as the darkness pressed in on her, her fears and doubts only grew.

Hearing her name called, she reluctantly picked up her bag and dragged herself downstairs. Maybe she would feel a little less miserable once the sun rose. The darkness of 5am was pressing in on her, exacerbating every black thought, and she was grumbling more than usual as she staggered into the kitchen and filled the kettle.

"Morning Rhi-Rhi!" Brodie said as he charged in after her, excitement in his voice.

She glared at him. "Hey."

He giggled as he grabbed a bowl from the cupboard and poured in some muesli. "How come you're so grumpy this morning?"

"It's hardly morning," she groaned. "Look, it's still pitch black out there. It's night-time. People should be in bed."

"You can sleep in the car if you must," her dad retorted as he walked in, sounding just as amused as her brother.

*Great, she was surrounded by the chirpy dawn chorus.*

Pouring a huge mug of coffee, she slumped into a chair and slugged it back, shaking her head when her brother offered her the cereal. "Not hungry."

Her dad laughed. "So, how will you and Tom survive without each other for two whole weeks?" he teased.

"I'm sure *he'll* be fine," she muttered. Then she mentally shook herself. She couldn't take her anger out on her family. It wasn't their fault. Time to make an effort to look a little more alive, and act a little more excited.

"Sorry, it's just been a crazy term," she said, gulping down more of her favourite brew. "I guess we should get this adventure started."

Brodie cheered, swallowed his last mouthful of cereal, then took his plate to the sink and washed it, before drying it and putting it away. "Ready!"

*When had he become so grown up?*

It was still dark when they stowed their bags in the car and piled in, but the glittering stars overhead lifted Rhiannon's mood. The still-asleep world was starkly beautiful, and she drew comfort from its shadows. For the first hour of the drive south to the ferry she dozed, trying to picture her and Tom reunited while pushing off the ghosts of her nightmare. But by quarter past six a faint glow began on the eastern horizon, and she gave up on sleep and focused on that.

The loveliness of the sky as it slowly lightened, transforming from black to grey to the palest shade of lavender, then through the whole spectrum of pink-yellow-orange as the sun spilled fingers of gold over the horizon, soothed her spirit. And while her heart still felt empty and scared about the yawning abyss of time before she'd see Tom again, a sliver of anticipation for their approaching journey finally stirred in her heart.

"So, Tom seems really nice," her dad said awkwardly.

"Uh-huh." She peered at him. How long had he been working up the courage to mention her boyfriend?

"And you did the right thing. I know I should be all modern and hip, and not admit to any concerns, but when he first walked in, it helped to know that he's Richard's grandson. Once we'd talked for a while I realised he was lovely in his own right, and it quickly became clear how much he cares about you, but for that first initial shock of meeting a new boyfriend? That was comforting."

Rhiannon winced. "Yeah, I'm sorry I ambushed you like that. I wasn't really sure how to bring it up."

"No darling, it's me who should apologise. I'm sorry we can't make it to Paris this trip to see Tom. And I'm even sorrier your mum isn't here to meet him. And, well, to help me deal with how grown up you suddenly are. But she would be so proud of you. And I am too."

"Thanks Dad."

He reached over and squeezed her hand, then they both lapsed into silence, lost in memories of Beth and how much they still missed her.

The ferry ride across the English Channel was rough, and Rhiannon held Brodie as he threw up over the railing, then smoothed back his hair and got him some water. "I shouldn't have had the orange juice," he whimpered, misery radiating from him in waves. "That's all I can taste now."

"I'm so sorry, buddy," she said sympathetically. "But we're nearly there. At least this is the quickest route – imagine if we were on the eleven-hour crossing!"

Brodie's face turned green at the thought, and she gave him a gentle hug while supporting his weight against the railing. The cold fresh air made both of them feel better, and they stayed out there for the rest of the journey, eyes on the horizon, faces lifted to the invigorating breeze.

As the ferry finally approached the French harbour of Cherbourg, their dad came up from below to announce he'd finished the last of his work, and was free for the next two weeks. "Now our holiday can really begin," he announced, and Brodie managed a wan smile.

When the ferry docked and they headed into the ship's belly to claim their car, they all felt a little green and wobbly.

"I know it's been a long day already, and you've both been very patient," their dad said. "Shall we stop in this town for lunch, and to get our balance back after the boat? There's a gorgeous old castle with pretty gardens on the outskirts of town, so we could have a picnic there. Do you think you could eat something buddy?"

Brodie rubbed his tummy contemplatively, then nodded. "As soon as we're on solid ground I'm sure I'll be able to have a bite or two."

By the time they got to the chateau, his appetite had more than returned, and he managed to polish off an egg and salad sandwich, a serve of hot chips, and half his dad's pie. Rhiannon was relieved that he felt better, and glad to finally eat too. Skipping breakfast when they got up eight hours ago hadn't been her wisest decision.

After wandering around the grounds, they hit the road for the two-hour journey south, keen to get to Mont-Saint-Michel before darkness fell. She let her brother have the front seat, and their dad turned up the music and sang in a loud and terrible but amusing voice, with Brodie joining in where he could. Tired and dispirited as Rhiannon was, their relentless cheerfulness eventually began to amuse her, and she figured she could probably survive two weeks.

The whole world was soaked in the rich golden light of late afternoon when they approached the bay where Normandy and Brittany merge, and saw the small island crowned with a gothic granite basilica in the distance. Rhiannon was enchanted. It had been a place of Christian pilgrimage for more than a thousand years, but their church buildings were constructed where the Celts had earlier worshipped their sun deity Belenus, and the Romans had built a shrine to Jupiter, king of their gods.

As they got closer, details revealed themselves. Rising up out of the white sand beach, the rocky tidal island was surrounded by battlements and ramparts, with a tumble of stone buildings spiralling up the hill, and the huge, sweeping abbey perched on top, its dark steeple reaching to the heavens. Water lapped the shore, and for the moment it was almost cut off from the mainland.

After checking into their hotel, with its gorgeous views of the ancient fortress, they set off to explore, crossing the causeway that had been revealed as the tide went out, and charmed by the historic buildings and vibe of the place. The cobbled spiral path that snaked up and around the island to the top was steep, but the little shops and cafes along the route were so captivating that they barely noticed.

When they chose a restaurant for dinner and sat at the small table with candles and a red-and-white checked tablecloth, a wave of emotion rolled over Rhiannon and almost drowned her. She could practically see her mum sitting in the fourth chair, telling them about her adventures in France before she'd settled down in their village, raising a glass of red wine in a toast to her husband.

Swallowing down the tears that thickened in her throat, she tried to be brave for her dad, who seemed to be similarly affected by the atmosphere of the eatery, their location on French soil, and his swirling memories of past love.

"Will we get to visit the castle at the top?" Brodie asked, breaking the silence that had settled over them.

Rhiannon grinned at the shocked glance of the waiter as he deposited a basket of bread on their table. "It's an abbey buddy, like a church or cathedral, but yes, we'll be able to go up there tomorrow and check it out. It will be an amazing view if nothing else," she said.

"But it looks like a castle from a faery tale!" Brodie insisted.

Chuckling in agreement, she offered him the bread basket and nodded. "That it does. And some would say it's just as magical as a faerytale castle, with religious visions, holy pilgrimages and spiritual epiphanies all taking place there over thousands of years, while the whole island dipped in and out of the mists."

That night Rhiannon's dreams were filled with chases up rocky paths, crucifixions, cliff falls, knights battling dragons, and herself locked up in a stone tower atop a rocky island, cut off from the world and all who loved her. When she jolted awake just before dawn, she wrapped the quilt around her and slipped quietly outside onto their balcony, too scared to drop back to sleep again and fall back into her nightmares.

Focusing on her breathing, she slowly calmed down. The view out over the ocean was stunning. Fog surrounded the island, obscuring it from sight, but every now and then the mists shifted, and a stone building or a turret appeared briefly before being hidden again. Brodie was right, it really did look like a faerytale castle from an ethereal realm, a place of myth and legend, and she shivered at how isolated it must have been during storms, when it was cut off from the mainland for long periods of time.

When she heard her dad and her brother stir, she went back inside, and they ate a quick breakfast in their room before heading out.

The fog had been burned away by the weak sunshine and blown away by the icy wind, and the old stone walls of the island were revealed in all their ancient splendour. Rhiannon shivered as they hurried across the exposed causeway, but it was from more than just the weather. Like the previous night, she could almost see her mother with them. Feel her comforting presence. Imagine her voice as she told them stories of magic and mystery.

As they climbed, it suddenly hit her how courageous her mother had been to stay in France on her own after her housemates went back to London for university. Here she was, lamenting two weeks away from her boyfriend, when her mother had spent months at a time on her own, or with strangers. Being brave. Being fearless. Being herself. Yesterday she'd complained about having to get out of bed early, while her mum had camped out in the middle of nowhere without a tent. While she whinged about the car ride and the comfortable ferry, her mum had hitchhiked around the country at the whim of whoever picked her up.

"Sorry I was such a baby yesterday Dad," she muttered.

He smiled at her. "You were fine. What made you say that?"

"I was just thinking about Mum, and how brave she was to travel on her own, without a plan, just turning up somewhere and trusting the universe would provide. Trusting her fate to whoever stopped to give her a ride, whichever farmer was offering money to pick fruit, or letting her sleep in their barn. I'm a complete wuss in comparison."

"Bravery comes in many forms darling."

Rhiannon shrugged. "I don't know about that. I've had it so easy compared to her, what with her awful childhood and cruel parents, yet I moan about the smallest thing."

"Hey!" Mike halted in the middle of the path and put his hands on her shoulders. "Darling, you lost your mother at sixteen, which is horrifyingly traumatic. And the way you've handled it has been inspiring, brave and incredibly mature."

She laughed, but there was a bitter edge to the sound. "That's not true. I fell apart for three months after Mum died, and was rude and crabby, and incredibly unhelpful, right when you and Brodie needed me the most. I can never forgive myself for that." Sadness swamped her, and she wanted to climb back into her hotel bed, drag the covers over her head and cry. Would the shame she felt over those lost months ever ease?

"Oh darling, you have to let that go. You were drowning in grief and trying to cope any way you could. And since then you've been the most amazing help to me, and such a wonderful, supportive sister. Brodie and I know how lucky we are to have you, and I won't hear another word against you."

Behind them, Brodie called out, and they turned around to see him with his face pressed to a shop window. "Look Dad! It's a kit to make your very own castle, um, I mean abbey. And a chocolate version as well. Can we go in and have a look?"

"Absolutely buddy, although shall we do it on the way back down the hill, so we don't have to carry it all the way up?"

"Yippee! Does that mean we can buy it?"

Mike laughed. "We can certainly go in and check it out. Now, do you need a piggyback for a little while?"

"Yes please. My legs are getting tired."

Rhiannon grinned at her brother, and followed him and their dad the rest of the way up the steep slope. It was beautiful at the summit, with amazing views back over the salt marshes of Normandy, and a fascinating huddle of buildings ahead of them. The weight of the ages pressed down on her as she explored, guide map in hand. The Romanesque church was impressive, the crypts and chapels built beneath it a little creepy, and the refectory and cloisters very moving. And Brodie was right – the courtyards, towers and ramparts did make it feel like a castle, although the golden statue of Saint Michael fighting the devil in the form of a dragon atop the spire reinforced its modern religious meaning.

It was Michael, according to legend, who had prompted construction of the first shrine early in the eighth century. A few hundred years later it became home to a community of Benedictine monks, then in the thirteenth century, the French king gave money so the monastic settlement could be expanded, and the beautiful gothic abbey that still crowns the summit was built.

The following century, the Hundred Years War led to the walls and many of the military constructions being added, which allowed it to survive a thirty-year siege. In the late 1700s, during the French Revolution, the abbey was secularised and used as a prison. And then, fifty years ago, a small group of monks and nuns returned the sanctuary to its original purpose, and now reside there once more, living the monastic life and giving tours.

Rhiannon was surprised to feel so much as she explored, although perhaps it was as much due to the island being located along the Apollo and Athena ley lines as its religious history. These lines of energy link sacred sites from Ireland to Cornwall to France, then down through Italy, Greece and the Greek Islands to Israel, stirring emotion and new knowledge in many. The thought of earth energies and druidic knowledge stirred a great longing in her, kick-starting her Tom obsession again, and reminding her how foolish she'd been.

Regret was starting to poison her and make her limbs heavy when Brodie sank onto a bench and announced he couldn't walk another step. Their dad leaned down so he could clamber onto his back, and they made their way back down the steep pathway for a late lunch, before popping into the store to buy the promised abbey kit and the abbey-shaped chocolate.

Then they hit the road again, heading off to the gorgeous cathedral town of Rennes, the capital of Brittany. Rhiannon loved their two nights there, and all the beautiful old buildings they walked past, but she couldn't wait to get to Paimpont, the tiny village on the edge of Broceliande Forest. She knew how much her mum had loved it there, and it had long haunted her imagination.

Chapter 24

# Written In the Leaves

### Rhiannon

A shiver of anticipation ran up Rhiannon's spine as they drove along the winding road through the enchanted forest of Broceliande. The ancient woodland was shrouded in mystery and magic, a shadowy realm of mist and myth, of chateaus on lakes, and lords who still hunted stags and wild boar. Thousand-year-old beech, oak and chestnut trees met overhead to form a shaded canopy, leaning in close to each other to whisper their secrets and protect their inhabitants. Lush green ivy curled around wide oak trunks, and deep emerald moss covered intricately twisted tree roots, providing the perfect hiding place for tiny creatures. Even the light seemed different, filtering through the greenery overhead and imbuing everything with a shimmering golden glow.

The mist-wreathed woods had long been considered the realm of faeries and Otherworldly beings. Of kings and queens, druids and knights, and figures of legends long lost. A place of pilgrimage for nature lovers, pagans, and those lured by its secretive beauty and the possibility of an encounter with the fae.

Rhiannon giggled. Would she meet a faery here? Find Viviane's fountain of eternal youth? Come across King Arthur's sister Morgaine? Stumble over Merlin's tomb?

"What are you laughing about?" her dad asked.

"Sorry, just wondering if I'll run into a faery queen. Isn't that what they say about this forest?"

Mike shrugged. "Don't be too sure you won't. Your mum had so many tales of magical encounters in this forest, and I don't think she even told me the strangest ones."

"Did you ever mind, the life she lived before you were together? The travelling, the adventures?"

"Not at all. Beth had a really tough childhood, but she said it was her time in France that allowed her to put it behind her. To let go of her bitterness and anger. All the experiences she had here, and the people she met, they made her who she was. Made her happier, and more able to love and be loved. She told me once that she wasn't sure she would have been capable of opening her heart to me, to all of us, without it. I remember – Hold on!"

Slamming on the brakes as a deer bounded out of the woods, her dad checked to see if she was okay, then laughed under his breath.

"What are *you* laughing about?" Rhiannon asked, heart racing. "We almost hit it!"

"Sorry, it's just that your mum had an encounter with a deer when we were in the Lake District on our honeymoon, and a long conversation with Elen of the Ways. It's like she's always with us isn't it, always managing to get a message to us that she's here in spirit."

Rhiannon wasn't convinced her mother would send a wild animal they almost crashed into as a sign, but she didn't want to disappoint her father by arguing. And she had felt her mother's presence, or something like it, in Mont-Saint-Michel, so who was she to judge?

Before she could reply, Brodie woke up, and sleepily asked if they were there yet.

Their dad grinned. "Actually yes, we'll be arriving any minute."

Right on cue, the sign to Paimpont appeared, and they turned off the highway. Rhiannon gasped. It was beautiful. A tiny village on the shore of a lake, at the edge of the forest, with a few sweet, old-fashioned buildings, and streets named after faeries. Her dad pulled up outside the tourist office and went in to get the keys to their place, a cute little house called Chalet of the Goblins, in walking distance of the lake and the abbey the town was built around.

After they unloaded their bags, Mike suggested that Rhiannon head out to explore, while he and Brodie bought groceries and made dinner. She tried to refuse, to insist on helping, but Brodie was proud to have a task, so she eventually shrugged and headed off before anyone changed their mind.

Late afternoon sunlight bathed the village in a gorgeous golden glow, and she breathed in the peace and magic gratefully, feeling it soothe her, body and soul. Time folded around her, and she marvelled that her mum had walked this same street when she was around her age. But Beth had been on her own, with barely any money and only limited French, with no plan, no back-up, no friendly face to encourage her. The comparison made Rhiannon feel young and naive, and reminded her all over again of how she'd left things with Tom. How could she have been so stupid?

Wandering through the grounds of the abbey, she continued to berate herself. If only she'd held her tongue, accepted his reassurance. Why had she instantly become so jealous? She groaned as she recalled the hurt on his face when she'd accused him of lying, and how crestfallen he'd been when she ignored his comment about seeing each other when she got home.

Shoulders slumped with misery, Rhiannon trudged back towards the chalet, eyes on the pavement, until a flickering light made her look up. There was a cute little shop tucked away down a small lane, with baskets filled with flowers suspended around the doorway, and a candelabra within. Bunches of dried herbs hung in the window, and there was an enticing display of magical books, crystals and jewellery below them. When she noticed a chalkboard offering tea-leaf readings, she shrugged and pushed open the door. She didn't really believe you could see your fortune in the bottom of a teacup, but if there was even a tiny chance of gaining some illumination on her situation with Tom, it was worth a go.

Gentle music and a soothing incense blend wafted around her as she entered, setting her mind at ease. Rose burned a blend just like it at some of her rituals.

A woman with long dark hair, wearing an emerald green velvet dress, looked up and smiled as she walked in. "Bonsoir, bienvenue," she greeted her.

"Hello," Rhiannon replied, kicking herself that she didn't have her French dictionary on her.

"Ah, welcome," the woman added, in sweetly accented English. "How may I help you?"

Rhiannon smiled and moved forward, then froze as the woman's face went white. She looked like she'd seen a ghost.

"Beth?"

A chill spread over Rhiannon at the sound of her mother's name, and she turned to flee, but the woman came out from behind the counter and touched her arm before she could.

"I am so sorry. Please forgive me, of course you are not Beth, she would be a middle-aged woman by now, like me. My sincere apologies, you just remind me of a girl I once knew."

"Beth is my mother," Rhiannon said softly. "She stayed here twenty years ago. Well, in this village anyway."

The woman laughed. "No, she actually did stay right here, in the room upstairs. My old room. Oh, I would love to see her again. Is she here with you? For how long are you visiting Paimpont?"

Rhiannon's face crumpled. "Um, no, she's not here. Mum died. My dad and my brother and I are retracing her footsteps, trying to feel closer to her, or something…" She trailed off, desperately wanting to escape this awkward situation, yet rooted to the spot, somehow compelled to learn all she could from this stranger.

Stricken, the woman took her hand. "Je suis vraiment desole," she whispered. "I am so sorry."

Tilting her head in acknowledgement, Rhiannon tried to remember her mum's stories. This must be the shop where she'd been taken in by Celia, offered room and board for a few hours of work a day. But Celia was dead too, wasn't she? A vague memory of her mum receiving a package from France, with a letter of farewell from her old friend, flitted into her mind.

"Lavender and lemon cake," she muttered. The recipe was in that package – and Rose had appeared a few minutes later with the same cake, still warm from the oven, freaking Beth out at the synchronicity. "Mum knew Celia, is that right?"

The woman nodded. "Oui. I worked here with Celia, goddess bless her soul, back then. And you are right, Celia was famous for her lavender and lemon cake."

All of a sudden Rhiannon could taste it, the sharpness of the lemon, the sweetness of the lavender. Reminded of the cake Richard had baked for the new moon ritual, she looked around, wondering if it was physical reality or something else flooding her senses.

"I make it now also," the woman said, gesturing to the far end of the counter, where a coffee machine and a cake stand stood. "Would you like a slice?"

"I'm okay," Rhiannon said, too embarrassed to accept. Part of her still wanted to run from... who was this woman? Awkwardly she introduced herself, hoping the stranger would respond in kind.

"Hello Rhiannon, it is a pleasure to make your acquaintance. Apologies, I am Jessica," the woman said.

"Hi Jessica. So, um, what was Mum like when you knew her?"

"Sadly I only met her briefly. Beth slept in my room while I was away, helping out in my absence. Celia offered for her to stay longer, to stay with us, but she said she had to move on. We spent a few days here, the three of us, before she headed for Paris. She was so wonderful, so carefree. And I never got to thank her."

Mystified, Rhiannon stared at her. "What for?"

"Your mother gave me the most amazing tea-leaf reading – it was so profound. I was going to leave Celia and move to the Auvergne to marry my boyfriend, but Beth told me not to do it. She said he was bad news."

Rhiannon gasped. Her mum never made black and white pronouncements, or told anyone what to do, or even suggested a solution. When she did oracle card readings, she shared the messages she got, offered the wisdom she'd learned, and presented all the options and their consequences, but she always insisted that the person make their own decision and come to their own conclusion. Was this why? Had she thought this reading of hers was wrong?

"How did you know she was right?"

Jessica smiled. "I didn't believe her at first, because I didn't want to know," she confessed. "I continued with my wedding plans, but a month later I found out he'd been cheating on me with a woman from his work. When I confronted him, he swore black and blue that nothing had happened, told me I was crazy, was imagining things, and convinced me it was my own flaws that made me suspicious of him. Then the night before the ceremony, the woman came to see me. She admitted they'd started an affair while they were away on a business trip, and said he'd promised her that nothing would change – that even after the wedding, they would still be together."

The floor tilted under Rhiannon, and her world started to spin. Cheating with a workmate on a business trip. "Where was the trip?" she whispered, although she knew the answer before Jessica said it.

"Paris."

For a long moment she struggled to breathe. Jessica caught her arm, steadied her, then led her to a chair. "Tea?"

"Do you have coffee?"

"Of course." While Jessica bustled around behind the counter making their drinks and cutting them both large slices of cake, Rhiannon tried to convince herself the story had nothing to do with her. Tom was not like this woman's ex-boyfriend. *She* was not like Jessica. She wasn't even French, for a start. But it niggled at her. Had she been drawn into this shop to hear this woman's story? Was it the universe's way of warning her?

A rush of sadness swept over her, but the aroma of the coffee momentarily lifted her spirits. It was wonderful, thick and strong, with a dollop of cream on top. The cake was delicious too, light and sweet and tart all at once. Jessica made small talk as they ate, telling her about a trip to England she'd taken a few years ago, then reminiscing about being trained by Celia to take over the store as well as her ritual circle after she died.

As Rhiannon gulped the last sip of coffee, Jessica took a deep breath, and a tentative look flashed in her eyes.

"Forgive me for saying so, but you looked sad when you walked in, non?"

Rhiannon grimaced. "I'm okay."

"I could do a coffee reading for you if you would like. No charge. I never got to thank your mother for my reading, so it would be an honour to do one for you."

A chill was numbing Rhiannon's fingers and toes, ice was settling in the pit of her stomach, and dread was creeping up her spine. "Thank you, that's very kind, but I really should get back," she stammered. "Dad will be wondering where I am."

"Aucun probleme," Jessica said kindly. "No problem. I will be here tomorrow if you change your mind."

Abruptly Rhiannon stood up, and searched her pockets for money for the coffee and cake.

"Non, non, it is my pleasure," Jessica insisted. "Please, to honour your mother."

Tears started to well, at this woman's kindness and the memories of her mother she was stirring, and Rhiannon muttered her thanks and ran out into the swirling darkness.

## Chapter 25

# The Witch In the Woods

### Beth

**P**ain needled at the jagged edges of Beth's awareness. She'd been swamped with relief when she made it across the ocean with her little family, after fearing she would be left stranded on the shore, yet it had been so frustrating to watch them climbing the steep path of Mont-Saint-Michel and exploring the narrow cobblestone streets without her. Exquisite torture to see them arrive in the tiny village of Paimpont, with its faerytale forest and the piece of her soul she'd left there so long ago.

And now, as she followed Rhiannon into The Magic Teapot, she was almost torn apart with longing. This was the place Celia had opened up to her, offering shelter, love and knowledge to a young English girl so bereft of wisdom and experience when she'd arrived, who blossomed in her presence, and in her encounters with the fae folk in the forest of enchantment.

It was lovely that Jessica was still there, running the store, doing the psychic readings and retaining its witchy origins, and it made her happy to learn that she'd helped her avoid a doomed marriage. But it was Celia who Beth couldn't stop thinking about. The woman who had meant so much to her, who had shaped her into the person she became, and helped her open her heart to love – of the friend, the mentor and the romantic kind.

"Excusez-moi?" Beth called out apologetically as she nervously entered the tiny village store. Her French was improving, but guilt still plagued her for not being fluent. It felt rude. The woman who emerged from the back room smiled at her and replied in strongly accented English.

"Welcome to Broceliande, Mademoiselle. My name is Celia. How may I help you?"

Beth shrugged, embarrassed. She didn't have much money, and the only hotel she'd passed was clearly way out of her price range. "I was wondering if there was anywhere to stay around here, just somewhere small..." Trailing off, she tried to fight the panic threatening to engulf her. She'd thought the friends she'd been travelling with were coming back for her tomorrow – until she checked her French dictionary, and realised they wouldn't be back for weeks.

The woman came around the counter, holding out her hand to her, and Beth smiled at her kind eyes and the tiny sweet-smelling flowers entwined in her long red braid. There was incense burning, and as she breathed it in, Beth felt calmer and more at ease. Less like an outsider or interloper. Less scared and awkward.

"I have a small room upstairs you are welcome to stay in for a few weeks," Celia offered. "The young woman who usually lives with me, and helps me in the shop, is away for a month."

Beth's whole body exhaled in relief. Yet could it really be that easy? How much would it cost? And was it safe? No one even knew she was here. What if this kindly woman wasn't as sweet as she seemed?

"There is no pressure," Celia said, eyes twinkling with mischief when Beth stared at her in alarm.

*Had she read her mind?*

"If you are able to help me a few hours a day in the shop, there will be no charge for room and board. But if you do not have time for that, I am sure we can come to some arrangement on a price."

"Oh no, I'm more than happy to help, if I can be of any use to you," Beth said quickly. "I have no real plans, and nowhere I need to be any time soon." She gulped. Was that wise to admit?

"Well, um, Mademoiselle –?" Celia gazed at her expectantly.

"Sorry, I'm Beth, and thank you for your kind offer. I would be honoured to accept."

Celia smiled. "Would you like a cup of tea Beth?"

Nodding gratefully, she followed her new friend behind the purple velvet curtain and out to a charming stone kitchen. A large kettle was perched over an old iron stove, and bunches of herbs hung from hooks in the low ceiling. Celia took a ceramic teapot painted with violets from a shelf, spooned in tea leaves from a glass jar, then filled it with boiling water. Next she pulled two pretty floral cups with matching saucers down from a cupboard and set them on the deeply scarred wooden table, then added a still-warm cake that smelled of lemon and lavender.

"Have a seat," she said, as she filled a pretty jug with milk from a glass bottle in the fridge.

Nervously Beth sat down. Her head spun as she tried to catch up with what was happening. She'd just accepted a month-long job she had no idea about, working with a stranger in a hippie shop in a tiny village of French speakers.

"There is no need to worry," Celia said, voice gentle. "The shop is not so busy during the autumn. And some of our days will be spent tending the garden, or out in the forest, gathering herbs. You may do as much or as little as you wish."

Summoning a smile, Beth cautiously took a sip of the strong tea and a bite of the delicious cake, then listened eagerly as the owner told her about the store. The Magic Teapot sold Celia's herbal potions, bath salts, medicines and freshly blended teas, along with a small range of homemade foods, local art and gifts, and she performed divination and tea-leaf readings too. Beth was fascinated, and nodded shyly when asked if she would like one.

"Okay, if you would take your last sip, I will spin your cup like this, then turn it over..." she explained, as she did just that. "And now I examine the patterns of the leaves left within."

As Celia gazed into the cup, Beth examined her, taking in the long, dark red hair, the pretty, softly flowing velvet dress, the silver charm bracelet that tinkled when she moved. She looked wild and mysterious, but kind. Someone her mother would loathe. A witch in a little stone cottage on the edge of the forest, but one with a heart of gold instead of bad intentions.

When Celia looked up and caught her eye, she gave an amused, knowing smile, as though she'd heard her thoughts. Yet she didn't criticise her, or deny it was true.

"Do not fear Beth. No harm will come to you here, and if you are open to it, you will find immense healing in these woods, and discover new parts of yourself. It is no accident that you find yourself in Paimpont, despite feeling as though you were stranded here, and deserted by your friends."

Beth gulped. That's exactly what she'd been thinking.

"You are supposed to be here right now, on your own, to give you the time and space to grow into yourself, and to assimilate all the things you have been learning and feeling and experiencing over the summer. There is a magical heart beating within you, and a healer's affinity with nature and the earth. You will learn much from the forest here, and although it won't make sense to you for a long time, there is peace for you in the countryside."

Beth frowned. She'd grown up in the countryside, and there had been no peace in her childhood. Give her a big city any day.

As though she'd spoken aloud, Celia smiled. "Four weeks here will be perfect. There is love and fulfilment for you in Paris, but first you must be ready."

By the third day, Beth was rising before the sun peeked above the horizon, as Celia did, and joining her new friend for a gentle yoga and meditation session before she tried to assist her in baking breakfast croissants – two each for them, and the rest for the succession of locals who popped in each morning for tea or coffee and a chat.

On the fifth day, Celia invited Beth on one of her foraging expeditions into the forest, and she fell in love with its deep and ancient power. The following morning, when she was given the day off, Beth borrowed her new friend's bicycle and pedalled out to explore the twisting wooded paths for herself.

It was breathtakingly beautiful, but within an hour she realised she was completely lost, and it was a struggle not to descend into blind panic. The forest was huge, and dark, so she couldn't see ahead or behind her. Celia trusted her to find her way though, and for some reason had faith in her competence, so Beth closed her eyes, took a deep breath, and forced herself to focus.

At first all she was aware of was bird song, and a soft rustling in the undergrowth that she hoped was just the passing of a small and harmless creature. Then she felt the sun on her face, and heard the soothing burbling of water. Following the sound, she stumbled upon a small spring. Was this Viviane's legendary Fontaine de Jouvence, the Fountain of Eternal Youth, which she'd read about in one of the books in Celia's cosy study?

Sinking to the ground, she felt the energy of the earth pulsating through her, and sensed the power of the water even before she ran her fingers through its icy flow. A high-pitched laugh startled her, and she gazed up to see a woman gliding towards her, a flowing silver dress billowing around her body, and long black hair swirling in the breeze that had sprung up.

"Dearest, you are not lost," she said, her voice deep and imposing. "You are just beginning to find yourself. And you must stay strong and be brave, because it can be painful, and challenging, but it is always worth it. To discover the truth of who you are is the greatest gift of all."

Startled, Beth gaped at her. "Um, how can I ever know that? How can anyone know that?" Who was this woman? Where had she come from? *How did she know anything about her?*

A smile flickered across the woman's face, somewhere between haughty and encouraging. "By doing what you are doing now Beth. Opening yourself to new experiences. Encountering people you imagine are so different to you, so strange, yet are not. Being alone with yourself, and examining your life and your choices."

*That didn't sound so hard.*

"And for you dear one, it is also about letting go. Releasing the pain and anger you are holding on to. The bitterness you feel towards your parents."

Suspicion flared in Beth's heart, and she stared at the silver-clad figure, unsettled. Had Celia told people about Beth? But the sweet French woman didn't know anything about the mother she was fleeing on this haphazard adventure. She gulped. The thought unnerved her. Was that the real reason she hadn't returned to England? Why she'd put her studies on hold to traipse around a foreign land, with no plans, and no point? Was this whole spontaneous journey just a cop out, rather than the brave, carefree quest she'd envisioned? Was she taking the easy way out by running away, instead of facing the cause of her pain?

The woman's face gentled. "Dear Beth, that is not what was meant. This haphazard adventure, as you call it, is very important. It is the best way to discover who you really are, and what you are capable of, without the limits others have set on you. Relying on yourself. Getting to know yourself. Meeting new people you can tell about who you are – who you want to be – in your own words, from your heart." She smiled. "And soaking up the healing power of this forest, this land and this water, that will help too."

Her eyes flickered down to the spring, and Beth shook her head. This couldn't really be the Fountain of Eternal Youth, could it? That was just a story. Yet if it was true, did that make the being standing before her Viviane? Priestess, fae queen, consort of Merlin?

This time the woman's laugh was impatient, even a little sinister. "People are fools to think that simply drinking some water will restore their youth or make them immortal, when they do not even know what to do with the life they have."

"So no restorative powers, no elixir of life?" Beth asked, surprised to find she was disappointed there was no truth to the legend.

What else had she read? One book referred to the fountain as the holy grail, but she was too scared to ask about that.

The strange being heard her question though. Sighing dramatically, she fixed Beth with a steely, impatient gaze. "Yes, it has been referred to as the holy grail, but the grail is about knowledge, and wisdom. It is about understanding yourself and your purpose so that your life is *full*. Not a longer life, or immortal life, but a richer, more *meaningful* life. Which is infinitely more precious."

Bristling at the scolding, Beth focused back on the water, and was instantly calmer. Perhaps that was all she needed, the calm of nature, the mental head space to look within.

"Now you are beginning to understand," the woman said approvingly. "Connecting with nature will help you connect with yourself. All waters can be healing, when you connect with the spirit of the element. Sacred springs, sacred wells, sacred fountains, sacred oceans too. The waters in this forest will help wash away what you no longer need. And this fountain, *my* fountain," she continued with a sly smile, "it is about forgiveness, letting go with compassion, and not letting bitterness weigh you down. Release your anger and your bitterness here, let it flow away with the sacred water, and feel yourself washed clean and pure."

"Celia, do you really believe in magic?"

The older woman regarded her coolly. "Don't you?"

Beth laughed. Then stopped abruptly. Gulped. "You're serious?"

Celia pointed at the bunches of herbs hanging above them. "What do you think they do? They help and heal, and soothe and nourish, and it's the magic of the earth, the life force of the land and the plants, that does that. We're all linked together, plants, animals, people, elements."

"Elements?" The strange woman she'd met in the forest had used that word too.

Celia smiled. "You'll learn all of this soon, I can see it, so there's no need to rush. But everything is made up of the four elements – earth, air, fire and water. As you walk through the forest, you'll see them all around you, breathe them in, feel them on your skin, on your tongue, in your heart."

"And these elements, these herbs?" Beth cast her hand around the room. "Are you a witch?"

When Celia nodded, she gasped. "Really?"

"I've been called many things, but kitchen witch is probably closest to who and what I am it." She laughed at the look on Beth's face. "All that means is that I embrace life. I honour nature. I work with the cycles of

the moon and the seasons. I do what I can to heal not harm. And this kitchen is the centre of my work, the centre of my life I guess."

Beth gazed around the room, taking in the jars of herbs, the warm loaf of bread fresh from the oven, the thick book she'd seen Celia write in over the past few weeks, after people had visited her for tea-leaf readings or healings. This warm, light-filled kitchen was so different to the cold, austere place her mother ruled over. And yet, she'd rarely seen Patricia Bishop eat, and *never* seen her enjoy it. Celia devoured everything with such joy and pleasure. Food. Books. Life. Was that her mother's problem? She was permanently hungry? Starved of warmth, connection, nurturing?

Not that Patricia deserved sympathy, or would even want it. The woman had ice water in her veins, and sustained herself on a diet of disapproval and cruel judgement, which no one could live up to, least of all her disrespectful, ungrateful, undeserving daughters – *her words* – and her perpetually disappointing husband.

"Beth?"

Shaking herself back to the present, she looked up at her new friend through blurry eyes. "Yes?"

"You can let go of all the judgement now. You're free. Don't waste your life defining yourself the way people in your past have. You can recreate yourself now. No one here knows you, so you can discover the essence of who you are and who you want to be. But you have to let go of what you're holding on to. Let go of the investment you have in their beliefs of you."

"I don't believe their view of me."

Celia smiled, but there was sadness in it. "Oh Beth, you do. And you use it as an excuse to stay stuck, to not strive for what you really want. You accept their limitations on what you're capable of. It keeps you safe. You don't have to worry about failing, because you never try. You live your life small, when you should be dreaming as big and wide as the universe. Reaching for the stars. Who cares if you fall short? What's the worst that can happen – you need to learn something new or try harder to get there? The tragedy of never risking is that you will remain within the narrow parameters set for you, I'm guessing by your mother?"

Beth nodded miserably.

"She's not here dear girl. Don't let her be *here*," she added, tapping Beth's forehead, right between her eyes.

Tears welled, but she sucked them down. Celia was right. Why was she lugging the weight of her mother's expectations and cruelty around France with her? That's why she'd left home – yet it seemed she hadn't actually escaped, not emotionally anyway. But she would change that, from this moment forward.

"Good girl. Now, off to the forest with you," Celia said, voice light and airy again. "I've packed a baguette for your lunch. I'll be out this afternoon, so is the chicken pie we made yesterday okay for dinner tonight?"

Beth nodded again, and finally smiled. "It's perfect. Thank you." And although she'd been starved of affection her whole life, and had little experience of human interaction, Beth walked around the table and hugged Celia on her way out. And felt something within her start to thaw.

The forest was a sanctuary. Beth listened to the whispers of the wind through the trees with great reverence. It was sacred here, almost like a church, an observation that would infuriate her mother. But she no longer cared what her mother thought. From now on, that woman was out of her head.

Closing her eyes, she focused on the wind as it brushed her face, lifted her hair, and swirled her skirt around her legs. Then she felt the sun kiss her cheeks, infusing her whole body with warmth and security. Slowly she became aware of a solidity from the earth, an energy that was awakening her even as it grounded her. And when she heard the sound of water in the distance, she laughed. Celia had promised she would encounter all the elements in the forest, and here they were.

When she heard an answering laugh, she whipped around in alarm, head jerking and eyes gazing wildly around her. But there was no one there. Was she starting to imagine things, now that she believed the craziness that someone could actually be a witch? What was wrong with her? This forest with all its myths and legends must be getting to her, weaving its hooks into her, and firing up her wild imagination.

The giggle came again, and she stared in consternation as she followed the sound and saw a...

No, it wasn't that. There was no such thing as faeries.

With a wiggle of its bright velvety-covered bottom, the mischievous sprite beckoned her down, and she sank to the grass until she was eye to eye with...

"I'm seeing things," Beth said flatly.

The little creature grinned. "I wish more people could see things." The voice was tiny and delicate, like a bell, but somehow she understood it. Then the feather-light fae being leaped up onto her hand, and peered right at her.

"Celia's right, as usual. You have an open heart and an open mind, and you're finally ready to start seeing the magic in the world, and within yourself."

"I'm not magical," Beth retorted. "I have no magic."

The little creature pursed its lips in disapproval. "Everyone has magic, silly. It's within all things, all life, and we can all make our lives magical if we choose to. Don't stay closed off to it, please."

"But what are you?"

"I represent the element of air, and the qualities of inspiration, awakening, and the imagination. You can call on me when you want to be more playful. When you're ready to imagine your life in new colour and joy and depth."

Beth's head spun. It was too much. Was she dreaming? *Hallucinating?*

A sigh escaped the...

"*Faery.* I'm a faery. Is that so hard for you to believe?"

A voice called out from overhead. "Give her time Fee, she's new to this..."

"Fine." The faery darted up and kissed Beth's cheek, then flew away in a shimmer of iridescent wings. Dazzled, Beth lifted a hand to her face in wonder. Did that really just happen? A faery kissed her? Or had Celia's conversation this morning filled her head with fanciful thoughts? Humans who were witches was stretching the bounds of credulity. Who would believe there were faeries in the world too?

But as she wandered further into the forest, she realised she desperately wanted it all to be true. She wanted to live in a world of witches and faeries and magic. Far from the money, ambition and greed she'd grown up around, the backstabbing to win at someone else's expense. She longed for the existence she'd glimpsed here. Did that mean she had to stay in Brittany though? Was the magic attached to this place? Is that why Celia lived in her little cottage on the edge of the forest, on the shore of the lake, in the in-between place that wasn't totally wild, but was far from civilisation? Would she have to give up her planned life in London?

Then she rolled her eyes and decided she must be going crazy. How could she live hidden away in a tiny French village? She couldn't work here, couldn't earn money, couldn't sign a lease. *Couldn't speak the language.*

Momentary lapse of reason quickly discarded, she followed the sound of the water, which got louder as she walked. There was a new vitality in the air, a slight crisp wetness to the breeze. Weaving around a corner of the path, she tripped and fell, right in front of a spring carved out of the rocks. Water was gurgling over them and pooling in the stone bowl below, but it wasn't the water that had brought her to her knees, it was the shadowy figure bent over it, murmuring words under her breath. A prayer? A lullaby? *A spell?*

Beth's eyes grew heavy, and she felt sleep descending on her. Blinking rapidly, she tried to force herself awake.

*What was she, Sleeping Beauty?*

The figure turned, and Beth froze, caught in the gaze of a woman who seemed older than time itself. Her eyes were dark and deep, with tiny sparkles twinkling within them like the night sky. Beth couldn't say what she looked like, because she couldn't drag her attention from those eyes.

"Beth." The word was a whisper, was a sigh on the wind, but she wasn't sure the woman had spoken, because she felt the name in her heart rather than hearing it with her ears.

She tried to break their connection, to focus on the world around them, but it had melted away. The two of them stood outside time, outside reality. Was this death, this absence of anything, of everything? She felt bereft, yet a part of her was growing, expanding. Something new was birthing itself within her. She wanted to be held by this stranger, and that thought scared her. It made her pull back, and try to break whatever spell she was under. Terror pulsed through her.

"There is no need to fear Beth, no need to run from yourself. Or to run anywhere. You are where you are meant to be right now, so trust that. Trust your own heart. Trust what you feel, even when you doubt what you see."

Trembling, Beth reached out a hand, and was shocked when she felt the flesh of the black-clad woman's cheek. It was smooth, and soft. Alive. Some part of her had hoped it was an apparition.

The woman's mouth turned up, and her eyes twinkled. "Beloved, I am real, although few people have the will to see me now."

"Why can I see you?"

She smiled again. "Only you can know that Beth. And you have the power to close yourself off from this Otherworld too, if you do not wish to see."

"I do! I want to see, I want to *know*." There was a yearning within her she hadn't felt before, and her fear drained away. All that remained was love, and longing, and the sense of peace the forest had gifted her.

"You do not need to remain here to retain that feeling, or that knowing. You can carry it within you wherever you go."

Relief suffused Beth. She'd been afraid of that, afraid the magic would disappear the moment she left the forest, left Celia's home, left her own free self.

"Oh Beth, you will always be free, if you want to be. It is not other people who decide that we are bound to them, it is we who decide to stay there. To stay stuck. Let all of that go now."

Emotion swelled within Beth. A tear formed, and glistened on her lashes like a diamond before spilling over and rolling slowly down her cheek. But this tear was not formed from sadness, or infused with pain – it was composed of relief and joy and freedom.

"Thank you." Her voice was a faint whisper, yet happiness raced through her veins and the blood throbbed loudly in her ears, drowning everything out.

Bowing her head, she tried to compose herself. There was so much she wanted to ask of this woman, so much she longed to learn. But when she looked back up, the clearing was empty. Sunlight filtered through the trees in twisting golden threads, and she heard a bird above her, darting past on furious wings. Taking a step forward, she knelt down where the woman had been, and gazed into the deep still pool of water. The surface was black, although she saw tiny silver stars within it, drawing her closer, as though into the eyes of the woman in black.

Startled, she watched as a series of images played out across the water. Drinking tea with Celia, doing tea-leaf readings alongside her, walking in the forest in the rain. Then it shifted, and she was standing at the foot of the Eiffel Tower, climbing the hill to Sacre Coeur, then wandering down a cobblestoned street hand in hand with –

She didn't know. Ripples expanded outwards as she tried to see who the person holding her hand was, but the visions were gone. The water was dull now, dark and lifeless. No twinkling stars or shimmering scenes stretched out on its surface. No promise of things to come.

Stumbling backwards, Beth fell in the dirt, and shook violently.

Eventually she managed to control the trembling, and gazed around the glade with wide eyes. She felt lost, yet somehow found. Perplexed and anxious to know more, yet calm. The images in the water had only sparked happiness in her, contentment. She would have to be okay with that for now.

Deciding that she may as well eat where she'd fallen, she pulled out the parcel Celia had packed for her from her basket, and unwrapped the ham and cheese sandwich made on a still-warm, freshly baked baguette. Surprised by how amazing it tasted, she wondered how something so simple could suddenly be so delicious. Had Celia already changed her, making her able to enjoy things with the gusto that she did?

To really taste things – food, emotions, love, life? It was such a stark contrast to her mother that she laughed.

Being stranded in this neck of the woods was turning out to be a blessing.

Dipping her hands into the spring, she drank deeply of the water. Its icy freshness soothed her within, and sated her hunger for progress. Standing up, she dusted off the back of her skirt and headed for home, this temporary shelter she'd grown to love.

The following day Jessica returned, and Beth had to give back the room she'd so loved being in. Celia insisted she was welcome to stay longer, that they would find space for her, but Beth knew it was time to move on. Winter was coming, she could feel it, and she'd woken up that morning with a sudden, desperate desire to see Paris, and meet the man the watery visions had promised her. She had barely any money, but if she'd gained one gift from Celia and the enchanted forest, it was to trust. She would find her way, or she wouldn't. It didn't matter. Life would unfold as it should.

And it did.

## Chapter 26

# Into the Woods

### Rhiannon

A cough dragged Rhiannon from sleep, and she groaned and rolled over in the narrow single bed. She was so tired, but the sound just got louder and more frequent. Throwing off her blankets, she sat up – and saw Brodie slumped in his bed, looking miserable, his small body shivering every time he coughed.

"Hey buddy, are you okay?" she asked as she crossed the room to sit on the side of his bed. "What's wrong?" Resting her hand against his forehead, she winced. He was feverish, his cheeks red and his eyes watering.

"My throat hurts," he gasped, then succumbed to another bout of coughing.

"Wait here buddy, I'll get Dad. Just a sec."

Hurrying to the other room, she woke her father, who pulled a dressing gown on over his pyjamas and followed her out to the hall.

"Why don't you head out for the morning, while I wait with Brodie and see if he needs a doctor? There's no point you staying inside on this beautiful day, and your brother will be devastated if he thinks he's ruining your holiday."

"I don't mind staying…"

Her father yawned, then smiled. "I know that, and so does Brodie. But the chalet owner left her daughter's bicycle at the back door for you, so you may as well make the most of it. I know how much you want to see the forest."

Finally convinced, Rhiannon dressed quickly and headed to the kitchen to see if there was anything she could scrounge up. A basket covered with a floral cloth sat on the bench, alongside three silver flasks, which definitely hadn't been there when she went to bed the night before. Peeking under the cover, her mouth watered. There were six croissants, some pain au chocolate and a few chausson au pommes, still warm and smelling heavenly. Mrs Corentin must have slipped in to drop them off in the last half hour. Wrapping a few pastries in a tea towel and picking up one of the flasks, Rhiannon popped her breakfast in the bike's straw basket and set off.

Breathing in the crisp early morning air, she tried to push her worries over Tom to the back of her mind. The sky was blue, the sun was hot on her shoulders, and she was in France, about to enter the magical Broceliande Forest.

Myth and legend soaked into the earth here, under the ancient trees and along the narrow pathways, and resided deep within the lakes and springs. Tales of knights and faeries, druids and wizards. Of enchanted fountains and sacred burial chambers, ensorcelled swords, and spells to stay young, charm a lover or break a heart.

And on a personal level, she knew how much the time her mother had spent here had meant to her. Would she be able to feel her here? Encounter the ghost of her mum as she was now, or perhaps the spirit of Beth as she'd been when she left home twenty years ago to explore the world, and had connected with magic for the first time.

Standing at the edge of the mysterious forest, Rhiannon smiled, eager to slip onto the nearest path and enter the woods. But suddenly a huge and ominous bank of black clouds pushed its way across the sun, and she shuddered as the whole world seemed to darken. The golden light streaming through the trees faded as though a switch had been flipped, and a swirl of icy fog gathered around her legs, reaching out cold, questing fingers that sent shivers up her spine.

Gazing up at the sky, she wondered what to do. If the storm broke while she was within the woods, would she get lost? Would it be dangerous in there if lightning struck?

A bolt of fear shot through her. Was it her anxiety and jealousy over Tom creating this storm? The man at the tourist office had insisted it would be blue skies and sunshine all week. The terror of those moments up on the tor last year – when she had unleashed the anger and rage that fuelled the storms, had *become* the thunder and lightning – returned, and she trembled in horror.

But no. It couldn't be that. She'd let go of all the fury that had convinced her she was controlling the weather and creating the storms in the wake of her mother's death. This had nothing to do with her. It would pass. Leaning the bike against a tree, she reached into the basket and pulled out the still-warm parcel. The sweet aroma of butter and sugar wove around her, comforting, soothing, and as she bit into the fresh, flaky pastry, she sighed with contentment. When she unscrewed the lid of the flask and discovered rich milky coffee, she grinned. No approaching storm would ruin her morning while she had coffee and croissants.

Somewhat fortified, Rhiannon peered into the trees. Which path should she take? Apprehension rippled through her, destroying her fragile, pastry-induced calm. The sun-dappled forest she'd expected was dark and foreboding. The atmosphere of the wild woods seemed more scary than enchanting. Tension thrummed through her body, through her bones, and her blood ran cold. She wanted to flee, wanted to be back home in her own bedroom. But that was crazy.

*She could do this.*

Pulling her jacket tightly around herself, she set off. One foot in front of the other. One step, then another, and another. She concentrated on her breathing, inhaling deeply, trying to centre herself, to calm her mind. Trying to focus on the beauty around her. Yet the tidal wave of emotion wouldn't abate, and she finally sank to the ground, dread pressing her into the earth. Why was she shaking? What was she afraid of? How had this magical moment turned so cruel? These woods were supposed to be healing. Instead she was breaking apart, terrified to be walking within them.

The tinkling of bells distracted her, and she peered into the gloom, trying to identify the source of the sound. A child's bicycle, heading up the path towards her? Or a faery, darting overhead to torment her?

She laughed at the thought – until a clap of thunder overhead made her jump, then a lightning strike right behind her forced her to her feet and sent her staggering down the path away from it, further into the trees. Too scared to notice which direction she took or which fork she chose, she just ran, blindly, deeper into the woods. When the heavens opened and poured down on her, the ground became slippery. She splashed through puddles, her shoes soon soaking wet and her jeans muddy and cold where they clung to her calves. Tears poured down her face, tears of anger and fear and frustration, but they were indistinguishable from the rain lashing stinging needles into her face.

Then she tripped on a tree root and found herself hurtling down a muddy slope, her ankle twisting painfully and her hands grazing on the rocks that bruised her as she slid and skidded ever downwards.

"Stop!" she screamed.

And it did. The rain ceased. The clouds parted. Her fall was broken.

A silent, yawning abyss stretched around her, almost as terrifying as the storm. And a tall, imposing woman stood above her, staring down at her, eyes inky black and intense, shadows making strange patterns on her skin. She seemed to be drawing the darkness of the woodland to her, where it swirled around her like a cloak.

Rhiannon shivered. She'd never felt as intimidated as she did right now, frozen to the spot by the stranger's harsh and penetrating glare. A heaviness crept into her bones, pulling her into the earth, and her eyes grew heavy. Goosebumps rose on her arms, and her stomach churned with trepidation. Who was this? What did the black-clad woman want with her? And why was she suddenly aching with bitterness and anger and grief?

Abruptly the mist-wreathed being reached out a strong hand to Rhiannon, and hauled her to her feet.

"Thank you," she muttered, embarrassed that her voice trembled.

The woman nodded. "Dear one, there is no need to fear me. Or to fear the forest. Or indeed, to fear yourself."

*Okay.*

The silence stretched out around them. There was no bird sound, no wind. Time seemed stuck. Rhiannon's heart rate slowly returned to normal.

"Everyone is afraid of the deep dark woods – of their subconscious, of their shadow side, of the wildness within them – but you should not be. It is where growth lies. It is where you will find freedom."

"Freedom?"

The woman's sigh shook the forest floor, and Rhiannon cringed.

"Freedom from bitterness, and from fear." The imposing figure's voice was stern, and commanding. "Freedom from the cycle of self-sabotage you are trapped within."

Rhiannon gaped at her. "Fear? Self-sabotage?"

*What was the woman talking about?*

"Fear of happiness, fear of being loved. And destroying a beautiful relationship for no reason at all."

"Now wait a minute." Rhiannon straightened up, a spark of anger and defiance giving her strength. "You don't know me. You don't know what happened. My boyfriend is going to Paris, the City of Love, with another woman, and he didn't tell me. He was weird and secretive about it. How can I trust him?"

"Oh Rhiannon, he did not confess to anything because there was nothing to confess. And he did not hide anything from you. He told you who he was going with."

*Hmm, yes, technically that was true.*

"Well, last night I was led to a place where Jessica told me her story, about the fiance who cheated on her on a business trip to Paris. And my mother was the one who warned her about it. Surely it was a sign, my mum guiding me there to listen, to learn."

The black-robed woman shook her head, and the sorrow on her face almost broke Rhiannon's heart. "That is Jessica's story, it is not yours. You were led to her because she is a link to your mother, and she has a message for your father."

*Oh.*

"Your relationship with Tom is strictly between the two of you. It has nothing to do with anyone else, and certainly no connection to a stranger from across the sea being betrayed twenty years ago by someone you will never meet. Look within, I beg of you. It is not Tom you are angry with. It is not him making you bitter."

Her voice was like thunder, and Rhiannon trembled before her. Yet she couldn't walk away, suspended in place by the woman's unyielding severity. "Do not invent reasons to protect your heart, or create situations to drive him away," she continued sternly. "Do not sabotage your relationship with a man who loves you, because of the harm someone else inflicted on you."

Confusion swirled around Rhiannon, like the mist rising from the cold forest floor that was starting to affect her vision. She couldn't peer through it, couldn't see ahead of her clearly, and couldn't make sense of the strange woman's words.

Finally she sighed. "I don't understand. What do you mean?"

"Dear child, you are transferring your anger at what happened to you long before you met Tom onto him. You are hoping that driving him to end things then blaming him for the break-up will make it easier to cope with your pain."

"Oh, you mean what happened in the woods? It's okay, I'm over that." Rhiannon laughed. The woman's demeanour had been freaking her out, but she'd got it all wrong. She was fine. She was healed.

"No. You are not fine. You are not healed. And you do not just 'get over' something like that. Betrayal, deception, physical pain. They leave a mark. A scar. They change you fundamentally. You may pretend all you like that it does not affect you, but it is still there, deep within you. It still controls you, and limits you. It makes you lash out at those who love you, and invent foolish reasons to avoid happiness. It means well, it pretends to protect, but it is a prison."

Gently she took Rhiannon's hand, and the compassion in her eyes took her breath away. This woman's own pain was deep and real. As old as time, and as bottomless as the lake within this forest. "But it is not these woods you are afraid of Rhiannon," she murmured, voice softer now. "It is *your* woods. And the woods within your heart."

*Her woods.* The words whispered and wove around Rhiannon, and her grip on reality started to slip. *Her woods.* Slowly, sinuously, a flashback of that awful night slithered into her mind. Her, standing naked under the full moon in the middle of the clearing, believing her friend's brother was helping her do a healing ritual for her mother. Believing that darkness was beautiful like the night, not evil like him.

A growing horror threatened to consume her. "No," she growled. "I won't go back there."

"Back where?"

"To that night."

"Which night?"

Tears welled in Rhiannon's eyes, but they were tears of anger. She glared at her interrogator. "The night in the woods, with Evan." Strangely, she felt stronger just speaking his name. It had taken a long time before she could stop referring to her attacker as "him", before the woman in red forced her to name him. And she had been right. Calling him by his name *had* lessened his power over her.

The woman in black was staring at her now, eyes glittering. "And what did he do?"

Rhiannon shuddered. Now she remembered that Aideen had also tried to make her say the word, but she hadn't been able to then. She didn't think she could do it now either.

"What did he do?" the woman thundered at her, and Rhiannon shook harder.

"The thing he did. *The thing that happened*." It was a whisper, her throat constricted with panic and fear.

This time, as though to purposefully keep her off balance, the woman became the embodiment of patience and empathy. "Dear child, you must name it before you can be free of it. Say it. I know you can do this."

Fury glinted in Rhiannon's eyes, and her fingertips sparked, but she drew herself up straight, took a deep breath, and forced herself to speak. "He raped me. Are you happy now? I was raped." Her knees buckled, but the woman caught her in strong arms, and held her tight as she broke down.

"Do not fight your emotions Rhiannon. Let yourself feel them. Acknowledge them." The tone was soft now, the manner gentle, soothing. "You cannot release its hold on you until you have spoken it. Named it. *Accepted it.* There is great power in naming something. It gives you back control. It puts you in charge of your story. It stops you seeing yourself as the victim, and gives you agency."

Perplexed, Rhiannon drew back. Could it really be that simple? Could the key to her healing be in the speaking of that word? Could the power to move forward reside in the claiming of it?

The reclaiming.

So simple, yet so hard. She said it again, voice shaky but firm, and the woman smiled sadly at her and pulled her back into her arms. The sudden sympathy and compassion cracked Rhiannon wide open, and she wept as she was flooded by images of that night, and memories of the pain, the shame, and the humiliation.

"What do I do?" she finally managed to ask through her sobs.

"Be gentle with yourself. Honour yourself. These things take time. Healing is a life-long journey, not a place you arrive at then leave, suddenly transformed and free. Some days the road will be smooth and easy to follow, and other days there will be obstacles and setbacks. But you must continue the journey, even when it feels too difficult to go on."

*She didn't know if she could do that.*

"Oh Rhiannon, you can. You absolutely can. You have strength and power within you. Your mother named you well. And it will get easier, I promise. The scar may twinge occasionally, to remind you of what you have endured, and survived, and transcended, but it will continue to fade, until most of the time you will not even notice it. And when fear comes up for you in response to any situation, think through your reactions, question your motives, and make sure you understand *why* you are responding the way you do. That you are reacting to the correct person."

Nodding, she thought of Tom, of the push-pull she felt when she was with him, one moment wanting so desperately to kiss him, the next terrified of him touching her. Now it made sense. She wasn't indecisive, wasn't leading him on. She was reacting to what she'd pretended to have forgotten.

"Yes." The woman smiled. "But now you are aware. Now you are conscious of what fuels your fear. It has been exposed to the light, so no shadows remain to trip you up. Acceptance and understanding are powerful tools. And now that you *are* aware, I beg you, do not let your bitterness poison you. Do not let your hurt become the hedge of thorns that cuts you off from the world, cuts you off from love. It will protect you, true, but you will lose everything. It almost made you lose your boyfriend, correct?"

Regret and trepidation rippled through Rhiannon. "Maybe it already has. I don't know if he'll be there when I get home, or whether I've already driven him away."

The woman's face softened, and she reached out a comforting hand to stroke Rhiannon's cheek. "Trust in what you have. And do not allow your fear to turn to resentment. Believe me, I know just how much acrimony and anger can harm a person, can destroy them. I have spent… forever… trying to atone for my sins, trying to gain forgiveness for what my rancour made me do. It is toxic. It slowly poisons you, poisons your heart and your hope, until you die inside. But you have the power to change this Rhiannon, by confronting the darkness not just of the woods, of the storm, but of yourself. Accept what happened. Take control of it by naming it. And when you are ready, you can lessen your pain by sharing your burden."

*What?*

"You can tell Tom, or Carlie, or your father, or Rose."

Rhiannon gasped in horror. "No way! No one can ever know what happened to me."

The woman smiled sadly. "This was not your fault dear child. No one will blame you, or think less of you, or change their opinion of you. They will just want to support you and love you. Please understand that you do not have to endure this alone. But it is your decision to make, or not make. Just know that those who love you will not stop loving you. And please accept that it was not your fault. It is time for you to finally emerge from the darkness of the woods, and the shadows of the forest."

As she spoke, the sun began to shine through the canopy of trees above them, and bright beams of light danced around them. The woman's eyes sparkled and her form shimmered, and Rhiannon was worried she would fade away.

"How will I know what to do? How to act? The way to keep the shadows at bay?" she implored.

Laughter echoed through the trees. "You already know. You have journeyed through the forest, by going within your self, within your subconscious, and within your heart. Think of all the faery tales. The hero or heroine must go into the woods and confront the darkness within, but they always come out, and they bring with them the wisdom they learned there, and the lost and broken pieces of themselves that they integrated. You have done the work. It is time for you to go back out into the world."

Rhiannon stared at her, mouth open in shock.

"So go."

The woman's voice was stern, and Rhiannon didn't wait to be told again. Quickly she turned and hurried back the way she'd come, praying she would find the right path out of the woods.

When she calculated that she was far enough away from the woman, she slowed her pace. It was so beautiful in the forest now that the sun had come out and banished the shadows, both from the light-dappled path she was walking along, and from within her. Green and gold swirled around her in a delicate dance, sunbeams spun between the branches, and the atmosphere of storm and rage she'd been surrounded by, and filled with, transformed from roiling tempest to soothing breeze.

Her breathing calmed, and she focused on the air that moved around her, gently buffeting her body, lifting her hair, clearing her mind. For a moment she pictured herself as a raven, lifted on the swirling currents, swooping down over the trees, and seeing far ahead from its vantage point in the sky. Closing her eyes, she tried to embed that sense of perspective within, to open her mind to other people's points of view. To Tom's point of view.

Tilting her head, Rhiannon heard melodic bird song, and picked out poetry on the breeze, a poetry of the earth, and of the soul. She heard the spirit of it all, and most importantly, the spirit of herself. And then it faded, and the wind whispered to her.

*Let go. Relax. Release it all.*

As foolish as it sounded, a weight lifted from her as she surrendered. It was time to stop holding on to her resentment and bitterness. To take the woman's advice. The wind died down to nothing, and she exhaled all the pain she hadn't even known she was holding on to, and sank to the ground, suddenly too weightless and insubstantial to hold herself up. But it was a good exhaustion. A good release...

Emboldened by the change of light and the burning away of the chill, Rhiannon breathed in the last whirls of mist, feeling it curl down into the very core of her being. Cooling her. Calming her. Somehow centring her into her own self. The rational and loving self. The woman was correct. That bitterness and fear, that jealousy and doubt, was not her, and she was devastated that her buried trauma had made her react that way to Tom. To question his motive.

*Question herself.*

He'd told her the truth. If he didn't want to be with her, he wouldn't be. If he wanted to be with Marie, he would be. She was embarrassed that she'd reacted from her own fear, rather than to his words and actions, but at least she'd figured it out now. She just hoped it wasn't too late.

Dragging herself to her feet, she stepped forward. A small kernel of knowingness ignited within her, coaxed out by the now-golden morning, and the memory of the mysterious black-robed woman she'd poured out her heart and soul to.

When she made it back to the chalet, Brodie was curled up in bed, and her dad had just put a pot of coffee on the stove. "How was the forest?" he asked eagerly as he poured her a cup. "Was it as enchanted as you'd hoped?"

"Even more so," she said, smiling as she remembered. "It was like another world in there, and it was fascinating to see the dramatic changes as I walked – the darkness of that crazy thunder and lightning storm, with the rain pummelling down on me, then the soft and mystical sun-soaked woodland that emerged afterwards."

Mike raised an eyebrow. "Storm? There was no storm, it's been hot and sunny all day." He looked at his watch. "How far in did you go? I guess you have been gone for hours."

She stared at him, puzzled. How on earth had that storm not reached the village? Had she somehow found herself in another dimension? Or, scariest of all possibilities, had she conjured it herself? And how had all that time passed?

"I suppose I walked for a long time, so I made good progress into the woods. And then the storm broke, and I started sliding down this weird rocky outcrop, twisting my ankle, cutting my hands, and getting filthy," she said, suddenly realising what a mess she must be. Yet when she glanced down, her jeans were only a tiny bit muddy along the hem, the huge splotches somehow evaporated.

"That sounds like Val Sans Retour, the Valley of No Return," her dad replied, not noticing her confusion. "It's said to be the domain of Morgaine, King Arthur's half-fae half-sister. At the entrance to her valley is Rocher des Faux Amants, the Rock of the False Lovers, which might be what you fell on."

Rhiannon stared at him quizzically as he found two mugs and got out the milk. Yesterday she would have said that was all stupid, the superstitions of people wanting to believe in myth and legend over reality. Yet she could picture a woman draped in black standing on that rock, gazing down at the lake below, heartbroken and bitter. "And what do they say about her?"

Mike laughed. "Well, according to the locals, Morgaine was trained in magic by Merlin here, studying her craft in this forest, learning about herbs, divining the future in the supposedly magical springs, and gradually developing immense powers. Yet she was betrayed, so the story goes, by her lover. He was a knight, and she transformed him and the woman he cheated with into stone – the Rock of the False Lovers. And supposedly she read the heart of every knight who entered the woods after that, and trapped those who were unfaithful. Which, sadly, was most of them, making her even more bitter and vengeful, and fuelling her spell."

The words of the strange black-robed woman from the forest echoed around Rhiannon. *I know just how much acrimony and anger can harm a person, can destroy them. I have spent... forever... trying to atone for my sins, trying to gain forgiveness for what my rancour made me do.*

Was it Morgaine she'd encountered? Had that sad, regretful woman transformed the cheating couple to stone, then become stuck in the valley until the end of time, trying to help others in penance for her actions? Not that they didn't seem at least somewhat justified, necessarily. How come the woman was always made to suffer when it was the man who was guilty of the crime?

"Coffee?"

She looked up, startled back from her memories of the woods, and her empathy for the much-maligned Morgaine. In all the retellings of the Arthurian stories she was cast as the evil one, yet what if she was just a woman badly hurt, trying to deal with the pain that had been inflicted on her? And trying to help others avoid her fate as a way to make amends.

Poor Tom. She really had to make it up to him. Apologise for her behaviour, and let him know she did trust him – that it was only herself she doubted. But no more.

"Coffee would be wonderful," she told her dad, and sent a silent prayer of gratitude to the woman in the woods.

## Chapter 27

# The Lady of the Lake

### Rhiannon

"Rhi-Rhi, will you play with me today?" Brodie asked.

After two days in bed, her brother was feeling much better, and Rhiannon smiled, relieved.

"Of course. What would you like to do? We could start at the Gate of Secrets, which looks really cool, then we could cruise through the abbey, and have a picnic on the shore of the lake."

Brodie squealed with excitement, and her dad looked over at her gratefully, but Rhiannon had just as much fun as her brother at the attraction. They posed with the sword Excalibur, which legend placed in the lake of Broceliande known as the Faeries' Mirror, then watched a few magic shows, examined old artefacts, and interacted with modern displays that brought the enchantment of the forest to them in a kid-friendly, no-walking way. She loved their exploration of the abbey too, and feeding the white swans on the lake before they fed themselves. All the problems she'd been stewing over left her while she hung out with her brother, which was a relief.

They didn't return to the chalet until late that afternoon, and their dad was already making dinner. Brodie told him all about their day then went to have a shower, and Rhiannon picked up a knife and started chopping vegies while she asked her dad what he'd done with his free time.

"I went to The Magic Teapot, and had a wonderful chat with Jessica. It was fascinating to hear about the time Beth spent here, and what she did and believed back then, and to learn more about Celia, who Beth always spoke so highly of. Standing in that kitchen, where Beth first learned about herbs and divination, where she said her heart started to mend, well..." he trailed off.

Rhiannon walked over and hugged him. "I'm sorry Dad."

"It was good though," he said, surreptitiously wiping his eye. "She showed me the room that Beth stayed in too, so I could see the view she looked out at every morning, over the lake, with the forest in the distance. It was so peaceful."

"It is really beautiful here. I can understand why Mum loved it so much, even though back then she thought she preferred the city."

Mike laughed. "It's incredible just how much our entire outlook can change over the years – or sometimes in a heartbeat. One moment of realisation..." Again he trailed off, and Rhiannon stared at him, frowning.

"Are you okay? Did something happen?"

Her dad's cheeks flamed red. "Well, after we drank our tea, Jessica offered to do a tea-leaf reading for me."

Rhiannon grinned. "Yeah, she offered me a coffee reading the other night, but I wasn't quite ready for that, so I ran back here as fast as I could." Her laughter faded when she saw her father's stricken face, and her heart constricted in fear. "What's wrong? What did she say?"

"She said there would soon be love in my life," he muttered. "But don't worry, that won't happen."

"Dad!" Rhiannon stared at him, aghast, her relief that nothing bad was about to happen making her voice sharper than she intended. "I know it's hard, but Mum has been gone for more than eighteen months. And she wouldn't want you to be alone forever. She wouldn't want you to cut yourself off from life, and love."

Some of Morgaine's words came back to her. *Do not let your hurt become the hedge of thorns that cuts you off from the world, and off from love. That will protect you, yes, but you will lose everything.*

"And Brodie and I don't expect you to be alone forever either, if that's what you're worried about," she said gently.

Mike looked up at her with tears in his eyes. "But Beth…"

"Mum loved you more than anything, so more than anything she would want you to be happy. And she told you that before she died, I remember. She made you promise you wouldn't close yourself off from love."

Reluctantly he nodded.

"Please don't barricade yourself away Dad, and deny yourself a chance at happiness. You'll honour Mum and the life you shared with her by continuing to love."

Stirring the pot on the stove, he smiled at his daughter. "When did you get so wise?"

She blushed. "There's a lot you can learn in an enchanted forest."

"And Tom?" he challenged her.

"Yeah, I owe him an apology. I'll make it right when we get home," she vowed. "But what else did Jessica say?"

"Hmm, nice change of subject." Her dad smirked. "Well, um, Jessica said I already know her, and that Beth approves."

*Laura. Could that be the person who would love her dad?*

Before she could mention her mum's friend, or consider how she would feel about her dad dating her teacher, Brodie bounded in and they sat down for dinner together. Watching her brother's enthusiasm as he recounted another story from the exhibition, Rhiannon smiled. This holiday had been the last thing she'd wanted, but she was glad she had this time with her family. And that she could almost convince herself they were all healing from their tragic loss.

Creeping out of her small shared bedroom in the misty pre-dawn, Rhiannon tiptoed to the front door and cautiously pulled it open. It creaked a little, but no one stirred, so she closed it gently shut behind her and straightened, peering around her into the fog-wreathed almost-dark. Although she hated getting up early, she adored this liminal time between night and day, when the whole world seemed poised on the edge of decision, and potential and promise swirled thick and deep.

Inhaling the cool crisp air and the scent of pine and jasmine, she steadied herself on the bicycle and headed towards the forest. It was even more beautiful this morning. She could feel the weight of the ages, the press of history and legend, and sensed something watching her every movement. She wasn't sure if it was human, animal or Otherworldly, but this time it didn't scare her. Today it was reassuring, that she was sharing this early morning adventure with someone, or something. A smile lifted the corners of her mouth and crinkled her eyes, and her heart expanded. She could feel her mother here, in the scent of the jasmine and the sturdy, eternal power of the oaks, and it was comforting.

"I miss you so much Mum," she whispered into the chilly morning with its slowly lightening sky. "I wish you were here to share this with me, to guide my steps, to hold my hand." It must have been her imagination, because for a moment it felt as though someone *was* taking her hand, enfolding her fingers in theirs, pushing warmth and healing into her body, and her mind. Tears pricked her eyes, but it wasn't sadness sweeping through her, it was a sense of love and hope, of wisdom encircling her and holding her safe.

Slipping within the trees, she waited for her eyes to adjust to the gloom, then marvelled to see the whole world slowly growing brighter as the sun inched higher, the faintest blush of colour glittering through the canopy, everything alive and infused with enchantment. It took her breath away.

Rhiannon closed her eyes and tried to drink in the magic, focusing on her other senses – the touch of the breeze on her skin, the warmth of the sun on her face, the sounds of bird chatter and wind through the leaves, the scent of the trees and vines, and the taste of the perfume of the flowers as she inhaled.

Opening her eyes, she walked onwards, then gasped in surprise. Before her was a huge lake, dark and mysterious and perfectly still, yet lit up with liquid gold where the sun pierced the trees and spilled out onto the surface.

This must be Miroir aux Fees, the Faeries' Mirror, believed to be the threshold to the Otherworld, and the dwelling place of the Lady of the Lake. Rhiannon shivered as she recalled the story she'd heard yesterday with Brodie, about the seven faery sisters who lived in the lake. They never came to the surface during the day, to avoid interacting with mortals. But one day the youngest sister ventured above, and fell in love with a knight. When her sisters discovered her secret, they murdered her beloved – so in order to revive him, she killed her sisters and made a healing elixir from their blood.

It wasn't quite the type of faery story she was used to. Far better to imagine Viviane, the Lady of the Lake, within the water's depths, rather than bloodthirsty, gruesome fae. Viviane was the wise, benevolent being reputed to have given King Arthur the sword Excalibur, and was also associated with the legends of chivalry and honour that spanned England, Wales and France.

Rhiannon wondered if her mother had met Viviane in these woods when she was staying with Celia. She could picture them chatting back then, and it made her smile to imagine them now, existing in some alternate dimension of this enchanted place, talking together still, about love and healing, nature and family, grief and loss, and life going on without you.

Gazing out over the water, Rhiannon sank into a memory of her mother, and smiled as a hazy figure floated towards her. Was it her mum's ghost, appearing at last to reassure her family she was still with them? Then she rubbed her eyes. Blinked several times. Told herself to stop being so fanciful. A woman was gliding towards her, draped in silver, as though she was drawing the light from the dazzling lake surface into the gossamer gown that clung to her.

Fear shot through Rhiannon, and she backed away, stumbling over a fallen branch, eyes wide with apprehension. But then the woman smiled, and her trepidation melted away.

"Do not be afraid."

*Easier said than done.*

A tinkle of laughter echoed through the trees, unwinding the anxiety within her. She offered a shaky smile.

"I am here to show you what you need to know."

Frowning, Rhiannon tried to understand. Was this a real person, or one of the women of the mists from back home? Or did every place of nature and magic manifest them? Who were they? *What* were they?

The peal of laughter sounded again, and Rhiannon blushed. She hated that they could read her every thought.

"Please do not worry about that dear one. We do not read your mind, only sense your emotions."

"And yet you knew I was worried you could read my mind – thus disproving your assurance."

The ethereal silver-clad woman looked startled, until Rhiannon giggled, and the tension between them began to ease. "I'm sure that's not the worst you can do," she conceded. "Now what is it you want to show me?"

"Come." The woman led her to the lake shore, and drew her down to the ground so they were kneeling in the dirt on the very edge of the water.

"Look."

Shrugging, Rhiannon gazed where she pointed, and wondered what she was supposed to be seeing. Peering below the lake's surface, she could just make out tiny fish, and plants that danced in a current she couldn't discern. She had no idea what relevance they had to her.

Then the woman put a hand on her shoulder, and a rush of images played out on the smooth clear silver of the water before her, startling her so much she almost fell in. There was Tom, standing first at a huge canvas painting her portrait, then walking with her up the tor for their own new moon ritual. As the visions changed, she saw them reading together on her couch, Tom bringing her a mug of coffee, and his face lighting up when he gazed at her.

God she missed him. And desperately hoped he would forgive her lapse of faith, and her immature school-girl reaction. She sighed. Did she even deserve someone as amazing as him? Didn't *he* deserve someone better than her? Less complicated, less messed up, less afraid.

She gasped at the word. *Afraid?*

"Yes, afraid," the woman said softly. "You must fight your fear, and conquer it. Do not be scared of being vulnerable. Vulnerability can be your greatest source of strength. And do not be afraid of opening your heart to love. Love is truly your superpower."

Rhiannon doubted she even knew how to open her heart to love, but she vowed to try. "If I still have a chance, and am not too late."

"It is never too late."

*She really hoped that was true.*

The images on the water changed again, and she saw Tom with her once more, at the Ostara ritual in London, in the secret garden the next morning, and standing in the kitchen with her, drying the dishes as she washed after their recent meet-the-parent dinner.

Then her heart lifted, and relief flooded over her. Now the two of them were leaping the Beltane fires together – and Beltane was still three weeks from now. All the other visions were of past events, but this suggestion that they would still be together in the future filled her with joy and hope.

Reaching out a hand to caress Tom's face, to touch his lips, she cried out in frustration when the image shattered into a million pieces and dissolved into ever-widening ripples, stretching out in a circular pattern towards the opposite shore.

But the woman touched her shoulder again, and the images on the lake surface shifted and formed again. It was her mother, reaching out a hand to stroke her hair, then beckoning her forward. Rhiannon leaned closer, trying to take the offered hand – then felt herself pitching forward into the lake.

When she opened her eyes, her vision was blurry, but she searched frantically for her mother, pushing past submerged rocks and waving reeds, her lungs burning. She'd just seen her mum, beckoning her into the water, so she couldn't be far. Finally she spotted her just ahead, and Rhiannon dragged her arms through the water in a frantic effort to catch up. As she drew closer though, Beth's face started to waver. Anxiously she reached out, trying to keep her mum with her, but her arms closed around nothing. Then awareness that she was under water hit her, and Rhiannon panicked. Her limbs thrashed as she tried to kick up to the surface, tried to hold her breath and not swallow any water.

As soon as her head emerged from the water, she breathed in huge, shallow gasps, desperate for air.

The woman in silver stood before her, waist-deep in the lake, and reached out a hand to calm her. "Be still dear one, you are safe."

"Where's Mum?"

"She is with you always." The voice was a lullaby, and Rhiannon felt the knowledge soak into her bones, comforting her more than she'd expected it to. "What you need to know is that you have the power of water within you. The power to wash away the effects of the past, and cleanse your heart of the pain you have experienced. If you do not do this, you will drive everyone away, and end up alone. Do not punish yourself, or anyone else, for what has happened in the past. Morgaine could not let go of her bitterness and anger – yet it was she who suffered for this, not the men she despised."

Rhiannon stared at her in shock. The woman in silver knew the woman in black?

Laughter drifted across the lake. "Morgaine and I have been part of each other's lives since before I can remember," she said, amused. "I tried to help her, but she was so bitter that she would not listen. Sadly in the end she punished herself more than anyone else, through her trickery and treatment of others. She was stuck in the loop of her curse, fated to live her days in misery. But you have the power and strength to move forward. To grasp new love, and a new life."

Water dripped down Rhiannon's back, and she realised she was still waist deep in the icy lake, her hair and clothes soaking wet. Yet she wasn't cold, wasn't uncomfortable, although she should be. She stared at the woman in consternation.

"Are you okay?"

"I think so," Rhiannon said, and to her surprise she realised she meant it. It sucked, what had happened to her, but it was in the past. She could wallow in self-pity, or she could accept it and gather her strength and move on, changed yet still herself. Evan would only win if she remained stuck here, denying herself the chance to love and be loved. Morgaine was right, she had to move forward, and go back out into the world. "Yes. I will be okay."

The silver-clad woman pulled her into her arms, and for a moment Rhiannon heard her mother's voice. "I know you are. You've always been my strong, spirited, resilient goddess girl."

Tears flowed, but they were happy tears. Her mother's presence enfolded her, comforting, supportive, empowering, and she relaxed into the warmth. Gently the woman released her, and stared off into the distance, eyes glazed.

Then she turned to Rhiannon and smiled. "It is time for you to go, time to meet your destiny." She handed her a large silver sword, heavy and razor sharp, engraved with swirling patterns of vines and animals, with a large sunset-hued carnelian stone set in the hilt.

"This is a symbol of your own bravery, of your own actions, of your own agency. Cut away your fear, and your lingering doubt, and feel safe to trust. There will be no betrayal this time, I promise you."

In a split second the woman disappeared, and Rhiannon was suddenly lying sprawled on the shore of the lake, hair streaming with water, mind spinning with everything she had seen and heard.

Dazed, she looked around. The sun was overhead. How long had she been... wherever she had been? And what on earth was she supposed to do with this sword she was clutching? Yet as she scrambled to her feet and started to retrace her steps out of the forest, the grand silver weapon crumbled to dust in her hand. She was sad for a moment, but relieved too. How would she explain a huge silver sword to her dad, let alone airport customs?

As she reached her bike, she realised her clothes were dry and her hair no longer dripped with lake water. This place was so strange. Pedalling back to the village, she felt like she was floating. Her head spun with dreams and shadows, memories and premonitions, and the love of her mother wrapped tightly around her. As she approached their chalet, she saw a vision of Tom leaning against the huge old oak tree out the front, arms open wide to enfold her, and she smiled, hoping it was a sign that he would be happy to see her when she got home. She couldn't wait to make things right with him, to let him know how much she'd grown in the short time they'd been apart.

But then he was running towards her, her wishful thinking brought to life, and she shook her head to dislodge the hallucination. It wasn't until he threw his arms around her and she felt his warmth and solidity, and the sense of safety his embrace always gave her, that her shock gave way to joy.

"What are you –" she began, but he drowned her question out with his kisses.

When they finally drew apart, he grinned. "Hey there you," he said softly.

"Hello you. Are you really here? God, what a stupid question. Um, how are you?" she asked, flustered. How dishevelled did she look after her morning in the forest – and the lake?

"I'm good, but I missed you too much," Tom said softly. "I begged a couple of days off so I could see you on the way to Paris."

Her cheeks burned. "I'm so sorry about all that," she whispered. "I don't know what came over me, being so silly, and so jealous. Of course I trust you."

Leaning down, he kissed her forehead. "I know. And it's okay. I apologise if I –"

"Nuh-uh, this was all me. I'm really sorry, and I won't be so immature again, I promise."

Before Tom could reply, her dad stuck his head out the front door. "Hey darling, hi Tom. Did you want to come in for a late breakfast, or early lunch? Brodie has been helping me with pancake mix, and we have a lot to spare."

Clinging to his hand, Rhiannon looked up at her boyfriend hopefully, an eyebrow raised in question. He smiled and nodded, and they headed inside.

"Hi Tom!" Brodie said as they all pulled up a chair at the worn kitchen table, and Mike poured out mugs of coffee. "It's good to see you again. We've been having the best time here. Are you going to stay with us?"

Rhiannon spluttered in shock, spraying coffee all over herself, while Tom tried not to laugh. "It's great to see you too," he replied. "And thank you for the kind offer Brodie, but I'm actually staying at a little place up the road."

No one missed the relief on Mike's face, and Rhiannon struggled to smother her giggle.

"I'm glad you could join us for... ?" her dad asked.

Tom smiled. "Just a few days, then I have to head to Paris for work. But it seemed divine timing. I popped into a little shop up the road that sells crystals and herbs, and the woman there said she had a room available."

"Divine timing indeed," Mike said, as he and Rhiannon laughed.

Taking a sip of coffee, Tom glanced at Rhiannon, then her dad. "You know the place?"

Mike nodded. "We do. Beth lived there for a month twenty odd years ago, helping the owner and learning about herbs and magic from her. And I was there last night, talking to Jessica, who knew Beth back then." His eyes gleamed with tears, but he forced a smile. "It was lovely to chat with her."

When they paused, Brodie jumped into the conversation, regaling Tom with tales of their time seeing the "castle" in Mont-Saint-Michel, his brief illness, and his adventures with Rhiannon since then. Showing no after-effects from being sick, he managed to eat as many pancakes as Tom, while keeping up an enthusiastic stream of chatter.

"Ooh! Dad and I can make dinner for you tonight Tom. We've been cooking lots and lots while we've been here, so Rhi-Rhi can have a break."

Tom glanced at Mike nervously, then smiled when he nodded. "I would be honoured to be your guest tonight Brodie, thank you."

"Yay! We'll have to go to the market though Dad," he said solemnly.

Agreeing good-naturedly, Mike ushered Rhiannon and Tom off to spend some time together. Tom had a rental car, so they journeyed north-east, to a part of the forest Rhiannon hadn't seen yet. On the drive she was quiet, still embarrassed by the way they'd parted, but Tom regaled her with stories of the nearby stone alignments and other sacred sites he'd visited in the past, and by the time they parked and set off along a winding pathway, her uneasiness had dissolved and their usual comfort with each other had returned.

The enchantment of the woodland soothed her, the secretive quiet of the trees weaving a spell around them, and the restless wind finally blowing her fears away. Squeezing her hand, Tom halted, then turned to face her. "I hope it's okay with you that I'm here," he said softly. "I didn't want to just turn up uninvited and interrupt your holiday, since I wasn't a hundred per cent sure you'd want to see me, but I couldn't wait two weeks..."

Her eyes widened. "Of course I want to see you! I'm so glad you came. I've been beating myself up over how we left things – well, how *I* acted – and terrified you wouldn't want to see *me* again."

Gently he pulled her into his arms. "You can't scare me off that easily," he said, and Rhiannon sighed with relief.

They spent the afternoon wandering along the tree-lined paths, pointing out ravens and mushrooms and hiding places for the fae, and talking about life and death, ritual, and the beauty of nature. They stumbled across Tombeau de Merlin, Merlin's Tomb, the stone dolmen thought to have sheltered – or imprisoned, depending on the tale – the druidic wizard. There were offerings on the rocks and in the tree next to it. Flowers, jewellery, candles, ribbons, poems, babies booties, crystals and many other personal items had been placed there to petition Merlin for wisdom, love and health.

Tom knelt down and placed a small crystal at the base of the stone, closing his eyes and whispering something Rhiannon couldn't hear. Not wanting to be left out, she took the ribbon from her hair and tied it to a branch, sending a silent prayer for love and healing out into the woods. Love of Tom for her, and self-healing so she could love him back.

When she stood back up, Tom was frowning. "Are you okay? You seem... different."

She stared at him, immediately anxious. "What do you mean?"

"It's hard to describe. Older somehow, yet younger too. As though you've been split open, then put back together even stronger."

*Oh.*

"Well, I have had some... interesting... experiences in the forest. Lots of memories of Mum, and realisations about things that happened in the past, and an epiphany or two. It's still not quite straight in my head, so I don't even know how to explain any of it, but some stuff is shifting, and things are becoming clearer. Sort of." She laughed nervously. "If that makes any sense?"

Tom smiled. "It does. And if you ever want to talk about anything, I'm here, but in your own time. I know how transformative this place can be. Just, well, as long as you're okay?"

"I really am."

And she was. Entwining her fingers with his, she ambled with him along the path under the trees, until they came to Viviane's Fountain of Eternal Youth, which nestled in a small, sun-dappled clearing. Rhiannon stopped abruptly. The silver-clad woman from that morning was hovering above the water, transparent yet visible, to her at least. Could Tom see her? And could it really have been Viviane, the mythical Lady of the Lake, she'd encountered earlier? The one who'd given her the sword? She blinked rapidly, and the image disappeared, but she could still hear echoes of her voice.

*You must fight your fear, and conquer it. Do not be scared of being vulnerable. Of opening your heart to love.*

Head spinning and body trembling, she leaned into Tom's steadying presence as she tried to pull herself together. Did this mean she was supposed to tell him about *the thing that happened*? To rip out her heart and take the risk of him being unable to love someone so... Scarred? Scared? Shamed?

"Oh, I have something for you," Tom said, stroking her hair. His soothing touch and presence with her here in the forest was all she needed, but that sounded too soppy to say out loud.

Tom reached into his pocket, then looked a little sheepish. "It's only little, and I'm sure you have loads of bookmarks... and, well, now it seems kind of silly, but when I saw it this morning in the Magic Teapot I knew I had to get it for you."

Opening the brown paper bag, Rhiannon grinned. It was a silver bookmark, an exact replica of the sword the woman in silver had given her, complete with a tiny but vivid orangey-red carnelian crystal. When she touched it, a soothing energy rushed through her, and the whispers of ages past floated around her.

"Remember," they murmured. "You are brave enough, and strong enough. You are enough."

She reached up and kissed him. "It's perfect, thank you. More perfect than you could imagine."

Drawn to the water, they crossed the clearing to the spring, sinking down until they were sitting on the rocks around the edge, trailing their fingers in the icy cold liquid.

Tom touched a finger to her brow, anointing her with the sacred water. "Did you know that many people believe the goddess Rhiannon later became known as Viviane, the Lady of the Lake?" he asked her. "Like all the old gods, transforming through time and tales, appearing in the guise of whatever was needed for people in each historical and cultural era, each geographical location."

She shook her head.

"Like you," he continued. "Shining no matter where you are, transforming according to your surroundings."

*How could he see so much in her, when she couldn't see a thing?*

Reaching down, Tom lifted her chin and stared into her eyes. "You are stronger than you know Rhiannon, and worthy of the deepest love. When you stop holding back, when you're able to trust enough to share your deepest heart, it will be spectacular."

Tears swam in her eyes, twinkling like stars on her lashes, but they didn't fall. Morgaine was right, she had to tell him what had happened to her, and risk his reaction, so that she could be her whole self with him. But not today. Not here in this magical faraway place, so soon after they'd reconciled.

"Thank you." Smiling up at him, she caressed his cheek, then gazed down into the surface of the spring. Remembering the images she'd seen that morning, she giggled.

"What, Miss Rhi?" Tom asked.

"This morning someone... well, um, I was shown a vision of us. First it was things we'd already done, like climbing the tor and being at the Ostara rite, but then I saw us jumping the Beltane fires together." As she said it, it became more real. She felt the heat of the flames, the touch of his hand in hers, and was suddenly very glad she *had* come to France, despite all her protests.

"I should think so," Tom said, mock stern. "It is the most important festival of the year for love."

A shiver of anticipation snaked up Rhiannon's spine, without the fear that usually accompanied it, and she relaxed and then lost herself in his kisses.

## Chapter 28

# The Golden Shore

### Beth

Gazing out over the water, Beth tried to pull the pieces of herself together, buffeted by the power of the waves as they crashed onto the shore, and swept up in the beauty of sunlight shimmering on the turquoise surface as the tides danced and swirled.

Water always soothed her, whether it was the gentle stream at the bottom of the meadow near home, or the lake she and Mike stayed on for their honeymoon, or the wild expanse of ocean thundering onto this sandy French beach.

Beth remembered this place. It was the pretty coastal town of Carnac, where she'd spent a week with Priya before her flatmate returned to London. She'd loved lying on the golden sands with her friend during the day, then sitting around a campfire at night with whoever turned up to join them. Stretching out under the stars, with the sound of the waves surging right beside her, had been so healing. It was before she went to Paimpont and Broceliande, so she hadn't been so powerfully aware of the magic of nature yet, but diving into the crystal blue waters, snorkelling and playing in the sea, and feeling the salty ocean breeze on her face, had soothed something deep within her.

One night a backpacker from Australia had joined them on the beach and told her about the nearby Carnac Alignments. Back then, Beth had no clue about the ancient rows of standing stones – close to three thousand, arranged in lines that covered forty hectares of countryside – or the burial chamber nearby. She hadn't appreciated their spiritual significance either, it was just fun to crawl into the darkened tomb and try to imagine a people long gone, who had buried their dead with such ceremony and ritual. Walking between the stones, the late autumn sunshine warming her shoulders and the breeze lifting her hair and keeping her cool, it had been enough that she felt such freedom there as she chatted with the Aussie girl about the wild and wonderful world.

Yesterday she'd found herself there again, hovering amongst the stones while Rhiannon and Tom wandered hand in hand down the rows. Her daughter's boyfriend shared stories about the spiritual purpose of the famous alignments, and the two of them paused to lay their hands on the stones, to breathe in the energy from the earth and the whispers of history, myth and legend.

They'd spent the whole day together, Rhiannon looking content and secure at last as she basked in Tom's attention. After a morning at the stones they stopped in a small village pub and shared a platter of cheese and salad and a freshly baked baguette, before continuing to explore the area all afternoon. Then finally, reluctantly, Tom had driven Rhiannon back to Carnac and dropped her off with her dad and Brodie, then sadly headed to Paris for his work event.

But as miserable as Rhiannon was to say goodbye, the fear she'd been racked with since her arrival in France had dissolved, and Beth was relieved that she was smiling again. It also made her happy to see the way Rhiannon and Tom treated one another, and spoke to each other – the consideration, patience and respect on Tom's part, the growing confidence and vulnerability on her daughter's.

And now, watching her two children on the beach together, Beth felt a yearning for the person she had been when she'd danced on these golden sands so long ago. Not that she wished away anything that had happened to her, because it had all made her who she became – magical, spiritual, loving and loved – but she wanted to wrap that poor, conflicted, agonised girl in a big hug, and let her know that all she was searching for was not too far off.

She'd have to endure a terrible relationship first, but after six wonderful months in Paris, she would shock herself by returning to her home village for her sister's wedding – and falling in love with Mike and staying there, the place she'd always hated. The place where she would slowly begin to see her worth, and eventually accept that Mike could really love her.

Desperately she hoped she'd instilled enough of that in her own daughter. It would devastate her if Rhiannon was plagued with the awful self-doubt and self-loathing she'd suffered as a teenager. When she'd given birth to Rhiannon and held her in her arms for the first time, Beth was filled with terror that she would be a terrible mother, but also an overwhelming sense of love and hope.

Hope. That was what kept her here now, in this strange, painful state, attached to her family and unable to move on, yet unable to reach out to them and help. The yawning pit of her own powerlessness swirled within her, threatening to tear her apart again and scatter her back out into the void.

Laughter dragged her from her memories, and she drifted down from the balcony of her family's hotel room to the hot sand, her heart lifting with joy as she watched her two children.

"Rhi-Rhi, wait for me!" Brodie called, then squealed as a wave drew up on the sand and covered his toes. "Oooh, it's too cold!"

Rhiannon smiled, then dove under a wave, coming up laughing and spluttering. Beth swooped down over the water and gazed at her closely, examining her face, her expression, even the way she stood, braced against the strength of the waves, laughing, and looking as though she'd released a lot of her bitterness and fear.

"Oh my darling, you don't know how happy I am to see you slip off the pain that has been holding you back, the trauma of that night, and the disappointment of how things went with John..."

Rhiannon whipped around, the salt water splashing with her exuberance, and peered into the air.

"Mum?"

Beth froze. Could her daughter really sense her?

Slowly Rhiannon turned away from the beach, so she was facing out to sea. "I've felt you so many times while we've been here Mum, which is what I was hoping for. I wasn't sure it was wise to retrace your steps, whether it would be too painful, especially for Dad, but it feels like you've been with us, hovering close, giving us permission to enjoy life again, if that makes sense."

Leaping over a large wave, Rhiannon continued peering around, searching for her mother. Beth floated closer, trying to wrap her daughter in a hug, but failing miserably, again.

"I don't know if you're here or I'm just imagining things Mum, but if you are, I just want you to know how much I miss you, and always will. It hasn't gotten easier to be without you, but the intensity has diminished a little. The jagged pain that was every waking moment has dulled around the edges. You're still with me, every second of every day, but I finally feel that I'm carrying you with me, in my heart, rather than being dragged under the ocean of emotions. No offence! It's not your fault, obviously. And I don't know if it's time, or this trip, or what, but I feel a little less... dark... in my outlook."

Pain stabbed at Beth, a sharp dagger of grief, but she was happy too. "Darling girl, I'm so glad. I wish I could tell you how much that means to me, how relieved I am. Not angry – never angry! – and not disappointed either. And I wish I could tell you how much I love you, and reassure you that I will be with you until your dying day, whether or not I'm still... here... in this form."

Reaching out her hand, Beth tried to touch her daughter, to embrace her, to connect with her in some way. And for just a moment Rhiannon flinched, then spun around again, gazing wildly into the air as though she'd felt her.

"Mum, could it really be you? If it is, thank you for being the most amazing mother I could have had. I know you had the worst, but I had the best anyone could dream of. I'm so grateful to you for encouraging me to be who I am, who I want to become. You let me see your magical life, explore it with you, even when I was too young to understand. And Rose has been a wise and wonderful mentor, and you gave me her too, as a grandmother, as a friend, as a priestess, so it still all comes back to you."

Beth laughed, the joy at her daughter's words lighting her up, making her weightless and buoyant with relief.

"And you taught me to be strong yet kind," Rhiannon continued. "I did forget that for a while, and needed my friend Carlie to remind me, but that was all you too. God, I wish you could have met Carlie. You would love her, I promise, she's so magical and mature – but most of all she's just the sweetest, kindest person I've ever known, aside from you."

Rhiannon paused to draw breath – and to wipe her eyes. Several tears had spilled over her lashes. One she caught on her hand, one fell into her mouth and was swallowed down, and another dropped into the ocean, becoming part of the soul of the world. Beth watched its iridescence swirl on the surface until a wave sent it crashing to the shore.

"And if only you could meet Tom as well. He's so lovely. Admittedly we had a few issues recently – well, I did – but since he came to see me, so far out of his way, I'm feeling much better, and am working on my trust issues. And –"

"Rhi-Rhi! Look at me!" Brodie called out, and Rhiannon turned away from Beth and swam towards her brother, splashing him until he squealed with laughter, then dragging him through the gorgeous green water as he kicked his legs, becoming more comfortable and confident with each wave he soared over. Beth smiled. She would never tire of watching her children, and seeing them grow closer, Rhiannon so protective of her little brother, and Brodie so grateful for the time she spent with him.

"Kids, are you ready for lunch?"

The voice of her husband flying over the waves made Beth swing abruptly in his direction, and she swooped over to where he

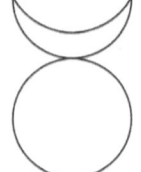

stood on the sand. He was so handsome. So lovely. So loving. Goddess she missed him, so desperately, and she could see he still missed her, in the frown furrowed on his brow even now, while he was on holiday and far from any work stress. In the way he didn't even notice the women sending admiring glances in his direction. Would he always be like this, oblivious to any potential new partner? Was there something she could do to help him? Reassure him in some way? Turn his eyes to the future and his heart to a new love?

A flare of fear made her hot, and her form wavered uncertainly. Rhiannon would start college later this year, and might move out to stay on campus. What would Mike do then? How would he cope if it was just him and Brodie? Or would that possibility stop Rhiannon from leaving home, maybe even stop her pursuing higher education? Beth hoped not. It would crush her if her daughter gave up her dream because her mother had deserted her and she didn't think her dad could cope without her.

She had to help Mike realise he was strong enough to cope – and ready to move on. Brodie would turn seven soon, so he wasn't completely dependent anymore. Surely Mike knew he could date someone else now. That he should. She'd been dead for more than eighteen months.

*Ugh!*

That thought still freaked Beth out, and she felt herself tear apart, her molecules dissolving and dispersing into the French sunbeams of that beach she'd once been so happy on.

## Chapter 29

### Rhiannon

"I like him more than the other boy," Brodie said, out of nowhere. Rhiannon stared at her little brother, shocked. "More than John? What makes you say that?"

"Tom is more fun, and he makes you happy, like Carlie does. Plus he really likes you."

Flabbergasted, Rhiannon's jaw dropped. "How do you know that?"

"He listens to you, and pays attention to what you say, and he never takes his eyes from your face."

They were on the ferry home from France, sitting out on the sunny deck drinking lemonade, and Rhiannon had been daydreaming about Tom. She looked up at her dad, a question in her eyes, and he beamed at her and nodded in agreement.

"It's true. He's a lovely guy, very considerate, and it's clear how much he likes and respects you. I hope you sorted everything out?"

"We did, thanks Dad." Rhiannon flushed with embarrassment. "And thanks for being okay with him turning up unannounced. I had no idea he was coming, I promise, but I'm so glad he did."

Mike laughed. "It was a relief for me too. It was tough watching you pine for him, and beat yourself up over whatever happened before we left. And it was okay that he turned up. I trust you darling."

Emotion swamped Rhiannon, and her vision blurred as her eyes welled. When her hat flew off her head, she was glad to jump up and chase it across the deck. What was wrong with her? Why was she almost in tears just because her dad said he trusted her?

By the time they arrived home late on Sunday afternoon, they were all tired, and Rhiannon was looking forward to a long bath and an early night. The light on their answering machine was flashing, and she dropped her bag and hit play.

"Hello everyone, it's Rose. I hope you had a magical time in Brittany, and I can't wait to hear about all your adventures. I've made you a casserole for dinner tonight, if Rhiannon wouldn't mind picking it up. Lots of love…"

Her dad turned to Rhiannon, and she smiled. "Sure, I'll just take our bags upstairs."

Another voice began, and Rhiannon froze. "Hi Rhi and Brodie, hi Mike. This is Laura."

Sneaking a look at her dad, she grinned as a faint blush coloured his cheeks. Had he also wondered if it was her teacher that Jessica had been referring to in the tea-leaf reading he had on the edge of the forest? The person he already knew, who Beth approved of, who would bring love back to his life?

"I'm looking forward to hearing about your trip tomorrow at school, but I just wanted to remind you about the summer festival the week after Beltane. Tickets were getting low, so I bought four, in case you want to go together, or you can have my ticket and take someone else if that's better."

Brodie's eyes widened with excitement. "Ooh, I love that festival," he said. "And Laura's a nice lady. Can we go with her Dad?"

"Sure buddy, that will be fun," he replied, glancing at Rhiannon then quickly looking away.

*Did he look guilty? Sheepish?*

"Do you mind popping over to Rose's now?" he asked, and she tried not to smirk. *Nice shift of topic.* "I'll take your bag up."

Laughing, she grabbed her keys and headed out into the golden afternoon. Laura, hey? She and Beth had shared a flat while they trained to be teachers, before Mike and Beth had started dating.

Would it be awkward for Laura that she'd seen their relationship grow and flourish? Would it be weird for her dad, wondering what secrets Beth had shared with her best friend about him over the years? And would it be strange for *her*, her dad dating her teacher?

Dating. Her dad had probably thought he never had to do that again, but now here he'd be, dating just like his daughter.

Her mind shied away from that thought, and she focused back on whether it would change her situation at school. It wasn't long until she and Carlie would graduate and be off to college though, so there was no reason Laura should worry about that.

She was still pondering the potential love match when she knocked on Rose's door.

"Sweet girl, come in. How was France?" Rose asked, leading her out to the kitchen and pouring water from the just-boiled kettle into the teapot. Like she'd known the exact moment Rhiannon would arrive.

"It was so amazing. I wandered up the winding cobblestone lanes of Mont-Saint-Michel, along faery paths in Broceliande Forest, and through the stone rows of Carnac." For some reason she didn't want to mention Tom. Not her fears and her silliness at the start, or the wonderful reassuring moments they'd spent together that had set her mind and heart at ease. "And it was nice to spend time with Brodie – he loved all the King Arthur associations of Paimpont, and the Lady of the Lake stories..."

Gulping, Rhiannon trailed off. Rose was staring at her, that priestess-focused, scrutinising observance that made her skin prickle and her throat dry up. Trying to swallow down her apprehension, she blundered on. "And it was great to see Dad relaxing too, and not worrying about work for a bit..."

Rose frowned as she steered Rhiannon to the table, drawing her down until they both sat, facing each other. She took Rhiannon's hands, her strong fingers soothing, even as her expression made Rhiannon shiver.

"I've been so worried about you," the priestess finally admitted. "I dreamed about you every night you were away. Are you sure you're okay?"

Composure slipping, Rhiannon forced a smile and nodded. "I'm good," she said, trying to make her voice sound more confident than she felt. "Tom managed to come down and meet us for a couple of days, which was lovely. We had a, um, a minor misunderstanding before I left, but we sorted it out, and it's going really well. And Dad likes him, which is a relief, and vice versa of course."

She was babbling now, she knew, but Rose's unflinching gaze was freaking her out.

"Your mother came to me too, in a dream. It was so vivid."

Rhiannon gasped. And noticed that her hands were trembling. She didn't know if she was angry that her mum could appear to everyone except her, or terrified of what Beth might have told the priestess. "I'm sure Mum would love Tom too," she whispered.

Rose frowned, and absently stroked Rhiannon's arms. It was so soothing, she wondered if the older woman was casting a spell on her.

"It was not about Tom, although I'm glad it's going well for you, and that your dad likes him. I know you were worried about that."

Biting her bottom lip, Rhiannon nodded reluctantly. "What did Mum tell you?"

"She said you've been trying to deal with something big, and that she let you down over it. And she begged me to help you."

Fire ignited within Rhiannon, scorching her heart, her skin, her very being, choking her so she couldn't speak, even if she'd wanted to. Not that she did. She couldn't talk about that. *Wouldn't* talk about it. Especially not to Rose, the woman who had been like a grandmother to her all these years.

"I'm fine." Her voice was raspy, disconnected. The room tilted around her, and she clung to Rose's hands so she wouldn't fall. Her breaths came in ragged, desperate gulps, and tears poured down her face.

"Sweet girl, you don't have to tell me what happened, although my dreams were disturbing, and felt painfully real, and your mum hinted at... things."

The flames rose, burning Rhiannon's whole body red. With embarrassment. With fear. With a faint stirring of anger. But mostly with shame.

"No." Her denial was loud, firm, strong. Until all her carefully constructed barriers cracked and crumbled, and her tears turned into wrenching sobs. Rose drew the distraught girl into her arms and held her tight, and for what felt like days, water leaked from her eyes down the priestess's back.

But finally, slowly, her crying subsided, and Rhiannon pulled herself together, and pulled away, scrubbing at her cheeks and sighing as she tried to pull herself together.

"I'm sorry," she murmured. "I thought I had this under control, that I was fine with everything, healed and resolved, long before I went away. But then in the forest in Brittany I, well, I had a conversation with someone, and discovered that I wasn't actually over it, not by a long shot. So I worked through things some more over there, and thought *that* would be the end of it, yet here I am in your kitchen, a sobbing wreck incapable of speech, as far from okay as you could be. Does it never end?"

The priestess handed her the tissue box and laid a reassuring hand on her arm. "Darling girl, I'm so sorry you're in so much pain. Could I do some healing on you?"

Hesitantly Rhiannon nodded, although she was suddenly shy and terribly unsure of what to do.

"Just sit there, and shut your eyes, and try to relax."

Convinced there was no way she could relax, Rhiannon was surprised to be bathed in a soothing warmth the moment she closed her eyes, as though she was floating in a hot, flower-strewn tub. She sensed Rose stand up and move behind her, then felt the priestess's hands settle on her shoulders.

Images flitted through her mind. A forest, but this one was sparkling, bright and welcoming, the opposite of the dark and spooky woods she dreaded. Laughter echoed between the trees, comforting her, and golden light surrounded her. It was familiar, and somehow related to her mother, but the connection remained elusive, hovering on the edge of her consciousness but never settling. The light permeated her whole body, making her smile, and lifting her heart with unexpected delight.

She came to a swift running stream, and marvelled as her anxiety dissolved and was washed away by the cleansing, pacifying power of the water, which soothed her with its music as it rippled over rocks, bubbled through a shallow pool, and eddied around a fallen log.

When Rose knelt and grasped her feet, Rhiannon giggled, and an explosion of tiny fae beings flitted about her head, blowing kisses to her, stroking her hair, and promising her peace and joy. Then there were cool lips on her forehead, and she heard her mother's voice.

*My darling, you are stronger than you know, and surrounded by more love than you can imagine. Trust in that, and allow them to heal you, to know you. Allow them to see you, the real you, because you are brighter than any star.*

A tear rolled down Rhiannon's cheek, but she was smiling. "I promise," she whispered.

Rose gently patted her shoulder and told her she could open her eyes, and Rhiannon spun around in confusion. "How did you get behind me again?"

"I didn't move sweet girl, I had my hands on your shoulders the whole time."

"But you were holding my feet, I felt it," she protested.

The priestess smiled as she took her seat, and Rhiannon's hands, again. "That wasn't me. But your mum was with us for a while."

That revelation should have broken her, but instead she felt empowered, and surrounded by love. "Thank you for helping me connect with her then. I imagined she was with me in Carnac actually, hovering in the air above me, but I know it was just wishful thinking."

"Don't be so sure," Rose said softly. "Now, how are you feeling?"

Shrugging, Rhiannon glanced down, and saw that her hands were no longer shaking. The soothing warmth still surrounded her. "I'm okay, I think. Thank you."

"Good." Bustling around the kitchen, Rose kept the conversation light until she'd poured them both cups of tea and sat back down. Rhiannon stirred in extra honey, needing the comfort, and the sweetness. She gazed at the older woman expectantly.

Lifting the cup to her lips, the priestess sipped the pungent herbal brew, before setting it down and taking Rhiannon's hands again.

"Sweet girl, when something traumatic happens to us – a death, a loss, some kind of violence – it will always be a part of us, no matter how many healings we have, and courses we do, and counsellors we seek. No matter how many people we heal. I understand, I really do, how you can feel like you've already processed it, resolved it, let go of it, and yet here it is again, another layer revealed, another level of hurt and pain and guilt, rising again to drown you."

The ache in her voice was so deep and ancient. Rhiannon thought of all the tragedy the priestess had endured. Losing her only child, then her husband, while still so young. And hadn't Carlie mentioned that Rose's parents were cruel and awful too? Yet she carried on. She helped everyone, and was loved and respected by all. She functioned so well despite – or maybe because of – those tragedies.

"I promise it will lessen its grip on you," Rose continued, smiling forlornly. "In time it will be swamped by better memories and visions. It will no longer control you, no longer burn within your body, crippling you from living, and loving."

Rhiannon shuddered as a flashback from the dark woods seared her mind. She wanted to bolt from this kitchen, from this woman who understood too much, and from what she was trying to tell her. But she knew she needed to hear it, knew she needed to deal with this so she could be normal again, whatever that was. So she swallowed down some of the tea, along with her reluctance, and lifted her gaze to meet Rose's sad eyes.

The priestess smiled at her, love and acceptance rippling outward as she spoke. "The things that happen to us, they make us who we are, and you are a wonderful, kind, compassionate and caring young woman, who will do so much good in the world, and help so many. But accepting that it makes us who we are is *not* the same as saying we made it happen, or wanted it, or should be grateful for it, or that we needed to experience it in order to grow, as some so-called gurus foolishly claim. It will always be a part of the book of your life, but it is not your fault, not your doing, not your responsibility."

Heat prickled on Rhiannon's skin, and her head spun, clouded with anger and grief and frustration. Maybe she couldn't do this. Couldn't cope. Couldn't be in a functioning relationship.

"Hey!" Rose said, lifting Rhiannon's chin, her eyes boring into her with strength and calm. "It's only a page sweet girl, not a chapter, and certainly not the whole story. And soon it will be nothing more than a passing sentence, or a passing thought, a footnote at the end of a long-forgotten story you barely ever think of. It does not define you. It cannot control you. And it absolutely will not destroy you, do you hear me?"

Finally managing a weak, barely-there smile, Rhiannon nodded. "I hear you."

"Good. Now, Carlie will be home from the healing centre soon –"

Panic shot through Rhiannon, but the priestess lifted a comforting hand to her cheek. "Your secret is safe with me. You can tell her when you're ready. But I'd best give you that dinner I offered, so you can all eat tonight."

Standing up and moving swiftly to the fridge, Rose pulled out a large crockery pot and handed it to Rhiannon. "Time is a great healer sweet girl, but so is sharing and empathy, and allowing people in to help and support you."

When Rhiannon opened her mouth to interject, the priestess held up her hand. "Only when you're ready. But pain and shame fester in silence and in the bleakness of isolation, growing and twisting and sending deeper roots. Letting in the light is the best way to conquer darkness, and talking about whatever happened is the most effective way to lessen your shame."

Putting an arm around her, Rose kissed Rhiannon's forehead, then led her gently to the door. "You are stronger than you know sweet girl, and surrounded by more love than you can imagine."

Rhiannon stared at her, shocked to hear her mother's words, but the priestess just smiled. "I'm glad you had a wonderful holiday. Please give my love to Mike and Brodie, and I'll see you soon."

As she made her way home, Rhiannon stared up at the stars just beginning to twinkle in the fading twilight, searching for answers, for assurance. Rose wasn't the first to advise her to reveal what had happened to her.

A memory of the woman in red in the woods by the fire, telling her to speak it.

Of stern and regret-filled Morgaine in the forest, demanding that she name it, and share it.

Of sweet Viviane by the lake, instructing her to let go of her fear and reveal her secret and her self.

But Rhiannon still wasn't convinced about the wisdom of telling. She couldn't tell her dad, as that would destroy him. Carlie had enough going on, enough tragedy of her own, and didn't deserve to have this drama dumped on her. And would Tom still be interested in her if he realised just how screwed up and damaged she really was?

She wasn't ready to put that to the test right now, and she wasn't sure she ever would be.

Chapter 30

# The Hungry Ghost

Rhiannon

Candlelight flickered, shadows danced on the walls, and incense smoke curled towards the ceiling in a heady blend of jasmine and lemongrass. Rhiannon grinned as she took in the purple cushions strewn on her bedroom floor, and the magical tools arranged on her small altar. It had been great to see Carlie when they returned to school yesterday, and she was really looking forward to tonight's coven meeting. She'd pretty much deserted her friend in the weeks leading up to their holiday, then had headed off across the sea for a fortnight, but with only two weeks until Beltane, she was determined to reconnect with her coven sister and catch up on her life, and weave some more of their grounding, comforting, healing magic.

When Carlie knocked on the door, Rhiannon greeted her with apologies for abandoning her, but her friend shrugged it off and insisted that having time alone had been good for her. They chatted about school and books and music while they made tea in the kitchen, but once they were in her room and breathing in the calming scent of jasmine, Rhiannon made one more attempt to set things right.

"I'm really sorry I put seeing Tom before our coven nights, especially as I was so mean to you when you missed just one to see Rowan," she said nervously. "And it was especially bad timing coming just before our French trip."

Carlie smiled as she gazed around the room. "It's fine, life happens," she insisted, walking over to look at the photos Rhiannon had just added to her pin-up board from her recent travels.

"That's me and Brodie at Paimpont Abbey," she said, enthusiasm warming her voice. "And me and Tom at Carnac…" She was grinning so widely she must look totally goofy, but Tom turning up to see her had meant the world to her, and she was so relieved that she was finally over her silly insecurities. That afternoon in the forest with him, and the following day, when they'd wandered through a field of stones and sheltered in a burial tomb – *who knew that could be romantic?* – were some of the best moments of her life. She was about to tell Carlie all about it, but her friend had frozen in shock as she peered at the photo in the bottom corner.

"Oh, that's Mum, from when we went to Brittany four years ago. This trip was kind of a remembrance, one we did in her honour, retracing the steps of the holiday we took with her. I don't know, it probably sounds silly –"

"That's your mum?" Carlie broke in, and her voice sounded strange, almost scared.

Rhiannon stared at her in surprise. "Yes, haven't I shown you pictures of her before?"

"I've only seen the ones from that dress-up party, when she was wearing a masquerade mask, and a few from towards the end of… well, from when she was really sick and had lost a lot of weight," Carlie replied.

"And lost her hair," Rhiannon said sadly. "But this is what she looked like before she got sick. She was so beautiful."

Carlie murmured her agreement, and Rhiannon walked over to stand beside her. It was deeply flattering when people said she looked like her mum, but Rhiannon didn't see it herself. About to offer some self-deprecating remark, she stopped when she realised something was upsetting her friend. What could be strange about a photo of her mother?

"What's wrong?" she asked, voice sharp.

"That's the woman I was talking to in the cafe that night, the one who reminded me of you," Carlie whispered.

Rhiannon stared at her blankly. "What woman?"

"Remember when I told you I'd met a woman who I didn't know, but who seemed to know me, and I tried to describe her, but she sounded like she could have been any of the women in Rose's circle? Well, it was her," she said, pointing to the photo.

"But she's –"

"I know," Carlie said flatly. "But she was wearing that exact same outfit too. And looked just as beautiful."

Rhiannon sank down onto one of the big purple cushions, photo in her hand, fear in her heart, but face filled with longing and hope. "What did she say?" she begged, then almost laughed, that she didn't doubt for a second that her friend had seen the ghost of her dead mother. She had no wish to query her on the specifics or even think about how impossible this whole thing was. Her mum had died nine months before Carlie arrived in Summer Hill, so it made no sense that she'd seen Beth's ghost. Yet it seemed that somehow she had, and Rhiannon wanted to know every single word she'd said, any tiny clue as to how she was, or where she was. Something to hold on to. *Anything.*

"The first thing she said was how much she loved the hot chocolate in that cafe," Carlie said, eyes gazing off into the distance as she tried to recall their conversation. "She was holding a mug of it, inhaling the scent, but I realised after she left that she didn't drink even a sip of it, which did seem weird."

Heart racing, Rhiannon's hopes rose. It had to be true. Only her mum would find a way to communicate from the other side and talk about hot chocolate. "That was her favourite treat. When we'd ask for pizza or chips or whatever, all she wanted was a mug of hot chocolate from Kylie's Cafe. Even when she was too sick to leave the house, she'd send me or Brodie out to get her a takeaway cup of it. But what else did she say?" she implored her friend.

"I asked her how she knew so much about me, and she said we hadn't met before, so I could stop thinking I was rude to have forgotten her. 'You could say I'm a friend of Rhiannon's,' she added, then told me that she knew I was worried about you, and she was glad we'd reconnected, and were such good friends, and that you would never intentionally hurt me."

Rhiannon stared at her friend, spellbound. "What else?"

"She said she could sense I was worried about Mike – it was after you'd told me he thought my mum hated him, and he'd let her down, so I'd copied some pages from Mum's diary for him, to reassure him that she'd always considered him a dear friend, and her only regret had been hurting him and Gran," Carlie replied.

"Wow, I didn't know you'd done that," Rhiannon said softly, jolted for a moment out of her frantic need to know. "Thank you so much for sharing that with him."

Carlie shrugged. "It was the least I could do."

Smiling absently, Rhiannon traced the outline of her mother's face on the photo she was still clutching. Then she turned to her friend, anxiety clear in the rigidity of her shoulder, desperate for anything more she could offer. But Carlie hesitated, worry creasing her brow.

"What aren't you telling me?" Rhiannon asked anxiously.

"Um, well, she said that I was kind like my mother, so of course I wanted to know if she'd known Mum, and she told me that she had, and that everyone in the village had loved her, and felt her loss when she left. Then she said she knew that Mike had never stopped loving her. Which made me mad, so I told her that wasn't true – that he had married an amazing woman who he adored, who he adores still, and whose children miss her terribly."

Tears welled in Rhiannon's eyes, and she was touched by her friend's faith, and her attempt at reassurance, when clearly Beth had been trying to offer Carlie a gift about her own mother. "Then what?" she asked, voice a haunted whisper.

"She said: 'I'm sure she misses them more than anything too,'" Carlie replied, then leaned over to embrace her friend.

Rhiannon smiled through her tears. "Thank you."

"What for?" Carlie asked, surprised. "I feel even worse now that it was your mum who said Mike always loved mine."

"Of course he did, and that's okay. It didn't diminish his love for Mum in any way, and it just made her like him even more, to know that he would always care about someone even when they were gone." There was a hitch in Rhiannon's voice. Had her mum always known she would die before her husband?

"She got confirmation from you that he still loves her, and I'm so grateful to you for that. I remember just before she died, when it was getting really difficult and she was so sick, I heard her telling Dad that she wanted him to find love again after she was gone. He told her that there was no way, but she insisted – she said she knew it wouldn't ever lessen the love he had for her, he would just find some more room in his heart for a new person."

Impatiently wiping her tear-filled eyes, Rhiannon tried to compose herself, but she was a mess. Carlie gave her an awkward hug, then went downstairs to make more tea and give her friend some space. Rhiannon didn't move, she just sat where she was, staring at the photo of her mother, trying to remember every word Carlie had said. Then anger and frustration bubbled up within her. She tried to shake it off, to push it down, but it was consuming her.

"How could you go to Carlie and not to me?" she cried. "I've been so desperate to see you, to talk to you, and she doesn't even know you! Didn't know to give me a message, because she had no idea who you were. Why would you ignore me in favour of my friend, my friend who gets everything! I'm the one who wants to see you so desperately. And surely I'm the one who *deserves* to see you?"

Furiously she scrubbed her wet cheeks, and tried to stop crying. Tried to control her breathing, and her tone. "I just want to see you so badly Mum. So bad it's driving me crazy. I'd swear you were with me in Mont-Saint-Michel, and I imagined I was talking to you in Carnac too, in the ocean, but you didn't say a word. Yet you show up in our favourite cafe and talk to Carlie? And appear to Rose in dreams? It's not fair! Why would you do this to me?"

Hearing footsteps on the stairs, she stopped speaking, but her body still shook with an anger she didn't want to feel, yet couldn't stop. Taking a deep breath, she forced herself to smile when Carlie handed her a cup of tea, then focused all her energy on her friend when she realised she was agitated too.

"What's wrong?" Rhiannon asked as she sipped her tea, grateful for the change of topic. "You look a little worried."

Carlie smiled. "Am I really that obvious? I'm just... well, I don't know... Do you think I'm going crazy, to be seeing things that aren't really there, to be having conversations with... um, what would you even call them? Ghosts?"

There was scepticism in her voice, and a hint of fear. Rhiannon sometimes forgot that Carlie hadn't had any idea about spirituality or new age healing or magic until she arrived in Summer Hill. "I don't know," she began, making her voice gentle. "I've never seen one, but obviously I very much want to believe that you did speak to my mother." She sighed, unable to totally mask her emotions. "Has it ever happened to you before?"

When Carlie hesitated, Rhiannon wondered just how much of her life she'd missed while being so distracted with Tom. Had she wanted to confide in her about this stuff before, and been frustrated that her friend never had time for her? Taking her hand, Rhiannon vowed to be there for her from now on.

"Your mum was the first one, but a few days after that I found the cottage again, the one in the mists, and Rowan was there," Carlie reluctantly admitted.

Rhiannon gasped. "You never said anything about that!" Then she reined in her indignation. When would her friend have told her? While she was rushing off after school to meet Tom? Standing Carlie up? Having dinner parties she invited everyone *but* her best friend to?

"To be honest, I thought you'd think I was going mad," Carlie said. "And it was the day you'd gone to see John, to break up with him. I knew you were hurt by his reaction, after you'd finally gathered the courage to reveal yourself to him, so I didn't want to start rambling on about ghosts and mists and things that were there but not there, if that makes sense. I didn't want to twist the conversation around to be all about me – I wanted to be there for you."

Rhiannon smiled. "I appreciate that." She was grateful – again – that her friend was so sensitive to her moods and emotions, and also surprised to recall that day. At the time, her break-up had seemed like the end of the world, the biggest and most dramatic decision of her life. But now, secure in her love for Tom, and overwhelmed by the immensity of her feelings for him, she couldn't even remember what she'd seen in John. Life was strange.

"What did Rowan say?" Rhiannon asked.

"Just that he loved me, and he knew that I loved him too, and that he'd felt the moment when I changed my mind and decided that I was going to choose both of you," Carlie whispered.

A shiver of regret pulsed through Rhiannon, and she grimaced. Her cruel ultimatum to Carlie, that she had to break up with Rowan or lose her friendship forever, was not her proudest moment, and she still cringed when she thought of it.

"And he wanted me to stop wishing it had been me that died instead of him – I'd said it wasn't fair because he had so much still to do, so much to give, so many people to help, but he insisted that I was going to do amazing things too, and he wanted me to know how much I am loved, and valued, and that I will make a difference too."

"That's beautiful," Rhiannon said, mortified that she hadn't been aware her friend had contemplated checking out, even for a moment.

"I guess," Carlie replied sadly, and her friend raised her eyebrows at her. "I mean, yes, it was beautiful, but I'd pretty much convinced myself I was just dreaming it, or imagining it, that it was some kind of wishful thinking, confirming to myself that he died knowing I loved him, because that's what I've been torturing myself over. Now that I know I saw your mum though, it makes it seem more real. But then I wonder why I haven't seen him again. Why has he left me?" she asked, voice broken, imploring.

"He'll never leave you," Rhiannon said emphatically. Desperately she wanted that to be true, for her friend's sake as well as her own. Because if her mum had managed to appear to Carlie, maybe she would eventually contact her too.

Carlie sighed and shook her head. "But I can't find him any more, and I no longer hear his voice either. The last time he spoke to me was a month ago, at Ostara, when Tom was tattooing me. He said he'll always be with me, but it's time to let him go."

Curiosity burned within Rhiannon. She was eager to know everything Rowan had said, but she waited for Carlie to speak.

This wasn't about her, or what she wanted to know, it was about what her friend felt ready to share.

"I don't want to let him go."

Her ragged, broken voice tore at Rhiannon's heart, and she leaned over and embraced her friend.

"Maybe my mum's words are for you too – that you can eventually love someone else, and it won't mean you love Rowan any less, just that you've made room in your heart for another person too. Like your mum did, and my dad too – they still loved each other, even when they both married someone else. And I know that if Dad does meet someone, even remarry, it won't diminish his love for my mum, or yours, or for the new person. His heart will just grow even bigger."

The front door opened then banged shut, and Rhiannon looked over at the clock by her bed. "Oh my god, how did it get to ten o'clock? We haven't organised a single thing for Beltane!"

Carlie shrugged as she tried to smother a yawn. "We'll have to do it next week, but we'll be fine. Maybe we can coordinate with Gran and share some of her wisdom while we help her prepare for the ritual. Not that she's been home much lately – she and Jake's grandfather have been seeing each other, so to speak, and I think it's getting serious," she revealed.

Eyes wide with excitement, Rhiannon stared at her friend. "Really? When did this start?"

"Oh yeah, I guess we've barely seen each other in the last month, what with exams and boyfriends and holidays," Carlie teased, and Rhiannon blushed.

"I'm joking! They'd been spending a bit of time together, gardening and stuff, and I know at first Gran was just helping him with his grief, helping him move forward. But after Ostara we were grinding herbs one night, and she brought up Jake, and suggested that there could be room in my life for more than one great love. And for some reason I called her on it – I said it was a bit hypocritical of her to tell me to move on and open my heart, when she'd denied herself love for more than twenty years."

"You didn't!" Rhiannon gasped.

"I'm afraid I did," Carlie said sheepishly. "It was a long conversation, and I was as gentle as I could be, although there were definitely some tears. But in the end she thanked me – because when she really opened up and looked within, she was shocked to realise that she *had* denied herself love, had walled up her heart, ever since Grandpa died. And despite healing so many other people, helping them become brave enough to risk everything for love, she'd never done it herself. She didn't think she deserved it."

"Wow," Rhiannon breathed.

Her dad knocked on the door then, and poked his head in to say hello, and the girls reluctantly packed up for the night. Carlie headed home in the inky black, and Rhiannon quickly got ready for bed. But as tired as she was, once she lay down in the almost-dark, she couldn't sleep. The message Carlie had gifted her from her mum spun round and round in her head. She was grateful for it, yet her anger hadn't totally subsided. It wasn't fair, she knew, but that didn't ease the bitterness.

"Mum," she hissed, trying to keep her voice low so she wouldn't wake her brother, but loud enough that if Beth's ghost was hovering around her, she would hear.

"I miss you, and I love you, but why would you go to Carlie and not to me? She didn't even know it was you. Why won't you talk to me, or to Dad at least? He is suffering terribly."

Wildly her eyes roamed the room, traversing the ceiling, and peering into dark corners not illuminated by the waning moon outside her window. Why had her mother appeared, fully formed and human-seeming, to her friend? With the power to lift a cup? And if it was back when she was breaking up with John, that was two months ago. What if Carlie had never connected the two, never been able to pass the message on?

Tears ran down her face, some trickling into her ears, others into her mouth. She was choking on her misery. On her grief. She'd thought she was coping with it all, yet here it was again, hiding in the shadows, ready to leap out and pounce on her at any fragile moment.

Trying to wrestle her emotions into some semblance of control, she softened her voice. "I just wish you were here Mum, so I could tell you all about Tom, and about our trip to Brittany. We thought of you the whole time we were there. And Brodie is so grown up now, you'd be amazed. He's such a great kid. Dad is still a bit of a mess, still hiding in his work, but he's functioning better than before now. And he did seem to relax a little on holiday, although I despair of him ever being able to give his heart to someone new."

She paused, feeling silly to be talking to herself, wishing so desperately that her mother would appear to her, like she had to Carlie, would wrap her arms around her and reassure her that she was still with her, still watching over them.

"I'm grateful for the message that you love us, and glad that your words might also provide some comfort for Carlie about Rowan. Do you know him? Are you in contact with each other over there, wherever there is? I guess that would be nice, if it was true. That you would find peace together."

Terror struck her as she thought that idea through. "Although if that is the case, he might have told you awful things about me. True things, but awful. Like how I was so cruel to Carlie. God, Mum, why aren't you here?"

And with that, she sobbed into her pillow until she finally fell asleep.

Chapter 31

# The Ache of Oblivion

## Beth

Swooping down from where she was floating on Rhiannon's ceiling, Beth settled on the side of her bed. It was breaking her heart to listen to her daughter's furious words. To feel her pain so tangibly, each sentence she hissed at her mother a barb through the heart. Focusing all her will, she tried to draw the molecules of her diaphanous form together, tried again to become visible, or at least weighty enough for her daughter to feel her presence, but she couldn't do it. She understood why Rhiannon felt betrayed, but she had no idea how she'd been able to appear to Carlie, or why she couldn't to anyone else.

At least Carlie had finally realised who she'd spoken to that night in the cafe, and passed on Beth's message to Rhiannon. She was glad Carlie had been able to talk to Rowan too – but her admission that she no longer saw him filled her with panic. What had happened to him? Carlie had last seen him a month ago, at Ostara, when he'd only been dead for three months. And now he was gone. Where had he disappeared to? Would she go to the same place, or did somewhere awful await her?

More importantly, did this mean *she* might disappear at any moment? Or had Rowan only moved on because he'd already resolved his unfinished business?

A memory of the flash of gold she'd seen the night she spoke to Carlie, when she'd sensed something trying to lure her back to the cemetery, smashed into Beth. She flinched, the shock of it tearing her apart, then felt herself scatter across the room and out the window into the back garden. Desperately she tried to pull herself together, to reconstruct her form and stay with her daughter.

But she couldn't. And eventually she let go and dispersed back into the ether, her spirit returning to the stars above, her awareness disintegrating into the void.

For the next few days Beth drifted in and out of consciousness. Dimly she was aware of her family moving around her – Mike heading off to work, Rhiannon and Brodie going to school, the three having meals together around the kitchen table at night. But it was the scent of honeysuckle and jasmine that drew her back fully to her strange semi-existence. The familiar sucking sensation as she re-awoke chilled her, but the spring flowers soothed her into unfurling and becoming present.

Wide eyed, she gazed around herself, surprised to discover she was out the front of Rose's cottage. The sweet perfume of the honeysuckle twining around the gate enveloped her in memories of love and magic, but she was confused. Why was she here? Was Rhiannon inside?

Focusing her will, she pushed her way through the door, offering a prayer of apology to Rose, and made her way through the house. But no one was home. Dejected, she floated back out to the front garden, then stopped abruptly. A woman she'd never seen before was sitting on the steps, shoulders slumped. A large wooden trunk had been dragged awkwardly onto the verandah beside her, and a small black kitten was threading unnoticed between her feet.

Confusion disoriented Beth. She swirled around the stranger, touching a hesitant hand to her shoulder in an effort to get a clue from her, then darting right at her and staring into her eyes, trying to glimpse who she was, and why she had called Beth to her.

Footsteps on the pavement made her spin around, and she saw Carlie approaching the cottage, dragging her feet, clearly shattered and distraught. Did she know the woman? For long drawn out moments Beth waited impatiently, willing the girl to lift her eyes and notice the figure on her doorstep.

Finally she did.

"Mrs Dunbar! Hello. I was just thinking about you," she stammered as she caught sight of the woman. "Are you okay?"

The elegantly dressed stranger stood up and hugged Carlie. "Please, it's Louisa," she said. "And I've been thinking of you too. How are you going?"

Beth stared from one to the other in bewilderment. Who on earth was Louisa Dunbar? And why – and how? – had she pulled Beth here to witness this strange, morose reunion? As much as she wanted to leave though, she couldn't look away.

The two sat down on the step together, the kitten pressed to Carlie's side, and Beth peered at them intently.

"I'm all right," Carlie said softly, trying to convince herself as much as her companion. "I miss him constantly, but Rose has been wonderful, and so patient, and I'm getting through the days."

"I'm doing okay too," Louisa offered with a faint, resigned air. "One day at a time, right?"

Beth smiled sadly. This must be the mother of Carlie's boyfriend Rowan, the one who had died so tragically.

Carlie was nodding, and Beth's heart tore apart at the pain the young girl had already endured in her short life. Both her parents lost, plus her home, friends, school, and country. Then on top of that, her first love. The only silver lining was that she'd discovered she had a grandmother she could stay with, and Beth couldn't think of a single better person for a guardian. The priestess had taken Beth under her wing when she was young and angry and warring with her parents, and she thanked the goddess every day for Rose's presence in her and her family's life.

But none of that explained why Beth was here now, witnessing this conversation between Carlie and a woman she'd never known. Returning her attention to them, she desperately tried to find a link.

"I'm moving up to Scotland next week to live with my sister for a while, so I wanted to say goodbye to you, and thank you for loving

Rowan so much, and making him so happy. And, well, I was packing up his apartment, and I thought you might like a few of his things," Louisa said, indicating the wooden trunk.

Carlie tried to encourage Louisa to keep them, but the older woman shook her head, insisting that the teenager accept the magical books and ritual tools her son had collected over years of druidic study and practice. Carlie was overwhelmed, and teary, but finally nodded and offered her gratitude.

"I know this sounds kind of weird, but Rowan mentioned to me not long before he died that if anything happened to him, he wanted you to have these," Louisa said, her voice a sigh.

Carlie recoiled in horror – and so did Beth. "You mean he knew that he was going to die?" she gasped.

"I don't know," his mum admitted. "I'm not sure if it was a premonition, or if he just loved you so deeply, and was telling me this to make sure I knew how much. But... oh, this will sound strange, but I saw him a few times, after he died," she said.

Beth hovered closer. Maybe this was why she was here. To figure out how to make herself seen, and known, to her own loved ones. She listened intently as Louisa detailed the occasions she'd seen her dead son, and her heart hurt for the woman's pain. No parent should have to endure their child's death.

"And you'll probably think I'm crazy when I tell you this," Louisa continued. "But the last time I saw him he spoke to me, and it was like he was there with me, talking to me, holding me while I cried. It was he who suggested I move back to Scotland to spend some time with my sister. And he reassured me that he would still be with me no matter where I lived, but that I had to start picking up the pieces and moving forward with my life."

Longing and hope overcame Beth. Could she appear to Mike in the same way, and convince him to move forward, to be open to finding love again? And could she make herself known to Rhiannon too, and offer her some comfort and reassurance?

Why couldn't she figure out how to do it? Dejected, she swooped around Louisa again, trying to catch her attention, then dove at Carlie. Her daughter's best friend had seen her that night in the cafe, but she was too focused on Louisa to notice her today. Had that just been a one-off, a rare conflux of emotions and energies and will? It had happened around Imbolc, after Carlie had done a ritual with Rhiannon, so maybe it was the seasonal gateway that had helped her appear. Excitement rippled through her. Beltane was approaching – would she have the chance to make another approach to her family then?

Forcing her attention back to Louisa, she tried desperately to learn anything she could about her ghostly sightings.

"But that was the last time I saw him, or heard him, and I hate that he's gone. It probably sounds selfish, because I'm sure he has somewhere better to be now, and I have to learn to go on without him, but I miss that, even if it wasn't real."

Panic struck Beth, and she broke apart, her phantom being disintegrating back into the molecules she seemed to mostly exist as – a swirling dust cloud of nothingness, a galaxy of pain trying to be made manifest. Would she disappear for good before she could connect with her husband?

Painfully and with great effort, she forced herself back into her ghostly form, in time to hear Carlie's emotion-drenched voice.

"I saw him too," she whispered.

Beth's heart ached for the girl as she shakily described her experiences to Rowan's grieving mother, of being held while she cried, and given advice and encouragement, and reassurances of love beyond the grave.

"But I don't sense him around me any more either – I haven't seen him or heard him for a few weeks, which makes me really sad. He said I had to let him go and start moving forward too," she admitted. "But I don't want to. How can it be selfish for us to want him to stick around?"

Louisa leaned across and hugged Carlie, and for a long time they sat like that, tears mingling, sharing their grief and finding some solace in being able to talk about the person they'd both loved so much. Beth ached with wanting to console them, to reassure them that yes, their lost loved one would never stop loving them. But was that true? Where had Rowan gone? And would she be dragged there soon too?

An idea bloomed. Was there a way she could find him and ask his advice? Or had he disappeared forever from the world and all that was beyond? The possibility chilled her, and she shivered. The tiny black cat swished her tail back and forth and stared at Beth.

"Maybe he feels that it's selfish of him to stick around and keep us from living our lives fully," Louisa said gently. "Especially you Carlie, you have your whole life ahead of you, and I hope it will be a life filled with love and happiness."

Carlie shook her head. "I'll never forget him," she said fiercely. "He changed me, in so many positive ways. I'm a better person now for having known him."

His mother smiled through her tears. "Thank you for telling me that. It helps me, to know that he did so much good while he was here. That he may not have been with us for a long time, but that he made a difference, however small."

Lost in their memories, they sat in silence, and Beth stared at them with sympathy. They were bound together by their grief, yet seemed so terribly alone. Should she leave them now? Their pain was so raw, and she felt increasingly uncomfortable intruding on it.

Before she could will herself away, Louisa told Carlie she had to go, just as the girl asked if she'd like a cup of tea. They smiled at the synchronicity, although the expression of joy soon slipped. Louisa offered Carlie her new address in case she ever wanted to get in touch, then the grieving mother clambered awkwardly to her feet and walked down the path to the street, and Beth prepared to drift back into the unknown.

"Wait."

Both women, one alive and one dead, turned back to Carlie.

"I've been meaning to tell you..." she began, then halted. Louisa and Beth both stood poised, waiting with bated breath.

"Please don't feel bad about my mum," she finally said, her voice cracked with pain. "Rowan told me you were worried his dad had hurt her, or worse. And he did, but she survived. She got away, and found her beloved, and had a wonderful life. She wouldn't have met

Dad if she didn't go through everything she did. So please, don't feel responsible in any way, or feel bad for her. You did nothing wrong."

Tears spilled down Louisa's face, and her body sagged with relief. Stumbling back along the path, she pulled the young girl into her arms. "Oh Carlie, thank you," she whispered, her voice croaky and thick with emotion. "You can't imagine how heavily that has weighed on me."

Beth froze in shock, and the rest of Louisa's words floated over her head, unheard. Carlie's mother was Violet, Rose's daughter, Mike's first love, and Beth's long-ago friend. The one she'd felt so guilty about, for not warning her against the man who seduced her into abandoning her parents and running away with him. Andrew, the man who had swept Beth off her feet just a few months earlier, then dumped her for her friend. The man she'd later discovered was married with a child.

All these years *she'd* been terrified that this man had hurt her friend, or worse. When Violet disappeared so mysteriously, Beth had felt partly responsible, but now Violet's daughter was absolving everyone of fault. Did that mean Beth could finally forgive herself? And was this the unfinished business that had been keeping her here, doomed to haunt her old life?

Would she dissolve away into nothing now?

Anxiously Beth waited...

And waited.

Long moments passed, and she was still hovering outside Rose's cottage, watching her daughter's friend as she stared at the woman who had been married to Andrew.

But wait, that meant... Rowan was Andrew's child. Carlie had dated his *son*? Her head spun and her mind reeled. Could the world get any smaller? Or weirder? And how had Carlie discovered the identity of her boyfriend's father – or coped with it once she had? Beth gazed at the girl again, recalling how she'd felt when she first spotted her, that Samhain night when she'd become aware that she was dead. She'd thought Carlie, walking at Rose's side, must have been the ghost of Violet, because she looked so much like her mother did when Beth had known her. Louisa must have recognised her too, when her son introduced her to his girlfriend. And goddess, had Louisa wondered if her own husband was Carlie's father? That would have been an awkward dinner conversation.

Again she wished she could find Rowan, wherever his spirit was now, and grill him. There was so much she needed to know about the past. About Violet, about Andrew, about herself.

And yet, did it really matter? That had all happened more then twenty years ago, before Rhiannon and Carlie had been born, before Beth had fallen in love with Mike.

Right now, all that mattered to her was contacting her husband and her daughter before she followed Rowan into oblivion. As she started to fray around the edges, Beth smiled. Violet hadn't held anything against anyone for falling under Andrew's spell, because it had led her to her soul mate. She'd found happiness after her heartache, and believed the pain she'd endured had been worth it, because she wouldn't have known the pleasure and bliss of true love without it.

That sweet psychic Bev had told her that Carlie would help her with some unfinished business, and she had. Her fear that she'd ruined Violet's life had been laid to rest. A weight lifted from Beth's heart, and she slowly faded away into the darkness.

When Beth next struggled back to awareness, she was wearing jeans and a red coat. Her taking-Brodie-to-the-park outfit. Floating down the hallway to his room, she grinned as he tried to comb his tousled blond locks. It had always been a struggle, and she felt a pang of longing, that she would never run a brush through his hair again. Never help him do anything again.

Watching him pull on his school uniform and tie up his shoes caused another wave of emotion. He'd had trouble with his laces while she was alive, but it was a breeze for him now. Sadly she followed him down the stairs, but picked up the pace when he laughed and raced into the kitchen.

"I know that smell Rhi-Rhi!" he exclaimed.

His sister turned and grinned. "Yes, I can't believe we haven't had Mum's special cinnamon-maple cereal for so long. I thought we could make it together this morning, and we can write out the recipe in our Memory Scrapbook tonight, okay?"

"That would be good," Brodie said, hugging his sister. "Thanks for still doing that with me. It's getting so big, we might need a new book soon!"

Rhiannon smiled. "Do you remember when we started it?"

Her brother looked slightly affronted. "Course I do! It was the night of the ghost plates, at the beginning of winter. Which means there must be another festival coming up, right?"

Pride swamped Beth, and she didn't know if it was her or Rhiannon who was the most surprised at Brodie's memory, and his recognition of the cyclical nature of the seasons and the corresponding rituals.

"That's right buddy," Rhiannon said, grinning at her brother and handing him a spoon. "We started the Memory Book almost six months ago, at Samhain, and next week is the opposite festival, Beltane, which marks the beginning of summer."

Beth flitted around the kitchen with them, soaking up every word her children uttered, every emotion that crossed their expressive faces, storing it all away in case she suddenly disappeared without seeing them again. After they ate, Rhiannon quickly washed the dishes, then hurried Brodie outside and walked him to school. Beth followed, her heart expanding with love and joy to be with them both, and relieved beyond measure that they were so close and considerate of each other.

When Rhiannon dropped Brodie at his school then continued on to hers, Beth stayed with her son. The clothes she'd returned in that morning revealed that she should focus on him today. Hovering at the entrance to his playground, she watched, transfixed, as he ran over to his friend Ben and started kicking a ball around, and chatting excitedly about a comic they were both reading. It made her happy to know he had such a great friend, someone he could read with as well as play sport and be active with.

A cacophony of sound exploded when the bell rang, and all the kids scrambled to get to class. Filled with curiosity, Beth followed Brodie and his friends, and was incredibly grateful to see Gabrielle Malling standing at the blackboard. She'd known Gabby for years.

They'd been to a few training courses together, done a joint fundraising campaign for a charity they loved, and shared a similar work ethic, dedication to their students, and daggy sense of humour. Brodie was in good hands with her.

After roll call, Gabrielle asked everyone to get out their homework, then moved around the room checking it.

"Great work Brodie," she said, placing a hand on his shoulder. "Did you have any trouble with this one?"

He smiled proudly as he shook his head. "I didn't even need Rhi-Rhi to help me."

"That's wonderful. Now, shall we try some maths?"

While some in the class groaned, Beth was amazed when Brodie nodded enthusiastically. Their teacher instructed them to turn to page thirty-eight in their text book as she moved back to the front of the room and began the lesson. Later, she had Brodie read a chapter of the book they were studying, and Beth was astounded by how much her son's comprehension and pronunciation had improved. Gabrielle looked just as delighted, and Beth was glad for the undercurrent of support present. It was things like this that made her so grateful they lived in a small town, where everyone knew each other, and everyone cared so much.

At lunchtime, Beth watched Brodie play games with several of his classmates, and during PE she was pleased to see him confidently taking part, and even leading one set of exercise drills.

When the final bell rang, she shadowed him outside and saw him line up near the buses, then jump on one with his friend Ben. Curious, she accompanied the boys back to Ben's place, and was happy to see Mrs Pearson welcome them inside for milk and cookies and a chat about their day, before shooing them outside.

Beth spent a wonderful afternoon swooping around her son as the two boys played in the fort they'd built in Ben's back garden. She loved that Brodie was still a little boy, getting to do little boy things, like pirate ship games and superhero adventures.

For a moment she'd seen a flash of pity in Mrs Pearson's eyes when she looked at Brodie, but it was replaced by gratitude and appreciation for the friendship the two boys shared, so Beth was reassured that it was a relationship on an equal footing.

Relief threaded through Beth like starlight, and she smiled. There was no need for her to worry on her son's account – he was more well-adjusted than she'd anticipated, close to his sister, thriving at school, and blessed with a wonderful friend.

There had only been one moment that day that Brodie had looked bewildered. It was in class, when they were chatting about the upcoming bake sale. The boy next to him asked what his mum was making for the stall, and what her favourite treat was.

Brodie's brow had furrowed in concentration, but before Gabrielle could reach him to intervene, he smiled at his fellow student. "I'll be baking with my big sister, which is always lots of fun. And Mum loved all sorts of treats. She taught me and Rhi-Rhi how to make star-shaped shortbreads, choc-chip cookies, delicious gingerbread biscuits, and her favourite spicy chai muffins."

It touched Beth deeply that he remembered those baking sessions, and she was grateful to Rhiannon for her efforts to keep their mum's memory alive for her brother. Her heart broke at the thought that some of his memories were blurring around the edges, and the knowledge that he would remember less and less of her as time went on. And if Mike did remarry one day, would Brodie forget her all together?

She still wasn't sure how she felt about being replaced. A tiny, jealous and bitter part of her wanted Mike to forsake all others, forever, and stay faithful and true to her. But that wasn't fair to him, or to their kids. At least Rhiannon would remember her properly – although would that make it harder for her to accept someone new in their life?

There needed to be a handbook on this, something to help grieving families decimated by loss work out the best way forward. Then again, she supposed it was different for everyone...

A thought struck her with the power of a hammer blow. Was that why she was still here? Was she holding on so hard for her own selfish reasons, and was it *she* who had to let go so that everyone else could move on? Or was she just here until Mike found someone, and then she would be allowed to drift off, to wherever she was going. Heaven? Hell? The Summerland? Back to the nothingness? That thought chilled her, but she supposed she would have no idea if that's where she went, since that was the very definition of the yawning void.

No awareness.

No knowledge.

*No her.*

## Chapter 32

### Rhiannon

"I had the strangest dream last night."

Sunlight was streaming in the window of the cafe, and Rhiannon was relaxed and happy. She hadn't seen Tom since France, so this morning she'd leaped out of bed early to make breakfast for Brodie, take him to football training and get a little homework done, then hurried excitedly to the cafe to meet her boyfriend.

And now he was wiggling his eyebrows at her and grinning mischievously.

"Not that kind of dream!" Rhiannon laughed. "It was about Mum. She was very much alive, and looked like she did before she got sick – long golden hair, unsunken cheeks, and a sparkle like stars in her eyes. She was wearing a gorgeous pinky-gold dress, with a crown of flowers on her head. Carlie and I had flowers in our hair as well – hawthorn blossoms, jasmine, white rose buds, violets and meadowsweet, all flowers of love, romance and new beginnings – and Carlie was in a pretty green dress, and I was in lilac. You were there too, and Jake. Everyone, it seemed…"

Trailing off, she lifted her cup and took a sip of the strong coffee, then bit her lip. Suddenly she realised her dream might offend Tom, since he was so close to his grandfather, and still missed his grandmother so much.

But Tom was smiling at her. "Then what happened?"

"This is crazy, I shouldn't even say it out loud."

"You can't tease me like that," he insisted. "And nothing is so bad you can't tell me. We're always honest with each other, remember?"

Forcing back a sigh, she nodded reluctantly. If she was really being honest, she would tell Tom that she loved him, that she'd fallen deep and hard and desperate. But she wasn't sure how he would take it, or whether he loved her in return. She knew he really liked her, and liked spending time with her – his trip to France to reassure her proved that he cared – so she didn't want to scare him off. Yet she was bursting to say it, to shout her love from the rooftops. It was getting harder and harder to keep it inside.

"Okay, you're right," she said instead. "And it was only a dream, it's not like it will really happen. So, we were all gathered in the meadow at the base of the tor, joined in a sacred circle, but Rose's friend Elsie was the priestess overseeing the ritual, because, um, Rose and your grandad were being handfasted."

Rolling her eyes, she laughed and drained the rest of her drink. "I know, it's silly, right? Clearly I have romance on the brain."

But Tom had frozen at her words, a forkful of lemon drizzle cake halfway to his mouth.

"What?" Rhiannon asked, surprised by his response. Was that idea so awful to him?

"Last night I dreamed about my nan, and she was alive again too. She looked like she did in her wedding photo, long before I knew her, but it must have been present day, because I was talking to her about you. Then she took my hand, clutched it to her heart, and implored me to help her. There were tears in her eyes, and so much urgency in her voice, which made me remember it so clearly when I woke up. And it was so real, like I really was talking to her."

A waiter hovered, and Tom paused and looked at Rhiannon. "More coffee?"

Nodding gratefully, she thanked the waiter then turned back to Tom. "What did your grandma say? And why are you blushing?"

Running a hand through his long hair, he smiled sheepishly. "It sounds silly now, but in the dream she was so insistent. She begged me to tell Pop that it was time for him to let love into his life. That it had been eighteen months already, and he had mourned long enough. She knew he would always love her, but life was too short to wait around. That she wanted him to have a rich life, a happy life."

Rhiannon grinned. "That's beautiful. Are you going to tell him? And do you think he'll listen to you?"

Tom shrugged. "I guess I could mention it to him. But that wasn't the weirdest part." Distracted, he stirred a spoonful of sugar into his coffee, which was weird, because he never sweetened his drinks, and looked unsure about whether to continue.

Reaching across the table, Rhiannon took his hand. "It's just a dream, right?"

"I thought that, until you told me yours. It's just, well, then Nan told me I had to visit the healer, and let her know she gave her blessing to their relationship. Then she handed me a white rose."

"Oh my god!" Rhiannon blurted out. "That could only mean Rose, right? I remember your pop telling us at dinner that Rose took herbal medicines to Marcy when she was ill, and sat with her for hours, so she has to be the healer she referred to. And how beautiful that it was a white rose – rose of lovers, of devotion and spiritual love, of hope and great esteem. And of Rose, obviously."

She stared at Tom, perplexed. "You look so worried, but that's lovely, isn't it? And Carlie did tell me that her grandma had been spending a lot of time with your pop, out in his garden, and helping him cook Marcy's old recipes. They seem to make each other happy."

Tom nodded. "I know. I'm just not sure what to do. I mean, Nan was so insistent, she made me promise to tell them both, but what if it was just a silly dream, and mentioning it makes things awkward between them, or between me and Pop? And what would Carlie think, me matchmaking her grandmother with my grandad? How could I presume to do that?"

"Hey," Rhiannon said, voice soothing. "Rose and Richard are both old enough and strong enough to do whatever they like, and you passing on those messages won't make them do anything they don't already want to. And whether it's Rose or someone else, letting your pop know that Marcy is at peace, and wants him to be happy and loved, can only be a good thing. I had to tell Dad the same thing recently. It's been eighteen months for him as well, and I think he'll stay in a fog of isolation forever if no one intervenes. I was so grateful Jessica gave him a tea-leaf reading in Brittany which said much the same thing – but he was terrified that I would think less of him if he dated someone, so I was glad I could clear that up."

Tom smiled at her. "Thank you."

"Maybe your grandfather is the same as Dad, and worries that it wouldn't be appropriate," Rhiannon said, warming to her theme. "That you or especially Jake would be upset if he started a romantic relationship. He might be wondering if you think it's too soon, or that he'd be disrespecting Marcy's memory if he dated someone."

"But he wouldn't be! It's been ages, and Jake and I would be thrilled if he allowed love into his life."

"See!" Rhiannon grinned. "He needs you to let him know that it's okay, with you and Jake, and also with Marcy."

Lifting his fork again, Tom nodded. "You could be right. But that's not the same for Rose. Aren't I the last person who should presume to tell her how to feel or what to do?"

Sipping her fresh coffee, Rhiannon tried not to roll her eyes. "Don't worry, if it's not what she wants, she won't feel pressured to do it. Besides, Rose knows about dreams and messages and divination, and understands that some are literal and some are more symbolic. You could just mention your dream and let her draw her own conclusions. Besides, I think it might actually help her."

Tom looked aghast. "How on earth could I help her? She's a priestess! And I've only met her once. Who am I to hurtle into her life with such a potentially life-changing message?"

"Who are you not to?" Rhiannon retorted. "But the groundwork has already been laid. Carlie had a big discussion with Rose recently, and made her grandmother recognise that she'd been denying herself love, and pushing potential partners away, for more than twenty years. She thought she was so together, so spiritually aware, yet her granddaughter turned her life upside down by forcing that realisation on her. Rose protested, and came up with a litany of excuses, but they talked it out until she was convinced. And Carlie ended up wondering if there was something going on with Richard, and when they would both feel comfortable enough to disclose it. So it could be that this is the exact message they both need."

"Okay, I'll tell Pop," Tom conceded. "But Rose?"

Rhiannon grinned. "Come on, be brave. How about we go down to the healing centre now, browse the books, look at the gorgeous jewellery, play with the crystals and the cards, and if you get a moment to talk to her, you can just casually mention your dream, then leave it with her. You don't even need her response, you can just say it and then we'll go."

He laughed. "You're very persuasive babe. Okay, I guess we should get it over with, right, and then can we wander through the woods and look for wildflowers?"

"I'd love that." And she realised she would. The thought of the woods no longer made her shiver in fear. She wanted to walk through them, hand in hand with her beloved.

She was making progress.

The bell over the door tinkled as Rhiannon and Tom walked into Rose's beautiful shop, and they were immediately drawn to the baskets of gorgeous colourful crystals, sparkling in the light of several candles. The burbling of a small water fountain added to the uplifting mood.

"It's wonderful in here. I'll have to do all my crystal shopping here from now on," Tom said, holding a large piece of selenite in one hand, and a moonstone in the other. "These are so powerful."

"Crystals just amplify the strength and power of the person wielding them, you should know that Tom," said a voice behind them. They spun around to see Rose, smiling at them in welcome.

"And the strength and wisdom of the person who selected them," Tom countered.

The priestess laughed. "Touche."

Rhiannon stepped forward to hug Rose, and the older woman held her tightly. "How are you doing today, sweet girl?"

"I'm good. Looking forward to Beltane, and to our planning on Tuesday night." She paused. Had the priestess just blushed at the mention of Beltane? "Are you still happy for me to come over?"

Hiding any sign of being flustered, Rose smiled. "Of course. Carlie has been doing some research today, so we'll have lots to discuss. And you Tom? Will you be down for the Beltane ritual next Sunday?"

"I'd be honoured, thank you. I have a ceremony with my coven on Saturday evening, but I'll be here in plenty of time for yours. Pop's really looking forward to it too."

This time Rose definitely had a flush of colour in her cheeks. Rhiannon grinned. "Speaking of which..." she said, nudging Tom.

He looked more nervous than Rhiannon had ever seen him, but he smiled bravely, cleared his throat, opened his mouth... then paused.

Rose took pity on him, leading them to the back of the shop, where there was a little alcove with a table and chairs, and a kettle that boiled as they approached. Rhiannon followed them, amused to see three mugs on the bench, with a jar of chamomile flowers and three silver heart-shaped tea infusers. While Rose and Tom sat down, she busied herself making the tea and trying not to laugh. Seemed Rose had been expecting them.

"What is it sweet boy?" the priestess asked.

Rhiannon handed him a mug of tea, and he thanked her before turning back to Rose. Breathing in the soothing scent of the chamomile, he finally began. "I'm not sure how to say this, and I would hate to offend you in any way..."

"Oh Tom, nothing you could say would upset me. You have a beautiful heart, and Rhiannon and Richard both speak very highly of you. And whatever it is, I know you have the best of intentions, which is all that really matters."

Encouraged, Tom gulped down some tea, almost choking on the heat of it, then held the priestess's gaze. "Last night my grandmother came to me in a dream..."

"Marcy," Rose said softly. "She was a lovely woman."

Tom nodded. "She and Pop were so in love, so happy together –"

Seeing the stricken look on Rose's face, Tom paused, until understanding dawned. "Oh, no! Please don't misunderstand. First she implored me to tell Pop that it was time for him to let love into his life. That he had mourned long enough, and while she knew he would always love her, life was too short to wait around. That she wanted him to be happy, and loved."

Relief washed over Rose's face, and she visibly relaxed, then turned to Rhiannon. "I think that's an important message for your dad too."

She smirked. "It is, but we're not talking about him right now."

Taking a sip of her tea, Rose chuckled. "Sorry Tom, go on."

"Well, after saying all that about Pop, she begged me to tell *you* that you have her blessing, and she handed me a white rose, just in case I wasn't clear on the message and who to deliver it to."

Tears shimmered on Rose's lashes, but she smiled, and her face softened. "Thank you sweet boy, for being brave enough to tell me, and for trusting in your vision."

Laughing, Tom took Rhiannon's hand and pulled her down onto his lap. "Actually, it was this one who gave me the courage, because she had a dream about her mum the same night."

The priestess's eyes twinkled as she gazed at Rhiannon. "I'm glad Beth was able to communicate with you, and I hope there was comfort in that."

"There was," she said. "And she seemed to be hinting at something deeper between you and Richard too, if that's not too forward of me to say?" A blush stained her cheeks, but Rose beamed at her.

"Beth always was a wise woman, and clearly you and Carlie are too. My granddaughter may have told you that she made me see the error of my ways. That I'd been denying myself love ever since I lost Louis, without even realising." She trailed off, then slowly sipped the herbal tea, an expression of calm smoothing out her features as the steam enveloped her. "So Tom, will you mention this to your grandfather?"

Tom grimaced. "Do you think I should? I don't want to freak him out. He might find it odd to hear about dream messengers and visions."

"I think he'll surprise you. He's far more open to all of this than you imagine." The priestess smiled, but when she looked up at Rhiannon, there was fear in her eyes. Her hand was shaking, so she put her cup of tea back on the table. "But what about Carlie, and Jake? Your final year of school is almost over, then there's university. Neither Richard nor I want to disrupt that, or make things awkward for them. Their feelings are far more important than ours."

Shocked, Rhiannon stood up and moved around the table. Crouching at Rose's side, she took her hands and gazed up into the face that was so familiar to her. Which was always so wise and certain, yet had all of a sudden become unsure. Vulnerable. "They would both be ecstatic to know that you two are happy together – and mortified if they suspected that you denied any of that for their sake. Nothing at all would change for them, except that you and Richard would both be happier, and that is all they want."

The priestess reached out a hand and cupped Rhiannon's cheek. "Thank you sweet girl, that means more to me than you could imagine. Your mum would be so proud of you."

Before they all started crying, one of the staff members came back to ask for Rose's assistance. Slowly the priestess got to her feet, hugged Rhiannon and Tom, then bid them farewell and headed to the counter.

"How are you feeling?" Rhiannon asked her boyfriend as they made their way to the entrance.

Before they could reach it though, Rose called out to them, and beckoned them over to the crystal corner. Picking up the large piece of selenite Tom had been holding earlier, she handed it to him. "I'd like you to have this Tom, as a small thank you for being brave enough to approach me with something so personal, and for trusting yourself and the message. I'm sure that wasn't easy for you, having known me for such a short time."

He looked like he was going to refuse the gift, but the priestess wrapped his fingers around the crystal and smiled. "You honour the giver by receiving graciously, you know that. And I am so grateful to you. I look forward to celebrating with you next Sunday."

Tom looked a little spaced when they made it outside, clutching Rhiannon's hand as though she was anchoring him to the earth.

"I'm feeling great," he insisted when she peered at him, although she sensed nerves beneath his ready grin. "Thank you so much for your support in there, and for your encouragement and faith. It means so much to me. *You* mean so much to me."

Rhiannon beamed at him. "Now you just have to tell your grandfather. Do you want to do it now? I'll race home and make some sandwiches so we can have a picnic in the woods, and meet you at yours in half an hour."

On Monday morning Rhiannon was climbing the front steps at school with Carlie, when Jake came running up to them, eyes sparkling with excitement.

"Oh my god, can you believe it? Isn't it amazing!" he cried, then stared at Rhiannon in panic. "Oh, um, can we talk about it yet?" he asked Carlie.

Carlie giggled, then nodded. "It's okay, Gran said we can share the news with Rhi. I was just waiting for you so we could be together when we spilled the beans. I think Gran knew it would torture us to have to try to keep it a secret from her."

"Guys, I'm right here! What is it?" Rhiannon begged, impatience and curiosity burning through her.

Jake smiled at Carlie. "Do you want to –"

"Oh god, someone tell me," Rhiannon shrieked.

Carlie laughed. "Sorry, it's just… well, you know how Beltane is all about –"

"Carlie, get to the point! Jake, what is it?" Rhiannon demanded.

"Rose and Pop are having a handfasting ceremony next weekend, as part of the Beltane ritual," he blurted out.

Rhiannon squealed and grabbed Carlie's hands. "Oh my god, that's so beautiful! How long have you known?"

"They told us on Saturday night, but you were off with Tom yesterday and we couldn't find you to share the news," Jake replied. "Carlie wanted to tell you straight away, don't worry. But isn't it sweet? They're so cute together."

Rhiannon couldn't wipe the smile off her face. She was so glad she and Tom had been brave enough to talk to Rose on Saturday.

There was no doubt that Tom's recounting of his dream to the priestess had had an impact, and clearly his chat with his grandfather had gone well too. Rose and Richard must have got together as soon as she and Tom left for the woods. She tried to look surprised, since Carlie and Jake should have been the first to know, but she was so happy for the priestess. So glad that the person who had given so much love to everyone else in Summer Hill all her life would finally accept something for herself.

When the bell for class rang, Jake rushed off to his with a cheerful wave, and Rhiannon turned back to Carlie.

"They want us to help during the ritual, if you want to," her friend said. "And Tom too, obviously. It's like we'll all be related in some way!"

"Oh Carlie, I'd be honoured," Rhiannon grinned. "How beautiful, after so much sadness. And Rose has given so much to everyone here, since way before we were born, so the whole village will be really thrilled that she's found happiness."

"I hope so," Carlie said. "She is definitely due some joy."

## Chapter 33

# Let Your Light Shine

### Rhiannon

Clutching a bouquet of wildflowers in one hand, Rhiannon knocked on Carlie's door for their Tuesday night magic meeting. When her friend welcomed her in, she followed her out to the kitchen, and presented the flowers to Rose.

"Thank you sweet girl, they're beautiful. From the heart of the woods, at a guess?" she said, eyes piercing into Rhiannon's soul. "Carlie, would you mind grabbing the green vase from upstairs?"

"Sure Gran."

Once they were alone, the priestess turned to Rhiannon. "Were you okay as you ventured into the woods?"

"I was," Rhiannon replied, and there was pride in her voice. "Thank you so much for your wisdom, and caring, and the healing last week. I wouldn't have been able to walk through there before that, but I was with Tom, which made me braver, and I could feel you with me too."

Rose smiled. "It's all you sweet girl. You're just letting your light shine from within, refusing to dim it for anyone or anything, and starting to recognise your courageous heart. It's beautiful to see."

She broke off when Carlie bustled back in, and the three of them made dinner, chatting about school and upcoming exams, and about Rhiannon's trip. When they settled down to eat, talk shifted to Beltane, but instead of rattling off the history, facts and meanings as she usually did, this time the priestess asked the girls about their favourite aspects of the celebration.

"I love that it heralds the beginning of summer," Rhiannon said. "In the middle of winter, when it's so cold and snowy, I always dream of Beltane, and remind myself that the wheel will soon turn and we'll be back there. And I love all the romantic aspects of it too. The tradition of leaping the Beltane fire with your beloved..."

Trailing off, she grinned as she recalled the vision she'd had in Broceliande forest, when Viviane had shown her the image of her and Tom jumping gracefully over the sabbat fire together.

"Ah yes," Rose said with a smile. "And the weaving of the maypole ribbons to represent the coming together of the god and the goddess."

A shudder rocked through Rhiannon at her words. That's what Evan had said in the woods, that they must come together as the god and the goddess. But no. He didn't have the power to affect her any more. She shook it off and turned to her friend, keen to change the subject. "How about you Carlie?"

"I'm excited that it marks the first day of summer, because I wasn't here for it last year, so I'm looking forward to getting to know the season up here – and to it not being quite as hot as an Australian summer! Oh, and I was reading about old traditions, so I want to get up early and bathe my face in the dew from our garden, to absorb the energy of vitality and abundance like they used to."

Trying to smother her laughter, Rose poured everyone more iced rose hip tea. "Sweetheart, I don't think you need that youthful boost quite yet, but it is still a lovely ritual to connect yourself to the Beltane sunrise, and the rising, whirling energy of the season."

Sighing deeply, Carlie reached for her glass and gulped some tea. "Summer solstice will be difficult for me though, because that will mark a year since Mum and Dad died. But I'm not going to think about that until I have to – it's still more than six weeks away, so all my attention will strictly be on Beltane." Her voice hitched, but she swallowed her pain and forced a smile.

Leaning over, Rhiannon hugged her friend. "We'll work out a beautiful way to honour your parents during the solstice."

Rose nodded, sadness clouding her face. "We'll honour them together. I'm so sorry I'm the only family you have left."

Stricken, Carlie reached across the table and took her grandmother's hand. "You are all the family I need Gran, I promise. And I'm surrounded by people here who are dear to me. I'm so sorry, I didn't mean to bring us down."

Standing abruptly, she cleared the table, put the kettle on, then filled the sink to wash up. Rhiannon started to get up to help, but Rose shook her head. "Give her a moment sweet girl," she said softly.

Nodding, Rhiannon took her seat and stared at the priestess. Screwing up her courage, she finally asked Rose what she'd been obsessing about since her friend's announcement the day before. "Of course, the thing Beltane is most about is love, and I've heard there will be a special addition to our ritual this weekend, is that right?"

A smile lit up the priestess's face, and she glanced at the wildflowers Rhiannon had given her. "Aside from my illuminating chat with you and Tom on Saturday, I'm sure Carlie has mentioned that Richard and I have been spending a lot of time together over the last few months."

Rhiannon nodded eagerly.

"At first he just wanted a hand with his garden, and with a couple of recipes, but after the Imbolc ritual, he asked if I could teach him a little about paganism and the cycle of the seasons, so we've been meeting up regularly to drink tea, eat cake and talk about magic."

"That's so lovely," Rhiannon said with a happy sigh.

Rose laughed. "Well, we would have gone on just having tea forever, and thinking nothing of it, until Carlie challenged me a few weeks ago, and I started thinking about Richard in a different way. I realised how much I enjoyed our time together, and how much I'd missed that kind of companionship, but I was content with the way things were, so I didn't say anything to him about romance."

"Then how did this happen?" Rhiannon asked, enthralled by the unfolding story.

The priestess lowered her voice. "He came to see me on Saturday afternoon, after Tom shared his dream about Marcy with him, and was totally flustered. A relationship hadn't occurred to him either – although he sheepishly admitted that he liked the idea, and felt we'd begun one without our even recognising it – but he was worried that I might assume his intentions weren't honourable, or that someone else might think he was taking advantage of me."

"No one would think that!" Rhiannon interjected.

Rose giggled, suddenly looking ten years younger. "I know. And as I told him, I've been just fine taking care of myself all these years. But Richard is more traditional than me, and was married most of his life, so he wanted a way to make his feelings public in order to protect me, so no one would think he wasn't serious in his courtship."

"That's so lovely."

"I must admit, it made me a little giddy, for someone to care about me like that, to be protective of me and my reputation."

A lump formed in Rhiannon's throat, and she was overwhelmed with a sudden rush of sadness. Rose had always been a warrior woman. The steady, strong rock who held the village together. The one who looked after her and Brodie when they were young. Who comforted them, and their dad, through the loss of Beth. The one everyone turned to for help and healing. But who had ever thought to check if she was okay? If she needed help, or healing, or a brief respite from all the responsibility she carried.

"I'm sorry," she whispered. "That none of us thought to look after you."

"Oh sweet girl, that's not what I meant. I have no regrets about my life and who has been in it, and to be honest this is more about Richard. He'd been feeling guilty that he was happy again, and falling... well, caring... for someone else. But Tom's dream reassured him that it was okay. And when he came over, we were discussing Beltane, and he asked about the handfasting ritual that is sometimes part of it. He wanted to know what it would mean if we did that."

Rhiannon gasped. "So he kind of proposed! And is it like a proper marriage? Is it binding?"

The priestess smiled mischievously. "Where do you think the expression 'tying the knot' comes from?"

"Really?"

"Of course. Long ago, when a couple wanted to commit to each other, and bind their lives together, the priestess would invite them to join hands, symbolising their free will to make the commitment, then their hands would be bound together with a cord that was tied in a love knot to signify their sacred union. Lots of pagan couples incorporate it into their weddings today, as a special part of the ceremony. I've performed a few handfastings over the years."

"Will you get married later?" Rhiannon asked, smiling at Carlie as she returned to the table with the teapot and three mugs, looking just as curious as she was.

"Oh sweet girl, we're too old for that. And it's far too soon in any case. Traditionally a handfasting is just for a year and a day, then you decide if you want to commit for longer after that. So this is just a lovely way to share our intentions, with each other and our friends. And for me, the most important thing is that it's a way to welcome Richard fully into our circle, so he knows he's not just a bystander in our rituals. It's a little intimidating for him to be dating the priestess, in a circle of mostly women, so I'm hoping that being part of this ceremony will put his fears to rest and help him truly understand the transformational magic we all work together."

As she poured the tea, Carlie grinned. "I'm so happy for you Gran, for both of you. I can't think of two people more deserving of a second chance at love. And it's also pretty cool that Richard is an Australian, despite having lived in England for so long."

Rhiannon giggled. Between Carlie, Jake and Richard, would they all end up with Aussie accents?

Her friend smiled. "Shall we start planning? What kind of flowers will be best for the ceremony Gran, and what food will you have for the celebration? And who's going to run the ritual in your place?"

A blush stained Rose's cheeks. "Gosh, I hadn't even thought of that. I'm sure Elsie will be happy to come down and do it though. Do you girls want to think about flowers while I call her?"

Nodding solemnly, they each pulled out their Book of Shadows. Rhiannon had a flashback of her dream, when her mum had been with them as they waited for Rose's handfasting. She and Carlie had flowers in their hair – hawthorn blossoms, jasmine, white rose buds, violets and meadowsweet. Flowers of love, romance and new beginnings. Had it been a prophetic dream? A premonition of sorts?

# Rhiannon's Book of Shadows

## Flowers For a Handfasting

*Hawthorn blossoms:* Considered the tree of love, pale pink or white hawthorn flowers are used in love spells and wedding rites, bringing abundant blessings to the newlyweds. Sacred to the goddess, they are believed to open the heart, ease pain, and offer hope, protection and healing. Also known as the May tree, for its association with Beltane and the beginning of summer, hawthorn wood was traditionally used to make the maypole, with the flowers used to decorate it. It's one of the Celtic faery tree triad of oak, ash and thorn, which signifies the presence of faeries when they grow together. And a legend from Brittany claims that Merlin lies in a tomb in an enchanted sleep in the forest of Broceliande (which I visited with Tom!), under the shade of a hawthorn tree, and that when the hawthorn buds each year, it is the soul of Merlin trying to come back to our world.

*Jasmine flowers:* The sweetly scented jasmine is associated with love, affection and romance, and is used in love spells, happiness rituals, and as an offering to the goddess. It's believed to penetrate the deepest layers of the soul and open a person up emotionally, and attracts both romantic and spiritual love. In the Philippines, the name of this flower, sampaguita, comes from the words for "I promise you", and represents a pledge of mutual love – couples traditionally exchanged jasmine necklaces instead of wedding rings.

*White rose buds:* Roses are universally considered the flower of love, and are associated with Aphrodite, the Greek goddess of love. White roses signify new beginnings, and denote devotion, great esteem, spiritual love, hope, charm and humility. White roses are referred to as the bridal rose, because of its long tradition as a wedding flower. And Marcy used a white rose to communicate with Tom about her approval of this relationship, so it should definitely be in the handfasting bouquet!

*Violet blooms:* *These gorgeous flowers symbolise love, loyalty and sweetness, and are associated with Venus, the Roman goddess of love, and thus with relationships and love spells. They represent spiritual wisdom, faithfulness and humility, which makes them perfect for Rose's bouquet, and she named her daughter for these beautiful purple flowers, so there's a bittersweet aspect to adding them, all steeped in love. Also referred to as heart's ease, they are a gentle, loving, protective flower with a beautiful fragrance.*

*Meadowsweet:* *This pretty white flower signifies love, truth, sincerity and grace. A member of the rose family, it keeps peace and cheers the heart, and is considered one of the most sacred herbs by the druids. It's used in love spells, and is known as queen of the meadow and bridewort, the latter because it was traditionally strewn on the grass at weddings for the bride to walk on. The Celtic goddess Blodeuwedd was created from meadowsweet, oak blossoms and broom flowers.*

*For consideration:* *We could also suspend some "kissing knots" around the healing centre for the celebration. Simply tie a white rose bud and a sprig of rosemary together with white ribbon, as they both signify love and honour. Then just hang them from a string across the door, where they will bring love and luck to everyone who enters, or pin them in door frames or on the walls.*

When Rose returned, both girls read out their lists, and the priestess smiled warmly and congratulated them. "You'll both need flowers too, if you're going to be my flower girls. Whether you'd prefer a bouquet or a wreath for your hair, or both, is totally up to you, but I have these two sweet little charms for you, which I thought you could incorporate somehow."

Smiling, she handed Carlie a small silver violet flower charm, with purple petals and green leaves. "For heart's ease Sweetheart, and for your mum. I'm sure she's with us always, and will be there for Beltane too, but I wanted you to have something physical to keep with you."

Nestling the charm in her palm, Carlie thanked her grandmother, then went upstairs to her room to find a chain to put it on.

As soon as they were alone, Rose offered Rhiannon a small silver key. "The key to your heart sweet girl. Because I think you're beginning to realise that you've held the key to unlocking it all this time, you just weren't ready to use it. But it's time now."

The room spun, and Rhiannon's breath hitched in panic. Suddenly she was back in the cloying darkness of an ancient stone temple, being pushed under the surface of the black water by the woman in blue, then told to look for the raven to find her love.

Then everything tilted, and she was in the deepest part of the woods, stalked by a huge raven who dropped a silver key into her hand instead of biting her. When she'd screamed in frustration and begged for answers, a voice had whispered on the wind that she would eventually discover how to unlock her pain.

But how was it all connected? The raven was supposed to indicate love, which hopefully meant Tom, but what did he have to do with her pain?

Her skin prickled as Rose's eyes bored into her, until she reluctantly looked up. "He's the right one sweet girl, and he's the key to moving forward," the priestess said gently. "The key to healing, to working through what happened, and being able to grow, trust and flourish in a relationship."

Rhiannon shuddered. Again with the having to tell.

Before she could reply, or retort, Carlie returned, the violet charm nestled at her throat. Taking a seat, she reached over and laid a hand on Rhiannon's arm. "Are you okay?"

Shaking off the visions, Rhiannon forced a smile. "Sorry, yes, I'm good. Just a series of things slowly falling into place. Cryptic signs to show me the way forward." She grinned when the priestess winked at her. "Now, I guess we should talk about food, right?"

Saturday morning, Beltane Eve, dawned full of sunshine and promise. Carlie and Rhiannon dragged themselves out of bed early and met on the slopes of the tor to gather the pretty white blossoms from the sacred hawthorn tree. After that they wandered through the woods, plucking meadowsweet and violets and chatting about the upcoming ritual.

"What would you have in your bridal bouquet?" Rhiannon asked, and was surprised when a dark cloud of sorrow crossed her friend's face.

"Something like Gran's I guess. I haven't really thought about it since..." She broke off, and quickly turned the focus back onto Rhiannon. "How about you?"

"Same. Um, are you all right? Sorry, I didn't mean to upset you."

Shaking her head, Carlie leaned down to pick another flower, letting her long dark hair hide her face. "It's okay," she mumbled, before slowly standing. "It's just, Rowan mentioned getting married, when I was ready, and for a moment I entertained the idea, picturing flowers and white ribbons and rings of promise. So it's tough to..."

Pausing, she took a deep breath and straightened her shoulders. "But this is about Gran, and I'm so happy for her. I can't wait to see how a handfasting ritual works, and for you to meet Elsie. She's so lovely. She and Gran have been best friends for forty years, which is beautiful. I hope we'll still be practicing magic and doing rituals together when we're proper grown-ups."

Rhiannon squeezed her hand. "I'm sure we will. Now I guess we need to get to the nursery to pick up the rose buds. This will be the sweetest smelling, prettiest bouquet ever."

Laughing, the two girls completed their floral tasks, then after a quick lunch at the nursery cafe, headed to Rose's cottage to pick the jasmine and begin their preparations for the ritual.

Carefully they laid out the flowers they'd harvested on the dining table, and divided them up. First was the handfasting wreath for Rose's hair. Deftly they wove the hawthorn blossoms and ivy with the jasmine flowers, white rose buds, violets and meadowsweet, speaking the words of a spell as they worked, infusing it with love and blessings. They crafted a bouquet for Rose too, then wove their own smaller floral wreaths and posies. The whole room smelled so sweet.

Putting them all in the fridge, they started working on the food for the celebration to follow the ritual. Laura was making a honey and lavender cheesecake, vegie goat cheese tarts and a green man cake, and Miri was supplying bottles of her much-loved mead infused with woodruff and other summery herbs for the celebration.

The girls had volunteered to make the main ritual cake though, and Carlie suggested a passionfruit cake in the shape of a heart, topped with cream cheese icing and crystallised violets.

"I still don't get how we can make a heart-shaped cake," Rhiannon said nervously.

Carlie grinned as she pulled down two baking tins from a high cupboard, then drew the pattern in the floury bench. "We make two cakes, a square one and a round one. Once they're cooled, we cut the circle in half, and put one half along one edge of the square, and the other on the edge that meets it. Then in the morning we'll smother it in cream cheese icing and decorate it with passionfruit as well as all the crystallised violets we're about to make, so no one will know it's not a single cake."

They also baked rose petal biscuits, honey joys and scones, and made a huge pot of lavender jam, which they'd serve with the scones the next day, and also bottle in small glass jars as a gift for everyone who attended. Then they prepped the strawberry and dandelion salad and the stuffed zucchini flowers that they'd complete in the morning.

It was midnight by the time the girls finished, but Rhiannon was wide awake as she walked home, the scent of the flowers still weaving around her, the small silver key charm held tightly in her hand.

The key to her heart. To baring her soul. Did she have the strength for that?

## Chapter 34

# A Menacing Flash of Gold

### Beth

In the mysterious chill of the pre-dawn dark, Beth found herself coming together up on the tor, in the swirling mists of that liminal point between night and day. She'd always loved this moment, when the whole world was poised between light and dark, between potential and possibility. When the air was alive with magic, and she felt so truly a part of the earth, a part of the web of interconnectivity between all of the elements.

It was Beltane morning, and she could feel the whirling energies, sense the shift of the seasons as summer sent its first whispers through the land. Gazing out over the darkened village, she tried to discern where her house was amongst the gathering shadows, but there wasn't enough light. She could pick out the ruined churchyard though, and the sweep of a car's headlights as someone set off for work. Then she heard footsteps on the path to the top of the hill. They were gentle, reverent, almost hesitant, and Beth peered into the gloom, trying to see who it was.

Desperately she hoped it was her daughter, because today, when the veil between the worlds was thin, would be her best chance of connecting with her. But if it was Rhiannon, surely Beth would already be aware of it, aware of her. And it couldn't be Rose either, come to wash her face in the healing, revitalising and magical dew of Beltane morning, because there wouldn't be this reticence from the priestess.

Beth wondered if she should drift off on the gentle breeze and leave whichever witch was seeking the solitude of the sacred summit to their ritual. Then she saw a flash of gold out of the corner of her eye, and panic swallowed her. Was it the eerie, elusive presence that had been following her since she'd become aware at Samhain? Had it been lying in wait for her up here, knowing before she did that she would find herself atop the tor this morning? Was this the moment she would dissolve away to nothingness?

Turning slowly, Beth tried to focus on where the chill of the strange golden aura was coming from, but before she could discover it, the approaching witch reached the summit, and her attention swung back there despite herself.

Silhouetted against the slowly lightening sky was Carlie, in a long green velvet dress and hiking boots. Beth hadn't considered that it was cold – she didn't sense things the way humans did – but the girl's body language revealed there was a chill in the air, even on this first day of summer. Mist danced around her, clutching and clawing at her dress with icy fingers, and wrapping around her shoulders and throat, as though it was trying to strangle her, or silence her.

Then suddenly the flash of gold Beth had been glimpsing for six months coalesced into a woman draped in sunshine yellow, and Carlie's throat came unstuck, and she started speaking to her.

Beth stared in wonder as they conversed. She wanted to know what they were talking about, and who the mysterious figure was, but she didn't dare approach them. She couldn't risk that this woman was what had been following her, the menacing presence threatening to drag her away from her family before she was ready.

But it was taken out of her hands when the woman in gold glanced over her shoulder, right at Beth. The shock froze her for a moment, then she started to disperse along with the mists. But the stern figure shook her head in warning before turning back to Carlie.

And now she could hear them speak, and ripples of memory were racing up Beth's spine. She'd met this woman before, when she'd returned to Summer Hill for her sister's wedding twenty years ago. She'd been walking home from Rose's cottage, lamenting the fact that she could never stay in this village and be herself, when the gold-clad figure had swirled into being in a pool of moonlight and fireflies right in front of her. It was she who convinced Beth the village could be her home. That she could be her whole self here, could love and be loved, and that she had magic within her. If not for that encounter, Beth would have gone back to France and lived an entirely different life. A life without Mike or Rhiannon or Brodie. Without Rose. Without magic.

Head spinning, Beth nervously floated closer, as though she could join their conversation, but it was clear Carlie couldn't see her. Saddened, she tried to follow the thread of the conversation. She'd missed the beginning, but it seemed that the mist-wreathed woman had just told Carlie she was a witch, much to the girl's consternation. Beth wondered if it was the word she objected to, or if she just had as little faith in herself as Beth did at her age?

"It is nothing to be scared of Carlie," the woman in gold said, voice soothing, like a lullaby. "You have worked hard, you have read widely, you have practised. You have spent time in nature, and attuned yourself to the energy of the moon and sun and seasons, to the magic of the earth. You have suffered much, yet you chose to become more compassionate, where others choose the path of bitterness and revenge."

"But I'm not like Gran. I'm not sure I believe in the goddess the way she does," Carlie whispered.

"But you are on a journey to discover what is true to you," the woman retorted. "You are on a quest both within and without, seeking knowledge and understanding, learning rituals and forging the confidence to change them to suit you. And you have opened your heart and your mind to experiences that would have made some people unravel, applying logic as well as intuition, and managing to marry the two without conflict. Most importantly, you hold nature as sacred and want to work in the healing arts, to aid people physically and emotionally. You spoke to Samantha – what could be more magical, more witchy, than protecting the earth and helping people to heal?"

Beth felt uneasy eavesdropping on Carlie's conversation, but when she tried to drift away so she didn't intrude, she felt a tug at her heart, a physical force drawing her nearer. Apparently she was supposed to be here right now.

The woman in gold winked at Beth, then turned back to the teenager and asked if she knew who she was.

"I'm guessing that you're the woman in yellow, or maybe gold," Carlie replied softly, nervously. "And friend to Brauna, Brianna and Aideen, which would make you the symbol of air?"

"Very good," she replied, and Beth grinned. The words would have sounded patronising coming from anyone else, yet this regal woman didn't have a drop of sarcasm in her. "My name is Liana. And what does air bring?"

"Is this a test?" Carlie asked wryly. Beth tried not to laugh, and Liana conceded a small smile as she reassured the girl there was no pass or fail.

For a moment Beth's attention was dragged away by the beauty of the sun slowly rising above the horizon. The first golden rays spilled across the three figures on the summit of the tor, illuminating Carlie's face as she sank down onto the wet grass and began haltingly to speak.

"Air represents thought, intellect, communication, clarity and truth," Carlie offered, voice barely a whisper. "It's about the dawning of a new day – moving forward, letting go of regrets and starting again, free of preconceptions and limitations. It heralds fresh starts and new beginnings, and the world and your life born anew."

Beth was impressed. Her daughter and her daughter's best friend were progressing well on their magical paths, with a good basic knowledge. She smiled as the woman in gold offered Carlie a velvet-wrapped package for Rose. Of course these Otherworldly beings would know and love the priestess. Drawing closer, she heard Liana tell Carlie about the new beginnings and new love that were coming for her, if only she would open her heart and let them in.

It saddened Beth that Carlie was so reluctant to accept this message, and she wished she could help her in some way. Feeling a heaviness on her chest, she raised a hand to touch the rose quartz pendant that had solidified around her neck. It had been a gift from the woman in gold all those years ago, a physical symbol to remind her of the message she was imparting. Beth closed her eyes as the memories flooded her.

"It will remind you that you are loved," Liana had told her. "That you need to trust. That you must open yourself to the love being offered. And when you doubt, it will reassure you that you are indeed filled with magic. It will also remind you that you are a part of this land, of this countryside, of this village, and that you are able to access the magic right here."

Is that what Beth had forgotten? Was Liana trying to remind her she could connect with her daughter if she opened up to the power of the land she had always been part of? And did she need to bear witness to Carlie's message, or could she go and find Rhiannon?

Opening her eyes, Beth looked over at Carlie, and wasn't particularly surprised that she was now sitting alone on the hill, Liana having dispersed back into the mists from which she'd come, which were fading now as the sun inched its way higher, bathing the whole summit in molten gold.

Watching Carlie stand slowly and make her way back down the hill, Beth hovered atop the tor. Stretching out her arms, she spun around, trying to recreate the sensation of freedom she'd experienced up here when she was alive, of being at one with nature and the elements. Where once she had been made of earth and water, bound within her body, now she was a being of air and fire, of liberty and light. Insubstantial as the breeze, yet she remained, buffeted by the wind currents, and somehow physical enough to have heard Carlie's conversation with the woman in gold.

Was it Liana who had been following her all this time? But for what purpose? And why hadn't she revealed herself earlier, instead of tormenting her with the secretive glimpses she'd allowed, the sinister flashes that had so terrified Beth?

And what did Carlie have to do with it all?

Collapsing onto the grass, Beth looked out over the paddocks full of sheep, the hills in the distance, the silver snake of the road weaving between green fields, and now she could see her house, where her little family was safely ensconced together.

*Without her.*

The reality of that finally hit her. She'd been clinging to the hope that she was still with them, still part of their life, yet she'd been denying the awful truth. For eighteen months she'd been gone, and they'd been trying to move forward. Maybe they needed closure as much as she did.

Movement above her dragged her back to the present, and she stared up at the black ravens wheeling overhead, impressed by their grace and power. Suddenly a white bird appeared, an angel tern, which dove right at her, then settled gently at her feet just before she broke apart with fear. Gazing up at her, head to one side, it regarded her with curiosity and a strange, wild intelligence. Then it opened its mouth – and instead of a caw or a croak, words tumbled out.

"Your daughter Rhiannon of the birds sought us out in her grief and pain, and we spoke to her of peace and hope, whispered to her of magic and healing, and reminded her that she held all that she needed within her. That she was far stronger than she thought she was, and much braver than she imagined," the bird said.

Beth gasped, too shocked to respond, and the feathered creature eyed her impatiently before continuing.

"Although it took her some time to accept our message, eventually she did. And now she is communicating with the ravens, and integrating their message and their medicine. Her spiritual rebirth has begun, and she is coming to terms with all the aspects of herself, and all the things she has experienced, the good and the bad. She will be wiser for it, and more resilient, so you have no need to fear on her account. She is surrounded by those who love her, who will soothe and heal her with their compassion."

"That's wonderful, but I don't know how you can know that, or how I can understand you and what you're saying," Beth whispered, still struggling to get her head around a talking bird.

"Does it matter?" the white bird asked irritably. "Surely the only thing worth focusing on is that your daughter will be fine."

That was true. She was an anomaly herself. Was a bird that could speak any stranger than a ghost who couldn't move on, or a woman in gold who emerged fully formed from the swirling mists? Finally she managed to shrug off the oddity and focus on the message.

"Both of your children will be okay Beth. You can focus on your husband now. You're here for a handfasting, are you not? There's something in that for you." And with that, the angel tern took flight, leaving Beth blinking into the rising sun, stunned by all that had unfolded that morning.

Her mind raced, thoughts jumbling in her head. She was so happy that Rose had found love, but she wasn't sure how that related to Mike. Was the key in the ritual itself? There were ribbons to tie their hands, and a Beltane fire the happy couple would leap over at the celebration. Who else would be there? Rose and her magical circle. Her own family. Carlie. Rhiannon's boyfriend Tom.

Then a flash of knowingness pierced her heart, and she sank back down on the grass, rocked to her core. *Of course.* Rose's companion Richard would be there too. Richard who had lost his wife eighteen months ago, around the same time Mike had lost Beth. Richard who had felt paralysed by guilt when contemplating welcoming someone new into his life, terrified that his grandsons would think less of him, or be impacted in a negative way.

That had to be the link. It was time for Mike to move on, to open his heart, but he was putting Rhiannon and Brodie before his needs, imagining them hostile to anyone they might see as taking their mother's place. Yet as Tom and his cousin Jake had made clear, they thought it was time for Richard to come out of mourning, and he had accepted their wisdom. Beth knew Rhiannon had said the same to Mike, but had he listened? Did he believe her?

Filled with determination, Beth closed her eyes and willed herself to her daughter.

She knew what she had to do now.

Chapter 35

# The Happy Phantom

### Rhiannon

A furious hammering on the door woke Rhiannon up, and she struggled out of bed and raced down the darkened stairs in her pyjamas, wondering who on earth was even up at this ungodly hour. It was Carlie, out of breath, freezing cold, her words tumbling out in a garbled rush.

Rhiannon ushered her inside, listening impatiently as her friend flitted from topic to topic. Jake, and friendship, then a woman in gold, and the promise of new love. Finally her foggy brain caught up.

"It's about time," she said, leading her friend upstairs to her bedroom. "I'm not sure how much longer he would have waited."

"Am I too late?" Carlie's voice was stricken with fear.

Rhiannon shook her head. "I don't think so, he doesn't seem the fickle type, but I wouldn't risk leaving it too much longer."

"But do I really like him?" Carlie asked, face screwed up in anguish. "And can I do this? And should I? I mean, what if I hurt him? I'd never forgive myself."

"Oh Carlie, you're hurting him by not giving him a chance. No one knows what will happen – hell, Tom and I could break up next week – but you can't live like that, you can't tiptoe through life in the shadows, too afraid to try anything just in case it won't work out, just in case it will hurt. You taught me that," Rhiannon insisted.

She paused to pull a dress over her head and grab a brush, then turned her attention back to Carlie. "Life is pain, yet it's also incredible joy. But you have to move out of your comfort zone. You need to take a risk sometimes, stop protecting your heart out of fear, in order to feel the joy."

Her friend laughed. "That's what I told Rose."

Rhiannon gulped. It's what Viviane and Rose had told her too. That she had to trust someone enough to let them in, had to be brave enough to tell Tom what had happened to her in order to heal and move forward. Her mind raced as she tried to figure out how she could broach the subject with her boyfriend, if she ever managed to find the courage.

Shaking her head to shake off that thought, she focused back on what her friend was saying. Something about a present for Rose, and the woman in gold offering her the gift of love.

"But she told me I have to go out and make it happen myself, that I have to take the risk." Carlie paused, eyes wide and uncertain. "I'm not sure I can though."

Rhiannon took her friend's hands. "This is Jake we're talking about, your friend Jake, your study buddy, your thank-god-you're-here-too, I'll-throw-up-if-I-have-to-watch-Rhiannon-and-Tom-kiss-each-other-again partner-in-crime. There's no reason to feel nervous about talking to him," she assured her, then grimaced as the words echoed back at her. If that was true, then she should have no problem telling Tom. So why did she feel so vulnerable?

Carlie sighed. "I guess you're right. But that reminds me, has Tom arrived yet? And do you think he brought his equipment?"

Rhiannon gazed at her curiously. "Yeah, he got here this morning, although he's been around at Jake's, seeing his grandad. And I imagine he brought his stuff – he never goes anywhere without it. But you can ask him yourself, he'll be here any minute."

A knock interrupted them, and the two girls rushed downstairs and threw open the door, Rhiannon suddenly aware that her hair was a mess and her tummy was rumbling with hunger.

Tom was bemused. "What's going on?" he asked, as he greeted his girlfriend with a peck on the cheek then peered curiously at her friend.

"Come in, come in," Rhiannon said, dragging him through the door. "I think Carlie wants another tattoo. And to kiss your cousin," she added with a grin, then raced back up to her room, the other two trailing after her.

After a brief catch up, Tom set up his tattooing equipment and Rhiannon left him and Carlie to it. Sweeping her unruly hair into a ponytail, slipping on her shoes and grabbing an apple from the kitchen, Rhiannon wandered out into the backyard. A trail of sunbeams marked a path to the gate in the back fence, and on a whim she took it, making her way into the lane behind her house and following the golden beams. As she got closer to the tor she felt its presence drawing her forward, felt the heartbeat of the earth and the power running through it. The warmth of the early morning sunshine caressed her face, and she smiled at the glittering sunbeams sparkling ahead of her.

Stepping out onto the lower slope of the sacred hill, Rhiannon closed her eyes and breathed in the apple-blossom-scented air. Sensed the energy of the land rising up and surging through her, calming her mind, soothing her soul and filling her heart. Peace enveloped her, then she felt an arm around her shoulder, pulling her into the most healing, comforting embrace. She grinned. Perhaps she was finally going to meet the woman in gold too.

"Oh my darling, I'm so proud of you," a voice whispered. A familiar voice.

Rhiannon's eyes snapped open, and she shook with disbelief and urgent longing. Her mother was standing before her, looking well again, like her old self. And almost solid. Not ghost-like in any way.

"Mum! What –? How –?"

"It's Beltane, so the veils between the worlds are thinner, and I've finally been able to gather enough power to appear to you."

"But you spent time with Carlie," Rhiannon said before she could stop herself, voice petulant and far more accusatory than she would have liked. "I mean…"

"I know. She could see me when you couldn't," Beth replied sadly. "That wasn't my intention, I promise. I've been trying so hard to connect with you, but you girls have different magical strengths. And believe me, Carlie would have much preferred to see her own mother."

Rhiannon's mouth dropped open. She hadn't thought of that. Now she felt bad for demanding so much from her friend.

"But I've always been with you darling," Beth continued. "Hovering during your coven meetings, and applauding your progress and growing wisdom. Watching you fall for John, then realise he wasn't right for you, then meet Tom. Wanting so desperately to comfort you when you and Carlie had your falling out."

"You mean when I treated her so badly and possibly caused the death of her true love?" Rhiannon sighed. "I deserved her anger."

"No my darling, you didn't, and you don't, and Carlie isn't angry at you. You've both learned and grown from your friendship, and all the ups and downs of it, and she understands why you were concerned for her now she's experienced the same worry about you with Tom."

Grudgingly Rhiannon nodded.

"More importantly, you know why Carlie was so sure of Rowan, now that you're with Tom," her mum added gently. "And he's a sweetheart by the way. You don't have to worry that he's anything like Evan. You can trust him."

The relief at her mother's words was tangible, and Rhiannon exhaled a deep sigh. Slowly the tension that had made her shoulders tight and her stomach clench drained away, and she realised a part of her had still doubted Tom, or her own judgement perhaps. Had wondered if she was making a mistake to give her heart again, or tell him her innermost secrets.

Beth beamed at her. "Darling girl, it's never a mistake to love, not when it's real. When it's a shared connection, and you feel able to be your true self with them. You held a part of yourself back with John, because deep down you knew, lovely though he was, he wasn't mature enough to handle all of you. But Tom is. He's kind and strong and compassionate, and you can trust him with your secrets, and share your truth. He will see you, all of you, and love you for it."

A shudder rippled up Rhiannon's spine, and sweat prickled on her forehead despite the cool breeze. She didn't know if she could do that. She was too scared

of rejection, of seeing disgust in his face at her failings, horror at her shame. But she pushed the thought aside. Her mother was here, for who knew how long, and she had more pressing things to discuss.

"Why can I see you now? And more importantly, will I always be able to see you at Beltane, and Samhain too? Are there other times? Is there anything I can do to make it happen more often?"

Beth smiled sadly and shook her head. "I don't think so darling. I have a feeling Liana is helping me appear to you, just until my unfinished business is complete."

"What do you mean? What unfinished business? And who's Liana?" Rhiannon demanded, voice shrill with panic. There was so much she wanted to know, *needed* to know, but she was terrified her mother would disperse back into the air at any moment.

Laughter echoed across the glade, and a golden haze shimmered in the air around Beth. "Ask Carlie about the woman in gold. That's not what's important right now."

"But –"

"Darling, shh, I need to apologise to you while I can. Ever since I became aware in this state, I've been tortured by the knowledge that I left you so soon after that night in the woods. That I wasn't there to help you heal from it."

Tears welled in Rhiannon's eyes. She would have given anything to have her mother then, to have her *now*, but she didn't blame her for any of it. "It's not your fault Mum," she whispered.

"I appreciate that." Beth smiled, and reached out a hand to stroke her daughter's face, before dropping it in despair when her translucent fingers slipped right through her cheek. "I know I failed you though, and as a parent that is always your biggest fear, the one thing you can never forgive yourself for. But it soothes my heart to know that you have had help with this, from Rose, from the women of the forest in Brittany, from the woman of fire in our own woods."

Startled, Rhiannon stared at her mother. She'd been in the woods that night when Aideen had demanded she speak her truth and face her fear? Had heard Viviane and Morgaine imploring her to say the word aloud, to tell people what had happened to her? How mortifying.

"I know they seemed harsh, but you're ready to move forward with your life now, to put it behind you," her mum said softly. "Not to forget it, or to forgive him, but to forgive yourself, and trust again. I should have known that between Rose and your father, and the women of the mists, you were in good hands."

A tear trembled on Rhiannon's lashes, and she swallowed, trying to stop the burning pain and the chill of regret from spilling out over the lump in her throat.

Her mother smiled wistfully. "I know Brodie will be fine too, because of you. Thank you for the project you're doing with him, to help him remember me. You are filled with wisdom my darling, and compassion and empathy and strength, and don't you ever forget that. You will make a wonderful grief counsellor, and help so many people."

Beth looked like she was going to cry too. Rhiannon peered at her, confused. Could ghosts cry?

But her mother spoke again before she could ask. "And Rose was right, I couldn't be more proud of the woman you're growing into."

This time Rhiannon couldn't stop her sobs, and she wiped a tear from her cheek as she tried hard to commit every word, every expression, every gesture of her mother's to memory. "Thanks Mum," she whispered, and saw pain and longing cross Beth's ghostly face.

"I think I've completed the last of my unfinished business."

Gold sparkles danced more vividly around Beth's shoulders, and Rhiannon's heart clenched in panic. She couldn't lose her mum now, right when she'd finally found her!

"Oh my darling, you haven't lost me. I will always be with you, in your heart, for as long as you remember me and hold me close. Just be happy for me, that I can be free now, that the fear that has trapped me here has finally been relinquished, and I can dissolve into the air and move into the light..."

"No!" Rhiannon screamed.

Chapter 36

Rhiannon

When Rhiannon opened her eyes, she gasped in shock. Her mother was still standing in front of her, as bewildered as she was, and gazing around the glade as though searching for someone.

Finally Beth sighed. "Perhaps this means I have to confess my terrible behaviour and my awful guilt to you, given Carlie and Rose are such a big part of your life." Regret vibrated through Beth's voice. Sadness and apprehension hunched her shoulders.

Rhiannon stared at her, confused. What on earth could her mum have done that was so bad it would hold her here when she wanted to move on?

"Oh darling, I appreciate your faith in me, so much, but I've been guilt-stricken for the last twenty years," Beth said shakily.

*What?* Her mum was the kindest, sweetest woman she knew. She had nothing to feel guilty about.

Taking a deep breath to steady herself – although did ghosts need to breathe, or was it just for Rhiannon's benefit? – Beth haltingly began her story. "I love that you think me incapable of anything bad, but I did something a long time ago, something thoughtless and selfish, which I feared had destroyed a friend. And I spent every day afterwards trying to atone for it. I was far nicer to people than was in my nature, I was more patient with you and Brodie than I might otherwise have been, and I loved your father with a fierceness and a constant need to prove that he hadn't settled for second best."

Rhiannon's head spun, a wave of dizziness washing over her as time and space folded in around her. "You've never been selfish," she insisted. "In fact, it was hard growing up in the shadow of how amazing you are, trying to live up to that."

A fleeting smile illuminated Beth's face, but it didn't reach her eyes. "I tried to be the best person I could be, to make up for what I did," she whispered.

"I don't understand," Rhiannon said, voice incredulous. "Dad adored you. I've never seen a more devoted, loving husband, or a stronger, more loving couple than you two. And you couldn't possibly destroy anyone's life. I don't believe you."

Her mother sighed, a sigh that shook the trees around the meadow, then braced herself to continue. "Your father loved Violet, Rose's daughter," she blurted out. "They were childhood sweethearts, and everyone thought they would get married. But then I came home from Paris for your aunt Jenny's wedding. I was lonely, depressed by the end of a terrible relationship, and bruised from constant arguments with my mother. When I met Mike I fell hard for him, because he was everything this other guy wasn't – he was kind and caring, and offered me friendship without a second thought. Even his girlfriend Violet took me in, becoming my friend, including me in their outings, inviting me to go on their dates, listening to me, showing me kindness."

Beth paused, and grimaced, but forced herself to go on. "Then the three of us went to a psychic course – and the teacher was the guy I'd been seeing in Paris, although he was using a different name then. And he wanted Violet."

A chill went up Rhiannon's spine, and she stared at her mother in horror. "Andre, the psycho shaman?" she asked, trying to recall what Carlie had uncovered about her mum's mysterious second love, the one who'd forced Violet to leave Rose and her dad, and caused such pain to so many.

"Yes, although I knew him as Andrew. I tried to stop him, I really did. I threatened him, said I'd tell Violet he had been cruel, and violent, but he said he knew how much I wanted to be with Mike, so if I kept my mouth shut, he'd help me work a spell to be with him, while he worked one on Violet."

"No!" Rhiannon croaked.

Tears poured down Beth's face. "I regretted it straight away, and tried to fix it, or cancel it, but he blackmailed me into going along with it. And whether it was the spell or just the way of the world, Violet fell for him. And then she disappeared."

For long moments Beth stood frozen, head bowed, wrapped in memories, and remorse. Rhiannon caught glimpses of visions – Beth, young and naive, pining after Mike, and a girl who looked like Carlie taking the hand of a much older man and walking away with him. "But Rose..." she murmured, then trailed off, too horrified to articulate the thought.

Beth's head jolted back up to face her daughter, and she nodded sadly. "It tortured me that Rose was so kind to me, so happy for Mike when we got together, so wonderful with you and Brodie from the second you were born. She was like the mother I never had. Loving, supportive, accepting, so much more than I could ever have hoped for. Yet I was always terrified that she'd discover what I'd done. So I was just waiting for her to turn her back on me."

"But Rose loved you like a daughter. The two of you were so close." Rhiannon was struggling to get her head around this disclosure, to rewrite her opinion of her saintly mother as someone who could have caused real harm.

As though she could read her daughter's mind, Beth winced. "She really did love me. And she did know, but loved me anyway," she admitted, wonder in her voice. "When I first got sick, she came to see me. Well, she came every day, to sit with me, to give me healings, to look after me, to offer me spiritual comfort. But one day, early on, she was holding my hand, and she looked up at me, eyes full of love, and told me that she knew what I'd done, and what it had wrought, but it was not my fault. That she forgave me, and I had to let go of the guilt and the shame, because it was making me sick."

"But if she'd already forgiven you, why do you still have unfinished business? Why are you still here?" Rhiannon asked.

A harsh wind roared around the glade, buffeting Beth's not-quite-there body, and making her sway. But she smiled at Rhiannon, and reached for her hand, and the wind died down.

"Because I was still terrified that I had destroyed Violet's life. That Andre had hurt her, or worse," she finally whispered.

Rhiannon felt the pain jolting through her mother like a physical thing in her own body. She knew from Carlie that the fear was warranted – Violet's friend Jasmine had worried about the same thing, and so had Rowan's mother Louisa, who was married to Andrew/Andre before he left her for Violet. What a tangled web it was. But surely it couldn't have all sprung from one tiny little spell her mum had cast?

"Oh darling, your faith in me soothes my heart, yet even Rose forgiving me couldn't really ease my guilt. Then the other day I was drawn to Carlie again, as she realised that Rowan was no longer around her, communicating with her or appearing to her. It made her so sad, although she tried to find peace and acceptance in knowing he'd been able to move on. And I hope you're able to get to that place too, with me."

Rhiannon shrugged. Nothing would make her be okay with losing her mother, but what did that have to do with Beth moving on? "How did that help you with Violet?" she asked.

Shaking her head, Beth tried to focus. "Sorry, the important thing for me was that Rowan's mum turned up at Carlie's place. They offered each other some comfort, but it wasn't until they were saying goodbye that Carlie provided closure for Louisa – and for me. She almost didn't say it, because she didn't want to cause the woman more pain, but thank goddess she did, because it not only eased Louisa's guilt, but mine as well."

"What did she say?" Rhiannon asked, impatient again. No offence, but she didn't know Rowan's mother. She was only concerned with her own.

"It wasn't anything momentous, and yet it was," Beth replied. "It's funny, that the briefest moment, the smallest action, can ease somebody's pain, set them on a new path, change a person's life. She just begged her not to feel bad about her mum. Rowan had told her that Louisa was worried his dad had hurt Violet, or worse. And he did, but she survived. She got away, and found her beloved, and had a wonderful life – and she wouldn't have met her true love if she hadn't gone through everything she did. Carlie promised her that she shouldn't feel bad for her mum, or responsible in any way. I could see how deeply her words affected Louisa – and they were everything to me too."

A tremor pulsed through Beth, and she faded slightly, becoming more ghost-like. Rhiannon reached out to her in panic, but her mum wasn't quite done.

"I saw the huge weight fall from Louisa's shoulders, and I felt it too. To know Violet survived Andre, and found her soul mate, and lived a life filled with love and joy... You have no idea what a gift that was for me as well as for Louisa. Carlie's words freed Rowan's mother from her guilt, allowing her to move forward with her life, and they've done that for me too, so I can move forward with my... death... I guess."

A fierce wind whipped up again, and a dark cloud covered the sun. Rhiannon shivered. Was her mum going to dissolve away to nothing right in front of her? That would be like her dying all over again, just when she'd found her.

"Don't go," she begged.

Beth smiled sadly, and lifted a hand to blow a kiss to her daughter. The clouds parted, and a stream of sunbeams illuminated Beth, bathing her in a golden light that made her sparkle like rainbow quartz. Translucent yet solid. Caught somewhere between life and death, between hope and despair.

"Thank god," Rhiannon whispered.

But Beth was shaking her head, upset, almost disturbed, to still be standing on the grass in the summer sunshine. She swore under her breath, then sighed. "I was hoping your father would realise this on his own, but it seems he's being wilfully stubborn and oblivious. It seems you'll have to help me with this one darling. And I apologise that it's awkward and strange, but I need you to tell your dad he should move on."

"Mum!"

"It's been eighteen months since I died Rhiannon," Beth said, the first hint of sternness in her voice. "I thought maybe he was coming to this conclusion himself, when Jessica gave him that reading –"

"You were there? You came to France with us?"

Beth's face softened, and she smiled at her daughter. "I told you I've been with you, as often as I could be. But I think I have to let you all go so *you* can move on. It can't be healthy for you guys, having me hanging around you, haunting you. Perhaps your dad senses me with him on some level, and won't consider anyone else while my shadow lays over him."

Hot tears filled Rhiannon's eyes then spilled over, falling like jagged diamonds down her red-blotched cheeks. "But Mum, I *want* you to stay with us always," she murmured. "Dad would too."

"I know darling, and I desperately want that as well. But I think I have to move on for my sake as well as yours. I've had a few reminders that I'm not supposed to be here, and as painful as it is to contemplate leaving you, and leaving all that I know, it's past time that I did."

"Where will you go?"

Beth laughed, a mirthless laugh. "Who knows? Back into the starless void perhaps. Or to the Summerland of pagan lore. Or maybe I'll be reincarnated. There has been no epiphany about that yet, but maybe that will come when I surrender. When I let go of what I have been holding so fast to."

Heart racing and tears pouring down her face, Rhiannon wrung her hands. "But I've just found you."

"And I'm so glad you have," Beth said. "It's such a relief that you know how much I love you, and how proud I am of you, and how grateful that you're looking after Brodie. And it will mean the world to me if you can reassure your dad that it's time for him to open his heart to someone new. To the possibility at least. Can you do that for me?"

"I don't want to."

"Darling!"

"Fine," Rhiannon grumbled.

Her mum reached out a hand to her, and Rhiannon sensed it as a gentle breeze, drying the tears on her cheeks, and soothing her soul. "It won't mean he loves me any less darling, just that his heart has grown even bigger. He has so much room for love in his heart, and in his life, but you will have to help him. Let him know it's okay with you, and with Brodie. That you won't be angry or resentful. That you will be happy for him."

"That might be pushing it."

"Do it for me Rhiannon, please. And for your father."

Reluctantly she nodded, and with a gentle smile, her mum kissed her on the forehead – a sensation she almost felt – then faded away, dissolving into a swarm of golden sparkles that danced around her head then flitted away like butterflies.

Sinking to the grass, Rhiannon's sobs increased, and sadness and regret slammed into her. Yet slowly, within this vortex of despair, she experienced a warmth and a joy she hadn't expected. She was suffused in her mother's love, and she would hold on to that forever. Most importantly, she knew Beth was finally at peace.

For a long time she sat there, breathing in the memories that swirled around her, wrapping her in coils of mist and reminiscence, until the cawing of a black raven overhead brought her back from the dreamscape she had slipped into. It was Beltane. Her boyfriend was waiting for her at her place, and she had to be at Carlie's soon to help Rose prepare for her handfasting. There was love and friendship surrounding her, and as bereft as she felt right now, she had to focus on that.

Springing to her feet, she ran across the green slope of the tor, down the wooden steps, and raced along the laneway, heading for home. Heading for her family, her friend, and her beloved.

## Chapter 37

# Into the Void

### Beth

Tears cascaded down Beth's face as she watched Rhiannon walk away. Happy tears, that she'd been able to communicate with her after dreaming of it for so long, but there was sadness too, and fear, and a desperate yearning that pulled at her core. She'd pretended to her daughter that she was at peace with her death and impending journey to... somewhere else. That it was better for all of them that she let go. But she hadn't convinced herself.

In despair, she closed her eyes. Pain rippled through her, and panic clutched at her heart. What would happen when she ceased to be? Where would she go? *When* would she go?

Silently she screamed into the void. A terrible wind battered her, the sun burned her, and her tenuous link to her form started to break down. She was at the mercy of a maelstrom of elements and emotions that were destroying her fragile hold on existence.

Was this how she would disappear... move on... pass over...

*What did you call it?*

Would she disintegrate into the elements and become part of nature? Dissolve into the air. Sink into the earth. Float away in the water. Burn up in the fire.

Maybe that was fitting. She'd always seen herself as an intrinsic part of the environment. And while she railed against having to leave, wasn't this how it should play out? The wheel of the year turning ever onwards, and the cycle of life, death and rebirth moving ever forward. Knowing how beautiful nature was, and how sacred its wheels and cycles, she couldn't be upset to become part of it, right? Clinging to life when she was dead would only upset the natural balance.

Conjuring the thought of calm, of the exercises Rose had taught their ritual circle to centre themselves, Beth imagined herself home. And when she opened her eyes, she was standing in her old bedroom, staring out at the blue sky and sunshine. And finally, so quietly and gently it was as though it had soared in on butterfly wings, a vision played out before her.

She was lying in a white hospital bed in a room filled with flowers of every colour, Brodie just born and snuggled up at her chest, Mike sitting in a cold plastic chair, holding her hand, tears of love and devotion in his eyes. Rhiannon, eleven years old, was sitting opposite him, a small hand on her new brother's head, and curious wonder on her face.

"My perfect family," Mike said, voice full of love, joy and awe.

There was a question in Beth's eyes, but he ignored it, sweeping down to kiss her rather than wasting his breath again on reassurances.

"This is what I always dreamed of," he continued firmly. "My own family. A love to rival all those you read about in the classics, with my precious wife and our two children, the physical manifestation of our deep connection."

A tear slid down Beth's cheek, and he tenderly wiped it away.

"I know you didn't have that growing up darling," he said softly, kindly. "But you have it now."

She nodded. It was true. She had all that she'd dreamed of too – work she loved, gorgeous children, and a husband, partner and friend she had loved since the moment they were reintroduced fifteen years ago. Her broken heart was soothed, and healed, as she finally comprehended this fact. Her husband wasn't pining for his first love, if he ever had, or for a different life. He loved *her*. She was enough. Her, just the way she was.

S miling through her tears, Beth floated over to the open window and gazed down at her garden, grateful for the immense well of beautiful memories she had to access. It would be those that kept her alive to her family. She was gone from their physical world, but she would reside in their hearts, woven into the fabric of their existence by all the treasured moments they'd shared. Mike, Rose, her children, her friends – they had all influenced her in myriad ways, had made her who she was, and she had done the same for them.

Now she would live on in the people they had become because of her. In the traditions they'd built together, in the phrases of hers they used, in the experiences they'd shared, and the personalities they'd developed out of their tight family unit. The legacy of her own cruel parents had shaped her early life, made her a person she wasn't proud of, and taken her a long time to get over. So she was proud that she had been a loving, supportive mother to her kids, helping them grow into the kind, clever, giving and compassionate people they were becoming.

And she and Mike had taught each other to love, and helped heal the other's broken heart. She would be a totally different person if she'd married someone else, and he would have been too. They had brought out the best in each other, and encouraged the other to be all that they could be. Beth thought of Carlie telling Rowan's mother that knowing him had changed her, and so, no matter who else she loved and what else she became, he'd always be part of her. That would have to be enough for Beth too.

The wind whispered through the leaves of the oak tree, and the scent of apple blossoms drifted from the direction of the tor. Beth missed walking this land, feeling connected to the earth, and she especially missed working in her garden. She'd spent so much time with her hands in the dirt, planting herbs, weeding flower beds, casting spells and weaving magic. Her sun wheel of summer herbs looked a little wild around the edges, but for the most part it had survived her absence. And her moon garden, filled with fragrant night-blooming flowers, could still be discerned.

A smile twisted the corners of her mouth as she recalled the nights she and Mike had lain there together on the grass, the silvery light of the full moon shining on their naked bodies, the sweet scent of jasmine and gardenias intoxicating her as much as his kisses, and the shadowy patterns of the blossoms appearing like a treasure map on their bare skin. A swell of yearning shuddered through her as she remembered Mike tracing his fingers across her shoulders, her stomach, her lips... Crushing flowers beneath them as they clung to each other in the inky dark.

She gulped. It was better that she leave soon, if Mike was going to find love with someone else. She wanted him to. It was the right thing to happen, because the living needed to live. But she couldn't bear to see it unfold. Couldn't be here to watch someone else in her room, in her bed, in her family. And she sensed her departure coming nearer, shadowing her wherever she went, pulling at her brittle centre. She'd expected to dissolve into the void once Rhiannon promised to talk to Mike about opening his heart again, but she was still here. What was left?

The vision of her in hospital with her family returned.

*Brodie.*

She closed her eyes and focused on her son. A sucking sensation almost tore her apart with fear, but then her surroundings settled, and she felt the sun on her face. Cautiously opening her eyes, she smiled. She was in her friend Laura's sunny apartment, and Brodie was sitting at the small kitchen table with her, wearing jeans and a green buttoned shirt, a fierce intelligence and curiosity burning in his eyes, and looking so grown up.

Running a hand through his blond curls, Laura poured him a glass of juice and offered a plate of sandwiches.

"Do I have to do anything today?" Brodie asked, picking up a salad sandwich. "I don't want to make a mistake and ruin Rose's special day."

Beth swooped closer, perching on the chair next to her son, drinking in every expression on her face, every word, every movement.

Her friend smiled at her son. "You couldn't ruin it if you tried Brodie. But no, there's nothing you have to do other than be there to help Rose celebrate. You're a very important part of her life, and it will make her very happy that you're sharing this special occasion with her."

"She's important to me too, and to my whole family. She was so kind to Mumma when she was sick, and even before that. Kind to everyone. Mumma always wished Rose was her real mother, instead of my mean grandma."

Laughter shook Beth at this revelation, then she wondered how her son had been aware of that at such a young age.

Laura was smiling too. "Yeah, we're all so grateful to have Rose in our lives, and I know how much she loves you and Rhiannon. You're the grandchildren of her heart."

"Do you have any kids?" Brodie asked abruptly.

Sadness shadowed Laura's face for a moment, but she made an effort to push it away. "No, unfortunately I wasn't able to have children. But I'm lucky because I get to teach heaps of young people, and share in their lives that way."

"Oh, I'm sorry," Brodie said, sounding older than his years. He reached out and patted her hand. "What about a husband?"

This time it was a far bigger struggle for Laura to force a smile. "I did have a husband, but he was desperate to have children too. We tried for a long time, but it only ever ended in heartbreak, and, well, he couldn't handle it. We're still friends, but he has a new wife now, and they have a baby boy."

A stab of pain ripped through Beth. She'd been there for her friend through her long battle to be a mum, had held her together after each miscarriage, and done her best to comfort her as her marriage struggled under the strain. But it was a shock to learn that her husband had left her – and even worse that he'd so quickly remarried and had a baby with someone else. It broke Beth's heart that Laura had endured all of that without her. How had she coped? Had there been someone else to support her?

She'd been so obsessed with her own family, that she hadn't spared a thought for her best friend. Now Beth glided over to Laura's side and tried to wrap her arms around her, but her translucent almost-form was too weak, and she was left clutching at air again. Guilt throbbed through her, and sympathy, and regret. The pain made her want to fade away, to disappear altogether, but that would help no one. Reaching out a hand, she stroked her friend's cheek, and for one hopeful moment she thought Laura felt her presence.

But it was Brodie she was reacting too. His small hand was on Laura's wrist in comfort as he peered up at her.

"Could you be my mum?"

Laura's eyes widened in shock, and she cleared her throat nervously, but Beth had seen the wild hope and longing in her expression, and once she got over her own astonishment, contentment washed over her. Maybe she didn't have to do anything to help her husband – maybe Rhiannon didn't need to either. Perhaps it would be her little son who brought love to Mike, healed Laura, and made his family whole again.

"I would love that Brodie, but it's not up to me," Laura stammered. "And it's complicated. Your dad loved your mum –"

"And they both loved you," he retorted. "You're Mum's best friend, and Rhiannon loves you too." He looked so hopeful. Laura knelt down at his side and hugged him fiercely, while Beth tried not to dissolve into a puddle of tears.

"I am always here for you Brodie, and for Rhiannon, all right? If you ever need me, just let me know, promise?"

Slowly Brodie nodded, expression serious, almost stern. "I promise. And if you ever need a kid to hang out with, I'm here for you, okay?"

Laura nodded solemnly, then returned to her seat.

"And don't worry about me," Brodie continued. "I'm okay with Dad and Rhi-Rhi, but it would be nice to have you with us. And we're going to the festival with you next weekend, just like a real family, so we can practise!"

Laura winced, but she was clearly touched by Brodie's offer to be her pseudo child, and her resistance to the idea seemed to be melting away in the hope she was feeling.

Pride in her young son overwhelmed Beth, and she swooped down and wrapped her arms around him. "I love you so much darling boy," she whispered. "And I'll always be with you, I promise."

He reached his hand up to his shoulder, where her hand was resting, and smiled. "I love you too Mumma."

Hovering next to him, Beth shook her head in amazement, while Laura gaped at him from across the table, then stared right at Beth, trying to see whatever Brodie was sensing. "Is your mum here?" she asked nervously, her cheeks reddening.

"Sometimes I feel her with me," he said with a shrug, as though it was nothing unusual. "Rhi-Rhi told me that Mum is always with us, that she's in the air we breathe and in the earth we walk on, the rain that falls and the flowers we see. Mostly jasmine for me, because that always makes me think of Mumma."

A clock struck the hour, and Laura glanced up at it in a daze. "Oh, we have to get to the ritual. Have you had enough to eat?"

Brodie nodded.

"Would you like to pick some jasmine with me on our way? So your mum is with us today?"

A smile lit up Brodie's face as he nodded again, and Beth sighed with relief as they left the apartment and headed to the garden, her son's small hand clinging tightly to Laura's. While it hurt her to see her replacement, it also soothed her worries. Her friend would take good care of her family, and their love for her would soothe Laura's pain.

So what now? Why was she still here?

The words of the angel tern came back to her. "You're here for a handfasting, are you not? There's something in that for you."

Taking a deep breath, Beth closed her eyes and willed herself to Rose.

## Chapter 38

# Precious Moments

### Rhiannon

Rushing in the back gate and up the stairs to her room, Rhiannon felt like a different person. Seeing her mum had broken her heart, but it had calmed her too, and given her hope. Maybe even provided her with the courage to tell Tom her secret.

As she burst into her bedroom, she stared at Carlie and Tom, seeing them in a new way too. Her eyes rested on her best friend, the delicate, damaged soul who was stronger than she'd ever been. The one she had woven magic with for almost a year. The one who had inspired her to find her career path, and encouraged her to follow it. The one who had forgiven her for trying to break up her relationship, for being so unsupportive. The one who had her back as she fell in love with Tom, despite her own heartbreak. The one who thought it was Rhiannon who was helping her to get over her own grief, when all along it had been the other way around.

A wave of emotion overwhelmed her, and she threw her arms around her friend and held her close. "I love you Carlie," she whispered. "Thank you for helping me to heal. For helping me to grow. For helping me to see the magic in the world. For helping me to love."

Carlie hugged her back, although she winced as her freshly inked wrist brushed against Rhiannon's shoulder.

Rhiannon giggled. "Sorry, I forgot. Let me see it!" she squealed, grabbing her hand and drawing it closer.

"Wow, it's beautiful. And it totally matches Jake's tattoo, with its candle flame and wave, and its rose quartz to his amethyst, and its white feather to his black." She glanced up at her friend. Golden sparks of light were swirling around her head, and her delicate features had lost their haunted look. When had she begun to soften? Was it from finally accepting Jake's love for her – and the possibility of her own for him?

"I'm so happy for you," Rhiannon said. "You deserve happiness more than anyone I know."

Carlie laughed. "I don't know about that, I think Rose is the most worthy of us all, and today is all about her. On which note, I'd better get home and help her get ready!"

Picking up her bag, Carlie turned to Tom. "Thank you so much for doing this for me. It means so much to me."

Rhiannon gazed proudly at her boyfriend as he leaned over and embraced Carlie. "It was my pleasure. And I know how much it will mean to Jake too," he grinned, making Carlie blush.

"Well, I'll see you both later," she said, and hurried out to the landing and down the stairs.

Carlie's whirlwind departure left a heavy, oppressive silence in the room. Tom gazed at Rhiannon, his dark eyes filled with joy at her arrival, and also desire. She shivered. There was electricity sparking between them, and an undeniable attraction. He was gorgeous, the best looking guy she'd ever seen, and she'd flirted outrageously with him when they first met. Suggesting she was more experienced than she actually was, in life and in magic. Trying to impress him with her knowledge of the craft, padding out the length of time she'd been doing rituals, and exaggerating her ceremonial closeness with their priestess.

His eyes widened as she bit her bottom lip, and fear snaked up her spine. She'd led him to believe she was more mature in other ways too. Had implied that she couldn't wait to be intimate with him, and that the thought of Beltane and its old rituals of love and sex filled her with excitement and anticipation.

And now here they were, standing together in her bedroom, alone in the house, her painfully aware of just how much she loved him, while knowing she wasn't ready to fall into bed with him, no matter how much she wanted to. Not with her secret stretching out dark and insidious between them, threatening to drag her under at any moment.

A wave of dizziness descended, and the next thing she knew they were sitting on her bed, fallen there, Tom's arms around her, holding her tighter than was probably wise. She could feel his hard muscled chest against hers, feel the strength of his body, and the proof that he really did want her. She gasped, in panic, in fear, and was stunned when instead of trying to kiss her, Tom put a finger under her chin and lifted her face so she was gazing right into his beautiful, mesmerising eyes. Eyes that now held only concern, rather than the desire she'd been so desperately attracted to, yet deathly afraid of.

"Baby, what's wrong?" he asked gently.

She stared at him, frozen, with no clue of what to say or how to proceed. Did she even know what was wrong? Her mum's words came back to her. Beth had told her she was ready to move forward, to love and heal and forgive, but she had no idea how to do that. Sadness and pain welled within her, and the pit of shame swirled ever wider and deeper in her stomach.

"Rhiannon, talk to me, please. Have I done something to hurt you?" Tom implored her. The concern in his voice was obvious, and her heart melted. He was such a beautiful person. At first she'd been attracted to his bad boy persona, to his long dark hair, his raw magnetism, and the motorbike he'd whisked her away on. But she'd soon discovered that behind his carefree exterior he was incredibly kind and clever, a great friend to Jake, a loving grandson to Richard, and the most considerate guy she knew. Perfect boyfriend material. It was a shame she didn't deserve to be with someone so wonderful.

"Hey," he breathed, and the hurt in his eyes was like a slap in the face. He really cared about her, but he wouldn't if he knew what she was really like. Knew what had happened to her.

"I'm sorry," she whispered. "I'm sorry I led you on, that I wasted your time. You deserve someone better than me." She leaned away from him, even though every instinct in her body screamed at her to move into his arms, not away from them, the space between them chilling her as the warmth of his touch drained out of her.

"I don't understand," he said, the words cracked with pain. He took both her hands, and held them tightly when she tried to pull them away. "You were so happy this morning. Did I do something to upset you? Was it wrong of me to do Carlie's tattoo today, when I should have been with you?"

She almost laughed. "Oh Tom, it's not you, I promise. It's me. I'm not who you think I am..." she admitted, trailing off as she tried to swallow the sadness that made speech so difficult.

"I know who you are Rhiannon," he said firmly, taking her hands. "I know you're the kindest person I've ever met. I know your little brother worships you, and that your dad is so grateful that you've helped them both through your tragic loss. I know your best friend adores you." He paused, and stared at her fiercely. "And I know that I love you."

She gasped at his words. Shocked, amazed, overwhelmed, and suddenly so desperately happy. Since the day they'd met, she'd been dreaming of him saying that. A smile illuminated her face, then was just as quickly gone, shadows darkening over her brow as a clap of thunder broke somewhere overhead.

"I love you too," she murmured. "But I'm not good enough for you." As she said the words, she felt something pass between them, through their joined hands. It wasn't the electricity she'd felt before, the raw throb of desire. This was warmer, softer, and so comforting. For a moment she felt peace, and hope. Then something passed back to him from her, and she snatched her hands away. She wouldn't let him read her mind. He couldn't know her shame.

"Baby, please tell me what this is about, I beg you. I know that you're good enough for me, and there's nothing you could have done that would change that."

More than anything she wanted to believe him, to trust that it was true, but she was too scared.

Then she heard her mother's voice in her head. *My darling, you are stronger than you know, and surrounded by more love than you can imagine.*

Heard Rose. *It does not define you. It cannot control you. And it absolutely will not destroy you.*

The words Tom had spoken to her in the French forest. *You are stronger than you know Rhiannon, and worthy of the deepest love. When you're able to trust enough to share your deepest heart, it will be spectacular.*

And the woman in silver, Viviane, the Lady of the Lake. *Cut away your fear, and your lingering doubt, and feel safe to trust. There will be no betrayal this time, I promise you.*

Cautiously she felt the truth of the words as they soaked into her body, into her soul. Everyone had promised her that love would be enough, and Tom claimed he loved her. And if she refused to tell him, she would lose him anyway, torn apart by suspicion and uncertainty, and the shame that poisoned her. At least if she shared it, there was a fifty-fifty chance they could work it out. *Wasn't there?*

"Here's to trust and being brave," she whispered.

Tom gazed at her steadily, patient and full of love. "Baby?"

Sighing, she stared over his shoulder, out the window, unable to meet his eyes. "I know I flirted with you, and went along with it when you talked about sex magic, and implied that I couldn't wait for Beltane because, well, you know. I wanted to impress you, wanted you to be interested in me. I wanted you to want me. But the truth is, all of that scares me…"

Her voice was small, and shy, and constricted by fear, and the words caught in her throat and stuck there. She thought she'd choke on them if she had to continue. But she'd dived off the precipice now, and there was no turning back. No way to climb up and out of this mortifying situation.

She felt his hand on her cheek, so gentle, so hesitant, and a kernel of hope unfurled within her. Tom turned her face so she had to meet his eyes. Which were shining with love, and light, and joy.

"That's not a problem my love. We can wait as long as you like," he said, voice strong and sweet. "I know in the beginning you probably thought that was all I wanted – and it's true that for a moment I thought of you as simply a pleasant way to pass the time while I was stuck down here with Pop. But that was only the first day, and only for the first few hours. By the time we kissed goodbye that night, I was smitten."

"Really?" she asked, wanting so badly to believe him, to trust him, to be able to open up to him.

"Of course. I wouldn't be driving down from London a couple of times a week if that was all I wanted."

Rhiannon smiled, and her heart lifted a little. Yet that wasn't the point, and her face fell again.

"But I'm not good enough for you," she stated, voice cold now, eyes empty, whole being devoid of warmth and feeling. "Just before Mum died, there was a guy... Oh god, I can't believe I'm telling you."

Tom squeezed her hand. "You can trust me my love."

"We were doing a ritual in the woods one night. He'd promised to help me create a spellcasting for healing, to cure Mum... I know, Little Miss Naive." She shuddered. "But then... then he forced himself on me..." she finally whispered, while tears ran down her cheeks.

"Baby, I'm so sorry," Tom said, leaning in towards her, wanting to hold her. But she recoiled from him, fear in her eyes, in her stance, as she shuffled away from him and curled up against the wall, trying to take up less room, less space, to not be seen. Nervously she pulled her long wavy hair around herself, trying to hide, to be invisible. Her shoulders shook, and hopelessness and disappointment washed over her, threatening to drown her.

"Rhiannon," he said, voice gentle yet firm. "This is not your fault. I'm so deeply sorry that you experienced that, but it is *not your fault*. You have nothing to feel bad about."

She stared at him through red-rimmed eyes. "How can you say that? I've been trying to pretend it didn't happen, pretend there's no need to feel ashamed, but how can you even look at me like that, how can you see past what I've done, what I am? How can you love me now?" she wept.

Tom watched helplessly as her shoulders collapsed and she tried to make herself even smaller. "Baby, the only person who should feel shame is this... guy. I wish I could make him pay, make him sorry for what he's done to you, but please believe me when I say there is no reason on earth that *you* should feel shame. This was *not your fault.*"

Hesitantly she peered up at him, the slightest spark of hope igniting in her heart. "But I feel so ashamed. Like I've been spoiled in some way, and am not worthy of you. Every time you look at me you will see my shame, see my ruin. How can you be with me now?"

He stared back at her, expression calm, soothing, although he was seething inside. Cautiously he reached out his hand to her, and slowly took hers in his. He was relieved when she clung to it, fingers entwined, but while he longed to scoop her up in his arms, he remained still, not wanting to spook her. Not wanting to force anything on her.

"You couldn't be more wrong," he said instead. "There is no shame, and no ruin. It devastates me that you've been hurt like this, especially when your mum was so sick, but you have absolutely no reason to feel ashamed. I love you Rhiannon, and if necessary I will tell you all day every day just how much, and I will reiterate until I'm blue in the face that this was most definitely not your fault, and doesn't reflect on you in *any* way."

The briefest of smiles flitted across her face, although the tears continued to flow. "Will this feeling of worthlessness ever go away?" she asked, voice a broken whisper.

"You are more than worthy my love. It is he who is not worthy."

There was silence in the room as they stared at each other, then Rhiannon sighed, and Tom frowned. "I want to help you my love, to take your suffering away, but you're going to have to tell me what to do. Have you been able to share this with anyone else, or have you been agonising over it on your own all this time?"

Slowly Rhiannon shook her head. It wasn't like she could tell him she'd revealed it to a mysterious woman in the woods, confided in the Lady of the Lake, and shouted it at the spirit of Morgaine. "I haven't told anyone. Mum knew something had happened, she found me that night in the woods, but she died the next day, so I just kind of buried it. I mean, compared to losing my mother it was nothing, right? How could I care about that when my little brother and my dad were falling apart? When I was falling apart…"

Tom pushed the curl that had fallen into her eyes back behind her ear, and smiled at her. "My brave girl, that's totally understandable. It's probably the only way you could survive, could get through each day. Did something bring it back up? Something happened to me last year, which made some trauma I thought I'd buried long ago re-emerge. I hope *I* didn't trigger anything for you," he said anxiously.

Rhiannon felt his fear. "No, of course not," she replied quickly. "But are you okay?"

"This is not about me baby, I'm fine. I got some counselling, and it really helped, so if you ever want to do that, I'll happily go with you, or give you a hand finding someone. And surely Carlie would be more than willing to support you in this?"

"That's actually when it first re-emerged," she said sheepishly. "Something happened with her and Rowan – nothing like this though, it was just a misunderstanding – but I over-reacted really badly. It was after that that I started remembering. And I would have told Carlie, I mean, I know she wouldn't think badly of me, but it happened to her mum, way worse than my… well, the thing that happened to me… so I couldn't burden her with it. I feel bad enough burdening you with it."

Her tears increased, and her shoulders heaved with pain. Tom squeezed her hand in reassurance and comfort, and fought his natural inclination to draw her close.

"Oh my love, it's not a burden at all," he said. "I'm honoured that you felt you could confide in me, because shame lives and grows in silence. It thrives on silence. The less you talk about it, the more powerful it gets, so the best way to defeat shame and fear is to talk about it."

He paused when Rhiannon's eyes widened in disbelief and denial, and rushed to clarify what he meant. "Your secret is safe with me, I promise. And you don't have to tell everyone, or even anyone, else. You just need to share it with one person, and

I am more than happy to be that person. To be your light, and shine love and acceptance into the darkest corners of your pain. Because shame requires darkness, it craves denial, and it's only in exposing it to the light that you can conquer it and start to heal."

Squirming at the intensity of Tom's expression, but touched by his consideration, Rhiannon tried to smile. "Thank you," she mumbled. She felt so awkward, so off balance, and she was terrified that despite his beautiful words, he would look at her differently now.

As though he heard her thought, he lifted her chin and stared into her eyes. "My love, it breaks my heart that you suffered this, but you are a warrior, a fighter, a survivor. You're not a victim in any way. You are not what happened to you," he insisted, softly yet firmly. "I see the sum of everything you are Rhiannon. I see *you*."

Tears misted in her eyes, but they didn't fall, because part of her was expanding, and growing, and pushing towards the light. The light that was Tom. Staring at him in wonder, she finally fell into his arms, her body relaxing against his as she released the breath she'd been holding all this time, and allowed herself to feel the love he had for her.

*He loved her. He saw her.*

A swell of joy washed over her, and hope, and her elation at seeing her mother and knowing she was at peace combined with the safety and love she felt in her boyfriend's patient arms. She felt transformed. Reborn. A butterfly feeling its wings for the first time.

They stayed like that for what seemed like forever, Rhiannon curled up in his arms, Tom gently stroking her hair, until they heard footsteps on the stairs. Her dad called out that he was dropping by the healing centre to check on preparations, and would meet her at Rose's place in twenty minutes.

Rhiannon leapt up, panicked. "I'm almost ready Dad," she yelled back, grabbing her dress off the hanger. "I'll catch you up."

They heard the front door open and close, and Tom stood up and pulled her into one last embrace. "I'd better get back to Pop's  and make sure he's ready too," he said wistfully. Kissing her on the forehead, he grudgingly released her and headed for the door.

Then stopped and turned back to her. "I love you Rhiannon."

Her heart broke open. A lump caught in her throat, and tears welled in her eyes. "I love you too," she murmured, and was relieved when he came back and wrapped her in his arms again. They sank back onto her bed, and for countless precious moments they lay there, holding each other close. Finally Tom rolled over so he was braced above her, and gazed down into her eyes. And just gazed at her. Soft. Gentle. Protective. Loving. No pressure. No kissing. No pushing her to do anything she wasn't ready to do.

She smiled. "Thank you." It was inadequate for all the emotions she was feeling – the deep gratitude, the love, the relief. But it was all she had. Well, except for... "I love you so much Tom."

His face lit up with a radiant smile. "I love you too Rhiannon. And I will see you very soon."

Reluctantly she ushered him out, then had the quickest shower ever, before pulling her forest green dress over her head, fastening the rose quartz heart necklace Tom had given her at Ostara around her neck, and brushing her hair until it shone.

Catching her reflection in the mirror, she grinned. She was glowing. Beltane had definitely woven its magic over all of them this year. Rose and Richard were speaking vows of commitment at their handfasting ritual, Carlie had finally decided to open her heart to someone new after the terrible losses she'd suffered, and Tom had told her that he loved her.

Spinning around in the middle of her room, the layers of her dress flying around her, she felt happiness bubble up inside her.

"Thank you Mum," she whispered, eyes on the clear blue sky and sparkling sunshine outside. "I love you so much. Be free now."

## Chapter 39

# The Ties That Bind

### Rhiannon

A golden haze swirled around Rhiannon as she rushed over to Rose's cottage, but whether it was the beautiful day or her own whirling mind that caused it, she didn't know. The sun was warming her face, birds were singing a sweet symphony in time with her hurried footsteps, the heavy scent of jasmine clung to her skin, and the light-headedness she usually only felt in the ritual circle was making her laugh, then cry.

She'd spoken to her mother, words of comfort and love and hope. Had felt the ghost of a kiss on her forehead, easing her loneliness and despair. Had promised to play matchmaker for her father. She cringed at this last bit, and pushed it aside. Already the wisps of her encounter with her mum were fading, like the remnants of a surreal dream she couldn't quite hold on to. The more desperate she became to remember, the further it drifted away.

Stumbling on a crack in the pavement, Rhiannon slowed her pace and tried to exhale the sadness. Her mother was content – as content as you could be in that situation – and ready to move on. That had to be enough for her.

Her mum had also assured her of Tom's good intentions, and told her to trust him.

*And to tell him.*

She hadn't wanted to, hadn't thought that she could, but when he sat in her bedroom holding her hand and declared that he loved her, she'd screwed up her courage and reluctantly revealed her secret. If their relationship was going to grow and deepen, if she loved him as she claimed, she couldn't hide such a big part of herself. Hide this thing that affected how she acted, and maybe even how she loved.

Her voice shook, her body trembled and her stomach clenched in fear, but she'd managed to croak out the words, then wait stoically for him to leave the room. Leave her.

But he didn't. He said again that he loved her. More than that, that he saw her.

Saw her pain, and soothed it.

Saw her blame, and reassigned it.

Saw her shame, and lifted it from her.

And now she was floating, weightless, as though she might leave the safety of the earth at any moment and drift off into the air. Peace from speaking with her mother cocooned her, relief at the outcome of her admission coursed through her veins, and love soaked deep into her heart and spilled out of her.

Love for Tom, and his love for her.

Love for her father and brother, for Carlie and Rose. For her life.

And finally for herself.

Flustered and out of breath, Rhiannon hurried up the path. Her dad was already standing at the front door, deep in conversation with Carlie.

"I'm so sorry I'm late, I came as soon as I could, and –"

Carlie smiled, distracted. "It's fine." Still listening to Mike, she handed Rhiannon one of the flower wreaths they'd woven the night before, which matched the more elaborate one they'd created for Rose. Entwined within the hawthorn blossoms and ivy were sprigs of jasmine and meadowsweet, and rose buds and violets – flowers of love, and flowers to represent Rose and her lost daughter Violet.

The wreaths were imbued with love, magic and blessings, and when Rhiannon settled hers on her head, she breathed in the gorgeous scent of the flowers and felt the weight of their spell, and was overwhelmed with the certainty of her feelings for Tom. Her friend caught her eye and beamed at her, as though she could sense the immensity of her emotions, and Rhiannon grinned back. Gratitude swelled within her, and she looked skyward, wanting to believe that her mum was there, hovering above them to bless the handfasting, and bless them all.

A tentative step in the hallway made Carlie spin around, and Rhiannon and Mike craned to see behind her. Rose appeared, smiling nervously yet radiating a happiness that smoothed out the lines on her face, erasing the visible signs of pain from all the tragedies she'd endured. As the priestess caught sight of her granddaughter, her demeanour softened, and relaxed, and Rhiannon could have sworn she saw a cloak of black raven feathers slide from her shoulders and dissolve at her feet.

"No longer must she be a warrior. She can rest now," a familiar voice croaked in Rhiannon's ear. She gazed around wildly, seeking the raven. She couldn't spot it though, and wondered if she'd just imagined it. Or was it part of her now? Was it possible to become one with an animal spirit guide? To be gifted its wisdom?

Rose caught her eye and nodded imperceptibly, then turned back to Carlie, thanking her granddaughter for coming into her life, for healing her heart and pushing her to finally accept love.

When her dad wiped a tear from his eye, Rhiannon was surprised, yet Rose had been like a mother to him all these years. He leaned forward and placed a gentle hand on Carlie's back. "I want to thank you too," he said, voice thick with emotion. "For helping Rhiannon to heal, and for bringing me peace. You're very much loved and appreciated here."

"Don't make me cry," Carlie warned, but she was smiling with love and pride. Rhiannon was also finding it hard to keep a lid on her wildly swinging emotions, and she sent a prayer of thanks to the heavens, for the blessings of all she did have. Was it her mother she implored, or the goddess? Or were they the same thing now?

"We really should get our act together and go," Carlie announced, excitement in her tone and body language. "We have a ritual to create, and love and magic to weave."

Her elation was catching, enveloping everyone in joy, and whispering through Rhiannon as she lifted the hem of Rose's pale gold faery-like dress. Her dad took Rose's arm, Carlie picked up the bouquets, and the four of them set off. When they reached the meadow at the base of the tor, a hum of voices and a profusion of colour greeted them, and she was thrilled to see how many people had gathered to celebrate with Rose.

The priestess's friend Elsie stood in the centre of everything in a flowing purple dress, with flowers in her hair, a wand in her hand, and a broom leaning casually against the altar she stood behind. And Laura was marshalling everyone into a circle formation around Elsie, with Brodie at her side.

Transfixed, Rhiannon stared at them, noticing the joy on her brother's face as he proudly tried to help Laura, and the kindness their mother's friend displayed as she shared what she was doing and made him feel involved.

Was it Laura who would bring happiness to her dad? Help to heal his heart, and hold his family safe? Rhiannon hadn't been sure how she really felt about the possibility, but seeing Laura with Brodie was a revelation. She'd worried that it might be awkward because Laura was her teacher, but her final year of school was nearly over, so that wouldn't be an issue for much longer. And she realised now how much better she would feel knowing there was someone who cared about her dad and her brother when she went off to college.

Sighing, Rhiannon shook the contemplation off. She'd have to sort out her future soon – decide with Carlie whether they'd do the long commute from Summer Hill every day, or rent an apartment close to campus. Would the time they saved doing the latter be eaten up by the guilt of abandoning their families? She knew her friend was concerned about leaving her grandmother too...

But she could worry about that later. Today was Beltane, a celebration of love, awakening and new beginnings. Of Rose's blossoming relationship with Richard. The awakening and unfurling and revealing of Carlie's feelings for Jake.

The healing of her own heart so she could open it to Tom, and the igniting of a love for him that was transforming her.

And the blue-skied, sunshiny day couldn't have been more perfect. A gentle breeze wafted the sweet fragrance of the flowers on the altar around the meadow, the flames of deep red and forest green candles in glass jars danced merrily, and someone was softly strumming a guitar and singing of love and friendship.

And in the middle of the circle, next to Elsie, stood Richard, a white rose bud in the buttonhole of his green shirt, the midday sun haloing him in shimmering golden light. The look on his face when he caught sight of Rose walking towards him brought tears to Rhiannon's eyes. Love, respect, compassion, kindness – and a touch of awe that the glorious priestess approaching him saw something in him he hadn't known was there. Rose had that effect on everyone. The power to see within and beneath, to bring out and nurture all that was good in a person.

Rhiannon still couldn't believe the priestess had thought herself unworthy of love, yet it made a sad kind of sense. Everyone had been bruised by something – a tragedy, a loss, a trauma, an injustice – and each of them was scarred by their experiences. No one could avoid the suffering of life, or escape being damaged in some way, but you could choose whether or not to be defined by it. You could view your scars as an excuse to hide away or lash out in anger and inflict hurt on someone else, or you could see them as a sign that you had endured. A dark counterpoint to make you appreciate the light even more. A badge of honour that declared you were healing, and able to open your heart to the world even wider than before.

Was she ready to open herself to life, and to love? Prepared to be vulnerable again, and risk being hurt, so she could experience all the beauty and depth of the heart-filled connection she'd been offered? It had taken Rose twenty years to let someone new in, and Rhiannon was determined not to make the same mistake.

And maybe it didn't even matter if you were ready. Maybe you never would be. Maybe you just had to jump in regardless. Close your eyes and take that leap of faith, and see what happened. If it all ended in tears with Tom, she knew now that she would get through it. She would be devastated, of course, but she had survived, and eventually thrived, through worse.

Whispers floated around her, darting like butterflies. Was it her mum speaking to her? Or the raven? Was it the mysterious woman in gold who'd been mentioned twice today? The same one she'd glimpsed during a new moon ritual, then later in London, at Tom's sabbat?

Or was it her own heart, finally beginning to comprehend the truth?

*Everyone is broken in some way, and we can choose to crumble and fall apart, or work towards healing and fall together.*

*We're stronger in the places we've been broken.*

*Everything is cracked, but that's how the light gets in. Everyone is broken, and that's how our light shines out.*

*There is nothing more powerful than a broken soul who has transcended their pain and is ready to risk again. To rise strong, and fight their way back up from the ground where they fell.*

A glimpse of this had been reaching for her through Tom's words of love and reassurance, and the acceptance and compassion in his eyes. But now she *felt* the truth of it vibrating through her body. Humming through her veins. Soaking deep into her bones. She had been broken, yes. She was damaged, and vulnerable. She was also strong, and powerful. She was everything, all at once. Her pain had ripped her apart, but she was putting herself back together with threads of gold. Wiser, brighter, more caring and more ready to risk than before.

Stronger in the places she was broken.

Capable of loving harder, falling deeper, and soaring higher.

Transforming in front of her own eyes.

"Welcome," Laura cried, and Rhiannon was jolted back to the present. She watched her teacher introduce Elsie as the priestess for the ritual, then step back into the circle, Brodie's small hand in hers. Mike and Carlie were still with Rose, walking her to the altar to meet Richard.

Smiling, Rhiannon's gaze slid to Tom, hovering protectively at his grandfather's side. When he looked up and right at her, she forgot everything else. The whole world receded and she was drowning in his eyes, in the depths she was discovering of him, and the magic he so sweetly wrapped her in. His piercing stare sent a thrill of desire shooting through her, and her heart raced. He was so gorgeous, so wise yet wild, and so kind and compassionate too.

The day they'd first met, when she'd been so entranced by his bad boy facade, tattoos and air of danger, she could never have imagined that he would be the one to hold her safe as she cried. To enfold her in love and understanding while she came to terms with her pain. To tear apart the shroud of shame she'd buried herself in, then take her hand and lead her out of it and into the light.

While Elsie greeted Rose and Richard, Tom's eyes never left Rhiannon's face, and the electricity between them dazzled her, shattering all her defences and thawing her frozen heart. It was hard to believe that this amazing man loved her, yet she could still feel the comforting warmth of his hand on her cheek as he'd insisted that he did. The strength of his arms around her, so protective, as he shielded her from the world. The gentle touch of his lips as he'd promised patience and understanding until she was ready.

She was overwhelmed by all the parts of himself he'd revealed, and the vulnerability he'd offered her when he declared his love. She hoped she was worthy of it.

A kaleidoscope of butterflies darted past, circling Rhiannon's head and dancing close enough that she could feel the beat of their wings on her face. Holding out a hand in wonder, she giggled as one paused, settling on her palm and tickling her with its tiny feet. Enchanted by its beauty, it took her a moment to realise it was speaking to her.

"You are worthy just as you are Rhiannon, and it's time for you to awaken to the beauty and lightness of life. You are a healer, a rock for your family, but you must also make time to be playful. To laugh and love, and allow the joy of this to bubble up within you."

Rhiannon stared in wonder. "Mum always loved butterflies."

"Yes, and we are with her now," came the tiny voice, then its owner flew after its friends, swooping around Rose's head as she stood at the altar. One alighted on her forehead to kiss her brow in blessing, eliciting a smile from the priestess, then they all glided off up the slope of the tor in the sunshine.

As though it was a sign, noise rushed back at Rhiannon, and she became aware of her surroundings once more. Rose had reached the middle of the circle, flanked by Carlie on her left and Mike on her right, and the three of them bowed their heads in greeting as they faced Richard and his grandsons. Then the four attendants released Rose and Richard into Elsie's care, and melted back into the circle. Mike headed over to where Brodie stood with Laura, and took his son's other hand. Rhiannon saw peace on his face, and the lifting of a weight he'd carried for far too long. And was there a glimmer in his eye as he looked at Laura, a new emotion and openness? She hoped so. She'd grudgingly promised her mum she'd help her dad, but she hoped he would figure it out himself and she could stay out of it.

Turning back to the altar, she watched as Carlie took Jake's hand and led him to a spot in the circle where they could clearly see both of their grandparents. Jake looked bewildered at first, confused by Carlie's new affection, but his expression turned to joy when she leaned in and whispered something to him.

Rhiannon grinned – then forgot all about them and their budding romance when Tom walked towards her. He laced his fingers through hers, then lifted them to his lips and kissed her hand, the sweet and gentle romance of it all making her swoon. Standing in the circle with him by her side made her feel strong and powerful, and deeply connected to the magic of the occasion.

"It's all you," he whispered. "The strength and power is yours."

She shrugged. "Can't it be ours?"

"Of course. It *is* ours. Just don't forget your own part."

"Deal," she said softly. "And thank you for this morning."

"It was my pleasure. I love you sweet Rhiannon."

Smiling radiantly, she focused on Elsie again. For a moment she had the strangest feeling that the woman conducting the ritual was... not quite human. There was an Otherworldly quality to her voice as she spoke, a fae-like shimmer to her long purple dress. Curiously she peered at the four women positioned at the directional points, dressed in the colour of their element.

Was that red-robed Aideen to her left, the woman of fire, and the south? The one who had challenged her in the woods that night, and forced her towards healing? Could she discern Brianna, the stern woman in green she'd met by the lake in Scotland, standing to her right, representing the element of earth, and the north? And was it blue-clad Brauna across from her in the circle, standing in the west and ready to welcome in the power and beauty of water?

Nervously she turned to the woman in the gold dress on the other side of Tom, who was clasping his hand but focusing intently on Elsie. Was she the woman in gold who had helped her mum appear to her this morning? Who'd given Carlie a gift for Rose, and promised her love with Jake?

But that was crazy. Her mind was playing tricks on her. She remembered Carlie telling her that Elsie was bringing four women from her own coven to help facilitate the ritual, so Rose's circle could relax and take part. Rolling her eyes at her over-active imagination, she determined to enjoy what was right in front of her.

And the handfasting was beautiful, the magical words flowing over Rhiannon, and the entire circle, leaving her with a sensation of love and bright potential. There was a golden shimmer around Rose and Richard when Elsie bound their hands together, symbolising their commitment to each other, and the whole circle laughed in delight as they jumped the beautifully decorated broom while bound to each other, signifying the sweeping away of the old and the making of a new beginning, on their terms.

Rose had confessed that she and Richard had no idea what they would do next, or where they would live, and they weren't in any hurry. Today was mostly about welcoming Richard into her life and her ritual circle, and acknowledging their mutual respect and growing bond. It touched Rhiannon deeply to be part of it, to see the priestess letting down her defensive walls after so long, and Richard opening up to magic, to the love of his grandsons, and to the most incredible woman everyone there had ever known.

She could feel it reflected in her own lowering of her guard, her own opening to love and peace and an enchanted future.

## Chapter 40

# Bitter Sweet Heart

### Beth

When Beth's eyes snapped open, she was momentarily blinded by the warmth of the sun and the golden light surrounding Rose. The priestess was heading towards the lower slope of the tor, arm in arm with Mike, while Rhiannon and Carlie followed in their footsteps, clutching sweetly scented bouquets and the hem of Rose's beautiful gold gown.

Beth gasped at the same time as her daughter when they heard the hum of conversation and caught sight of the large, colourful group gathered in the meadow, each person draped in vibrantly hued clothes, with bare feet, sparkling crystal jewellery and fresh flowers in their hair.

A cheer rang out when they saw Rose approaching, and Beth felt a thrill of joy. The priestess had guided and protected her all of her adult life. Had loved her, challenged her, mentored her. To see her so happy meant the world to Beth, and she was suddenly grateful that she hadn't been swallowed back into the void after seeing her daughter. Being here now made her feel complete, like she'd come full circle to witness this rite, the first she'd been part of where Rose wasn't the priestess.

Floating ahead of Rose and her attendants, Beth smiled sadly. Laura was encouraging everyone into a circle formation, Brodie at her side, wide-eyed and eager to help. This would have been her job, if she was still alive, and the dejection and regret threatened to split her apart. Sensing her daughter behind her, Beth spun around and headed back to the comfort of her instead.

The roughly formed circle parted to allow Rose in, and she walked forward to the central altar with Carlie and Mike on either side of her. Rhiannon didn't follow them inside the boundary, instead clasping the hands of the people on either side of the opening and closing the sacred circle. Allowing the magic to activate. Beth stayed with her, disappointed that Rhiannon didn't sense her this time, but her intrigue with proceedings outweighed her devastation.

Ghost mother and vibrant daughter stood together and watched as Rose and her escorts approached Richard, who was standing arm in arm with his grandsons at the flowery altar. After a few words with the purple-clad priestess facilitating the ceremony, Carlie took Jake's hand and led him into the circle, and Tom clasped his grandfather's shoulder then made a beeline to Rhiannon, taking her hand, bringing it to his lips, then whispering something in her ear that made her light up like a dawn sky.

But Beth was fixated on her husband. She smiled as Mike kissed Rose on the cheek, then made his way over to Brodie and Laura. Swooping across the circle to them, she hovered as Mike took Brodie's other hand. A sigh of deep longing rippled through her, but when she saw Laura smile warmly at Mike, and her husband grin back then lean forward to straighten her flower crown, Beth let go of her tension and relaxed. Her family would be in good hands if Mike ended up with Laura, and it salved her conscience at abandoning Rhiannon and Brodie to know they'd have someone who already cared about them in their life. It also made her happy that two of her favourite people in the world had a shot at love.

A gold flash out of the corner of her vision made Beth whip around. Liana was standing beside her.

"Beloved, how are you feeling?"

Beth blinked a few times, trying to formulate the words. "I'm okay I guess. Or at peace with things, is that how I should be speaking? I'm so relieved I was able to speak with Rhiannon –

thank you for assisting me, if that was you. I hate leaving her, but I know now that she will be okay. She's found someone who values her, but most of all she values herself, and that helps."

She smiled, trying to be brave, to ignore the pain and convince herself she would be able to survive never seeing her family again. "And I got to see Brodie with his teacher, and watch him in the classroom and with his friends, so I'm confident he'll be fine too. He's resilient, and he's surrounded by people who love him, so how can I complain about that?"

Liana bowed her head in acknowledgement.

"And then there's the guilt I hadn't anticipated, that I'd carried with me all my life. Discovering that Violet found happiness despite me turning her life upside down, that she didn't hold anything against me, and I hadn't destroyed her... I can't even begin to describe my relief over that. And I love that my daughter and Violet's are best friends. That they understand and accept each other, and inspire the other to be even more, to reach their full potential. She didn't have that with her old friends."

Eyes welling, Beth gazed at her husband, her chest aching with loss, with the anguish of a future that would never be, and a bitter-sweet heart broken yet grateful for this closure. "And I think my beloved is finally ready to move on, which fills me with sadness and joy in equal measure."

Liana rested her hand on Beth's shoulder, and soothing warmth flowed into her. "It will take them some time to find each other, but Laura will be a wonderful support for your family whether or not it turns romantic with Mike. He will be all right, I promise you."

Beth tried to smile bravely through her tears. Tried to focus on the comfort this knowledge gave her, rather than the dagger of pain at having to let go.

"There is one more thing," the woman in gold said. "Come, Ailia has an offering for you."

Mind racing, Beth stared at her in confusion. Who was Ailia? And what could she possibly give her?

Liana took her hand and led her into the middle of the circle, right in front of Rose. Beth panicked, terrified they would ruin the ceremony, but the purple-clad woman conducting it winked at her.

"Beth, this is Ailia," Liana said. "Ailia, Beth."

"Hello Beth," the woman in purple said with the faintest smile. "There is no need to worry about disrupting things." She tilted her head to indicate the people surrounding them, and Beth gazed around in wonder. Everyone in the circle was frozen in place. Everyone but her, Liana and Ailia.

"We are outside of time for a moment Beth, do not fear. We are granting you the space to complete the last of your unfinished business before –"

Liana cut the woman in purple off with a fierce glare, and Ailia shrugged her elegant shoulders, but stopped talking.

"I have finished," Beth protested, then bit her tongue. Should she admit that? Yet it was clear her time was coming to an end, so there was no reason to withhold the truth. "Brodie is growing up well, surrounded by friends, family, and a fantastic teacher. Rhiannon is starting to heal, held safe by her dad, her best friend, and a boyfriend who loves her, and my dear husband finally seems to be open to the possibility of loving again. I've even found peace over Violet, thanks to her generous daughter."

"Are you done?" Ailia asked, eyebrows raised. "May I continue?"

Embarrassed, Beth nodded, and apologised, then watched in awe as the purple-clad being waved her hand subtly in the air, and in response, Rose turned towards her.

"Dear Beth!" The priestess held out her arms to her, and Beth fell into them, not understanding how Rose could be seeing her, or how she had become physical body enough for the priestess to hug her, or how time had stopped to grant her this blessing. But it didn't matter. There was so much she wanted to say to Rose. Too much to put into words, and so she found herself sobbing instead, and soaking up every precious moment of reassurance from the woman who had been a mother to her.

With great effort, she pulled herself together. "Thank you for caring for Rhiannon when I failed her.

For caring for Mike when I deserted him. For caring for me when I didn't deserve it," she blurted. "Oh Rose, you were everything to me, and I never even told you."

"Darling Beth, there was never any need for words. You showed me your love every day through your actions, through your kindness and generosity, and your friendship. You were everything to me too, a dear friend, a coven sister, the daughter I'd lost."

A stab of pain like an electric shock raced through Beth, and she drew back in alarm. "But it's my fault you lost your daughter."

The priestess regarded her with serious eyes. "It was never your fault darling girl. You should have no regrets about Violet. She made her own choices, and created her own life. And she found the person she was meant to be with in the end, and had a wonderful marriage, and a wonderful daughter, so we can't be sad for her."

"But even if she ended up okay, you didn't," Beth retorted, tears streaming down her face. "I robbed you of a life with your daughter, a life as a mother."

Drawing her back into her arms, Rose held the distraught ghost-woman tight, and Liana edged closer, placing a comforting hand on Beth's shoulder. The warmth soothed her, like a spell, and she eventually managed to get her weeping under control again.

Ailia cleared her throat, and Beth stared at Rose in panic, knowing her time with the priestess was drawing to a close. "I'm just so sorry, for everything. I hope you can find it in your heart to forgive me."

A radiant smile transformed Rose's face, and she took Beth's hand in hers. "Darling girl, there is no need to apologise, and no need to seek forgiveness. You and Mike were perfect for each other – just look at the children you created together – and you welcomed me into your family when I lost mine. I will never be able to repay that honour. You gave me a gift when everything was torn away from me, and I owe you everything for that. So please, wherever it is that you go now, know that I feel only love and gratitude for you, and always have. And I will care for your family for you Beth. They will never forget you, I swear."

The purple-robed woman gazed at them sternly. "Liana, you need to help Carlie. And we need to proceed with the ritual."

"Yes, of course." The woman in gold turned to Beth. "Come, you can watch with your daughter." Together they glided across the circle to where Rhiannon stood, hand in hand with Tom, and Liana smiled at Beth and left her there.

The handfasting was magical, and Beth savoured every minute of it, overjoyed for Rose and the new love blossoming in her life, and overwhelmed by the beauty and truth of Tom's feelings for her daughter. And it didn't hurt that he was related to kind and steady Richard and Jake, or that Rose thought so highly of him.

It was a thrill to be with her coven sisters again too, even if it was only in spirit on her part. She wished she could hug each and every one of them, and thank them for embracing Rhiannon and welcoming her into their magical circle. Fervently she hoped that her daughter would grow up with the compassion of Laura, the kindness of Glenda, the wit and fierce intelligence of Miri, the empathy of Belinda, and the joy in life of Paulette.

Then before she knew it the handfasting was complete, the rest of the ritual had been conducted, and people started to drift away to the healing centre for the celebration. With a full but heavy heart, Beth watched Rhiannon and Tom walk down the hill, then pause on the side of the road to kiss, becoming so lost in each other they didn't notice there were no more cars coming.

Relieved by their joy and trust in each other, Beth turned to look for Mike – and was shocked to find herself face to face with Liana. Feeling complete didn't mean she was ready to leave the world.

"Beloved, I sincerely hope that it helped you to be here today."

Panic and fear enveloped Beth. If she said no, would she be able to stay longer?

One look at Liana's face told her there was no wiggle room. And she *was* beyond grateful that she'd been able to remain for this long. But now she was scared of what lay ahead. Where would she go? Would it hurt? Would she still be conscious, still be herself?

She steadied her expression. "I suppose I have to be ready, right? We all have our time, and mine is up. It just hurts to know I'll never see my family again. Never be able to talk to Rhiannon."

Liana smiled. "Sweet Beth, that is not strictly true. You may see her again."

"*What?*" Her heart thudded. A shiver ran up her spine. Hope ignited and burned through her veins. "I can stay?"

A flutter of blue butterflies flitted around her head, swirling so fast they dazzled her. As she tried to maintain her balance, she heard their voice again, as she had that long-ago day atop the tor, and almost fell over. "You have been transformed. You are a light in the world, a light to others, and we can see the inner beauty that illuminates you."

What did *that* mean to a ghost?

Liana held out a steadying hand. "I allowed you to see me this morning, talking to Carlie, so you would know our purpose. See how we help those who seek the magic and healing of the earth, the sacred wisdom of nature."

Mind whirling, Beth tried to make sense of her words, but she couldn't. Who was *we*? Who were *those*?

"And Aideen told me you saw her in the woods with Rhiannon one night, which shocked her as much as it shocked you..."

"The woman at the fire. She was... like you?" Beth shuddered as she remembered how scared she'd been, and how indignant, to come across a stranger with her daughter. "She said she was a guide of sorts. Is that what you are?"

"Guides? I suppose you could say that." Liana paused, wondering. "Yes, we aid and guide. We offer advice and comfort. We help someone to see the truth of their situation. We challenge them to be better, to be more. Guardians perhaps."

Another memory surfaced. "And you bestow gifts." Beth's hand rose to her throat, feeling the soothing warmth of the rose quartz pendant Liana had given her when she was a twenty-year-old girl full of pain and self-doubt.

"To remind you of your magic when you doubted yourself." The woman in gold smiled at her, expression tender. And was that pride in her eyes? *For what?*

"Dear Beth, how could you doubt that we would all be proud of you? We know how much you suffered as a child, we know what your previous relationship cost you, and we know how much you helped and healed others your entire life."

Could a ghost blush? Beth's cheeks, still wet from her tears, felt warm, and she was certainly touched by the praise. Yet she had no idea what Liana was talking about. What did any of this have to do with her, or with seeing her daughter again?

Instead of answering, Liana turned back to the altar, and Beth noticed a huddle of women surrounding Rose. Three of them broke away and glided towards her.

"Greetings beloved," said the woman in blue. "I am Brauna, the Lady of Water."

Beth gasped. "Yes, I remember! I met you in the park one night with Violet. She said you were the embodiment of what Rose calls in with the elements, the directions and the deities. That you're the spirit of nature, the manifestation of an aspect of the goddess."

Sorrow crossed Brauna's face. "Dear Violet. I am so sorry you lost her. But she was correct. We are a part of nature – the nature that you have held as sacred for so long."

Perplexed, Beth stared at the blue-clad figure, trying to take it all in. "Okay, so you're the Lady of Water. And Liana, I learned this morning, is the Lady of Air. Yes?"

Brauna nodded, then the woman in green extended her hand. She had long red hair that flowed down over her shoulders and was entwined with flowers, and her dress seemed to be made of the leaves and vines of the forest itself. "I am Brianna, although some call me the Lady of Earth. I have helped your daughter with her magical work, given her ritual tools, and challenged her worldview. She is wise and good. You should be very proud of her."

Beth paled, not sure she could handle these strangers telling her about her own daughter. "I know she is, and I am." Her voice came out snappier and less gracious than she'd hoped, but the panic and apprehension was wearing her down. Nothing made sense. Had she fallen down a rabbit hole to some other land, or dimension?

Before her anger overflowed, the woman in red stepped forward and bowed her head in greeting. Despite her long black hair, white skin and severe, blood-red lips, she was far less intimidating today.

Or maybe Beth was less afraid now than she'd been in the woods that night as she watched this... woman... eyeing her daughter over the leaping, all-consuming flames.

The mouth she'd thought cruel back then turned up in a smile. "I apologise for startling you that evening Beth. I had never before been seen by someone I was not appearing to, and it rattled me. But I am Aideen, Lady of Fire, and I am honoured to make your acquaintance under more joyful circumstances."

Laughter burst from Beth, she couldn't help it. "More joyful? I am glad for Rose, don't get me wrong, but in case any of you have forgotten, I'm dead, and Liana has implied that it's time for me to... disappear... So forgive me if I'm not in a celebratory mood."

In an instant the woman in purple was at her side, somehow breaching the distance from the altar in the blink of an eye, and Beth glowered at her warily. Was she the one who would... dispense with her? Was she the leader of this strange, Otherworldly band of mist-wreathed women, and the one to send her into oblivion?

"You give me too much credit," Ailia said, a gentle smile softening her unyielding features. "I am the woman of spirit, the Lady of Light, but I am here for Rose, to help her finally walk out of the darkness and into the light."

"So why am I here?" Beth growled. She wanted to scream. She wanted to flee. What did these strange women want with her? *Why was she still here?*

Liana stepped forward again, full of apologies. "I am so sorry Beth, please forgive me. I have never done this before, and my initiation was so long ago that I do not remember the details."

"Done what?" This time Beth's challenge was just a whisper, because fear was pumping through her veins, constricting her voice, strangling her of speech and thought. *What initiation?*

The gold-clad woman took her hand, her eyes kind, her manner soothing. Beth felt some of her knots of tension unbind.

"It is I who is going Beth, not you. I have been doing this since long before Rose was born, and it is time for me to dissolve into the air. I need you to take my place. That is why I have been following you. I never meant to scare you, but I had to be sure that you would be capable of helping people heal, guiding them through their tragedies and trials, encouraging them to follow their hearts, inspiring them to protect the earth, and reassuring them that they hold magic within them."

Hysterical laughter swooped around the meadow, until Beth realised it was coming from her, and forced her mouth shut. She felt delirious, unhinged. Perhaps she had already crossed over, and hell was this quagmire of absurdity. "I'm sorry to disappoint you Liana, but I am the very worst candidate for your position, whatever it is. Every single person at the ritual today would be more suitable, would do a better job. You really can't be serious."

*And yet.*

Abruptly she stopped talking and stood silent, a flower of hope blooming in her chest. Rhiannon had met some of these women, and so had Carlie. "So wait, if I accept this job, I'll be able to see my daughter again, talk with her every day, help her with her problems, see how she's going? Watch her grow up."

It was dangerous, this hope, but excitement was flooding Beth now, clouding her mind and drowning all her doubts, and joy was bubbling up within her and threatening to spill out. Sensing movement, she looked down. Her pale pink dress had turned the same golden colour as Liana's and was swirling around her calves, and she felt the comforting protection of her butterflies again as they started to spin around her.

Ailia looked stern again, and shook her head, but Liana smiled at her. "You will help many people Beth, the way Aideen and Brauna helped Rhiannon. You may see your daughter occasionally – if she has need of you – but we women of the mists have a far greater purpose, far removed from our former lives and our former ties. Now come, we have much to teach you."

Overwhelmed with confusion, disbelief and a wild, yearning hope, Beth glanced over to where Rhiannon and her boyfriend still stood on the side of the road, completely lost in each other. Perhaps feeling her eyes on him, Tom drew back and looked up.

Shock crossed his face as their gazes locked, but he quickly masked it, and smiled at her, then lifted a hand and waved. Rhiannon peered in her direction, curious to see what had caught her boyfriend's attention, but clearly couldn't discern anything. She shrugged, kissed Tom again, then took his hand and led him towards the village.

A single hot tear fell from Beth's lashes, landing on the grass and shimmering in the sunlight, but already she felt removed from reality, disconnected from her personal feelings and swamped with a love and affection for all of life and humanity. It was... strange. Uncomfortable. Unfamiliar.

Before she could descend into panic, movement at the altar caught Beth's eye, and she felt herself drawn along in the wake of the five colourful, mist-wreathed women. Rose stood there, alone, Richard a little way off with Mike and Laura, who were still holding Brodie's hands between them.

The priestess lifted her head as they approached, and summoned a smile. She looked so tranquil, so accepting, and Beth was awed by her demeanour on such a huge day. Until she realised that Rose thought they were coming to take her away. She was preparing herself mentally for her own death. Beth almost cried out to her, but Aideen placed a hand on her shoulder and bid her be quiet.

"Greetings, not-Elsie," Rose said calmly.

The purple-clad woman bowed her head in acknowledgement. "Greetings beloved Rose, I am Ailia. And please, worry not. I am not here to take you. That would be the cruellest blow, would it not? To have endured so much, and then to finally find love and happiness, yet lose it all in the next moment."

"I'm not worried for me, I'm concerned about Elsie. Is she okay?"

Beth smiled. Of course the priestess would be more concerned about someone else.

"Elsie is fine. Well, she was a little unwell, but there is no need to panic. I am here instead because it is time for you to walk out of the darkness and into the light. You have more than earned your happiness dear one. And we all want to thank you, for being such a light in the world."

The priestess nodded, then turned her curious gaze on Liana. "Thank you for the gift this morning, and for your wisdom all those years ago, when I wasn't sure I wanted to marry."

Beth gasped in horror, but Rose smiled at her and squeezed her hand. "Sweet Beth, it was nothing like that – it was all wrapped up in my cruel mother and our monstrous relationship, nothing to do with poor Louis."

The priestess turned back to Ailia. "You will look after Beth?"

"Of course we will. She will be safe with us. It is Liana who is saying goodbye."

Wonder swamped Beth as she watched Liana enfold Rose in her arms and kiss her forehead, then step back. Rose bowed her head, whispered farewell, then joined Richard, who put his arm around her and guided her off to their celebration.

A cloud of blue butterflies appeared, as if by magic, and surrounded Liana's glowing golden form. "Thank you Beth," she called out, a radiant smile on her face as she appeared to meld with the delicate winged creatures and melt into them. She rose into the air, encircled by butterflies, then floated across the meadow until she faded from sight.

A sharp stab of agony and regret pierced Beth's heart, then receded, and she was enveloped in warmth and comfort again. A spell no doubt, but she couldn't bring herself to be upset about it.

Slowly a delicate, swirling mist materialised in front of them, solidifying like something alive. It sent out soft fingers to stroke Beth's arms, and soothe her red cheeks, and all the pain and fear she had been holding in her body drained away from her. Her long golden dress swished around her ankles, and she felt herself softening and growing stronger at the same time. Awe filled her when she looked down and saw her skin glowing gold in the sunshine, and her hair lengthening and shining like a beacon.

Aideen beckoned to her. "Come Beth, we have work to do."

Nodding joyfully, she followed her new friends into the mists.

Chapter 41

Rhiannon

Dazed with love, and the joy of the handfasting, Rhiannon clutched Tom's hand as they finally stopped kissing and made their way to the village. They caught up with Carlie and Jake outside the healing centre, and Rhiannon linked her arm through her friend's as they climbed the stairs to the ritual room.

"I'm so happy for you," she said, voice low. "And so is Tom."

Carlie blushed, but didn't shush her. There was too much happiness in the air, too much love, to doubt anyone or anything.

The room was beautiful, transformed by flowers and candles and twinkling faery lights, and full of all the friends who had helped Rhiannon and her family through their loss. A community that supported each other, and was overjoyed to be there to honour Rose and give thanks for all she had done for them over the years.

For the first half hour, Rose and Richard were swamped by well wishers, all wanting to congratulate the happy couple and welcome Richard to their lives and their hearts. Then there were speeches, some funny, some moving everyone to tears, before Laura brought out the ritual cauldron and lit the apple wood within it, and Rose and Richard leaped over the Beltane fire hand in hand, to wild cheers.

"I haven't seen Pop this happy in for ages," Tom whispered to Rhiannon. "And I haven't been this joy-filled for a long time either."

She beamed at him. "Same!"

"So, shall we jump the Beltane fire too?" he asked, eyes alight with mischief.

Grinning, Rhiannon nodded. Then swayed as dizziness overcame her. Her skin prickled with heat as she remembered the look of horror and condescension on John's face when she'd asked if he would leap the fires with her. Then she felt gratitude, because if he'd agreed to do it, she would have stayed with him, and never met Tom.

Pushing the memory away, she smiled as another vision closed in around her. This was the one she'd seen on the glittering surface of the lake in Broceliande forest, of her and Tom soaring over the Beltane fire together, publicly sealing their love and commitment to each other. They were even wearing the same clothes from the vision today, which she hadn't registered until now.

Tom's arms had wound around her the moment she began to sway, and she soaked up the sensation of safety and security she felt within his embrace, the strength of his body and his heart as he held her close. Protecting her, healing her, yet walking beside her rather than ahead, wanting her to blossom and bloom on her own terms, to call on her own strength, and her own wisdom. He offered her love as well as freedom, and he celebrated her just the way she was. Finally the truth soaked into her bones. *She was enough.*

Her eyes shone as she looked up at him, and she saw the love she felt for him reflected back at her. "Yes!" she said, voice loud, clear and totally sure. "I'm ready to leap with you. And to fall for you."

Grinning, Tom kissed her, then they moved to where Glenda was directing those who wanted to jump.

There were loud cheers as, hand in hand, they cleared the flames, cheeks flushed and eyes sparkling. Rhiannon marvelled at how far she'd come from that night in the woods with the woman in red, when she'd been terrified of the fire, of the transformative power of its heat, and of what it would reveal of her.

Now she felt naked, stripped of barriers and defence, and of any need for them. She was strong, and free, and more totally herself than she'd ever been. She was seen, and she was loved, for her true self, not some masked version she thought people would like better.

Standing on the edge of the room, she held Tom's hand, and laughed as he raised his other one so that together, one hand each, they could clap on the other jumpers. When Carlie and Jake leaped the fire, she cheered even louder, then as the last couples jumped, and the flames and excitement died down, Miri and Laura began to serve the Beltane feast.

Rhiannon found herself seated next to Rose, with Tom on her other side, and the priestess's eyes twinkled. "Thank you sweet girl for all your help today, you have made me so happy."

"I didn't do anything," she insisted, blushing red at the praise.

"Oh Rhiannon, you did. You and Carlie gathered and wove together all the beautiful flowers, you cooked most of the food, but most importantly, your love and support of my growing feelings for Richard mean so much more to me than I can express."

Before she could reply, Richard approached with plates of food for him and Rose, and he thanked Rhiannon and Tom for their bravery in sharing the messages that had led them all here, to this moment. Rhiannon's eyes blurred with tears, but she was laughing too, caught up in the whirlwind of love and joy that this Beltane had brought for all of them.

Later she lost herself in the dancing, thrilled to be back in Tom's arms. She remembered their first night up on the tor, when she had seen the black ravens wheeling overhead, and imagined the white angel terns dancing with them across the sky, and hoped that one day she and Tom would dance together too. Now, the music and the twinkling faery lights overhead added to the magic and possibility that permeated the room, and her heart was full when she saw Carlie and Jake dancing, her head on his shoulder, his arms around her as though she was the most precious thing on earth.

She smiled as Richard spun Rose around in a circle then caught her again, his eyes filled with love, then she looked over Tom's shoulder for her dad. He was sitting with Brodie, deep in conversation, but stealing occasional glances at Laura, who was hovering close by, tidying the platters of food and checking candles.

"Just a second," she said to Tom, and moved towards them. Ruffling Brodie's hair on the way, she took the plates from Laura's hands and dragged her over to Mike, then pulled her dad to his feet and placed his hand in Laura's. "I'll hang out with Brodie for a while. You two should dance," she said firmly, and gave them a little push. Then she took a seat with her brother, smiling as Tom joined them, and the three chatted about the ritual, and the cauldron fire, then Brodie quizzed Tom about his motorbike.

Catching her dad's eye, Rhiannon smiled as he mouthed his thanks to her, then spun Laura around and caught her with a delicate hand on her waist.

"I'm looking forward to all of us going to the festival with Laura next weekend," Brodie said, and Rhiannon stared at him in surprise.

"Really?"

He shrugged. "She's a nice lady, and she really cares about Dad, and about us. And she needs us too."

Before Rhiannon could think of something to say, Miri came over and pulled up a chair. "You two lovebirds go dance. Brodie and I have plans to discuss."

"*What?*"

Brodie giggled. "Miri is going to help me work out how to build a skate park," he said. "Now go dance, you two."

Laughing in wonder, Rhiannon took Tom's hand when he offered it, and they made their way back into the swirling mass of people.

Later, as people started to drift home, Rhiannon offered to help clean up, but Miri shook her head. "Glenda, Belinda and I are on duty tonight, and we'll do the rest in the morning. The night is too beautiful to be inside, so go now, and a blessed Beltane to you both."

Her eyes twinkled, and Rhiannon hugged her, grateful again for the love of her mother's friends.

Soon Rhiannon and Tom found themselves outside on the pavement, the rich inky darkness swirling around them, the shadows more soothing than scary. She remembered how nervous she'd been when she contemplated this moment, back when they'd planned to go up to the tor for their own Beltane rites. But as Tom gently stroked her cheek, all the fear fell away.

"So, shall we climb the tor?" she asked.

"My love, I don't expect... I mean, we don't have to..."

Standing on tiptoes, she reached up and kissed him, love and passion making her heart race and desire throb through her.

"I know, and I'm very grateful to you for that. But where better to sit and watch the stars, and talk together all night, than up there, in our special place."

He grinned and slung an arm around her shoulders. "Let's go."

It was beautiful up on the summit, cool and silent, with not a soul to be seen. Sinking to the ground, they smiled at each other as the clouds cleared and the sky was dotted with stars. The air around them shimmered in the faint light.

"You look like you're about to float off into the air," Tom said, holding tightly to her hand in case she did.

Rhiannon smiled. "No, I'm not going anywhere. I'm exactly where I want to be, with the person I most want to be with."

Eyes shining with joy and illuminated by starlight, she pushed him back onto the grass, then leaned down to kiss him.

"Out of suffering have emerged the strongest souls.
The most massive characters are seared with scars."
*Kahlil Gibran, Lebanese-American poet and artist*

"Above all, be the heroine of your life, not the victim."
*Nora Ephron, American filmmaker*

# Thank You!

Thank you so much for reading this book, and
sharing the magic of Rhiannon and Beth's stories.
As an indie author, I rely on word of mouth and reader reviews
to get the word out. If you enjoyed *Into the Air*, I would be
so grateful if you could take a moment to leave a review on
any book site. Reviews help improve sales and ranking,
and are of immense help to all indie writers.
Even a single sentence will make a difference.

If you'd like to stay in touch and receive free exclusive content,
be the first to hear about book news, events info and giveaways,
win prizes and more, you can sign up for my newsletter at

## www.sereneconneeley.com/subscribe.

(And don't worry, you can unsubscribe at any time...)

With love and gratitude,
Serene xx

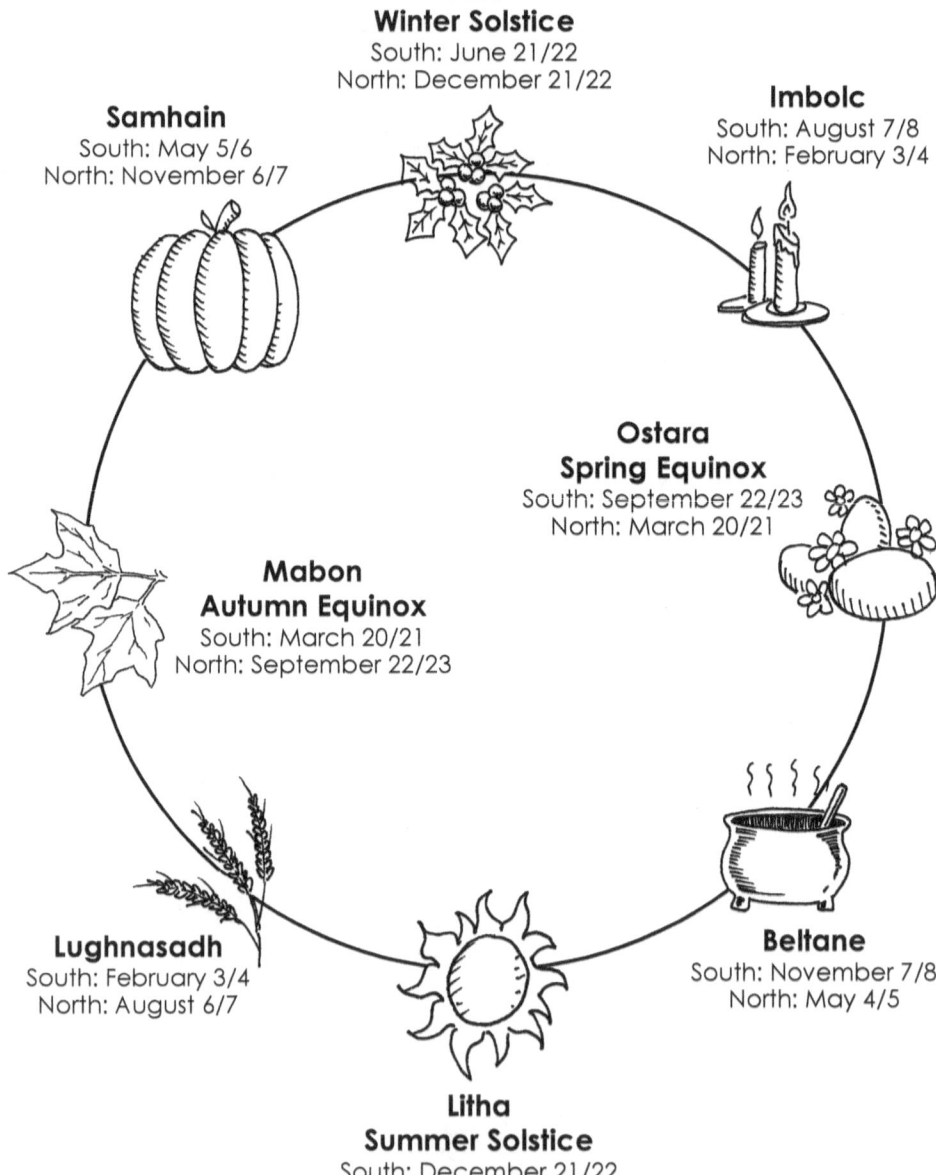

**Yule**
**Winter Solstice**
South: June 21/22
North: December 21/22

**Samhain**
South: May 5/6
North: November 6/7

**Imbolc**
South: August 7/8
North: February 3/4

**Ostara**
**Spring Equinox**
South: September 22/23
North: March 20/21

**Mabon**
**Autumn Equinox**
South: March 20/21
North: September 22/23

**Beltane**
South: November 7/8
North: May 4/5

**Lughnasadh**
South: February 3/4
North: August 6/7

**Litha**
**Summer Solstice**
South: December 21/22
North: June 20/21

# The Wheel of the Year

Rose and her witchy circle, including Beth and Violet in the past, and Rhiannon and Carlie today, celebrate the eight sacred sabbats, or festivals, of the Wheel of the Year, as ancient druids, priestesses and magical practitioners once did, and modern pagans around the world still do. In *Into the Air*, the story begins a few weeks after Imbolc, weaves its way to London for Ostara, and culminates at Beltane, the first day of summer, and the major fertility festival, where love, abundance and fertility are honoured.

A powerful way to become more aware of your inner world is to harness the natural magic of the cycles of the seasons. The shifting energies of the earth's turning have been celebrated and utilised for thousands of years, and even today, when most of us are so far removed from nature, you can still tangibly feel the introspection of winter, the crisp change of autumn, the potent energy of summer and the vibrant power of spring, and see the changing moods reflected in the colours of nature and the behaviour of plants and animals.

Attuning yourself to the vibrations of the eight sacred festivals that make up the enchanted Wheel of the Year will fill you with strength, magic and a sense of grand possibility and potential. You will become more in sync with your inner self and your intuition, and start to connect with your own emotional tides as you connect with the earth's.

These special days, determined by the position of the earth in relation to the sun, mark the beginning, midpoint and end of each season, and are measured today by astronomers and scientists. In the past they were calculated by druids, the philosophers and scientists of their age, and recorded in stone circles and cairns, or by shamans who created calendars in pyramidal structures. These events have been honoured for thousands of years in cultures throughout the world, so the imprint of their energy can be tapped in to and absorbed.

Long ago, when life revolved around agriculture, and the sun and the moon were considered deities to be worshipped, the Celtic peoples of Europe, and many others around the globe, were in tune with nature. They had to know when each season began and how long it would last so they could plant and harvest crops, hunt migratory prey and prepare for the harshness of their winters. They divided their year by seasons, not months, and honoured each change, celebrating eight festivals that marked the cycles of these seasons and the energies of the earth.

There are four astronomical and four agricultural festivals. The astronomical celebrations are determined by the position of the sun, and include the spring and autumn equinoxes (Latin for "equal night"), which occur when the sun is directly above the equator and the length of day and night is equal, and the summer and winter solstices (Latin for "sun stand still"), which occur when the sun is at its northern or southernmost extreme, the furthest it ever gets from the equator. These four events are the midpoint of each season – thus the summer solstice being referred to as Midsummer's Day and the winter solstice as Midwinter. The agricultural celebrations are known as cross-quarter days, because they fall midway between the astronomical festivals. Traditionally they were tied to agricultural events such as the sowing and harvesting of crops, and they mark the beginning of each season.

Even today, when most of us no longer live in harmony with the earth's rhythms or agricultural cycles, magical practitioners celebrate the Wheel of the Year as an honouring of nature and an acknowledgement of the continuing cycle of life, death and rebirth, both literally and symbolically. Literally this refers to the changing seasons – the planting and rebirth of spring, the fertility and vibrant life force of summer, the harvest energy of autumn, and the introspection and endings (death) of winter. Mythologically it was tied to the story of the god and the goddess. At the spring equinox they meet and court, before consummating their love during the rites of Beltane. At the summer solstice the goddess blooms into the mother, pregnant with new life, and the sun god reaches his energetic peak. He weakens through the harvest time of Lughnasadh and the autumn equinox, before journeying to the underworld at Samhain to learn new wisdom. Then he is reborn at the winter solstice, when the goddess gives birth to the infant sun god, and the Wheel turns again, playing out the cycle on and on through time.

Once this creation story was regarded as fact. Today some people still think of it as a literal retelling of a historical truth, while others feel it is simply a parable that humanises and anthropomorphises nature. Either way, it's now the symbolic meaning that's most relevant to our lives – planting the seeds of our dreams in the metaphorical spring, watching them grow and manifest in the world, then giving thanks for our literal harvest, and allowing the things that no longer serve us to die off or be released, before starting all over again with new dreams as we celebrate our own rebirth.

Becoming aware of the seasonal shifts and the patterns of nature wherever you live, and celebrating these ancient but still relevant festivals, is a simple way to tap in to the magic of the earth and start to connect with nature and your inner self. Channelling this energy and creating meaningful rituals in your life doesn't conflict with any religion or require a belief system, as it's a celebration of the science of nature and the cycles of the planet. Many pagans, like Rose and her friends, call on gods and goddesses, and have a personal concept of the divine as a universal creative force, but others don't believe in any form of deity, simply revering nature as sacred and as the source of life, and believing that divinity is an inner not an outer power, an energy within themselves and every other person alive.

Check the sabbat dates in your time zone at
www.archaeoastronomy.com
Check sunrise, moonrise, moon phases and equinox and solstice
times in your region at www.sunrisesunset.com

# *Ostara : Spring Equinox : Blossoming*

The spring or vernal equinox, known to pagans as Ostara, is celebrated around March 20/21 in the northern hemisphere, and September 22/23 in the southern. It's one of only two times in the year when the length of day and night is equal, as the sun sits directly above the equator on its journey north or south, creating equal light and dark.

This equinox is about growth and passion, and the unfurling and release of the immense potential within you. On a universal and a personal level, it's a period of balance and harmony, of union between the physical and the spiritual, and the integration of your heart and your soul. This can be harnessed to anchor your dreams in reality and enhance your own inner harmony as the balance of universal outer energies is reflected within. Relationships are also harmonious now, making it perfect for weddings and for healing rifts.

It's a time of growth and fertility, when new crops are sown, new shoots break through the earth, buds on the trees open, birds build nests and lay eggs, and new life is celebrated. Thanks was traditionally given to the fertility goddess Ostara, whose symbols were an egg and a hare, and who is still honoured around the world today, albeit unknowingly, in the form of chocolate eggs and the Easter bunny.

Energetically it's also a very fertile time, as the seeds you sowed of your goals at Imbolc begin to sprout and gain momentum. Paint some hard-boiled eggs with symbols that represent your desires, or buy or make the chocolate version, meditating on your own metaphorical fertility and your ability to manifest dreams into reality. Choose an affirmation related to your desired outcome, then write it down and pin it up where you'll be able to see it often.

Go outside during the day and breathe in the fresh spring air, filling your heart with new energy and inspiration as you fill your lungs with oxygen. In many ancient cultures, including the Roman one whose calendar we have based ours on, the spring equinox was the first day of the year, and the sense of new hope and optimism reflected in this time remains today. It's a celebration of new life, hope, passion, growth and energy.

# Beltane : First Day of Summer : Growth

Beltane, the festival of love and fertility that marks the end of spring and the start of the heat and energy of summer, falls in early November in the southern hemisphere and early May in the northern. It's the third fertility festival of the year, and celebrates the fact that the days are continuing to lengthen and the temperature is increasing.

Mythologically, this was when the god and the goddess were balanced in power and age, when they were lovers and equals. It was a time of sexual union – in some magical traditions it was the day the goddess conceived; while in others it was when she married the god.

Astronomically, this cross-quarter day occurs midway between the spring equinox and the summer solstice. In the southern hemisphere, the sun is halfway between the Equator and the Tropic of Capricorn on its journey towards the southernmost latitudes, and rises in the same position as it does three months later at Lughnasadh, when it's heading back north to the Equator.

Beltane, also known as Bealtaine (bright fire), May Day, Walpurgis Night, the Festival of Flowers and Floralia, marks the first day of summer. The evidence of new life is everywhere, in abundant blossoms, the hatching of birds, and bees pollinating flowers. The seeds planted in spring have germinated and sprouted, and the land is warm, buzzing and green. Brightly coloured flowers were traditionally brought inside to symbolise fresh beginnings and the power of nature, and pretty white blossoms were gathered from the sacred hawthorn tree, as Rhiannon and Carlie did, which was associated with Beltane and used for love spells, in marriage rituals, to make wands and maypoles, as well as for protection and healing. Women would bathe their faces in the dew gathered from their garden on Beltane morning to harness the energy of youth.

At the four cross-quarter days the veil between the worlds is considered to be thinner, and at this one people connected with the energy of the faeries, who were believed to emerge into the human world on this night to dance, find a lover, impart their wisdom and teach the odd lesson before withdrawing back into the mists.

Beltane was the major fertility festival of the Celtic year, and lovers would leap over bonfires hand in hand to renew their vows of love, then come together in sacred union in the fields to bless the crops with fertility. Maypole dancing, representing the union of the god (the pole) and the goddess (the ribbons), was performed to join the forces of masculine and feminine, and May Day was, and still is, one of the most popular days for marriages in the northern hemisphere.

But in the southern hemisphere the Beltane festivities fall in early November, which coincides with Samhain/Halloween. While some pagans don witch, vampire or ghost costumes for trick or treat parties, they're just as likely to dress as faeries and wood nymphs to represent the gentle, bright and light fae energy and the vitality and heat of the season, and perform rituals to boost love and fertility.

The festival of Beltane, no matter when it is celebrated, is a time of sunshine and abundant growth, of lovers and spells to attract love, and of celebrating the fertility of life, not just physically, but also of our dreams, ambitions and creativity.

## Ways to Celebrate

Beltane is a celebration of summer and of life, fertility and joy. In Ancient Rome it was called the Floralia, and was a flower festival in honour of Flora, their goddess of plants and nature. It was believed that she caused the trees, flowers and crops to grow, and also brought to fruition the blossoming of the human heart.

Hers was a sensuous festival, with rituals, games, erotic dancing, theatre performances, flower-clad altars and people swathed in colourful robes and ribbons. Golden torches lit up the night so the revelry could continue until dawn, and people abandoned themselves joyously to the rites. Legend recalls that Flora had a magic flower that would make any woman who touched it fall pregnant, which ties in with the energies of the Celtic festival too, which was all about the fertility of the earth, the animals and humanity.

As the land thrummed and surged with energy and growth, and flowers bloomed and sap rose within the trees, people also felt the wildness of nature. The Green Man, the spirit of nature, was honoured at this time, along with Cernunnos, the horned god and deity of Beltane and the summer. Many children were conceived at this time, and the Great Rite, also called the Sacred Marriage, was performed to symbolise the joining of god and goddess. Re-enacting this ceremony, which people believed created the universe, reassured them life would go on. It also united the two forces of masculine and feminine and the elements of yin and yang so central to nature-based religions.

The Great Rite was consummated literally, with a priestess playing the goddess and representing mother earth, and a priest embodying the god. At other times it was the king, wedding the land to retain his royal power, who channelled the god and joined with the goddess. This rite ensured the fertility of the land, and is still performed today in many magical traditions, although for most it is done symbolically, not literally, with a ritual involving a chalice and athame.

Huge bonfires were lit on Beltane Eve, to represent fertility, purification and healing, and they burned through the night. Cattle were driven between them to be cleansed on their way out to the summer fields, and the fires were also the focus of Beltane celebrations, with dancing and revelry continuing around them all night. Couples leaped over them together as a vow of commitment, to bring luck to their union and to publicly pledge their love to each other, as Rose and Richard did, and the ceremony represented a contract of being together for a year and a day.

This energy makes it a wonderful time to repledge your love to your partner. You don't have to build a bonfire and leap over it, although you can ☺ Simply lighting a red or gold candle as you stare into each other's eyes and speak your love and commitment will invoke the power and passion of fire. If you're single, make a commitment of some kind to yourself, nurture a friendship or sing your intention and wanting of a romantic partner to the universe.

Love spells are also performed at this time, to take advantage of the universal energies swirling around. It can be as simple as lighting a pink candle and making a wish, holding a rose quartz as you list the qualities you long for in a partner, or soaking in a bath filled with pink rose petals. Or it can be as involved as you want to make it, with moon phases and invocations and a lengthy list of ingredients. Just don't cast it on anyone specific, as this contradicts the magical principle of never interfering with someone's free will – and you could end up binding a psycho to you and have trouble getting free!

Instead add a little magic to your life by empowering yourself, increasing your confidence and your attitude. If you want to draw a partner to you, don't go for a specific person, just focus on manifesting someone with the qualities you desire, as there may be someone you don't know yet who is perfectly suited. This is why spells often end with: "This or something better..." because you don't want to limit yourself just to the possibilities you can imagine. So, put your desire out to the universe, and trust that the perfect person will respond.

Beltane is also considered the festival of the faeries, and during the long, bright evenings of early summer you can almost see them dancing in your garden, flitting from vivid coloured flower to gently waving leaf. You can connect to the energy of the day by opening up to the faery realm. Paint, draw, write about or hang pictures of these magical winged beings, or perform a divination reading with a faery oracle deck, drawing on their wisdom to gain insight into your future and any issues you are facing. Dress in long, loose, swirling clothes with flowers in your hair, and dance barefoot on the grass, soaking up the vibration of the earth and of this powerful, potent time. The magic and beauty of the fae's archetypal energy stirs something deep within and touches the heart, bringing joy and inspiration, while their vibration can alter ours and bring lightness to the soul.

## In Your Journal

Beltane is about fertility, both literally and metaphorically. Symbolically this day marks the igniting of the fires of creativity and passion, and the fertility of your dreams being made manifest. Embrace this energy and do all that you can to nurture and further your goals, because any form of action will be supported at this time. Check in on the projects you started at the spring equinox, and write about their progress and the ways in which they've sprouted into reality. If you need to fine tune anything, learn a new skill, or let go of an aspect so they can germinate further on their own, now is a good time.

At Beltane, when the god and the goddess are equals, neither mother and child nor maiden and wise old sage, aim to rebalance the masculine and feminine energies within yourself. Make sure you give equal power to your gentle, intuitive, feminine side as you do to your more outgoing, active, masculine side. This has nothing to do with gender, but simply the myriad aspects of your deeper self. Most people overlook, bury or neglect one side of themselves at times, but both are crucial to feeling loved, loveable and loving.

This is a festival of passion – for life, for love, for your dreams – so revel in what you feel most passionate about. Celebrate the fertility of life by conceiving new ideas, or do some word association until you discover a plan or goal that fills you with joy. Begin a new project, sign up for a course or start a new hobby, knowing the universe is bursting with energy you can tap in to simply by breathing it in.

It's also a day of love, so it's a good time to focus on self-love. Write a list of all the qualities and attributes you love about yourself, and all the reasons you are so loveable and so worthy of love. If it gets hard, take a deep breath and keep going, as it means this is an important exercise for you. (I still find this one hard, and have lots of pauses and struggles and tears when I do it, but it's worth persevering with.) Sit within a sacred space and light a white candle for innocent love, a pink candle for pure love and a red candle for passionate love. Focusing on each in turn, write something positive about yourself that fits with that energy. Let the fire of the flame take you deeper inside yourself so you can connect to your essence and see yourself as you truly are, with all your kindness, your strength, your caring, your beauty and your light brought to the surface.

The Beltane fires aren't only for couples – they can be jumped over alone or with friends as part of a personal ritual of purification and preparation, leaping out of your past, burning away the relationship issues that have kept your heart closed, and towards a future where love is possible. You can do this symbolically, stepping over a candle flame rather than a fire, as you let go of all the old, false thoughts you have held on to and the mistaken beliefs that have made you think you are unworthy or unready for love. Or simply visualise yourself leaping into a future free of doubt. Focus on yourself as a being of love, and manifest this into reality by holding on to this deeper truth and reminding yourself often.

# Magical Sabbat Recipes – Beltane

Beltane marks the first day of summer, and is representative of vitality, fertility and the energy of the sun, so its foods include luscious fruits like cherries and strawberries, green leaf, herb and flower petal salads, oat or barley cakes, dairy foods and honey. Mead, a type of honey wine, is popular. White wine, white grape juice or mead is often infused with sweet woodruff and served with strawberries to capture the essence of the season, and fruit juices and light floral teas match well too. Herbs of the season include sweet woodruff, meadowsweet, calendula, marjoram, thistle, angelica, apple, cinnamon, vanilla, rose, violet, jasmine, all-heal, cinquefoil, clover, honeysuckle, ivy, lilac, rowan and St John's wort.

Beltane is a festival of love and romance, so roses and other flowers can be added to food, used as a garnish or table decoration, woven into a garland for your hair or used in spells for love, which can be as simple as soaking in a bath filled with pink rose petals. You can also leave a little dish of nuts, berries and flowers out for the faeries, as this is another cross-quarter day when the veils between the worlds are thin, and their energy can be drawn on.

## Edible Flowers

Many flowers are edible, and summer is the perfect time to add some pretty petals to your recipes and strew them in salads. Some edible flowers include marigolds, nasturtiums, violets, pansies, primroses, calendulas, carnations, jasmine, sunflowers, dandelions, lemon verbena, lavender and hibiscus, as well as the flowers of sage, thyme, dill, chives, basil, coriander, bee balm (wild bergamot), sorrel, rocket and borage, plus zucchini and squash blossoms, apple blossoms and banana blossoms. Do always make sure your flowers are fresh and pesticide-free, and that they are the type you think they are, because some plants are poisonous. With some flowers, such as roses and chrysanthemums, only the petals should be consumed. For others, such as violets and nasturtiums, the whole flower can be eaten. And with others, like dandelion and calendula, you can eat the whole plant, although sometimes the petals are the tastiest part.

**Flower butter:** Combine 250g of butter with half a cup of chopped flower petals, and leave, covered and in a cool dry place, to stand overnight so the flavour of the flowers infuses the butter. Stir again then refrigerate. Use this pretty butter on breads, scones and muffins, and in cake, cookie and dessert recipes.

**Floral Ice Cubes:** Half fill an ice-cube tray with water and freeze. Once frozen, place a violet flower, apple blossom, jasmine bloom or rose petal into each ice-cube hole, top with water and freeze again. Serve in drinks to add a sweet summery look and a romantic vibe.

**Crystallised Flowers:** Beat an egg white and a few drops of water until foamy but not stiff. Using a small paintbrush, paint clean dry flowers such as violets, geraniums, pansies and rose buds with the egg white mixture, then sprinkle with super-fine sugar (use icing sugar or blend white or raw sugar in a blender), covering the whole surface of each blossom. Leave to dry for a day or two in an airtight container, then use to decorate cakes, ice-cream, desserts and drinks.

## Rose Petal Biscuits

**Ingredients:**
- ☆ 200g butter
- ☆ ½ cup icing sugar
- ☆ 1 cup plain flour
- ☆ 1 tblsp lemon zest
- ☆ 1 tsp rose water or pure vanilla essence
- ☆ Handful of rose petals (chemical free)

**What to do:**
★ Cream the butter and icing sugar, then fold in the sifted flour, lemon zest and rose water or vanilla essence. When well combined, gently stir in the rose petals. Cover the dough in plastic wrap and refrigerate for an hour or so to keep its shape while baking.

★ Roll out onto a floured board to around 1cm thick, and use a cookie cutter or the mouth of a glass or a jar to shape into cookies.

★ Place on a lightly greased cookie tray and bake in a preheated 180C oven for around 20 minutes, or until firm and golden. Cool on a wire rack then serve on a pretty floral plate.

# Rose Water

Rose water can be served as a drink, added to other drinks for an exotic flavour, stirred into pastries, and used instead of vanilla essence in baking (and vice versa). It's also a great beauty product, with anti-inflammatory and hydrating properties, and the scent can reduce stress and cortisol, and improve the mood.

★ Place half a cup of firmly packed fresh rose petals, or organic dried roses, in a bowl or a glass jar that has a lid. Pour 1 cup of boiling water over them. Cover with the lid and let the petals steep overnight, or until the liquid is at room temperature. Strain the rose water, and squeeze all the water out of the petals too. Store in the fridge in a sterilised jar, or freeze in ice-cube trays so you have small amounts ready to hand when needed for recipes.

# Rose Petal Tea

Rose tea has a light flavour, a sweet scent and a calming effect.
★ Using one cup of fresh rose petals, cut off the bitter white bases from the petals and rinse well. Place in a teapot and pour two cups of boiling water over them. Allow to steep for five minutes – the petals will darken and become discoloured, which is normal. Strain the rose petal liquid into teacups and add a little honey if you like.

# Fresh Rose Hip Tea

Rose hips are the small apple-like seed pods that form after a rose blooms (roses are part of the apple family). They have more vitamin C than citrus fruits, and are renowned for their power to help prevent and ease colds and flu. They also contain vitamins B, C, E and K, pectin and organic acids, and help strengthen immunity.

★ Pick or buy some rose hips. Wash, dry, then place in a dry, dark place for up to a week, until the outer skin of the rose hips start to dry up. Once dried, cut the hips in half and remove the seeds. Put the hips back in the dry dark place to continue drying – it will take another week or two to dry fully. Store in a plastic bag in the fridge, or freeze. To make tea, place a rose hip or two in a cup and pour boiling water over the top. Steep for half an hour, then enjoy.

# Calendula Cookies

**Ingredients:**
- ☆ 125g butter
- ☆ 1 tsp pure vanilla essence
- ☆ 1 cup plain flour
- ☆ 2 tblsps fresh calendula petals, finely chopped
- ☆ ½ cup raw sugar
- ☆ ½ cup milk

**What to do:**
★ Cream the butter, sugar and vanilla until soft, pale and creamy.
★ Stir in the milk, then add flour and finely chopped calendula petals.
★ Roll tablespoons of mixture into balls. Place them on greased baking trays and press down with a fork to flatten.
★ Bake in a preheated 180C oven for 15 minutes, or until golden. Serve warm, or allow to cool before storing. The calendula petals add a golden glow to the cookies, and anything else you put them in.

# Lavender Jam

**Ingredients:**
- ☆ ¼ cup dried lavender flowers or ½ cup fresh
- ☆ 1 cup boiling water
- ☆ 1 tblsp pectin
- ☆ 2 tblsps fresh lemon juice
- ☆ 1 cup sugar

**What to do:**
★ Pour the boiling water over the dried or fresh lavender flowers, and allow to steep for 20 minutes.
★ Strain the lavender water into a saucepan, and discard the lavender flowers (put them in your garden for a nutritional boost). Add the lemon juice and pectin and stir until the pectin dissolves.
★ Bring the mixture to the boil and stir in the sugar. Allow it to boil furiously for around five minutes, stirring occasionally as it firms up into a jammy texture. You can stir in a little more pectin and keep it on the heat a bit longer if you want it thicker.
★ Pour your jam into sterilised glass jars and refrigerate. The jam will be a pretty deep pinky-mauve colour, as the acid of the lemon juice reacts with the pigment of the lavender to change it.

# Flower-Infused Syrup

This sweet flower syrup will bring a taste of summer year round. Experiment with different flowers for different flavours and colours. ★ Place one cup of edible flower petals, one cup of water and three cups of sugar in a saucepan over a medium heat. Bring to the boil, and continue boiling for 10 minutes, or until it becomes syrupy, stirring occasionally. Strain into a glass bottle and refrigerate. Serve as a cordial with mineral water, or use the summery syrup in desserts or poured over pancakes or plain sponges.

# Honey Joys

**Ingredients:**

☆ 100g butter
☆ 3 tblsps raw sugar

☆ 3 tblsps honey
☆ 4 cups cornflakes

**What to do:**

★ Stir the butter, honey and sugar over a medium heat in a small pot, until butter is melted, sugar dissolves and mixture is frothy.
★ Pour over cornflakes in a large bowl and mix well, then scoop into paper patty cases that are sitting in a muffin or cupcake tray.
★ Bake in a preheated 180C oven for 10 minutes, then allow to cool.

# Beltane Passion Cake

**Ingredients:**

☆ 90g butter
☆ 1 cup raw sugar
☆ 3 eggs, separated
☆ 2 cups self-raising flour
☆ ½ cup fresh passionfruit pulp
☆ 1 tsp pure vanilla essence

**Icing:**

☆ 250g cream cheese, softened
☆ 2 tblsps honey
☆ 4 passionfruit

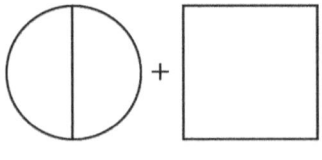

**What to do:**

★ Cream the butter, sugar and egg yolks together in a bowl. Stir in the flour and the passionfruit pulp.

★ Beat the egg whites until stiff, then fold in to the cake batter.

★ Pour half into a lightly greased square cake tin and half in a round tin, and bake in a preheated 180C oven for around 30 minutes, or until golden brown and cooked through.

★ While the cakes cool, prepare icing by combining cream cheese and honey, then stirring passionfruit pulp through. Cut the round cake in half, place the square cake on a serving platter and tilt so it's a diamond shape. Place one half circle of cake against the top left side, and one half on the right, to form a heart shape. Cover with icing and serve surrounded by rose petals or other flowers.

## Summer Salad

**Ingredients:**

☆ 3 cups greens – spinach, rocket, dandelion leaves, oak lettuce etc
☆ 1 Lebanese cucumber, sliced
☆ ½ red capsicum, sliced
☆ ½ avocado, sliced
☆ 1 cup fresh strawberries, sliced
☆ ¼ Spanish onion, sliced (optional)
☆ Handful of alfalfa or other sprouts
☆ ½ cup sunflower seeds
☆ 2 hard-boiled eggs, sliced

**Dressing:**

☆ ¼ cup olive oil
☆ 1 tsp honey
☆ 1 garlic clove
☆ ¼ cup lemon juice
☆ 1 tsp Dijon mustard
☆ Parsley
☆ Freshly cracked black pepper and sea salt to taste

**What to do:**

★ Divide the greens into separate bowls or one large one. Arrange salad ingredients on top. Combine dressing ingredients in a blender (or chop parsley finely and shake in a jar), and serve over salad.

# Litha : Summer Solstice : Fruition

The summer solstice, known to pagans as Litha, is celebrated around June 20/21 in the northern hemisphere and December 21/22 in the southern. It's the longest day and the shortest night of the year, and marks the peak of energy and solar power for the year. On this day the sun reaches its northern or southernmost latitude before it turns and heads back towards the equator, so near the poles daylight lasts for twenty-four hours – the sun just doesn't set for weeks at a time. In nature, everything is ripe and abundant, and life is blooming.

It's a time of high, hot and active energy. Creativity and expression is at a peak, so stand in your power and express your needs, saying what you want rather than assuming that people know. Whereas the winter solstice is slow and introspective, its opposite is fast and effective. Make use of the active energy – this is a time to do, to get out there and harness the energising earth power and make things happen.

Follow your passion, take a chance, say yes to new opportunities, and express your creativity and your inner self. This is not the time to be withdrawn or shy, it's for getting out amongst it and making your dreams come true. It's also a time when relationships – and you – will mature, and you'll apply new wisdom and forethought to your passion. So give thanks for the lessons you've learned, and allow the person you are maturing into to unfold.

It's a time of celebration too, of acknowledging how far you've come and what you've achieved. Enjoy the happiness and abundance of this season and soak up the sunshine and festive atmosphere. Traditionally people stayed up all night on solstice eve, partying around bonfires or within sacred circles of stone, then watched the sun rise the next morning, feeling it bathe them in warmth and light.

At dawn, stand with your arms outstretched and breathe in the sun's life-giving power. Let it wash over you with its healing energy and burn away anything you no longer need. Take note of how your dreams and goals are manifesting into the world, and meditate on anything that could be blocking your progress. Be open to letting go of whatever isn't working so you can move forward in a new direction.

# Lughnasadh
# First Day of Autumn : Gratitude

Lughnasadh, named for the Celtic god Lugh and also known as Lammas, is celebrated in the first week of August in the northern hemisphere and the first week of February in the southern hemisphere, and marks the end of summer and the beginning of autumn. It's the first harvest festival, traditionally a time of feasting and of thanksgiving for the life-giving properties of the grain and nature's bounty, as well as a recognition of the cycle of sowing and reaping of the crops.

It is also the time to honour the things you have grown and created in your life, a day to harvest the fruits of your labours, and acknowledge your successes and what you've achieved in the past year. Celebrate the goals you've reached and have your own festival of gratitude, in whatever form that takes. Toast your success, throw a party or do something special to mark the occasion – maybe reward yourself for your hard work with a gift you've long wanted, or some precious time off to rest and chill out. Make a list of all the things you've gained over the past year – the new talents you've developed, the friends you've made, the experiences you've had, the healings you've received, the gifts you've been given – and give thanks for it all.

Then, out of gratitude and in the spirit of the ancestors who shared the bounty of their harvest with those less well off, pay your good fortune forward. Donate to a local charity or collect food for the homeless, as Rose and her friends do, lend to a business in the developing world (Kiva.org does great work), or give your time to help someone, ensuring the energy of abundance continues and is strengthened. Give joyfully, with no expectation of receiving anything in return. And work out small ways in which you can make a difference to the people around you all year long as well.

As the energy begins to subtly slow, this is also a time to be patient and to trust that everything is as it should be, because there are still harvests to come. Not everything has to be achieved right now – some things take longer to manifest. The lesson of the Wheel of the Year is that everything continues, everything happens when it should, and everything is eternal.

# Mabon : Autumn Equinox : Harvest

The autumn equinox, known as Mabon and celebrated on September 22/23 in the northern hemisphere and March 20/21 in the southern, is characterised by the length of day and night being equal as the sun travels back across the equator to the other hemisphere. From this point on, the days will become shorter and cooler, but this is a moment of balance in nature and within – a point of harmony and calm.

Vibrationally Mabon is a season of withdrawal, of being alone to meditate, recharge, reassess and ponder where you're at in life. The energy of the earth retreats and goes within, as does your personal power, but from this introspection you'll emerge with strength and wisdom. It's a time to honour your achievements, experiences and growth, and to ensure balance by integrating all parts of your self. Acknowledge and celebrate what you've reaped in your own life. Feel fulfilment from each goal reached, releasing what no longer serves you in order to move forward. In the wild, old growth is cleared. In your life, cut out anything that's preventing new life and love from flourishing, whether it's work, people, a belief system, regret or the past.

On this day, when all is balanced, witches traditionally renewed their magical commitments, and you can renew any vows you've made or pledge a new one, be it to do with magic, love, friendship, career or anything else. As the shadows lengthen, it's also a good time to scry for insight into your future. If you can, light a fire and stare into the flames, allowing your mind to go blank and your vision to blur a little, or go outside and watch the clouds scuttling across the sky, analysing the shapes and symbols you see within flame or cloud. Without over-thinking it, write down what they mean to you.

Pyromancy (fire reading) and nephomancy (cloud reading) are forms of divination that have been used for millennia. You should develop your own dictionary of symbols, as you know better than anyone what any shape or image means to you, but you can begin with standard readings, such as a heart indicating romance, a cat referring to a need to trust your intuition, a tree meaning you will make new friends and a plane foreshadowing travel.

# Samhain : First Day of Winter : Death

Samhain, which is celebrated in early November in the northern hemisphere and early May in the southern, is a cross-quarter day marking the end of autumn and the beginning of the cold and dark of winter.

Symbolically it is about rest and renewal, of preparing for what's ahead and withdrawing a little to conserve your energy, and releasing the things you've been holding on to, in order to ready yourself for new challenges and experiences. It's also the night when the veil between the worlds is said to be at its thinnest, when people honour their ancestors and try to commune with the dead. Some set a place at the dinner table for any loved ones passed over, as Rhiannon and her dad Mike did at their Samhain ritual, while others cast spells to bring their spirit back, or use divination to converse. This magical time and its purpose has been conserved in the modern festival of Halloween, which celebrates ghosts, witches and restless spirits.

The beginning of winter is a period of reflection, so spend time in contemplation. If you've lost someone close to you, light a candle and remember them. Look at photos or letters and feel their presence with you. This shouldn't be morbid – you're celebrating their life and all they mean to you. Also honour those who are here now. Call your mum and dad, visit your grandparents, or write to someone who meant a lot to you when you were growing up and thank them.

Long ago, Samhain was the end of one year and the start of the next, so it's a powerful time to let go of the energy and old memories of the previous year so you can move forward with lightness and strength, and new resolutions. Light another candle, and by its flickering illumination, write out all the worries, frustrations, regrets and seeming failures you've held on to. Then burn the list in the flame as you visualise the element of fire burning them all away, helping you release your attachment to those emotions and their power over you. Breathe in this positive new energy and feel refreshed.

This is the time to prepare yourself for the rebirth you'll experience at Yule, but for that to happen there must be death – the death of fears and doubts, and anything holding you back.

# Yule : Winter Solstice : Rebirth

The winter solstice, known to pagans as Yule and Midwinter, falls around December 21/22 in the northern hemisphere and June 21/22 in the southern, and marks the middle of winter. It's the shortest day and the longest night of the year, and marks the transition between dark and light, both emotionally and physically. It's the lowest point of the Wheel in terms of daylight and energy, with the sun rising later and night falling earlier. The land is barren and cold, there is less light, and energetically people feel tired and unmotivated.

Winter is a time to rest and reflect, to acknowledge sadness and loss – of dreams, of friendships, of parts of your self – and conserve your energy. But the solstice is the turning point in this time of darkness, introspection and dreaming. Considered the dark night of the soul, it also marks the period when the dark half of the year relinquishes its hold to the light half. From this time forward, the days will start to lengthen, the sun will become stronger, and the energy within and without will start to increase and build.

In pagan times an evergreen tree was brought inside as a symbol of the hope of spring's return, and Yule was a time of feasting, celebration and gift-giving in honour of the birth of the sun god – traditions that live on today in the Christmas tree we decorate, the presents we put under it, the huge meal we cook for family and friends, and the celebration of the birth of the son of God.

To attune yourself to this festival of rebirth, light a candle on solstice eve to symbolise the sun and its activating energy, and list your dreams for the coming year. Traditionally people stayed up all night to await the return of the light, but if you can't do that, get up for the sunrise to toast the dawn and give thanks for this energetic reawakening. Open yourself to the promise of new growth and achievement, and the rebirth of your own self and your creativity, as the sun is also reborn. Symbolically and energetically it's a time to honour your inner wisdom, consider the lessons you learned during winter's introspection, and integrate them into your life so you can start to initiate change and prepare for the rush of growth of the coming springtime.

# Imbolc : First Day of Spring : Purification

Imbolc, which is celebrated in the first week of February in the northern hemisphere and the first week of August in the southern, is a cross-quarter day marking the end of winter and the start of spring. It celebrates the return of light to the land, and to our own hearts, and is a time of hope, renewal and fresh starts after winter's sluggishness. Energetically it's a time of awakening, rebirth and re-emergence. Nature fills with life force and quivers with the energy to grow again, and we start to emerge from the chill of winter, shaking off our lack of motivation and re-engaging with the world, making it a great day to sow the seeds of what you want to achieve in the coming year.

Imbolc is dedicated to Bridie, the goddess of inspiration, creativity and fire, who was later supplanted by Saint Bridget, whose festival is also celebrated at this time. Talk to Bridie – or Bridget, or the higher-self aspect of yourself – or write her a letter, and tell her what you want to create in the next twelve months. Meditate on your goals and what you hope to achieve. Don't worry about how to do it, as that will be revealed later in flashes of inspiration, guidance or outside help.

Physically it's a time of purification and cleansing after the long dark of winter, so clean your house and clear your space, sweeping out old energy and thoughts so the new will thrive. It's a good time to write about your beliefs and examine how you feel about your spiritual path too, exploring the reasons you think the way you do, and perhaps questioning if there are other viewpoints you might also embrace.

Imbolc is all about new beginnings, and in some magical traditions it is the day chosen for initiations and rededications, so if you want to make a pledge to a new path or a new goal, or a personal vow of any kind, you will be supported by the energy of the season. You may also like to ignite a candle to represent the coming back of the light, and do some candle magic. Stare into the flame as you concentrate on what you want, then blow it out, sending your desire out to the universe. Making a wish as you blow out the candles on your birthday cake is a magic that has survived from pagan times, and is a potent way to begin manifesting your wishes into reality, whatever day it is.

"It is so much darker when a light goes out,
than it would have been if it had never shone."
*John Steinbeck, American writer*

# With Thanks

I am so grateful to my sweet hubby and precious beloved, for his love, support and belief in me. For reassuring me when I hate the story, listening patiently as I brainstorm/panic, making me tea while I write, and asking for Rhiannon's story (not sure we knew what we were getting in for there – I thought it would be a small, *Mists*-sized book, not the epic three-year trilogy it turned into!). Thank you for our enchanted life together, and our magical adventures at home and away.

I am more grateful than I can express to amazing artist Selina Fenech, for allowing me to use her beautiful paintings for my book covers, and for serendipitously creating the perfect one at the perfect time. You are the sweetest person I know, my favourite artist, a wonderful writer, and I'm so excited for our gorgeous upcoming project.

Love and gratitude to my writer besties Selina and Kim, for their honesty, encouragement and wisdom sharing, and for laughter, long conversations, occasional venting – and support, focus and action.

Love and many thanks to inspiring author Kastie Pavlik, for her beautiful words, beautiful vampires and beautiful conversations.

Love and blessings to Felicity Pulman, Lucy Cavendish, Juliet Marillier, Sheena Cundy and Menna van Praag. To my NaNoWriMo and Insta-Writer buddies, to Fiona Lloyd, L. L. Hunter and the Story Queens, and to all the indie authors who share this crazy journey.

Much love to my gorgeous hubby and my faery friend Daniella for the illustrations. To sweet Voula for coffee and chats. To Jo for faerytale fun and deep discussions. To Janine, Claire, Mindy, Susanne, Amy, Autumn and my fit group friends for strength and sanity.

And all the love to my wonderful family who support me always. And to Petie, my Other Dad, for a lifetime of love and laughter, music, mayhem and sport, political debate, spiritual discussion and campaigning together for a better world. We all miss you so much ♥

*With much love, Serene xx*

# About the Author

Serene Conneeley is an Australian writer with a fascination for history, travel, ritual and the myth and magic of ancient places and cultures. She's written for magazines about news, travel, health, spirituality, entertainment, and social and environmental issues, been editor of several preschool magazines, and contributed to international books on history, witchcraft, psychic development and personal transformation.

She's the author of the original Australian faery tale *The Swan Maiden,* the Into the Mists Trilogy – *Into the Mists, Into the Dark* and *Into the Light* – the Into the Storm Trilogy – *Into the Storm, Into the Fire* and *Into the Air* – and the non-fiction books *Faery Magic, Mermaid Magic, Witchy Magic, Seven Sacred Sites* and *A Magical Journey,* and creator of the meditation CD *Sacred Journey.*

Serene is a reconnective healing practitioner, and has studied magical and medicinal herbalism, bereavement counselling, reiki and many other healing modalities, plus politics and journalism. She loves reading, drinking tea with her friends, working out, and celebrating the energy of the moon and the magic of the earth. Her pagan heart blossomed as she climbed mountains, sat in stone circles, climbed into ancient burial mounds and stood in the shadow of the pyramids on her travels, and she's also learned the magic of finding true happiness and peace at home.

*www.SereneConneeley.com*

# Books by Serene

The Swan Maiden: An Australian Faery Tale

## The Into the Mists Trilogy

Into the Mists

Into the Dark

Into the Light

Into the Mists: A Journal

The Into the Mists Trilogy Hardcover Omnibus

## The Into the Storm Trilogy

Into the Storm

Into the Fire

Into the Air

## The Magic Series (with Lucy Cavendish)

The Book of Faery Magic

Mermaid Magic: Connecting With the Energy of the Ocean
and the Healing Power of Water

Witchy Magic

## The Sacred Series

Seven Sacred Sites: Magical Journeys That Will Change Your Life

A Magical Journey: Your Diary of Inspiration,
Adventure and Transformation

Sacred Journey: A Meditation To Connect You
To the Magic of the Earth (CD)

Sacred Sites: Egypt

Sacred Sites: Glastonbury

Sacred Sites: Hawaii

Sacred Sites: Peru

Sacred Sites: Stonehenge

Sacred Sites: The Camino

Sacred Sites: Uluru

Rhiannon's story was first told in the Into the Mists Trilogy, which centres on Carlie and her mum Violet. But there are two sides to every story, so Rhiannon got her own series too...

# Into the Mists

Enter the swirling mists of an enchanted land, and open your heart to the mystery...

"I can't put this book down. It's so compelling and beautifully realised – there's so much magic. Absolutely recommended!"

*Lucy Cavendish, author of Spellbound and White Magic*

"This is Amazing with a capital A. It's healing, empowering, inspiring and, like all the author's work, truly magical. It's one of my favourite novels ever. It opened my heart and inspired the magic within me."

*Sarah Byrne, reviewer*

# Into the Dark

A best friend. A forever love. A promise.
A betrayal. An ultimatum. A choice...

"A compelling novel that haunted my dreams while I was reading it, and lingered in my mind long after I'd finished. It's very powerful writing, and very real – and very haunting, the mark of a good novel."

*Felicity Pulman, author of I, Morgana and The Janna Chronicles*

"Serene Conneeley's magical and very intoxicating new novel *Into the Dark* has me totally under its spell – I relish every shiver Carlie's descent into darkness is giving me. *Into the Mists* was wonderful, but this is another level, a huge leap. I LOVED this book so much – it just ended way too soon!"

*Lucy Cavendish, author of Spellbound and White Magic*

# Into the Light

A friendship torn apart. A love lost forever...
A curse to break. A mystery to solve.
A heart to heal...

"I'm absolutely blown away by this book and this series. It is beautiful from start to finish – magical, realistic, gentle, harsh, sad, joyful... I've been on a total rollercoaster ride, and am now feeling so bereft at the thought that these wonderful people will no longer be part of my life. These books are just beautiful."

*Kylie Matthews, reviewer*

## The Into the Mists Trilogy

The three books of the Into the Mists Trilogy are also available in a beautiful hardcover omnibus.
"A mystical, magical tale. I couldn't stop reading once I started – I had to know what happened next!" *L. L. Hunter, author*

## Into the Mists: A Journal

**Awaken your inner voice and unlock the power and strength within you...**

"This is *divine!* The lovely quotes are inspiring, and the feel is heart-warming. It sits on my bedside table for writing in during quiet times of reflection. Just beautiful."

*Cheralyn Darcey, eco artist and author*

## Audiobooks

*Into the Mists*, *Into the Dark* and *Into the Light* are also available as audiobooks, narrated by British voice actor Gabrielle Baker, from Audible, iTunes and Amazon.

# Also by Serene Conneeley

**Seven Sacred Sites: Magical Journeys That Will Change Your Life** is part spiritual adventure story, part history, part travel guide. Discover what makes these places sacred, when to go and how to get there, the fascinating histories, the rituals performed there, the cultural and magical significance of each sacred site, both now and in the past, and the many ways in which they still inspire, touch and initiate growth and learning in all who visit.

*"By far the best travel book this year. Her style evokes the great travel writers like James A Michener, who weave cultural anthropology into an entertaining traveller's tale – a recipe for pure reading pleasure."*
Joanne Lock, Spheres magazine

**A Magical Journey: Your Diary of Inspiration, Adventure and Transformation** combines a diary where you write the story of your life with a guidebook that includes the physical, mental and spiritual health benefits of journalling, and tools to release emotional blockages and unleash your authentic self. Make a wish come true using the cycles of the moon, celebrate worldwide festivals, and create magic in your life by harnessing the sacred energy of the seasonal turning points of the year.

*"This helped me connect to self, and venture forth with boldness and compassion. I am so much more aware, and I thank the author from the depths of my heart and soul for the opportunity to grow."*
Marissa Clarkson, bereavement counsellor

**Sacred Journey: A Meditation To Connect You To the Magic of the Earth** is a CD of seven guided meditations set over beautiful music. Each runs for around seven minutes, and can be done on its own, or all together as a fifty-minute journey. Attune yourself with the sacred elements and energies of the earth to soothe your soul, uplift your spirit and heal your heart.

*"A gem to treasure. Serene is a gentle, loving, wise teacher of wisdoms we can all benefit from. This takes us on a sacred journey into the earthly and heavenly elements and realms, and into history, spirituality and self-love."*
Lucy Cavendish, creator of As Above, So Below CD

**Sacred Sites: The Pocket Guides To Your Magical Journey** are seven mini books that are perfect for travelling or collecting. They include each of the places in *Seven Sacred Sites*, with extra practical information and websites added, plus pages for your notes, the better to plan your magical adventure.

**Witchy Magic** (with Lucy Cavendish) is an enchanting adventure into the Craft of the Wise, with clear guidance on how you can access this ancient knowledge and connect with your inner wisdom to create the life you dream of. Witchcraft is an earth-honouring spiritual path and an empowering, beautiful way to be at one with the universe, taking responsibility for your life and transforming every word and action into an alchemical tool of change. Step into the world between the worlds and the wisdom of your inner witch to create an inspiring, magical life.

*"This is a definitive reference for the would-be witch, and entertaining and enlightening for the witch-curious... For the history buff, nature lover and ritualist, to the magician, pagan and spiritualist, and well beyond."*
*Kylie Matthews, book reviewer*

**Mermaid Magic: Connecting With the Energy of the Ocean and the Healing Power of Water** (with Lucy Cavendish) is brimming with sea magic, inner journeys, marine conservation and rich research, and will help you develop a deep connection with the element of water. Work with the ocean and its creatures, learn about tides and lunar phases, divine your future with sea oracles, absorb the healing energies of sacred wells and springs, become an eco warrior, and discover the beauty of mermaid lore and love.

*"This is a wonderfully inspiring read. It really made me want to shed my twenty-first century shackles and dive into the ocean to embrace its wonderful healing powers. Thank you magical ladies for the journey!"*
*Sabina Collins, freelance writer*

**The Book of Faery Magic** (with Lucy Cavendish) is rich in tradition, history, research and lore, and filled with whimsical interactions with the fae, grounded guidance on how to work with them, and beautiful ideas for reconnection with nature and the magical realms. Whether you believe that faeries are truth or fantasy, *Faery Magic* is your portal to a state of being where fun and healing energy will help you fulfil your dreams, transform your life, and improve your relationship with the earth, your self and others.

*"The ultimate guide to all things faery – entertaining, informative and enthralling. Whether you believe in faeries or are just curious, there is much to learn in this book, from their history and legends, their magical gifts and nature sites, to the unique beings from around the world."*
*Larissa Chapman, Good Reads*

*www.BlessedBeeBooks.com*